Black Widow
of Penleigh Court

Black Widow of Penleigh Court

Eliza Laval

authorHOUSE®

AuthorHouse™ UK Ltd.
1663 Liberty Drive
Bloomington, IN 47403 USA
www.authorhouse.co.uk
Phone: 0800.197.4150

Published by AuthorHouse 10/21/2013

ISBN: 978-1-4918-8114-9 (sc)
ISBN: 978-1-4918-8115-6 (e)

For My Family and Friends—and all their support

To

Dawn + Gavin

With Love + Best Wishes
To A Great Sister + Brother-in-law

Love Val
xxx

CHAPTER ONE

(Returning Home)

Richard Penleigh, second son of Henry and Alice Penleigh, the Duke and Duchess of Warren, of Penleigh Court in Cornwall, stepped into the hall of his luxurious town house in Mayfair. He had just returned home after two years travelling in Europe, to a foggy, damp and cold November day. What a great time he had had, a smile crossed his face as he remembered the people, or at least some of them, in particular, the ladies whom he had managed to charm. He had always found himself to be attractive to the fairer sex, even the ones who were unattractive to him. He was tall, and broad, with a very athletic body, his hair was black as a raven's, and curling down on his collar, his jawline strong and firm, with chiselled features. His large brown eyes were fringed with long dark lashes, and when he walked into a room, the ladies would turn their heads, his gait very straight and his strides long—he certainly made a dashing sight in Society in his black frock coat and trousers, cut tight to show strong leg muscles, and with his bright white shirt, and snowy cravat, with a ruby pin, hardly surprising that the ladies saw him as a potential husband. With his good looks, and easy manner, he had a good rapport with his male friends, and a charming way with the ladies, even the mama's were taken with him, though they had most certainly heard of his reputation, they chose to ignore it. He would certainly be a good catch for some young debutante, and although only the second son of a Duke, his income was not to be sneezed at and his prospects were good.

There had been a couple of young ladies, in Venice, who stood out in his mind and one in particular, Lady Drucilla Maltby, who he felt sure would have welcomed an offer from him. In truth, rumours had already started as such, she was beguiling, and handsome, but he had no intention of being caught yet—after all, he was only seven and twenty, no age to tie himself down to one woman. It wasn't as if he needed to marry, no, there was more fun to be had before he would look for a woman to shackle himself too. One of the reasons he was so eager to travel was to free himself from the clutches of the mama's who couldn't resist throwing their daughters in his direction, and even after two years, he was still no nearer to going down that route. Besides, the woman that he chose as his lifelong partner, would have to fit the bill—she would have to be beautiful, and if not wealthy, at least of some standing, she would need to be amusing, and have a good mind, would he ever find a woman to fit his criteria, perhaps not. A dowry would be expected, but not necessarily a large one essential, he was wealthy in his own right, so he would be the one to choose his bride, not they him. He was well aware that he was a target for all the young woman searching for an eligible gentleman, looking for comfort and security for the rest of their lives—but he wasn't going to fall into that trap. No, he would require someone who could fit his criteria. Most of the young women giggled and whispered behind open fans, and if not, they held romantic notions, and talked of nothing but love, some of them even believing they were in love, but he wasn't convinced about love at all, those sort of things only existed in the female mind and in novels in his experience, he would hold no such fancy notions, and he had no desire to court a simpering chit. Anyway, he knew better from growing up with his own parents, their marriage after all, was purely one of convenience, and that led to nothing but great unhappiness, he could never resort to that. If he couldn't find a lady, amongst the ton, who could fulfil all the qualities he was seeking, then he would put off marriage until he did, he would never marry like his father or brother, his father had married for money and standing, and to gain an heir to the Dukedom, his brother to do his father's bidding, which amounted to the same, he could think of nothing worse. Eventually, he would inherit his grandfather Ritson's estate, Fernlea House, but only on the death of his mother, and that, he hoped, wouldn't be anytime soon. He did, however, have a sizeable allowance from his father, besides his Mayfair home, which was more than satisfactory to his needs. The Ritson estate, when he eventually inherited, was reported to do very nicely, it drew in a steady profit by all accounts, and the money in the coffers there, was very healthy indeed, hadn't his father attempted and failed, to make claim on it over the years? Fortunately it had been entailed, so the estate was safe and intact, otherwise, by the time it came to him, there would be nothing left, the Duke would have used it to fund his gaming habits. Come to think of it, the last time he saw Penleigh Court, there were definite signs of wear and tear, though he suspected that Maria's dowry would have taken care of that. Although the Ritson estate was much smaller than his father's estate, it was certainly large enough for his needs, even with a family. The house was a large red brick manor house, set into a hillside in South Devonshire, with large stable block and sweeping gardens which led down to a winding coastal path leading to the beach below, it seemed very impressive, it looked very grand. The estate also boasted a large apple orchard, which produced the apples for making cider, and of which the estate had recently started producing their own cider over the last few years, yet another business venture, that was proving to be successful for the estate, though the land did border with Somerset, the county known for its cider, Ritson cider was becoming well known. The estate was also situated less than a day from Penleigh Court. His tenants were farmers, who lived in small cottages on the estate, and who worked the land, for the time being there was an estate manager to oversee the running of both the estate, and the cider business, who had been appointed by the his grandfather's solicitor, Mr Harold Twine, of Twine and Fellows, so he could rest assured that it was all in good hands—he could see himself as the gentleman farmer, and excited by the prospect of a thriving estate, he smiled to himself, yes—once he inherited, everything would fall into place and there would be plenty of time to settle down and take responsibility then.

"Welcome home sir", his butler, Reeves came forward with a warm smile, breaking into Richard's thoughts, he turned with a start, "good afternoon Reeves" he replied, the man seemed pleased to receive him home after his long absence, it gave him a warm feeling to receive such a welcome, Reeves stood at the ready, Richard handed him his hat, placed his gloves inside, which Reeves placed on the hall table, before helping his employer out of his overcoat and hanging it on the stand next to the table. "I trust you had a good trip sir"?

"An excellent trip, thank you Reeves, but this English weather is foul, though to be expected at this time of year I suppose, perhaps you could arrange for a fire in the library"?

"Yes sir, it's all ready for you. Mrs Chalmers wondered if you would care for an early dinner tonight, she thought as you would be cold and hungry on your return, she is cooking your favourite—roast pheasant, just the way you like it Sir, with plum dough to follow". Reeves was a small man, who was getting on in years, he had a shock of white hair and black, beady little eyes, he was still as smart in appearance as he had ever been, and he stood very straight, but nothing slipped his notice, his mind was as bright and active as it had been twenty years previous, and Richard knew that he could trust him with his life—a more loyal servant he could never have wished for. He had been with the Ritson's family long before coming here, he was devoted to his grandfather, and his own mother, for as long as Richard could remember, so offering him work in his London residence, seemed the obvious solution, and one which suited everyone, not to mention delighted his mother, and he was very glad that he had. After all, there was but a skeleton staff left at Fernlea House, with little need of his services, so he would be more gainfully employed here, until Richard came into his inheritance, then he hoped that Reeves would return with him to Fernlea House. Richard was fond of him, he had always had time for him and Edward when they were boys, visiting their grandfather, now it was his turn to repay that loyalty.

"Excellent Reeves, and perhaps you could decant a bottle of my best port. But first I would take a hot bath and freshen up",

"Yes sir, as you wish, the fires are already lit, and your bed has been aired for you".

"Thank you Reeves".

After a hot bath and freshen up, Richard went down to his library, he opened the door and looked around the room—how good it was to back in his familiar surroundings, his solid oak desk, and chair with the burgundy red leather seat, they looked exactly as he had left them, just over two years ago. His large solid oak bookcase, and the musky smell of the old volumes lining the walls, the thick damask burgundy red curtains, were drawn against the late afternoon chill, and a bright fire was flaring in the grate—yes, he was glad to be home. He went in and closed the door, his eyes rested on the silver tray on the oak sideboard, and on it two crystal glasses and two crystal decanters, one half full of golden liquid, the other stood empty. The flames from the fire dancing and throwing shafts of colour, and patterns reflected in the glass, giving a warm orange and red glow of light to the room, so warm, inviting and welcoming on this cold autumnal afternoon—he picked up the decanter half full, and poured some of the golden liquid fire into one of the glasses, before taking his seat at his desk—there was a pile of papers in front of him, they would all have to be dealt with, but before he did that he picked up his glass and tossed the golden liquid down his throat—that felt good, and it warmed him. Now, he had best look through the papers to see if anything was urgent. As his fingers worked their way through the paperwork in front of him, his eyes rested on a letter with the Penleigh crested seal, which he knew had arrived from Cornwall, the home of his family. That is where he would start. He broke the seal and started to read the familiar hand, which he knew to be his dear mother's.

My Dearest Son,

I trust that you are well, and that you have enjoyed your travels. It would be such a delight to see you again, if you could spare a little time for a visit, I do so miss our conversations, and walks together, even though your brother is a good son to me, and I have his family for comfort, I constantly think of you, and how your life is working out.

Your brother Edward and his wife Maria, have just been blessed with their second child, another girl, I adore them all, though Maria can be somewhat cold at times and I do wonder if she really has your brothers best interests at heart, but your brother clearly dotes on them. I know your brother would welcome a visit from you, and to think that you haven't yet met Maria, let alone your nieces, Millicent and Rebecca. Such pretty names for two lovely children—I do so wish that I could have had a daughter, your brother and you have been a great blessing to me, a daughter would have been nice, but it wasn't to be, so I shall not waste time with regret, I shall enjoy my granddaughters all the more, and look forward to your visit.

Anyway, take care of yourself Richard, my thoughts and love are with you as always.

Your Beloved Mother

She was his only contact with his family, his brother didn't write, no doubt he would have his time taken up, running the estate, his father would be keeping him busy, what with finding time for mother, and now with his wife and daughters, but he could trust his mother to keep him informed of the news from home. She had written him several times while he was away, first to let him know that his brother had married, and then later to inform him that his brother's wife, Maria, had given birth to a baby daughter—his mother was delighted, a smile touched Richard's lips, his father only had time for boys, so his pleasure would be less so. Edward having daughters, would not have sat well with him, he could hear his father's voice "you deliberately defy me—your wife giving birth to not one chit but two, do you join forces against me? All that has been required of you is to provide a son and heir, and you can't be trusted to fulfil your part in that" as if he had any choice in the matter. In his father's mind, there was only two things that woman were required for, and that was for a man's pleasure and to carry son's for their husbands, beyond that, they were surplus to requirement, so his granddaughters would never have a relationship with their grandfather—although slightly sad, in this case it was probably a blessing in disguise. Mayhap it was kinder that he didn't have any sisters, as much as his mother would have welcomed a girl, her life would have been miserable, just as his mother's life had been. His father was a harsh man, some thought him to be a tyrant, and Richard, thinking about it, had to agree with them. His brother Edward was not like him, he was a gentle and kind man, he wouldn't hurt a soul, their tenants loved him, and the local gentry all showed him respect, all except their father, who at best held him in contempt and at worst, despised him for his mild manner. Edwards features were similar to that of his brother, and by all accounts they were both very dark and very handsome as the Duke had been in his youth, or had been according to his portrait, but Edward was slighter and shorter than himself, his face was longer and he had much lighter eyes, with a fringe of shorter lashes, but there the resemblance ended. His father had even chosen a wife for Edward, and although he had courted a lovely girl, of standing, who was the daughter of a local squire, and a girl who Edward had befriended as a child, his father soon put an end to that—his son would only be allowed to marry someone worthy to be a Duchess and a squires daughter certainly didn't fit that bill. So, as he couldn't trust his son and heir to choose a suitable wife, his father chose for him. His mother had told of this in her letter, but he might have known anyway, Edward certainly wouldn't have been trusted to choose the next Duchess of Warren.

At least he wouldn't be having any of that—thankfully he had his own life, and in truth he was probably more like his father in as much as he was known as a rake, but although his nature was very different to his brothers, he could never be blatantly cruel as his father had been, certainly not after watching the way his father had treated his mother, he could never respect his father's ways. Edward had always, even as a child, feared Henry Penleigh, they had both suffered beatings as children, at their father's hand, though his brother had always fared worse than him. As children, he had been the most mischievous of the two, and far more rebellious than his brother, yet Henry allowed him a great deal more leniency.

He had no problem, letting his father know exactly what he thought of his treatment towards his mother, for what it was worth. He hated the way that his mother had been dispensed of and cast aside after fulfilling her duty of giving him two sons, she had, after all, brought a sizeable dowry to the marriage, and although that would all have been spent—that was, one of his main reasons for choosing her. Henry still held his wife to certain rules though, even now, she was still his wife, and she would be allowed to live as she chose, as long as she stuck to his rules, and one of those meant that on the odd occasions if they received invitations, to dinner, or a ball, or somewhere where the Duchess's presence was required, he enforced that she go, for social purposes only, of course, but as long as she carried out her duties, then the remainder of the time, he ignored her existence, and she was free to do as she pleased, so long as there was no scandals or anything which affected him. Her money had clearly been short lived, as his gambling debts were large and losses very heavy at that time, and he needed it to gain control of a serious situation, but when she had fulfilled her part, by providing him with two sons, and the bulk of the money had run out, so had his wife's charm. His father ruled his household, and his family were dependant on his mercy.

His own reason for leaving the family home was mainly due to his determination to run his own life, and avoid watching his mother's sad lonely one. He could never follow his father's wishes, nor did he have any desire to watch the rest of his family, bow and scrape to the tyrant, so once he had finished his time at Eton, he decided to leave Penleigh Court. He had to admit though that his father for some reason, had made things easier for him, he had always been the favourite, though he never understood why, and strange as it was, he was the only one in the family that his father showed any respect for at all, and he made no attempt to hide the fact. This had never caused problems between him and his brother, but his father would throw up remarks such as he should have been the heir to the title, instead of Edward—after all, in his opinion, Edward was fit for nothing, he was useless and a coward, and should have been born a useless female for all the good he was. All of this made Richard feel very uncomfortable, especially when his father made these unnecessary comparisons in front of his brother, he actually loved Edward, and as brothers they had very different personalities and ways, but they were very close all the same, and he would have hated a rift such as this, to come between them. Richard was surprised however, when his father took him aside and told him that he could do as he pleased with his life, and sanctioned his desire to move to London—he was even more surprised when he favoured him with a free hand and a large allowance, he should go out and make something of himself—and that's what Richard had done. He had taken his town house in Mayfair, and led the life of his choosing, although he had felt guilt at first, as he knew that his brother could never experience the same pleasures, he soothed his conscious by telling himself that his brother had no interest in doing the same things as he.

His lifestyle very soon became widely known to the ton, where he was recognised as a rake of the first degree, no doubt he would have his reputation tarnished as they would liken him to his father. But he knew that he wasn't like his father, yes he appealed to the ladies, and he was known to enjoy a flutter at his club, but he never lost more than he could afford and even with the ladies, he could always be seen in the company of one lady or another, but he never caused a scandal, in fact he was particularly careful as he could not afford to be caught compromising any of them, as that would lead to the inevitable marriage, which he was not prepared to do, so he enjoyed their company but stuck to the rules. He took a series of mistresses, to supply his needs, far simpler that way, but they came and went. Even so, many mamas had still set their sights on him for their daughters, and after spending much time attending balls, soirees and such, he decided that it was time to get away and travel, away from speculation and wagging tongues, and the traps waiting to snare him into a marriage which he didn't want, no, he was certainly not ready for all that, he was still full of life, and he would make the most of it—to charm the women was one thing but why take a wife, when you could have a dozen mistresses.

There came a knock at the library door and the butler entered, interrupting his thoughts yet again "Yes Reeves"

"Dinner is about to be served in the dining room sir"

"Good—I will be along directly"

As he sat down to dinner, he found that he was hungrier than he had thought, the food was good, he just hadn't remembered how good, it certainly was his favourite meal, and Mrs Chalmers knew the very way to cook it to his liking, just as Mrs Breton had at Penleigh when they were children, she would always cook the things which the boys enjoyed, unbeknown to their father, when they were ill, or if the servants thought they had been given a beating which was not deserved, there were times when the servants felt sorry for the two boys and their mother, they knew the way things were, but only dare speak of it in hushed or whispered tones, and behind closed doors, had their father heard as much as a whisper, they would have been slung out without a reference or a penny.

Thinking about his family was making him homesick for Penleigh Court, to see his family again and be a part of it all, maybe he should go and visit his family in Cornwall, not straight away, he needed time to settle back into his home—he had some visits to pay, and things to attend too first, and a visit to his tailor wouldn't go amiss, but maybe in say a month. His mother's letter had been dated one month before he returned, which probably had coincided with his plans to return earlier than he had, he had hoped to return in September, before the cold set in, but he had been having too much fun with Lady Drucilla in Italy, to just cut his stay short, she had been good company, though he couldn't summon any thoughts to take it further—a pastime, but a pleasant interlude, one that held his attention a little longer than he had planned. But now, perhaps he should make a visit to Cornwall for Christmas, do as his mother had suggested, she would indeed be thrilled and excited to see him. Yes, that's what he would do, it would give him a whole month to get his things in order, and he could still leave for Cornwall the week before Christmas. It would of course mean that he would miss some good parties in town, but balls and parties had been in plenty while he was abroad, it wouldn't hurt him to take a few weeks in the country, and spend Christmas at Penleigh Court. There would still be Social events taking place, although on a lesser scale than in London, but even London entertainment would be scaled down at this time of year, many families would be returning to their country homes to enjoy their seasonal festivities.

Remembering their own festivities as boys, Penleigh had been a hive of activity, they had always thrown a huge ball on Christmas Eve and invited all the gentry within a twenty mile radius—the carriages poured up the drive, and the jewels and finery were a sight to behold. The food was laden on the large tables and the wine flowing in plentiful. An orchestra was hired to play for the dancers, Richard could remember how he and Edward had watched from the spy nook, which looked down on the great hall, the large tree decorated with trivialities, and candles burning in their sconces, garlands of holly and ivy, and sprays of mistletoe, hanging above doorways, the luxurious gowns of the ladies, and the elegant cut of the men, as they danced and swirled the night away under the large crystal sparkling chandeliers, it truly was a sight to behold. But that was in the days when they were all still a family, at least in front of guests and the servants, but now, although his mother would join the family for Christmas Day festivities, things would be very different—as for his parents, he would be surprised to see one word pass between them, but now his brother was married and there were children in the house again, even though girls, it just might bring activity and excitement back to the house once again.

His mother had moved, with her maid, to the East wing of the house, while the rest of the family occupied the West wing. His mother seemed to be a lot happier and more content to live this way. At first, she was constantly heartbroken, she lived on her nerves, never knowing where Henry's anger and contempt would strike next, he had broken her heart not only for her own treatment, but that of her elder son, Richard had feared for her sanity, until Edward had suggested that she move into the rooms which were unoccupied, in the East wing, once she decided and agreed to move into her own quarters, and away from all the ire of her husband, she started a quiet and simple lifestyle, things had settled down, her two sons were regular visitors, as was Nanny Grey, who had been her own Nanny, before her boys. She had taken up the post when his mother was but a small child herself, so when the Duchess married the Duke, she took her old Nanny with her, she was given a roof over her head, her food and a small retainer until her own boys were born, so she could then take up their care. Now Nanny Grey had grown old and arthritic, his mother determined that she should stay with her as a companion, where she could be looked after if necessary, so Nanny moved into the East wing along with her loving Alice. The Duke had allowed this, more from disinterest than care, as long as they stayed out of his way, and the Duchess did nothing to cause a scandal, he had no further interest in his wife or what she did.

Richard finished his food, swallowing the last bite before pushing his chair back from the table, he headed back to his library. He went in shutting the door behind him. He walked straight to the sideboard and picking up the decanter of dark red liquid, which Reeves had now decanted for him, he poured some into a glass, then he walked to the mantelpiece, the fire was dying in the grate, and he kicked the embers with his boot, sending sparks flying in every direction. He had made up his mind, he would go to Penleigh for Christmas, and he would stay a few weeks, he may have too in any case, if the weather turned bad. He would take the carriage, he would need to organise gifts for the family before leaving for Cornwall, there was so much more choice here in London. But first, he must deal with this wretched paperwork sat on his desk. He went to his chair and sat down at his desk—his fingers started flipping through the papers lying there—he would deal with these in the morning. He leaned back in his chair, throwing his long lean legs up onto his desk, and stretching his body, until he could feel his muscles and sinews firming then relaxing as he did so, arms resting behind his head. Then he picked up his glass, placed on the desk beside him and swirled the red luscious liquid round, before throwing it down his throat, he sat looking at the empty glass, and thinking what excellent port it was—he would need to attain more of that quality—he would take some to Penleigh Court with him, his father would surely appreciate a port that good. He had planned on visiting his club, but that would wait for another day, he was now beginning to feel very weary, perhaps tomorrow—for tonight, another glass of port and then his own large, warm comfortable feather bed.

Chapter Two

(The Shock)

Richard woke early, opening his eyes and stretching his long body to its full—a small ray of light was seeping into the room, through a chink in the curtains. His head hurt, when he tried lifting it off the pillow, the room started to spin around him, so he let his head drop back down again. He put his fingers to his throbbing temples, and tried to fix his mind on last night, it was no good, he could remember nothing. He must have had a very good night or he wouldn't have been feeling so bad this morning, James, his valet would have no sympathy—he would shake his head and say "Self-inflicted", as clearly it was, each time he did this he vowed never to do it again, but where was the fun in that. He closed his eyes again, suddenly, in a flash, last night's adventure came rushing back to him, he had gone to White's and met up with two of his oldest and best friends.

He had met Russell Hinton and Jasper Trent while at Eton, they had got on well together from the first, they had remained good friends ever since. Before Richard went on his travels they met frequently, to pass the time. They were always getting into scrapes together, and would make stupid bets between themselves, such as racing their thoroughbreds through the park, and who would get to dance first with a certain young lady, at Almacks. They really had been the bucks of the season then, and truth be told, although several years older now, their behaviour hadn't changed so very much.

Last night, they had gone to White's and had several hands of cards. He smiled to himself, remembering that for once he had won, and taken quite a sum of money from his two friends, that was a first, he normally lost, although he never lost more than he could afford to lose, they would of course be eager now to win it all back.

He suddenly remembered the little matter of his friend Russell, yet another confirmed bachelor (or so he would have them believe), yet only last week, at the Roland's ball, he had danced three times with Clarissa Martin, and one of those being the supper dance—that was serious, and if that wasn't enough, he had been seen on two afternoons later, driving his phaeton in the park, with the same young lady, and by all accounts it wasn't for the first time—marriage was definitely on the cards. He and Jasper had taunted Russell to distraction, until he had finally admitted that she was the loveliest creature he had met. Clarissa was very attractive, that was true, she had a round face, with a small turned up nose, and large warm brown eyes, that glinted like gold when she smiled, her golden locks surrounding her face, hanging down to her shoulders in soft golden curls. Russell was the heir to his father's estate, and although his father's heir, he preferred living at the family town house, which looked down on Hyde Park. His father didn't seem to have a problem with that, as long as he spent only the season in London, but spent the rest of his time at the family home. Consequently, he spent a great deal more time in London than at his estate, extending his London stays, as often as he could. Due to the Martins staying on for the small season, it gave him the excuse not to return to his country home—it was clear that he had made up his mind to offer for Clarissa Martin, but clearly he needed the time to gain the courage, before telling his parents about this, in the meantime, he was making the most of her company. It had been Clarissa's second season, she was the third daughter of Joseph and Belinda Martin, and although she was very attractive, being the third daughter, her dowry didn't amount to very much, her parents needed to find the best match possible for her, so they had thought to give her the best chance that they could, and staying on in London for the little season, could be profitable, especially now, seeing the way things were going with Russell and knowing that he was an heir to a fairly large estate in Yorkshire. As for Russell, he wasn't concerned about her dowry, he was taken with the girl and nothing was going to change on that score, she herself seemed to welcome his advances—his parents might not be so eager for this match, but Russell would do as he pleased, he was wealthy enough to make his own decisions, and certainly when it came to choosing a wife.

Another smile crossed Richard's lips—how long before White's would be running a book on Jasper and himself—they would wait a long time for him. Jasper, on the other hand, was more of a rake than either of them, and if his past behaviour was anything to go by, he could well find himself saddled with a chit before much longer. He too was a second son, but he had no direction whatsoever. His father had given him a good allowance, and although they had hoped that he would eventually go into the church, he had no intention of doing so. That would be quite ridiculous, a less likely minister there had never been. Perhaps his father had thought to calm his son's wayward ways—but Richard knew that Jasper was far beyond that. He had already got himself a whole load of trouble, when he had compromised Lady Henrietta Spalding, what he would have given to see Lady Hamilton's face, when she came upon them, she would have relayed the story many times, and each time a little more shocking than the first. He had been abroad when this all took place, but his friend had relayed his predicament in a letter. Being a second son, and with little prospects, Lady Henrietta's father, Sir George Spalding, had told him in no uncertain terms that he had no desire to condemn his only daughter to such a wastrel for the rest of her life, even though she had brought shame on the family, and he forbade Jasper to have any contact with her again. Jasper had been quite relieved, he had no intention of doing so anyway, she had been nothing more than an amusement, if a very pretty one, but that was all. His fear, that he would have been given no choice but to marry her, was thankfully, behind him now. Sir George did not see him as a suitable husband for his daughter, and by taking her back to the country in rather a hurry, had her married her off to a local squire, who had apparently, asked for her hand in marriage earlier and been refused, clearly her father had changed his mind now, and saw him as a more suitable contender than her seducer, and as the gentleman's interest had not waned, even though he was aware of the situation, he did not blame the Lady Henrietta, he had even agreed that were a child born from this little indiscretion, then he would care for it as his own. They had been married within the month, at least her reputation had been laid to rest, and the ton would soon forget what had happened, but Jasper had earned the reputation of a scoundrel, something which seemed to amuse him greatly.

Russell, although a good catch, wasn't the handsomest buck of the season— he had a shock of red hair, and a mass of freckles, giving him almost a boyish appearance. He was very thick set, with a square jawline, and his small, pale blue eyes, which sank back into his head, were fringed with eyelashes that were hardly noticeable, they were so fair, but he had a jolly appearance, and a winning smile, with little lines at the corners of his eyes, which creased and made his eyes twinkle when he smiled or laughed, and it was this that drew people to him. Jasper on the other hand, was very handsome, he was of average height, and build, but he had fair wavy hair, which surrounded his round face, with bright sparkling turquoise eyes, fringed with long fair lashes. His mouth was full, and when he smiled, there were silver sparks in his eyes making them twinkle, and shine, and with his straight even teeth, the ladies were drawn into him like a moth to a flame. How many times had Richard seen that happen—women were so gullible, behind that easy smile was a scoundrel stalking his prey. Richard knew his friends as well as anyone could, and he had to admire them both in their own different ways. One thing was sure, they all enjoyed a game of faro, at Whites, and they all liked a drink—they got up to the same pranks, although each very different in their looks and manner, they were three of a kind—that's why they were such close friends, and they trusted one another implicitly.

A tap at the door brought him back to earth, his head still ached, but it was time to get up, he couldn't lay a bed all day. He shouted "Come", he pressed his palm to his forehead. The door opened and James, his valet entered.

"A good night was it sir—did you not vow to avoid this situation again, and only three nights ago"? His valet was tall and lean, and stood a good head above the other servants, though he was about the same height as Richard, he stood with a wry smile on his lips.

"Yes, I believe so—but damn it all James, a man has to have a few pleasures, would you begrudge me mine"?

"Certainly not sir, but nor would I choose to spend a day under the weather as a result of a few hours pleasure, but it is your choice sir, not for me to comment" that was rich, it didn't seem to matter whether or not it was up to him to comment, but he always did—what did he know of having a good time, let him think what he would, he would have his say anyway.

"Obviously not, but incidentally, I have no intention of feeling ill for the rest of the day—in fact, I have decided to go for a ride this morning, that should soon set me to rights, and you are quite right, the fact is it isn't up to you to comment—but that has never stopped you yet"

"No sir, as you say, we are all entitled to our opinions" with that James walked over to the bedside and placed a cup and saucer down on the bedside table, before going to the window and throwing back the curtains. Light immediately flooded the room, a bright shaft falling across Richards bed, and hurting his eyes—Richard squinted and ventured an arm from under the bedcovers to cover his eyes, it was freezing, he quickly thrust his arm back and pulled the cover back up to his chin, and shuddered. James had gone into his dressing room and was taking out clothes that were suited to Richard's ride. He looked back to the window, there were long tendrils trailing all over the inside of the window pane, like sparkling diamonds in the bright light, which portrayed a hard frost, but at least the day was sunny and bright—just the morning for a ride, that's what he needed to see him right. James had left the room, but he soon returned carrying a pitcher of hot water, which he placed beside the bowl, steam puffing whisps of mist above the jug, inviting him to wash and shave.

"I shall be back shortly sir, drink your tea while it's hot, then I shall return and help you dress"

"Thank you but I can manage this morning—I am quite capable of dressing myself" he had had enough of a lecture in this fragile state.

"As you wish sir" and he left, closing the door behind him. Damn and blast the man, he wouldn't be patronised, he would decide his own pleasures, he really didn't need to have someone showing him the error of his ways—he may as well have stayed at Penleigh Court and let his father rule his life.

Richard pushed himself up in the bed, and reached for the cup sat beside him, he drank the warm and welcome liquid, before throwing back the covers and climbing from his bed, after a wash and shave, he went into his dressing room, he quickly dressed in the clothes which James had already laid out for him, and pushed a comb through his hair, it was too cold to tarry—he had started to feel a little better already.

Once dressed and ready, he ran downstairs and out into the courtyard, to the stables, he ordered that his stallion be saddled and made ready, took hold of the reins, thrust his leg into the stirrup and with one large leap, jumped up into the saddle, throwing his other leg over Tyson's back, before riding off at a steady pace, into the cold morning air.

Richard returned a couple of hours later, he felt much better, his head had stopped aching, and he felt fresh, cold and exhilarated. He had taken Tyson for a good canter, across the park and it felt wonderful, it certainly seemed to be the cure for his hangover, and it had blown the cobwebs away. He had looked for his two friends, in the park, but neither were there to be seen, though it was still fairly early and neither were early risers, and if they had been feeling anything like him this morning, he wouldn't really expect to see either of them before noon.

He jumped down from Tyson's back, and handed the reins to a waiting groom before heading back into the house. Inside, he threw down his riding crop and took off his hat, and gloves in the hall, before going through to the dining room to find his breakfast. He felt that he could eat a mountain today. The fresh air had done him more good than he cared to believe. He walked over to the sideboard, where breakfast had been laid out in silver dishes with lids. He removed each of the lids in turn, his stomach started to rumble at the divine smells coming from the dishes, he was certainly very hungry and ready for this, he helped himself to a large portion of eggs, bacon and devilled kidneys, and a hot steamy cup of coffee, then he sat down at the table, and ate his hearty fare.

After having his fill, he went into the library, he had dealt with all the paperwork which had awaited him on his return to London, thank goodness that was done, it seemed hardly possible that three weeks had passed since his return home, he had made his decision to go to Cornwall for Christmas, and if he was to keep to his decision, then he would be leaving this weekend. He still needed to purchase a few choice gifts for the family, before setting off.

Already since returning to London, he had fallen back into his old habits, he was beginning to wish that he hadn't made his mind up to go to Cornwall after all, but his mother had expressly asked him to pay a visit, he at least owed her that much, after all, he couldn't remember the last time he had seen her, it had to be almost three years, surely not, but he had been travelling for two, no, he must go. His father would probably welcome a visit, though he wouldn't show as much. In all truth it would be highly bad manners, not to go and visit his brother too, after all he hadn't seen him for about three years either, and he did miss him from time to time, it would look awfully churlish to avoid meeting his new sister-in-law, and now of course, his two new nieces—no, he wouldn't give Maria a chance to think him rude and dislike him even before meeting him. He would shop this morning, and leave for Cornwall by the end of the week, as planned. He went to the fireplace, and pulled the bell cord on the wall, within a few moments, he heard footsteps in the hall, slow and precise, the door opened and Reeves entered.

"Ah Reeves, could you have the carriage brought round please, I have decided to visit Penleigh Court, I shall be staying there for Christmas and through the New Year, but I don't want them notified, it's to be a surprise for the Duke and Duchess—my brother too, I must meet his wife and my two nieces who I haven't met yet. But meanwhile, if I am to spend Christmas with them, then I must go out shopping for a few gifts for the family"

"Yes sir, I shall see to it straight away"

"Thank you Reeves"

Shortly afterwards, Reeves knocked and opened the library door

"The carriage is ready and waiting at the front door sir"

"Thank you, I should be home for lunch, if you could let Mrs Chalmers know"

"Yes sir—I shall tell her"

Richard got up, and went out into the hall, Reeves helped him on with his great coat and handed him his hat and gloves. Then he held the door open, Richard bowed his head as he stepped through the door, and down the front steps, where his carriage was waiting, a footman dressed in the Penleigh livery of blue and gold, opened the door and pulled down the steps of the carriage for Richard to step up, but he didn't use them, he sprang up into the carriage in one leap, before seating himself in the corner and leaning back against the blue plush padded interior. Once the carriage had pulled away, Reeves stepped back inside and closed the front door—he must let Mrs Chalmers know so that she would have lunch ready for his lordship today, he wasn't in the habit of being at home for lunch since he returned from abroad. He must also inform Mrs Denton that Christmas and the New Year would be a quiet affair for the household, with their master spending time in Cornwall, their festive celebrations would be a quiet and intimate affair—she would be very relieved to hear it.

It was two in the afternoon when he finally returned to his Mayfair home. He wasn't fond of shopping, that was better suited to women, but it had to be done. That at least would be one task a wife would take from his shoulders, marriage did have its benefits. Never mind, it was done now. He would have Mrs Denton the housekeeper, wrap the items, after all, he couldn't take them unwrapped, that would never do. Mrs Denton would be able to make the ladies gifts look very pretty with ribbons and bows and such like, all the little fripperies which woman seemed to hold so much store by, he hadn't the time or inclination for such things himself. A footman carried the packages into the hall and placed them on the table, Reeves helped him out of his coat and took his hat and gloves, before heading straight for the dining room. Word was sent to the kitchen of the master's return, and lunch was served immediately.

After he had eaten, he went to his library, he poured some of the golden liquid from the decanter, into his glass—the brandy warmed him—he was still trying to thaw from his mornings ride, although the sun was shining brightly, the frost was rimy and heavy, coating everything it touched, in a shroud of white, with the sun sparkling on the frost, it truly looked a winter wonderland out there today. The sky was a lovely pale blue, with not a cloud to be seen, it would have been a beautiful winter's day had it not been for the bitterly cold brisk North wind, which blew right through his clothing and sank into his very bones. He shivered as he thought of it. He poured himself another glass of brandy, and sat himself down in his chair. He only hoped that the snow would keep off, or it would make his trip to Cornwall difficult indeed.

He crossed to the fireplace and pulled the bell cord, within minutes Reeves entered.

"Reeves, could you please ask Mrs. Denton to come and see me, as soon as possible"

"Yes sir, of course sir, right away"

Reeves closed the door behind him and Richard sat listening as his steps moved across the tiled hall floor and died away in the distance. He opened one of the drawers in his desk, and pulled out some labels, Mrs Denton would wrap the gifts he had bought, but he must write labels to go with each gift. He picked up his pen, and dipped it into the ink—then he pondered over each label, before writing something on each one. Once that was finished, he stood up and made his way back to the fireplace, where he picked up the poker and prodded at the large piece of wood, burning in the grate, the wood melted, turning to ashes before his eyes, although beneath was hot red embers, sparks flew out from the red hot glow, Richard took another piece of wood from the basket in the fireplace and threw it on to the red ashes, in seconds flames were leaping up, around the new piece of wood, throwing out a heat to break through the chill, before seating himself once again. A tap at the door, and Reeves entered "Sorry to disturb you sir, but this letter has just been delivered—he walked to the desk and handed Richard the sealed letter which was lying on the silver salver. "thank you Reeves", he looked at the note in his hand, Reeves walked round to the fire and went as if to make it up, but realizing that it had already been taken care of, he took a step back. Richard was studying the note, he recognised the seal straight away, it was his mother's handwriting, perhaps she would suggest he visit for Christmas, and a smile caught the corners of his mouth, that would spoil his plans. Reeves walked to the door, and quietly slipped out, closing the door behind him. Richard broke the seal and started to read through the note.

My Dearest Boy,

I am writing to you in a heartbroken, devastated state, the most terrible thing has happened which I fear I shall not recover from. Only yesterday your brother rode into town in the afternoon, but he never returned. When his horse returned without him, it was evident that something was very wrong, so a search party was sent out to find him, but it was too late, there had been the most terrible accident, he had taken the cliff path, and you know how narrow and hazardous that route can be, I cannot understand what made him go that way, but whether his horse was startled and threw him, or whether he stopped for some reason and slipped, he fell to his death on the rocks below Devil's Point, I doubt we shall ever know the truth of it all.

It is hard to believe this could have happened, I still cannot fully take it in, as both you and your brother were brought up here, you were both well aware of the dangers which exist in this wild and craggy countryside. Why on a windy winter's day, would your brother even have ventured along that path—it was difficult enough on a still summer day, but at this time of year, it was virtually impassable.

My poor, darling boy—how can I go on without him, it is only his love, and that of his family, which keeps me going, living here, with my loneliness as I must—how can I survive now?

My darling Richard, I do so hate to ask, but I so long to see you, I do so wish that you could visit, I miss you so very much—and now, with your dear brother gone, you are all that I have. Just a short visit would mean the world to me.

I am so sorry to have to bring you such terrible news, I trust that you are well, but I implore you to give thought to your family, who loves you so much. You are now my one and only son, and I need you to come home, so I am begging you to consider.

My love to you as always,
Your Loving Mother

Richard sat back, the letter fell from his hands on to the desk, he could feel the blood drain from his body—his hands were shaking, he was still staring at the writing, although he read the words, he couldn't believe what they were saying, and he was staring at the letter in disbelief. A knock came at the door, which broke through his thoughts. He jumped, startled, before taking control of himself and the situation

"Come in"

"You wanted me sir"?

"Mrs Denton, I'm sorry but this is not a good time, I have been given bad news. I will speak to you later"

"Yes sir"

He could see by the way she crossed her hands at the wrists, and gave a sniff, that she wasn't pleased, but he couldn't deal with that now. He stood up and went to the sideboard, where he filled his glass with the golden liquid, his hands were shaking and he had to try very hard not to spill the contents of his glass, while returning to his seat. He picked up the letter once again, and re-read the words. He had read this right—his dear brother Edward was dead. Why indeed, would he have gone that route at this time of year, hell, it was hazardous enough in high summer, but in winter, it was treacherous, had Edward lost his mind? He kept going over and over the same question, more than anything else, he couldn't believe that Edward could have acted so recklessly, or had he . . . . no, that didn't bare thinking about, surely he hadn't gone that way deliberately, he knew that his father had always treated him harshly, but surely that wouldn't have driven him to take his own life—and besides, he had a wife and two daughters to think about now—he loved them dearly, his mother had told him that—no, he had everything to live for, that couldn't be the case. He must get home, and as quickly as he could. He would have Mrs Denton wrap the gifts, though that was now of little importance, and he would leave in the morning. He picked up his glass, and swirled the golden liquid round inside, and then it dawned on him, if Edward was dead, then he was his father's heir—he would one day take his father's title and estate—his dream for the future gone, in a puff of smoke. He didn't want the Dukedom, but what choice did he have, he was the heir and what he wanted, and all the plans he had made, would now vanish. He lifted his glass and threw the golden fire down his throat, he could feel the burning as it slipped down, at least he knew he was alive. He would be expected to marry—and to produce an heir—the thing which he had put to the back of his priorities for so long, would now be expected of him to fulfil his duty. He could not believe what was happening to his family, what had happened to his brother or why, and now, because of it, his own world would be turned upside down too. He realized that he was shivering, though not from cold, it must be the shock, he was stunned, and so many thoughts were crowding his head, he couldn't seem to think straight anymore. What would become of Maria and her daughters, he would have to look after them—his brother would at least expect that of him. He could make sure that they were taken care of, and he would need to see that the girls were properly educated and eventually given a season, and both found good husbands, but that was a long way off—though it was the least that he could do. Maria would always have a home at Penleigh Court. But for now, he must go to Cornwall, immediately. What had started off as a pleasant interlude, and a pleasant visit, was now turning into nothing short of a nightmare. He walked over to the sideboard, and poured another shot of golden liquid into his glass— and tossed it straight down his throat.

He would speak to Reeves, and then to James. His trunk would have to be packed immediately, and made ready for him to leave first thing in the morning. He once again called for Mrs Denton, this time he requested that she wrap the gifts which he had bought that morning, before finding James, to pack his trunk and make ready for his trip, he would take James with him, he had never been to Cornwall before, and he expected that he would have something to say on the matter, but his services would be required, so he had better inform him directly, he must then make sure that everything here was up to date, as he could not be sure of returning in the near future. He must write notes for his good friends, as they would surely wonder at his absence. So many things to do, and he couldn't concentrate on any of it.

He picked up his pen and a sheet of paper, dipped his pen in the ink, and started penning a letter to the first of his friends, he would explain briefly, but he couldn't say when he would get to see either of them again.

23

He wrote the first note, then folded and sealed it, then he did the same again—that done, he could now go back to the thoughts which were crowding his mind.

Only this morning he had planned to spend a few weeks away, now he was leaving and didn't have any idea when or even if he would be returning. He had planned his life out to the letter, he knew exactly where he was going, and how he would get there, but now he felt apprehensive, his life had never been so uncertain, bile rose in his throat but he gulped it back—all he did know was that he must fulfil his family duty and he had to get to the bottom of his brother's death and he wouldn't rest until he had. A strange feeling was creeping over him, it wasn't good—something about all this wasn't right—and it sent cold shivers down his spine, just as if someone had walked over his grave, he tried to shake himself free of this feeling of foreboding, but it persisted, he would definitely get to the bottom of this matter, and nothing would deny him that.

CHAPTER THREE

(The Journey)

Richard awoke with a start—he gave a shiver and drew his great coat closer around his body—the rattle of the carriage wheels and the bumps as they hit the potholes and ruts in the rough country roads, and the clip clop of the horse's hooves, as they rumbled on. This was the second day he had spent sat in this wretched carriage, having his bones shaken to distraction. He had stopped at a small coaching Inn the previous night, he had thought to get some sleep and rest the horses before continuing this difficult journey. The place had been warm and dry, and the food very good, a short respite from this infernal buffeting, was a short and welcome relief, the room was clean and serviceable, but there was little comfort in the bed—it was large and looked welcoming enough, until he had tried to sleep in it—hard and very lumpy was the only way to describe it and he had not slept a wink all night—he had eventually got out of bed and stoked the dying fire in the grate, then ripping a blanket from the bed, he pulled a large and comfortable chair to what was left of the fire, and wrapped the blanket around him—he still didn't sleep much, but at least he could doze in fitful comfort.

Though the bed left a great deal to be desired, his lack of sleep was probably not solely due to the comfort of the bed—he could think of nothing but his brother's death—he tried desperately hard to make sense of the facts which his mother had given him, but even with a large stretch of the imagination, he couldn't comprehend any of it—it just didn't make any sense, all he could hope for now was that once he arrived at Penleigh Court, things would become clearer, maybe by now his family would have a better idea of what had happened. Something had to make him take that road, but what—that was proving allusive to him at present. For the life of him, he couldn't understand. That feeling of foreboding had not left him either, and every so often, it shot through his body as a shooting star through the sky, the feeling becoming harder to ignore each time—the feeling hung in his mind, like a ghost, waiting to appear, he shuddered to think of it.

He sat back in his seat, leaning back against the plush interior, and gazed out of the window—the day was bitterly cold, and still with a brisk wind, the sky was hung heavy with grey clouds, it gave the sky a white appearance, edged in grey, with a pinkish tint. That was a sure sign of snow—he hoped that it would hold off long enough to complete his journey, though he wouldn't be too sure. All around him the countryside was flat, with clumps of heather and bracken, dusted with a light touch of white sparkling frost—they must be on the Devonshire Downs road, that would mean that he still had another two or three hours journey. He was starting to feel hungry, it must be past lunch time by now, he reached inside his coat, and took the watch from his waistcoat pocket, it was ten minutes past one, he closed the watch and returned it, before opening the small package which the landlord of the Lamb and Flag had insisted he take. He looked at the food inside, it certainly looked appetizing, there was a large piece of venison pie, a lump of cheese and some crusty bread which had presumably been baked fresh on the previous day. He had filled his hip flask with brandy to help keep the cold at bay. That should keep him going until he reached Penleigh Court, he had enjoyed a large breakfast before leaving that morning, and he certainly had no intention of stopping again, they needed to keep going if they were to reach their destination by nightfall, and now with snow threatening, their journey could be slowed to a walking pace, and they would then be fortunate to arrive before midnight. He sat back in his seat, and started munching his way through the food, it really was very good, once he had finished, and every morsel had gone, he took a good nip from his flask. Now he would try and close his eyes once again.

The carriage clattered on, while he drifted in and out of strange dreams and weird thoughts, although not asleep, he was not fully awake either, his mind had drifted back to the cliff path above Devils Point, he could see two young boys walking there with their governess, the sun was shining brightly in the sky, feeling warm against their skin, and he could hear her warning them to watch their steps and keep to the track—while he watched, suddenly a stranger came out of nowhere, the sun had gone now, the sky had darkened, he couldn't see a face, the body was covered from head to foot in a black cloak, the hood pulled down, hiding the face from view, there was no way of telling whether the intruder was male or female. Hands alighted from the cloak, they were long and very thin, but it was still impossible to tell the gender of the stranger. Suddenly they locked on to one of the boys, pushing his body out, until he hung over the precipice, suspended only by the offending limbs, over the treacherous rocks below—the child started to scream, as did the governess, she reached out to try and grab the boy, the dark figure let go of the child, its hands disappeared, the child fell, shrieking, to the rocks below—when he looked down over the edge of the cliff, the child had become a man, and all he could see was his own face but pale and lifeless, his eyes staring but seeing nothing, his body ripped apart on the treacherous rocks below—he looked away, the path was empty—not a soul in sight. The dream had gone, and he was awake and alert again—his breathing shallow and coming in short sharp spasms, he shuddered, yet beads of sweat ran down his face, the awful memory stayed with him still. He sat up straight, trying to shake off whatever it was that had haunted him, his mind playing tricks on him, nothing more—his senses told him to forget it, after all, it was no more than a bad dream. His breathing steady once again, he gazed out of the window, the road was taking a sharp turn to the left, and he could hear the sound of rushing water, he knew then that the cliff edge was just over the horizon, and that the rushing sound was the sea, breaking against the jagged rocks beneath, even though he wasn't near enough to see any of it—he could taste the salt on his lips. Then he noticed the fluffy white specs of moisture, dropping from the sky. The countryside was becoming more craggy, from the right carriage window, he could see hills in the background—they had reached Cornwall at last, the sky had turned completely grey with a darkened hue, thank God he would soon be home. The carriage blundered on, the small white specs which had started by melting away as they touched the windows, were now growing in size, and dropping with more speed and gusto, the wind was howling, and there was a white blanket covering everything in sight. The carriage started to slow, the wind was blowing with such gusts, that the coachman clearly feared it would overturn. Now the direction of the coach was turning once again—the road was curling round to the right, away from the coastal road, and heading back inland—Richard closed his eyes, he could hardly feel movement, but they were moving at a slow rate—he reached in his waistcoat pocket, and pulled out his watch again, twenty minutes past three, they would be hard pushed to reach Penleigh Court before dark now, but with the weather having turned, he knew that they could go no faster. The wind was whipping the large fluffy white snowflakes which were falling thick and fast, causing it to drift across ditches and hedges as it went, the best that they could hope for now, was to reach Penleigh Court this side of midnight, and in one piece. Richard gazed from the window again—the bright white landscape all looked the same, then, as he watched, he noticed a landmark that he knew very well, telling him exactly where they were—as boys, he and Edward had a fearful fascination with this place, there was a crossroad just ahead, called 'Gallows Cross', they had just passed the gibbet, from which hung a half rotted corpse—though he was now a grown man, the place still made him shudder, he wondered who the poor fellow was, and what he might have done to deserve his fate. The body had been swinging in the wind, and was now covered in white glistening snow, such an eerie sight. The carriage trundled on slowly, the horses moving at little more than a walk, and to make matters worse, the road had started to climb quite steeply, they were wending their way into the village. Richard looked out to the left, knowing full well what he was looking for next, the ground was completely covered, but he could make out the headstones of the graveyard, and a little further on, the church, with its lych-gate, close to the track road, and a path leading up to the entrance with snow covered box hedges, on either side of the path, now hidden from view beneath the whitening mass. The carriage ploughed on, a building came into view—a three storey building, made of grey stone with snow covered ivy, winding its way up, and covering one side of the house, it had a small porch over the front door, and many windows, with glowing lights shining from two of the downstairs rooms, reflecting through the panes of glass, down on the newly laid snow, causing it to glitter like diamonds in the twilight. He remembered the rectory, where he and his brother would go on summer days, as their cook, Mrs Preen, would always offer them a glass of lemonade and a biscuit, freshly baked from the oven. He remembered the wonderful lawn at the back of the house, which ran downhill from the terrace, and the rose gardens with blooms the colours of the rainbow, then further on down to a gate at the bottom, which connected with the graveyard, and to which the vicar would walk to the church, to take the morning service.

The carriage still lumbered slowly on—climbing upward toward the village, there was no let-up in the weather, and the sky was turning to night, very quickly now. Then as they rounded a curve in the rutted road, the village came into full view, over the little stone bridge, where normally the water from the stream would run and trickle over stones in its path, but which was now frozen solid, and in the last light of the day, he could see ducks, unable to swim, slipping and sliding, through the virgin snow, trying to locate water, but finding only snow covered ice. Just across the bridge, the road swung round sharply to the left, the stream now to the left of the carriage, to the right, a small coaching inn, with a lantern burning over the door, next to it the stables, and then the blacksmith. How little things had changed, directly past the blacksmiths, a row of small stone cottages, all belonging to his father's estate. Behind the cottages, a lane leading up to a tiny shop, selling all sorts of small items and bric-a-brac.

Suddenly the carriage came to a halt—Richard shouted to the footman to ask the reason for this untimely stop. One of the footmen came to the open doorway "I'm sorry sir, but there is something lying to the side of the road, right over there", he said this pointing his finger, arm outstretched, to a small opening in the snow covered hedgerow, running up from the bend in the stream "There was no telling what it is sir, but we thought as we should check it out as it seemed to be moving—anything out tonight will freeze to death without a doubt sir" Richard jumped down "Of course, I shall check it out myself" he stepped briskly through the deepening snow, the wind still whipping the white flakes as they fell, piling them up against the hedgerow, making his steps difficult, the snow half way up the length of his polished hessians. He reached the heap lying almost hidden, at first he thought it to be no more than a bundle of old rags, but on closer inspection, he realized that this bundle was a young girl, she was cold and shivering, and he could see that she couldn't stand. At first he thought her unconscious, but as he neared, she looked up. Richard's only thought was to get her inside the carriage, and out of this cold and unforgiving night. He scooped her up in his arms, and with a few long strides, reached the carriage, his footmen following him, collecting the girls basket which had fallen into the snow covered grass beside her. Richard, still with the girl in his arms, leapt up into the carriage and laid her on the opposite seat to where he was sitting. Her cloak, covered in snow and sodden, no longer held any warmth, he reached down and removed it from her person, brushing the snow from her cheeks and eyelashes, he then removed and shook off his own great coat, and wrapped it around the girl, in an effort to warm her. Her teeth were chattering and her face was white as the snow, she tried to speak but Richard held his finger to his mouth to quieten her. He took his flask from the inside of his great coat, and held it to her lips—"Take a little, it will warm you" the girl did as she was told, then instantly coughed and spluttered "It's alright, you are quite safe now. My name is Richard Penleigh, you have nothing to fear, what is your name, and where do you live?"

"My name is Clara Penrose sir and I live at the old rectory, my father is the local vicar, thank you for coming to my rescue, I am most grateful for your kindness" Richard could hardly see the young woman's face, and strained his eyes in the darkness which had now encompassed the inside of the carriage, to see the owner of such a soft, well—spoken lyrical voice. "Don't give it another thought, I am glad to be of assistance". One thing was for sure though, she wasn't one of the estate tenants, she was of gentle birth, the vicar's daughter, he couldn't remember the vicar having a daughter, in fact, he couldn't remember the vicar ever having a wife either, so clearly a new vicar had been installed in the local church, since he left. The footman had now lighted the lamps on each side of the carriage, but the light from the lamps lit only the roadside, and not the inside of the coach, he would just have to wait until they arrived at the rectory, to see the face of the girl, with the hypnotising voice, who he had rescued from the elements.

"Where are you hurt Miss Penrose"? The girl tried to lift her head up, in an effort to show him that it was her ankle "please, don't try to move, I shall have you home shortly, my first priority is to get you home and in the warm, if pneumonia is to be avoided, then a doctor can be called to attend to your ankle"

"Thank you sir, you are very kind"

"Not at all. Tell me Miss Penrose, how did you come to be lying there on such a night"?

"Every week, I call on the elderly and the very poor of the village, to take them food which my mother instructs our cook to pack into a basket for them—I had been to visit old Mr. Hogan, who lives in the little cottage at the top of West Lane, while picking my way back in the snow, I caught my foot in a hedgerow, which I was unable to see, due to the snow, and my ankle twisted, throwing me off my balance and on to the ground—I tried to get up, but couldn't stand or put any weight on the ankle, and what with the weather, there was no one who's attention I could attract, I hoped that by now my father would have sent someone out to look for me"

"then clearly we chanced by at the right moment" he shouted to the footman, to turn the carriage around, and instructed him where they were bound—the door slammed and within a few moments, the carriage was slowing wending its way, at a walking pace, but back in the direction from which they had just come.

When they arrived at the rectory, Richard sent his footman to rap on the door, a few minutes later the door swung open and a young maid stood there. Richard leant forward, picked up the girl, still wrapped in his great coat, and stepped down from the carriage. Mrs Penrose was starting to worry for her daughter's safety and was in the process of getting a search party together to go out and look for her, she hurried up behind the maid as Richard stepped into the hall, the girl, safely lodged in his arms. "Oh my goodness, your hurt" Ada Penrose spoke to her daughter, both hands went up and she pressed her flat palms against her mouth in shock, then she quickly turned "bring her in here sir", this time to Richard, before turning on her heels and scurrying to a door and pushing it open, then standing back to allow him to pass. He carried Miss Penrose into the drawing room, it was a large room, and although the furniture was a little sparse, it was of good quality. There were three settee's in total, all upholstered in pale green silk, with darker green silk curtains at the windows, the walls were papered with dainty pink flower clusters. There were a few little wooden tables dotted around the room, and a selection of large potted ferns. Two armchairs facing each other, upholstered in pale pink silk, stood either side the fireplace, facing each other, and a grand piano stood at the other end. There was also a small writing table under one of the large windows, which Richard knew would face down the terrace and across the sweeping lawn, although the curtains had been closed against the evening. A large fire burned brightly in the grate, the flames making patterns on the wall. In the centre of the mantelpiece, an ormolu clock, with candlesticks either end. Richard placed the girl on the settee nearest to the fire, before standing back to take in the view. For the first time, and by the light of the lamp, Richard had his first real sight of the girl he had rescued. She was older than he had first thought, and the prettiest girl he had ever set eyes on. He thought perhaps her age to be twenty, she had a small heart shaped face, surrounded by dark brown locks of hair, that shone different colours of red in the firelight, and which hung in ringlets down over her shoulders and down her back. Her eyes were soft warm hazel, that twinkled like gold, and her lips, although still a little pale, he felt sure were normally pink and inviting, long lashes fluttered against her pale cheeks, and her skin like ivory silk. When she smiled her teeth were as white and straight as pearls set into a perfectly set necklace, with dimples in both cheeks, which appeared each time a smile crossed her lips, adding even more to her appeal. Miss Clara Penrose—he would not forget her face or voice in a hurry.

As Richard studied her, she too had been trying to take in his handsome good looks, she had noticed his warm eyes and soft gently curling raven hair, and the cut of his clothes, which screamed of excellent taste. His large hands, and his tall frame, with his very athletic body, made her heart skip a beat. The way that he had just picked her up, as if she were nothing more than a rag doll, and carried her through the snow, which was half way up his highly polished hessians—she could easily fall for a man such as this, but that could never be, this gentleman had said that his name was Richard Penleigh, her heart sank, this man was not of her social standing, she was a vicars daughter, he was the heir to a Dukedom, she must put him from her mind. She was very grateful though that he had probably saved her from freezing to death this afternoon.

Mrs Penrose had disappeared, but a few minutes later she returned and entered the room carrying a blanket, "I have sent word to Dr. Somerville, so he should be here shortly, but in the meantime, let me wrap you in this to keep you warm, Daisy will bring you some hot chocolate to warm you". Mrs Penrose took Richards great coat, which was still wrapped around her daughter, and covered her with the blanket instead, handing the coat back to Richard and turning to him she said "I must thank you sir, for rescuing my daughter, though we haven't been introduced, I can't bear to think what may have happened, had you not found her when you did. Could I offer you some refreshment"?

"That is very kind of you ma'am, but I must resist your hospitality. My name is Richard Penleigh and I am headed for Penleigh Court where I had hoped to arrive before nightfall, now I must be on my way, but I should be much obliged to you ma'am if you would permit me to call on Miss Penrose, perhaps in a few days, to check that she is in fact on the mend"?

"But of course, my lord—I'm sure that Clara would welcome the company"

Richard inclined his head to the ladies, and Mrs Penrose dropped a curtsy, "until then—good evening ladies"

Richard turned and left the room, pulling his great coat on, and tightening it around his body to keep out the chill. Daisy, the maid scurried to open the door, and Richard took his leave.

Back in the coach, the snow was still falling hard and fast, though not quite so hard as before, the flakes shimmering silver in the light from the lamps, though there was no let-up with the wind, it had settled very deep on the already rutted road, making the carriage wheels slip and slide with each turn. The coachman, and footmen, although very tired, wet and cold, were also eager to be on their way, no doubt their thoughts now on a hot meal and a comfortable bed.

Richard sat back once again, in his seat. He too, was very eager now to arrive at Penleigh Court. He wondered if he would have ventured on this journey at all, had he known how miserable it would prove to be— although, a smile slowly crossed his face, had he not made this journey, he would never have met Miss Penrose, and that would have been a great shame, as he felt a strange thrill at the prospect of getting to know her better. She would certainly provide him with a little amusement, while in the area.

The carriage slowed almost to a stop, then suddenly, a sharp turn to the right, Richard knew that they had arrived, they were turning into the drive, through the large iron gates, past the gatehouse, then up the long sweep of drive, past the lake to the right of the drive, now frozen solid and covered in driving snow, and shielded by the ghostly shrouded trees, before heading on up to the house. He could just see the lamplight from the downstairs windows, giving off a welcoming glow, as the horses turned into the circle leading up to the main entrance, the wind whipped up a frenzy of sparkling white flurry, and adding it to the already large snow drift mounting up between the four columns, and building up to a mound before the large, heavy solid oak front door.

Finally the carriage came to a halt. Richard sighed with relief as one of the footmen opened the door, and dropped the steps, for him to exit, before lifting down his trunk and following him inside the hallway. The butler, Newbridge, had opened the door, it squealed on its hinges, even before they had alighted, he must have heard them coming. Here at last. As he stood in the hallway, looking around him, taking in the scenery, that feeling of foreboding welled up inside him once again, Newbridge helped him out of his great coat and placed his gloves inside his upturned hat, placing them on the large hall table, which already housed a large potted plant. "It's good to see you my lord, the Duke will be along directly" "thank you Newbridge, perhaps you could arrange for me to take a bath, I am cold and hungry and as you can imagine, the journey has been somewhat trying, so I would take a bath before dinner if you please" "yes, of course my lord, I shall send someone to see to it straight away" "thank you Newbridge". Newbridge had been with their family since he could remember, the Duke held great store by him, though Richard believed that the old man was more in tune with the Duchess, as were most of the servants, but though their preferences were only whispered behind closed doors, they knew better than to disobey the Dukes orders, therefore endearing them to him, as much as that was possible. His mind wandered back to his brother, if he was looking for answers to the questions which were in his head, then there was a good possibility that he should speak to the servants, he would have to be discreet, but he was determined that whatever the cause of his brother's death, he wouldn't rest until he got to the bottom of it, so what better way to start than to speak with some of the servants, he knew they had opinions, and they probably knew better than any, what had been going on, it was just getting them to talk to him—he would see what he could do.

CHAPTER FOUR

(Penleigh Court)

"Richard dear boy, what an unexpected pleasure" the Dukes voice boomed out across the hall. He had heard a commotion, and left his library to see what was going on. "So, you have decided to honour us with your presence—I had thought that you were still in Europe, obviously got it wrong"

"Indeed father, your prodigal has returned. I actually arrived back in London two months ago, but am here now, due to a letter which I received from the Duchess, but a few days since—informing me of my brother's tragic death"

"I see, so, you thought it a good time to visit, well, as you can see" he replied stretching out his arm and waving his hand across in front of his body, "This is a house in mourning, so there will be no dancing and parties here—you would have done better to stay in London, I'm sure it would have proved to be a little more entertaining for you, especially as I see you are still in need of a wife"

"I am well aware that we are all in mourning sir, that's as it should be, and I am in no hurry to find a wife, though I am very interested to hear how my brother met his death. First however, I am very wet and cold, and have been travelling for two days, I should be grateful for a bath and a change of clothing before dinner, in fact, I have already taken the liberty of requesting Newbridge to organise such for me".

"Yes yes, of course, you had better go into your old room" he turned and shouted loudly "Newbridge", the old man came walking slowly and upright, from the direction of the kitchens "Your Grace?"

"See that my son has his old room made ready—and then prepare a bath"

"Yes your Grace, preparation is already under way I believe the room is being prepared as we speak"

"Good, and get someone to move that trunk out of the hall, its damned untidy"

"yes your Grace, I shall see to it directly" and with that he disappeared once again toward the kitchens.

"Dinner is at eight o clock sharp, you know that I won't tolerate tardiness" said the Duke, turning back to his son

"Of course father, I had not forgotten, and as it happens, I'm rather hungry anyway—my brother's wife, she will no doubt be joining us?"

"I expect so" Richard gave his father an incline of the head before turning and ascending the stairs.

He opened the bedroom door, it all looked very much as if time had stood still—the huge four poster solid oak bed, with its carved solid wood headboard, the grand focus of the room. The drapes around the bed, which had once been lovely, bright blue brocade, were now very worn and faded, the matching curtains, now closed to the cold winter's night, and counterpane of silk, of the same blue, were also worn and faded. The room had looked exquisite when his mother had first taken charge of the re-decoration, but it had long since become tired and worn and the thick Persian rug also of similar colour, was thoroughly worn and threadbare. Either side of the bed, stood matching bedside cabinets of solid oak, a candlestick on each, with a table, housing a lamp and a comfortable winged armchair, close to the fireplace. A large solid oak chest with a plush blue velvet covered lid ran across the bottom end of the bed, he had not seen that before. His eye then went to the large oak door leading from the bedroom, to his adjoining dressing room. His mind wandered to his own house in Mayfair, where he had a separate room for bathing, but that was a very fashionable house, and Penleigh Court was old, hundreds of years old, a pity really but there it is, and his dressing room was hardly large enough to house a bath, so he would have to wait for a bath to be brought in to the bedroom and filled, before he could enjoy washing away the dust and cold of the journey, at least it would be warm in front of the fire, and God only knew he was ready for some warmth and comfort, after his bone shaking carriage.

Then came a knock at the door, a servant with his trunk entered, Richard ushered him into the dressing room, and pointed out where the trunk was to be placed—his valet, James would be here in a few days, they had eventually agreed that James should follow on with the remainder of the luggage, and with the weather as it was, and taking into account that they would spend at least one night, if not two nights or more, at staging posts along the way, he would have to manage without a valet for a few days, Richard didn't really mind the inconvenience, in fact, he was quite capable of dressing and taking care of his own toilette, though if he ran into problems, the Dukes man would probably be only too pleased to help out, at least he would have a little peace and quiet for a few days—and knowing James as he did, no words of reproach, or disapproving looks.

He went to the chair by the fire, and sat down, he could feel the warmth now, the flames shooting out in all directions from the wood crackling in the grate, as he stretched out his long, tight muscled legs and leaned back against the cushions. A few minutes later came another knock at the door and this time it was his bath, followed by two servants with large pitchers of water—once his bath had been placed in front of the fire and filled, the servants left, closing the door behind them. Richard stood up, if he sat in that chair for very long he would be falling asleep and that would never do. He stripped off his clothing, and stepped into the bath—it felt so good, after the long, cold journey, and a night with no sleep—he soaped himself all over, before lying back and enjoying the lovely warm water encompassing his body. Ah, this was the luxury he had been looking forward too since leaving London—sheer bliss.

Once bathed and dressed in clean clothes, he descended the large staircase. He stood and looked around him—the staircase was very grand, it was very wide, sweeping down from the landing, the carved wood hand rail curling round to the left and right at the bottom, the banister rail on either side, was made of solid oak, he could remember as he stood there, watching with Edward from their hiding place, the balls when his mother would silence the crowd as she descended the stairs, in one of her beautiful ball gowns, she had been a very beautiful woman when she was younger, some said stunning, he and Edward had always been very proud of her, even from a young age, but it had faded over the years, probably the worry and heartache that she had suffered, she had certainly had more than her fair share of that—the last time he saw her she was looking fragile—he would pay her a visit after dinner, as he wanted to surprise her himself, if the servants hadn't told her of his arrival already.

At the top of the stairs a landing, wide and long, curling round to both sides of the hall, with passages to both the right and left, leading off the landing, with bedrooms branching from the passages. He looked up, to the right, there was the hideaway, well disguised from here, the priest-hole, where Edward and he would hide, and look down on the hall to watch the dancing when his parents entertained, the ladies in their colourful gowns, and the men, dressed in their finery, giving him and his brother their first taste of social occasions. Down in the hall, was a raised dais at one end, where a grand piano lived, and where the orchestra would reside, on evenings of balls or soirees—this was the ideal place for social gatherings due to its size. The large, tall potted palms, standing beside the dais, would move home on such occasions, being placed around the edge of the room at intervals, disguising the small tables and chairs set up half hidden behind them, for couples wishing to be discreet to sit, chat and sip wine. A large hall table, close to the entrance, housing yet another potted plant, with a large ornate mirror on the wall above, and a stand for overcoats and umbrella's the other side of the doorway. From the other end of the hall, was a passage, leading to the downstairs rooms—and the two large chandeliers were the pride of it all—they were large and crystal, and shone like diamonds twinkling when all the candles were alight, though at present the candles were few and spaced in the large settings, and although throwing out enough light to see by, was nothing compared with how they had looked on social occasions—that had once been his mother's delight, but she rarely even gazed on them these days.

Richard turned at the sound of swishing petticoats, coming down the stairs, to see his first glimpse of his sister in law, Maria, or at least that's who he assumed her to be. She was tall and elegant with blonde hair, piled high on her head, her eyes were a piercing blue fringed with golden lashes, her mouth small, and her lips thin and narrow, her nose small and neat, and turned up at the end. She was tall and slim, almost fragile, with her small features, but she walked very straight, with a certain assurance in her stance. The black gown that she was wearing, was cut low, but fitted to best accentuate her tall and slender figure, although in mourning, the colour became her well. Richard watched as she worked her way towards him, her fixed gaze never once faltering. Richard gave a bow, and took the hand she had extended to him—lightly brushing it with his lips—"so you are Edwards brother, Richard, I can see the likeness, though I believe you are more handsome than he" her voice was soft and sweet like a tinkling bell, Richard was not fooled, he immediately thought that her eyes, a little too close together, and the line of her straight taut mouth, were hiding a very different side to this woman, and there seemed to be so little sign of grief for someone so newly widowed. Everything about her was immaculate. He couldn't imagine how Edward would have managed being married to a woman like this, he was very gentle, but he was also too laid back, and unconcerned about everything, he had never, even as a boy, let anything bother him, other than the Duke, he wouldn't have noticed or even bothered if he had holes in his clothes, and he cared not a jot for fashion, it had only been his mother's influence which had kept him smart in his appearance, he much preferred older comfortable clothing, and spending time on the estate and down at the stables, rather than meeting and greeting socially, he had no interest at all in the finer things expected of him, though his mother would always be relied upon to cover for either her sons if ever the need arose. He was getting the distinct impression that Edward's wife was the complete opposite of her husband—even in this short time of meeting her, he felt there was a ruthlessness about her that was quite startling, she would have been more attuned to his father than his brother, and he could see that this woman was used to getting her own way, Edward would have no doubt, allowed this woman to influence him, indeed he would have depended on it, but even so, this did not appear to have any bearing on his untimely death, allowing his wife to influence his decisions, even to have free reign with his money, was still a far cry from influencing him into taking his own life, and to what purpose, had Edward lived she would one day become Duchess, now her rosy future had disappeared, surely she would never have done anything to jeopardise that—he had a feeling that was her main reason for marrying him in the first place. There was still a great deal here to learn but he couldn't believe that Edward had died at his own hand—no, there was more to this matter than met the eye, and he felt even more determined now to find out exactly what. His mind suddenly returning to the lady stood in front of him, waiting for him to speak

"Thank you ma'am—and you must be Maria, my mother has told me about you and I am delighted to meet you" she was looking straight at him, with a steady gaze, in fact, she hadn't taken her eyes from him once since he had noticed her, coming down the stairs.

"Dinner is ready, shall we go in"? she asked, now smiling yet he noticed that the smile didn't reach her eyes

Richard held out his arm to which she rested her hand on top of his, before they walked silently toward the dining room—followed close behind by the Duke, who had by now walked up behind them.

"I see that there is no need to introduce you to Maria" said the Duke

"Indeed not father, we have just become acquainted"

"Good, then let's eat", with that he entered the dining room and went straight to stand behind his chair, while Richard saw Maria to her seat, before walking to the other side of his father, and standing behind his chair, waiting for Maria to be seated first, before seating themselves.

The Duke sat at the head of the table, with Richard to his left and Maria to his right. Why did he get the feeling that there was tension between his father and Maria—there was definitely something, there certainly seemed to be little said and no eye contact between them, no doubt his father was angry with her about something. Had they quarrelled before his arrival?. He had hoped to discuss his brother's death with them at dinner, but decided to leave this until a more appropriate time, at least until the servants had left them. Perhaps after dinner would be a better time. Richard enjoyed his dinner—he was even hungrier than he had thought—the food tasted delicious, and he savoured every bite. His father had enquired of his travels, and about London, he hadn't been there for a while, but would shortly be expected to show his face in the House of Commons, at least now Edward would never have to face that, he knew only too well that that prospect horrified him. Richard would one day be following his father's footsteps, but for the time being he was more than happy to let his father fulfil his duties in London, while he was content to acquaint himself with Lincroft, the Dukes estate manager, and the running of this estate, maybe he would learn more information of his brother's dealings if he did, perhaps even something to help him understand what had happened to him.

Once dinner was over, one of the servants placed cheese and fruit on the table, and the decanter of port—this seemed to be the cue for Maria to leave them, she got up and excused herself, without casting a glance in the Dukes direction, she looked straight at Richard as she did so, giving him one of her warm smiles, before leaving the room and closing the door behind her.

"I see that things are not well between Maria and yourself father, surely, after the sad death of my brother, who was Maria's husband, we should all be united in our grief, and cast aside our differences, for now anyway"

"Is that so, damn the woman, tis hoped that she will now take her brats and move out, not that it has anything to do with you—she failed to do her duty and now she sees fit to burden me with her welfare, clearly she neither cared for her husband or his family standing, or she would have been more intent on fulfilling her duties, if you are looking for answers to your brother's death, speak to her, to think that I chose her for the next Duchess—pah, and this is the way she treats me" the anger flared in his now black eyes. He was a large man, every bit as tall and broad as his younger son, he would once have been very attractive, but with age his waistline had expanded greatly, and his hair, although still thick and wavy, was now streaked with grey. His nose was large and spread, and while he spoke of Maria, his nostrils flared with anger, and his eyes had turned from grey to black dots. He may have grown older, but he was still a force to be reckoned with. Richard thought that there had to be more to their disagreement, but the Duke would disclose no more.

"We are speaking of Edward's wife father—surely, he would expect Maria and her daughters, to be given a home—a roof over their heads, fed, clothed and an education for the girls—it's the very least that we can do, and as for his death, what could Maria know of that, unless you believe

41

that he was embroiled in underhand dealings, and I cannot believe my brother would have entertained such things. The fact that no heir was born, was of no consequence, had my brother lived, then there would have still been the possibility of such, we cannot condemn her at fault for that"

"Condemn her"? his father's face turned crimson "Had your brother been half a man, then perhaps he would have already produced an heir, but as it was they neither did their duty by me, so I have no intention of putting a roof over her head, or food in her stomach, why would I waste my money on her or her brats, she may stay here until we are out of mourning, I am not a harsh man, as you say she is a widow—on that I have agreed, but after that, she must make her own way in life, I am not a charity for every waif and stray of the area" Richard thought that he would have an apoplexy, but he wouldn't stand by and watch Edward's wife and children be treated this way.

"I'm sorry father, but I will not see her thrown out on the street with her two small children—they are merely babies and my nieces, would you have them starve on the street"?

"Do not question me boy, as I have already said this matter is no business of yours" his voice was raised higher and louder than ever, and with acid tones "If you are so worried for her future, perhaps you should consider marrying her yourself, you are in need of a wife, and no nearer I see, to taking one. Though perhaps you would do better to forget her, and find a wife who would be sure to provide you with a son and heir, I fear that the best that woman could offer is a bastard, and I won't have a bastard inheriting my estate and God knows who, my title"

"That sir is a ridiculous notion—I have no desire to marry anyone at this present time, and when I do, I shall make my own choice of bride. But the fact remains, we cannot see Maria and her children—Edward's wife and daughters, thrown out on the street to starve—those children are your flesh and blood sir, there is no question that they were Edwards daughters, surely Maria cannot be blamed for not giving Edward a son or Edward producing a son, that decision was not theirs or ours to make. We must give them a home, father, whatever your differences, I will not allow them to be turned out of their home, to face starvation.

"Then you shall be extremely disappointed—may I remind you that I am master here, in my own house, and until I'm dead and gone, I will have the say who stays and who goes in this house, and I will thank you to keep your opinions to yourself. When you are master, then you shall decide, but until then, I shall have my way—do you understand?" He was shaking with temper now—his black eyes bulging from his head, and his face crimson. Richard looked at him but he decided against saying more—he did not after all wish to be the death of the old man before him. He had seen him angry with Edward, but never in a state like this before.

Richard said no more, he could see that it was pointless taking this conversation further, he stood up and left the dining room—he had intended speaking to his father about Edward's death—it was plaguing him all the more now, but not while he was in this frame of mind—he would get nowhere and had no desire to make his father ill or worse, one death in the family was more than enough in one week,—no he would wait until his father was a little more amenable again. He walked down the passage, this would be a good chance to visit his mother, he hoped that she would be happier to see him than his father had been, it would also give him the chance to calm down, as his own ire had risen to meet his father's, though he shouldn't have expected any different. His father was impossible, he would never follow in his footsteps, he was known for a tyrant, and he could well see why the Duke was named thus, that was for sure, but he wouldn't allow his father to throw Maria and her two little ones, out on the street, he would have to think of a way of making sure they were taken care of, but at present he would concentrate on the Duchess, there was time enough to face this problem later. He followed the passageway round to the connecting door, before opening it up, and stepping through to the East wing.

It was a good job Richard remembered to take a candle with him, as the passageway, unlike the West wing, had only candlelight at intervals, throwing out no more than a dim glow, and although the rooms that were occupied by his mother, or her old nanny, would be lit according to their needs, much of the East wing was still covered with dust sheets, and unused. There was only one servant in this part of the house, and she took care of all her mistresses needs. Even their food was prepared and cooked, then carried through from the West wing, on trays. Although his father was content for the Duchess to live in the East wing, away from the rest of the house, and he had agreed for her to keep Nanny Grey as her companion, he was not prepared to spend unnecessary money on servants and the likes, and as such, one servant was her allowance. Gracie attended to everything for her and Nanny Grey, though everyone seemed happy with this situation. Even his mother's personal allowance was very small, not that she had many needs nowadays, she rarely went anywhere, and she never spent any time in London, she had two new evening gowns a year, and several new day dresses—which was more than adequate for her needs, which were but few. He held the candle high, and strode down the corridor, until he reached the living rooms of the Duchess. He stopped outside the small parlour door, and listened, he could hear the muffled voices coming from inside, though he couldn't hear what they were saying. He smiled to himself, blew out the candle and tapped the door, before opening it, and entering.

The Duchess looked up immediately, once she saw him stood there she threw her hands in the air, and reached out for him "Richard, I can hardly believe my eyes—you came, and in such terrible weather too. Come closer my dearest, let me look at you, pull up a chair and seat yourself here with us by the fire" Richard went forward and embraced his mother, kissing her cheek. Then she pushed him back, so that she could get a better view of him. "You look so well, my dear, perhaps a little thin, but now you are home, I shall be able to keep my eye on you."

"I had thought that the servants would have let you know of my arrival earlier this evening" then he turned to the other large comfy chair, placed the other side of the fireplace, "Good evening Nanny Grey, and how are you"? Nanny Grey smiled he turned and leant forward, planting a kiss on her cheek also "Oh I'm as well as can be expected, thank you young man, though riddled with pain, but that's the joy of growing old I suppose" Richard smiled, then he looked back to his mother "I had intended to visit for Christmas, but now, with the news of Edward's death" he looked at his mother's face, tears spilled from her eyes and ran down her now wrinkled face "my poor dear Edward—he was too young to die—he truly cared for me you know, he was so good to me, and now he's gone".

Her hair, once a rich dark brown, and swept up on top of her head, with little stray ringlets, escaping to frame her face, had now turned grey, the ringlets gone. Her eyes, once light brown, flecked with gold, that sparkled when she spoke, and her smile, that touched her eyes, bringing them alive. Her full red lips, and small turned up nose, she had been such a beautiful woman once, the Duke should have been proud of her, not indifferent. But now, the tears spilled from her eyes, she took out her lace handkerchief and dabbed at her cheeks—Richard took her hand, they had always been long and thin but now they were long and bony, the skin paper thin, and stretched to tearing point, covering her bones.

"His death was a great shock to all of us mama, but I am determined to learn how my brother died". She looked up into his eyes, the sparkle and fire had now gone, and in its place was hurt and a faraway look he had never seen before. Her small features making her look older than her years, her body now so thin, she looked frail, her black mourning gown accentuating her white pallid skin. A great contrast to the Duke, who evidently had a good living, his mother was week and feeble, it had been a real shock for him to see her, he knew that she was looking older before he went away, but now she had become a different person—the death of her eldest son certainly had an effect on her, but the years hadn't been so kind either. He wanted to scoop her up in his arms and hug her.

"You say you want to find out what happened? It was a terrible accident— Oh dearest, promise me that you won't go near that awful place, I couldn't bear for you to risk your life there after what has happened—you are the only son that I have now Richard, I couldn't bear to lose you too"

"Lose me? My dear mother, I have no intention of being lost—I am here to cheer you, so think no more of losing me. Come, tell me, how are your granddaughters?

"They are charming, delightful, have you met them yet?" she replied sniffing back more tears

"I'm afraid I have not yet had that pleasure, but I intend to rectify that tomorrow"

"Nanny Anson brings them to see us every day, of course they are but babies, but they are the joy in my life"

"I am glad to hear it"

"Please forgive me Richard," she said, dabbing her tear filled eyes "but do sit down, pull up a chair dear boy, and sit next to me, I want to hear all about your trip to Europe, and all about the young ladies you met there" she tried to smile at him, but he could see that the smile never reached her eyes, which were now red, and her face covered in deep pink blotches, from her tears.

"I can tell you about my trip dear mama, but I'm afraid that there are no young ladies of consequence to speak of" she patted his hand

"I cannot believe that not one young lady has fallen head over heels in love with you—you are so very handsome, as was your father at your age" he laughed out loud "would you see me married at such a tender age"?

"A tender age indeed" now she had come to life, and patted his arm with her closed fan, "Your father was married at five and twenty, and I only just twenty, but you must not marry for anything but love—I want you to promise me that you will not marry unless it's with a young lady who you love and who returns that sentiment—I would not wish you to marry for anything less—promise me"

"I promise mama, I have no intention of marrying until I'm sure it's what I should do, though I cannot share your sentiments of love, I believe that is for women only, but I shall only marry someone when I feel the desire too, you need have no fear of that"

"While in mourning, it's unlikely that you will meet many suitable young ladies, but I should like to see you with children before I die"

"Then I have plenty of time—and I shall do whatever I can to oblige". She smiled again at this, and once again patted his arm he did so love teasing her. Then he pulled up another chair and placed it beside hers.

After a long conversation about his travels in Europe, the places he visited and the balls and assemblies which he attended, they had talked for over an hour, until sleep started to overtake him, and he needed to go to bed. He gave a loud yawn, patting his hand to his mouth.

"I'm sorry mama, but I think it's time to retire, it has been two very long days, and I've had very little sleep since I left London—and I have tired you out also, I have no desire to wear you out completely—we will speak again tomorrow,—I shall come and take tea with you then if you wish" "That would be wonderful my dearest—I shall look forward to seeing you then, in fact, your nieces visit in the afternoons, so you will get to meet them too"

"Splendid, I shall look forward to it" Richard stood up and bent to kiss first his mother's cheek, then he turned to Nanny Grey, brushing his lips across her old, worn and battered cheek also, though she had already started dozing in her chair. "Goodnight ladies, sleep well, until tomorrow". Then he picked up a candle, lighting it from the lamp, and left the room, shutting the door behind him.

He made his way back to his room, where he undressed and climbed straight into his big comfortable bed, already warmed with a warming pan and so inviting. Although his mind still full of the thoughts filling his head, he had no more information than when he first arrived earlier this evening,—he thought with a sigh, and that now seemed like a month ago, rather than just a few hours—there were also the problems between his father and Maria too, they would have to be addressed and settled but at present, after going against his father and taking Maria's part, the Dukes anger had been highly inflamed, so he had best wait until his anger had abated somewhat. He would not see his sister in law, with her two little children, thrown out on the streets with no money, and left to starve—he would have to find a way to settle this matter, and there was the Duchess to consider, she had told him herself that her granddaughters were her joy, and God knows, there was precious little of that in her poor sad life, he would not see that taken from her. Tiredness overtook him once again, his eyes started to close, he could no longer keep them open. Still tomorrow he would face it all, for tonight, all he wanted was to give in to his tiredness, and blissful sleep. The bed felt wonderful, he lay back against the pillows and closed his eyes, suddenly he was back in the Rectory, the beautiful face of Clara Penrose floated into his mind, he wondered how she was, and he promised himself that in a few days he would ride over and find out—he was happily eager to get to know Miss Penrose better, then within moments he had drifted into a calm and peaceful sleep.

CHAPTER FIVE

(Maria's Secret)

Richard woke late the next morning he climbed from his large warm bed, and padded to the window—shivering as he drew back the curtains to the pale winter sun, throwing off a paltry glow. The world outside covered in a thick white blanket even though the snow had now stopped falling, and the wind had died down. Off in the distance, the grey expanse of ocean, thundering in against the black rocks, and throwing up a white frothy foam, the sky was white with tinges of grey, looking eerie in the morning light.

He washed and dressed, then left the house to go and seek out the estate manager, Melvin Lincroft. His office was down by the stables, the building was a small grey stone building, built In the same vein as the house itself, although many years later, and detached from the main house. Though it was situated alongside the stables, the entrance was round the corner, and out of view of both house and stables. He had wondered if his father would be there, and if he had woken in a better frame of mind this morning. That issue still needed sorting out, but for now he wanted to find out more about the estate and its manager, who he hoped would be able to throw some light on Edward's dealings. He had never met this man before, Melvin Lincroft's father had been the estate manager when he was last here, Ernest Lincroft had been a sweet old man, and he had been at Penleigh Court for as long as he could remember, but he had died just after Richard had left, so it seemed the natural thing to do for his father to employ the son, who had returned around the same time. He did wonder though, why his father had seen fit to offer him the Gate Lodge for his home, instead of the cottage on the estate which was where his family had always lived before—he knew that Melvin had been sent away to his grandparents, for his education, but more than that he had no idea. He was eager to make this gentleman's acquaintance.

When he arrived at the estate office, he could hear voices coming from inside, and decided to stop for a moment, in order to find out who the visitor here was. Intrigued, he was drawn to the conversation that he was listening too. A man's voice first, followed by a woman, he knew that soft voice, it came from his sister in law—but why would she visit the estate office, she would surely have no business here. He decided to listen further, he got up close to the window, an all but thin rectangular slit, letting in a little light, and situated right next to the stables, there was no sign of the grooms, they must be inside—he wanted to overhear the conversation, perhaps he could even learn something to his benefit this way. He pressed himself flat against the stone wall, and listened carefully, straining to hear what was said

"I have a little something for you" that was the man's voice

"For me, here?" the voice low and smooth

"You would want me to give you something special here?"

"Tell me, how special, is this little something?

"Very special, I promise that you will be delighted, but my darling, not until later—be patient, I'm sure you will find it well worth waiting for"

"I am intrigued, and I shall look forward to—later"

"But you must go now—we wouldn't want anyone to see you here like this"

Richard half turned to allow him a quick view of the couple inside, they had fell silent—they had their arms about one another and the embrace had melted to a full kiss. Richard jumped back against the wall again, so, his dear sister in law was having an affair with the estate manager. He had talked of later, obviously a secret assignation—he wondered if Edward had known of this, and how long it had been going on, perhaps his father was aware of this affair, maybe that's why he was so angry toward Maria, but if that were so then why had Mr Lincroft been given the Gate House, and wouldn't the Duke have sent the man packing? Suddenly he heard the click of the latch on the office door—it brought him out of his thoughts with a start—he looked about for somewhere to hide, before Maria came round the corner, the only place to go was to slip into the shadows of the stables, he couldn't allow her to find him here spying on her and her lover. He stepped into the stable, and just as he disappeared from view, Maria came striding round the corner, back straight and head up, looking magnificent in her black riding habit, with her top hat and black net covering her face. She was carrying a riding crop, she had obviously been out for a ride. He waited until she had entered the house, then he stepped out of the shadows again and made his way around the corner, and opened the office door. Melvin Lincroft was sat at his desk, he had a ledger open which he was perusing.

"Good morning Lincroft"

"Good morning my Lord—please call me Melvin, your brother always did" Lincroft stood up as Richard walked through the door, and he gave a little bow.

"How can I be of service to you my Lord"

"Well Melvin, as you probably already know, now that my brother has gone, I am the Dukes heir, so I shall be looking to you for help and guidance in my dealings with the estate. I have no desire to make changes, certainly not at present, but I am eager to see the books, and learn as much as possible about the running of the estate.

"Of course my Lord, but you need have no worry of the running of the estate, that is the reason the Duke has employed my services, and I can assure you that I'm more than able to fulfil my duties, if a problem should arise, then I shall bring it to your notice, you have no cause to concern yourself with these things"

"Yes, well I have no worries of that, but I do intend to take an active part in the running of the estate in future, so I trust that we can work together from now on. But first, perhaps you would like to tell me a little about the estate, and how it runs, about the tenants, and I thought that it might be a good idea to ask you to introduce me to all of them—for a start, we could perhaps take a ride around the estate and meet the people at the same time, at a time that suits you of course, I realize that you are a busy man and have plenty to do."

Melvin Lincroft's face was now wearing a frown—so his brother had little dealings with these things, otherwise he would not have been so put out. He didn't trust this man, he was now well aware of the affair between him and his sister in law, but he had a feeling that there was much more involved in all this, certainly more than he had imagined. Richard thought that it would be wise to try and keep on this man's good side, at least for the time being, he would play this man's game, but he would not trust him, Richard would look into his dealings and get to the bottom of it all, but if he was to find anything out about Edward's dealings, or more to the point, his death, then he would need to be able to prove it—he had this feeling of foreboding telling him to tread with great care, this man could be dangerous. Richard looked up and fixed his gaze, he may tread carefully, but he wouldn't back down

"I see, perhaps you could accompany me one morning when I visit the tenants, if you are eager to be introduced to them" he said carelessly

"Splendid, then I shall return at a later date, and you can introduce me to all the tenants, and I will go through the books with you then" he knew that was the best offer that he would get. Richard turned and went to the door, but something made him stop—he must ask Melvin about the accident, he couldn't help his feeling of foreboding lurking in his head, but he felt this man may be able to shed some light on the situation. He turned to face the man once again Melvin Lincroft had been watching him walk to the door, now he looked him in the eye

"My brother, have you any idea what made him take the route which he did, on the day of his accident?"

"I'm sorry my Lord, I've no idea—I know that he had an appointment with his solicitor that afternoon in Truro he often went that way when he wanted to be alone—but more than that I couldn't say my Lord" Richard was watching his expression—but he could read nothing—was he lying, or not?

"I see, so his business was nothing to do with the estate?"

"Not at all my Lord, he would surely have said if that were so"

"Yes, I expect that he would—and who found him?"

"It was old Tom Lennin from one of the cottages, he works as head gardener here, but you would know him of course—there was a good party of us all went out to search, once his horse returned without him—all the grooms and some of the house staff went out—it was late afternoon, and starting to get dusk, there had been a lot of rain the night before, so the ground was wet and slippery and the wind was blowing a gale, we all went off, separating to cover all the areas where he might have been, then old Tom, who was covering the beach, must have seen him and sent his lad back to alert the rest of us—we all gathered down there, and two of the servants managed to retrieve his body and we laid him in the trap, and brought him home. It was dark before we got back to the house. The doctor was called, but nothing could be done, he was dead so that was an end to it, a terrible accident. And that's about it. The funeral took place yesterday, the Duke wanted it seen too early, and he was laid to rest in the family crypt in the churchyard—all done before lunchtime, and before the weather turned too".

"Yes, thank you Melvin, you have been very helpful."

Richard didn't want people to think that they were being questioned, though it was natural to be inquisitive as to the incident, but he would have to be very careful about the way he handled all this, he didn't want people to think that he was suspicious in any way, and already he could tell he had made this man before him suspicious of him, and besides, there was nothing to say that Edward didn't just have a nasty accident after all. With that he turned and opened the door, as he turned back to Melvin, he couldn't help but notice that Melvin was still watching him closely, he had made an enemy already that was clearly apparent

"Good bye my Lord" Melvin seemed to make this statement final, before sitting back down in his chair and casting his eyes back down to his ledger which lie open on the desk before him.

"Good day Melvin" Richard said no more but left, closing the door behind him.

❦

Melvin had explained what had happened, the explanation was viable and Richard could easily see why his death was readily thought to be an accident, were it not for the fact that he knew that his brother would never have ridden there at this time of year by choice, then he would not have questioned the fact—he could of course be right, but there were still certain things which didn't add up, why had he rode into Truro to see his solicitor that afternoon—especially as it had no bearing on estate business, could it have had anything to do with finding out his wife was having an affair with his estate manager? Or maybe something else, which Richard had yet to learn. Edward had only married Maria for his father's sake, so there were no feelings involved. He had thought Maria very cold—she had shown no signs of grief over her husband's death at all—and other than the fact that she wore black, no-one would have thought her to be newly widowed, she clearly had no feelings for Edward, but she seemed to make no pretence of the fact either, perhaps Lincroft proved to be a better lover, or after hearing the conversation in the office, perhaps he plied her with pretty trinkets, though if that were so, how could he afford it on an estate managers wage. There was also the ill feeling between her and the Duke, yet he had chosen her as Edward's wife, and she would have become the Duchess had his brother lived—then on speaking to his father, he had grown very angry, more than he had ever seen him before, and he was talking of throwing her and her children from his house, had he realized what was going on? Perhaps he believed her daughters to have been the fruits of her affair, and not his flesh and blood. Though his father had not been faithful to the Duchess, so why would he take his anger out on her, but do nothing about Melvin Lincroft? Nothing made sense—and there were too many secrets. He went into the stables once again, and requested one of the grooms saddle him a horse, he had a real desire to go for a ride, he wouldn't be able to take the cliff path, as much as he would have wished to visit the place, with the heavy snow and the slippery ground, the cliff path would be lethal but a ride would perhaps give him time to think everything through, he really needed to do that and see if he could make sense of any of it, and if there were any more clues to his dear brother's untimely death, that he had failed to realize—he had skipped breakfast, he had been rather too late for that anyway, but a ride before lunch would help to clear his head, and also give him an appetite, at least that's what he hoped.

Maria climbed the stairs and strode into her room, her mind abuzz with what Melvin had just promised her. She wasn't hungry, she had had a good breakfast, so she was too excited to have lunch, she was too eager to get to the Gate Lodge and receive her gift, more jewels—her trunk was filling slowly, and of course, to meet her dear Melvin—the time they shared together was getting less, and she was worried now with Richard's arrival, that he would intrude on her ventures—but they would cross that bridge when they came to it. Now her mind drifted to Richard—he had been a far better prospect than she had at first thought—so handsome, he almost took her breathe away, she would forgo her lover for that man, indeed she would do all in her power to have him marry her—that way, all was not lost, she could still carry the title of Duchess, and to be married to a man like that—who wouldn't give everything for that. She washed her face, and changed her clothes, a lovely black velvet, low cut dress would be suitable— this damned mourning was already proving to be difficult for her—after all, she had all those beautiful gowns, which she felt sure that her dear Melvin would much prefer, and Richard too for that matter, but now it would be a whole twelve months before she would able to wear them. She would normally call for her maid, but as she was going out again, it was better to keep her movements as quiet as possible—she couldn't allow the Duke to find out her secret, as if he wasn't causing her more than enough problems now, nor could Richard find out—she would do nothing to jeopardise a future with him. She would have to find a way, to have him seduce her, that way she could force his hand—though she would rather he offer for her willingly, but she would see how things went. She put her hand over her hair, a stray strand had come loose and she tucked it back in again, and slid in another pin from the pot on her dresser—that looked better, one quick glance in the mirror, now she was ready to go—she took out her thick wool cloak, and threw it around her shoulders, pulling the hood over her head, before opening her bedroom door and slipping out.

Maria slipped out of the side door, and round to the back of the house, she would use the back drive which was rarely used these days, it would take her round the back of the lake, and back to the Gate Lodge through a small spinney of trees. This was the route she always used when visiting Melvin, she could go this way without fear of being seen. The only time that people came this way was when there was a pheasant shoot, then the Duke and his party used this road which led directly to where the shoot would take place—but she would know when a shoot was on, Melvin was expected to attend, and you could clearly hear the guns from the house. Today however, there was no-one in sight. She trudged along in the deeply laid snow, and made her way on up the slippery rutted road. Once at the end of the road, she turned right between the trees, and came out a few moments later, opposite the Gate Lodge, before stepping from the shadow of the trees, she stood still and listened, checking the main road to the house, right then left—not a soul in sight, only the chirp of the birds overhead. She crossed the road, and trudged up the snow covered pathway, and into the cottage gate—then she went to the door, and without a backward glance she opened the door and slipped inside.

Melvin heard the latch of the door, and walked out into the hall to meet Maria. Without a word he went straight to her, unfastening her cloak, and kissing her hard on the lips. Their warm embrace seemed to last an age, before he pushed her a little away from him, and hung up her cloak. There were no fears of servants here—Melvin looked after himself—he had a large fire burning in the grate of the small drawing room, which could be felt as you walked in the door, Melvin quietly ushered her in.

"Come my darling, you are early today, you were not seen?"

"No—there was no one around at all—everything is quiet, but I am early as I am eager to receive my gift" she smiled up at him coyly

"Your gift, I might have guessed, you would rather have your gift than I?" he was teasing

"Not at all, but I am curious" he could see that he had touched a nerve, her cheeks had gone pink

"First, my love, we need to get you out of your widow's weeds"

Maria laughed out loud, and turned her back to him, to allow him to undo the buttons on her gown. Once he had removed her dress, he then went on to slowly remove the rest of her clothing, kissing her neck as he did—when they were all in a heap on the floor, he turned her around and drank in the beauty of her naked body. He pulled her to him and started kissing her, hard and passionately, all the time softly caressing her, before removing his own clothes and leaving them in a pile next to hers. To one side of the fireplace was a painted screen, with a large potted palm—Melvin then went behind the screen and stepped out again with a velvet box in his hand.

"Turn around my darling, if you are to have your gift"

Maria never spoke, she gave him a beaming smile, her eyes espied the black velvet box and her gaze never strayed from it, Melvin could see the box excited her

"Turn around my love" he said in a hoarse voice

She said nothing and turned away from him. Melvin went up behind her and started placing small butterfly kisses along the back of her neck, and placing one arm around her, caressing her as he did so—then he opened the box with a click, and took out the beautiful large ruby necklace which was lying there. It was one huge ruby, with several smaller rubies on either side of it, and it was set in a large solid gold setting with a gold chain, this was certainly a stunning piece of jewellery—he smiled as he reached over her and placed the necklace around her throat—Maria caught her breathe with pleasure, her hand came up and touched the large ruby as the firelight caught it's glow, flashing shards of light through the dimness of the afternoon. She turned around in Melvin's arms and threw her arms about his neck.

"Oh Melvin, it's beautiful" she whispered

"But not as beautiful as you my darling. Though you know that you cannot wear it at least for now, once we are married, we will leave this place and go abroad somewhere, then you shall wear all your new jewels, but for now—only when you are here with me—you do understand why, don't you my love"

"One day I shall wear all my precious gifts for all to see, I shall have such pleasure showing them all off, but for now, it shall be for your eyes only" she replied reaching up and kissing him—the kisses grew harder, more passionate, until they sank on to the rug before the fire, adorned only by the sparkling ruby necklace, and made love. Afterwards, Maria dressed and crept back out into the snow covered late afternoon dusk, and made her way back to the house along the back path. The necklace placed safely back in its box, which she carried in her hand, beneath her cloak, hidden from prying eyes.

Once back in her bedroom, with cheeks pink and bright, she smiled to herself, laying back on her bed, she opened the clasp of the box to take another look at yet another prize possession, it really was beautiful, Melvin was so good to her, she had quite a collection of gifts from him, such a pity that they had to be kept hidden, but they couldn't take the risk. Then a thought suddenly registered in her mind, her trunk, what would she do about her trunk now? She snapped the clasp shut, she hadn't thought about that—it was too late to have it brought to her room, she would now have to decide what to do—she could not let Melvin know, he would want her jewels for safe keeping, she would have to hide this box somewhere else, until she could decide what to do.

Richard had a good ride, and although he didn't push his mount, due to the weather, he felt fresh and alive, but his mind was on other matters. He came to the decision that the Duke wasn't aware of the situation with Maria and his estate manager, and he certainly wasn't going to be the one to tell him, besides, it was none of his business what Maria did now. He was still puzzled over his brother's actions on that fateful day, but until he could learn more facts, speculation was pointless, the thoughts nagging in his head were still there, but facts were what he needed—and he had none. After a very pleasant ride he decided to head back to the Court for lunch—he was getting very hungry, and who could think seriously on an empty stomach.

Once he had returned to the house he went straight to the dining room for lunch, the Duke was already seated when he arrived

"Did you forget the time?" he asked as Richard entered

"I've been for a ride, and have only just returned father" he replied

"So I see—have you been to meet Lincroft?"

"Indeed—I am going round the tenants with him one day, many, no doubt I shall remember"

"You will need to rise a little earlier, if you are to accompany Lincroft. I take it that you are used to spending half the day a bed, and half the night in gaiety"

"I rose late this morning, but have always been an early riser, even in London—though after my journey here it was little wonder that I awoke late this morning" trying to keep his voice steady

"And your valet, I take it he is to follow?" he was still spoiling for an argument, but Richard was determined not to give him the satisfaction

"Indeed sir, he should be arriving any day, with the remainder of my trunks"

"So I suppose you will be poaching Chester until then?"

"Indeed I shall not—I am more than capable of looking after myself until James arrives." Richard decided that while they were alone he would broach the subject of his brother.

"Have you any idea father, why Edward went to Truro the day that he died?"

"How should I know—your brother never discussed very much with me"

"I only wondered if it was an estate matter or not?"

"An estate matter, if there had been an estate matter I would have sent for old Truscott to come here—not go gadding half way round the country to get to him"

"It must surely have been a personal matter then"

"I have no idea, why the interest?"

"I just found it hard to believe that Edward would have travelled along the cliff path at this time of year—that's all, the place would have been lethal, and he would have known that" he stated

"You should ask his widow—mayhap she could answer your questions"

"I shall go and speak with her after lunch, thank you"

He wasn't likely to get much joy there—his father really was a bad tempered man, he had become more so since Richard went away.

As soon as lunch was finished, Richard got up and left the dining room and went in search of Maria—but he couldn't find her anywhere—she may have gone visiting and decided to stay for lunch, that would make sense, but with that in mind, he then realized that he had heard her and Lincroft making plans to meet later—so, he would call in at the office, just to see if Lincroft was still there or not. As soon as he walked around the corner, he could see that the place was quiet and looked uninhabited, trying the door latch, his assumptions were confirmed—they were both missing, so she was probably in the midst of receiving her special present that Lincroft had been promising her earlier. He smiled to himself as he walked back to the house. He would speak to her later—anything he had to ask her would keep.

CHAPTER SIX

(*Meeting Richard's Nieces*)

He had promised to go and see the Duchess this afternoon—he returned to the house, and along the passage leading to the East wing. Although still daylight, several candles had been lit in the hallway of the East wing. The day was very overcast and dull, so night time would fall early tonight. Snow was once again threatening, for the sky had that pinkish hue, Richard had picked up a taper, though had not lit it yet, for he would need it to return, as he had promised to have tea with his mother and Nanny Grey, and he was looking forward to meeting his nieces for the first time. His nieces, he so hoped that were true, after learning what he had this morning, even he was having second thoughts as to the legitimacy of Maria's children now. He opened the door to his mother's drawing room, and was greeted with a large smile, before placing her long bony finger over her closed mouth. Richard quietly tiptoed across the threadbare rug, and held out his arms, the Duchess hugged her son, like she would never let go, then Richard stood back and looked at his mother, Nanny Grey was fast asleep and snoring in the chair opposite, and there was a bright fire burning in the grate so they talked in whispers

"How are you today?" Richard asked

"So pleased that you are here dearest boy—I had not expected to see you yet, but I'm glad that you've come—Nanny Anson won't be in with my little ones for a while, she usually brings them in about half past three, so that we have half an hour with them before tea, but it will give us a little while to talk first—Gracie will bring us a cup of tea to wake Nanny Grey about three o clock"

"I'm in no hurry mama, I have come to see you, I shall stay for tea as promised, so that I may meet my nieces then"

"What have you been doing with yourself this morning? Have you met the Duke's new estate manager yet?"

61

"Indeed I have—I have asked him to take me round the estate with him on one of his visits, and he has agreed, though rather grudgingly so" his mother smiled

"He is not like his father—since going away and coming back with an education, he seems to have risen above his station, not at all like his father—but the Duke seems to be content with his services—I don't trust him Richard—your brother didn't like him either, he used to say that he felt uncomfortable in his presence." so Edward hadn't trusted him either—could he have found them out?

In the next moment Nanny Grey awoke, she roused herself up, and opened her eyes

"Edward, dear boy, I didn't hear you arrive" she said struggling to sit up in her chair

"I'm not Edward Nanny, it's Richard—I'm sorry if we woke you though"

"You didn't wake me, I wasn't asleep—I only close my eyes to rest them for a bit" Alice glanced at her son giving him a smile and with raised eyebrows, a small shake of the head to warn him not to argue with Nanny, and he smiled back at her knowingly

"Of course you were not asleep, I realized that, but I didn't want to intrude on your peace and quiet"

"Don't you mind me—we are pleased to see you young man—your brother used to visit but we don't see anything of him anymore, haven't done for some years—he must be very busy" she said vaguely

Richard looked puzzled at his mother, who just shook her head

"I expect so, Nanny" Richard managed to reply, obviously Nanny was becoming confused lately—after all, she was in her late eighty's, it was to be expected.

"Tell me Richard" said his mother "Have you seen Maria today?"

"Briefly this morning, I believe that she had been riding, for she was wearing a black velvet riding habit and carrying her riding crop, though I didn't have chance to speak to her" Richard answered truthfully

"We haven't seen anything of her for several days either—have we Nanny?" she said, looking over at Nanny Grey

"And a good job too if you ask me—that one as gets well above her station—I don't understand why she came to live here" said Nanny Grey with a venom in her voice

"She was Edward's wife Nanny, don't you remember?" answered Alice

"You wouldn't have known it—gadding about with all the young men that one" said Nanny Grey

Alice looked at Richard and shook her head

"Take no notice" she whispered softly for his hearing only, "she gets very confused these days".

They talked between them about Richard and his life in London, and of his mother's wish for him to find a wife. As his mother was talking to him, his mind drifted back to Clara dear sweet Clara, he must have had a faraway look in his eyes, as she asked

"You are far away dearest, tell me your thoughts"

"It's nothing mother—you were just reminding me of someone, that is all" with that his mother smiled "so there is a young woman" she moved forward conspiratorially in her chair, waiting to hear further

"No mother, not really, I had just remembered someone who had just hurt her ankle, and I had promised to enquire for her health, and had almost forgotten about it, until you reminded me—perhaps I shall visit her in the morning"

"Then she lives locally?"

"Not too far away" this time he was smiling as he answered—there was no way that he was telling his mother about Clara, in truth, there was nothing to tell anyway. He himself was looking forward to visiting her, but that was all—he was merely doing his duty, though she was the loveliest creature he had beholden.

"And is she someone with whom we are acquainted perhaps?" his mother persisted

"I shouldn't think so mother—and there is nothing to tell in any case, I saw her home safe after she had fallen and hurt her ankle—that is all there is to tell"

"That is a good start, but I'm sure that she must have fallen in love with you dear boy—how could she not, with someone so handsome and charming, especially when you helped her in her hour of need" she was smiling at him—poor mama, she believed all the woman in the world would be in love with her wayward son, Clara probably hadn't given him another thought.

"Nonsense, my dear mama, as I have already told you, I have no intention of marrying just yet, I realize that it will be expected of me in the not so distant future, but for the time being there is no-one who I would give up my life for, or to be shackled too"

"My darling I do understand, but tis hoped that you will meet someone who will catch your eye, and who you will want to "shackle yourself" too"

"I very much doubt that, so please mama, don't pin your hopes in that direction"

"We shall see" she looked at him with adoration in her eyes, and a large smile on her lips—this smile did reach her eyes. Richard felt sorry that he would deny her anything, least of all this wish, but he wouldn't marry for convenience, and since love wasn't an option, then it could be a long wait for his dear mother, before she would see him settled and with a family of his own.

A knock came at the door, Gracie entered with a tea tray and three cups which she placed on a small table next to Alice. Then, she went round the room lighting all the lamps, before she gave a curtsey and left the room, shutting the door behind her. Alice poured the tea and handed one over to Nanny, and which Richard stood up and placed on the little table beside her, though she was drifting off to sleep again. Then Alice poured a cup which she passed to him, and one for herself. They talked of lots of things, Richard had told her about his life in London and his two good friends, who he had left letters with, when he set out for Cornwall, until a knock came at the door, and Nanny Anson had arrived with her two wards. Holding the eldest child by the hand, and carrying the little one in her arms, she entered the room. As soon as she was through the door, the eldest little girl ran to her grandmother and scrambled up onto her knee—she was a very attractive child—she had long dark curls falling down around her shoulders, and a little round face, with small features and a turned up nose, she had very large dark brown eyes, with lashes that fringed them and lay against a soft warm little cheek. She looked at Richard and couldn't take her eyes from him, but she clutched her grandmother as if this man would steal her away, never to return.

"Don't be frightened little one, this is your uncle Richard, he is very eager to meet you" she said gently. The child, still watching Richard, clung to her grandmother as if her life depended on it. Richard stood up and offered Nanny Anson his chair, as she was still stood holding baby Rebecca. Nanny Anson nodded her head in thanks and took the seat offered. Richard leaned down and tousled the little girl's hair, she immediately hid her face in her grandmother's bosom, then after a few minutes, she looked back at him.

"Talk to her Richard, she will soon get used to you" said his mother

"So you are Millicent are you?" the little girl pressed back into her grandmother once again, but this time she nodded her head.

"And how old are you" he asked, the little girl said nothing—but stared, her great large eyes, almost like that of an owl, peered at him a little less frightened now. She reached out toward the diamond pin, which was sparkling in his cravat, he leaned down low, to allow her to touch it—then she pulled back—she was starting to get used to him a little now. Then Richard turned to Nanny Anson

"And this little lady is Miss Rebecca I presume?"

"That's right, my Lord" Nanny Anson answered

Richard looked at this tiny bundle lying in Nanny Anson's arms, her head being the only thing which was not wrapped tightly in the blanket. She was sleeping, so he couldn't see the colour of her eyes, but she had little hair, and a tiny little round face, her lashes too, though very fair, were long and resting upon her small cheeks, and her cheeks were rosy. Although she had no hair, there was something resembling a fair fluffy down all over her head. She was a totally different colouring to her sister, yet the shape of their faces was very much alike. Millicent was definitely his brother's child—she was so like Edward, with her dark look. There could be no mistaking that, he couldn't believe that his father could even doubt that for one moment, but Rebecca, maybe it was still too soon to tell—he had heard that babies change quite often, though he had no knowledge about such things himself. He thought about Melvin Lincroft—he was very fair, but so too was Maria, Lincroft he supposed was a handsome man, with blue eyes, though there was something about them that Richard couldn't put a finger on. He was of large build and he had huge hands— but he couldn't tell if Rebecca was his daughter or not. Millicent caught his attention again, she jumped off her grandmother's knee and went to Richard, lifting her arms in the air for him to lift her up—this was a turn in the right direction, he lifted her up in the air, and swung her round, she giggled and laughed out loud—she had a lovely infectious laugh, Richard laughed at her. Soon he was swinging her round as if she were flying through the air, and all the time she giggled and chuckled, which had them all laughing, until his mother suggested that he would make her sick if he didn't stop. He pulled up a footstool, and seated himself, stretching out his long legs in front of him, Millicent plonking her little body down on his hard muscled thighs. He wrapped his arms around her, and cuddled her up close to his body—she was a soft warm bundle snuggling against his large chest—within a few moments her little thumb went into her mouth and as she snuggled up tight, her eyelids started to flutter and close, soon she was fast asleep. Once he had taken Millicent from his mother, Nanny

Anson had placed the baby into her arms—it suited his mother, she had always loved babies, he could see the pleasure that these little children gave her. Nanny Grey drifted in and out of sleep, but once she had even referred to Millicent as Edward—she was back in their nursery when they were children. He looked down at the little bundle he was holding, watching all her little expressions as she slept—Nanny Anson looked at the clock on the mantelpiece and stated that it was time to return to the nursery, and that they would return again the next day. Richard stood up and told Nanny Anson that he would carry Miss Millicent back to the nursery for her, been as she was asleep it was a pity to wake her, and although he felt that Nanny Anson wished to state something, she said nothing and nodded her head in agreement. Richard, still holding the child, went to his mother and kissed her cheek and promised to see her again soon, before following Nanny Anson back to the nursery.

He had now met his two nieces—they were charming, especially Millicent—she was definitely his brother's daughter, there was no mistaking that—in that moment he had decided that whatever happened, he would take care of those two little girls and their mother, he owed it to Edward, whatever his father said—he could never not care and protect them. He ran down the stairs and into the library—he thought the Duke may be there, but he wasn't—Richard went to the sideboard, took the stopper from the whisky decanter, and poured the golden liquid into a crystal glass and tossed it down his throat. He had so many questions, and so much to find out, yet he had already, in one day, learnt things which he would rather not of uncovered—he dearly hoped that his brother's death had nothing to do with his wife.

CHAPTER SEVEN

(*Renewing Acquaintance*)

Richard sat down to breakfast, the Duke had already eaten and left. Moments after sitting to the table, Maria walked into the dining room, and joined him.

"Good morning Maria" said Richard as she entered

"Good morning Richard, and how are you settling back in here? Are you comfortable enough?"

"Indeed I am" he replied swallowing the food in his mouth

"I wondered if you would care to ride with me this morning?" she asked

"I'm sorry but I must decline your offer this morning, I have to call on someone who I promised to visit, perhaps another morning instead" he replied

"Yes, of course—and the person you're calling on, is an old friend?" Maria was inquisitive, but Richard had no intention of telling his secret

"No, nothing like that—just one of the villagers who twisted her ankle, I helped her home before I arrived, and told her I should look in on her in a few days—nothing more than that. Anyway, I wanted to ask you something. I wondered why Edward was visiting his solicitor in Truro, on the day that he died, and thought that you could perhaps enlighten me"

"I'm sorry Richard, I'm sure that it must have been something to do with the estate, he didn't discuss anything with me—he never discussed anything with me. So, this lady in distress, perhaps I could go with you on your visit? "

"Oh, that is very kind of you Maria, but I did promise to call, and feel that I should do so alone on this occasion—perhaps another time"

"As you wish—I only thought to assist you, but as you say, another time" Then changing the subject Maria said

"I hope that you haven't forgotten that Christmas is in a few days, I realize that this year will have to be a quiet and intimate affair, but I wondered if you think that we should still house the carol singers on Christmas morning—they always come and sing for us in the great hall, and we offer them refreshments afterwards—surely that could still be arranged"

"I don't have a problem with it—but you would have to ask the Duke—he is still the one who makes the decisions here, as he has already pointed out to me"

Maria laughed before saying

"Yes, well, I was hoping that you wouldn't say that—I don't think that he likes me very much these days—I had thought that we could speak to him together, perhaps he would listen to you more than me"

"Ah, I see, you wish to have me on your side against the Duke, I am more than happy to oblige, but, truth be told, I don't think that my influence is much better than yours".

"It really is good to have you here with us you know, Edward spoke of you often—I feel we are going to get along famously, you and I" she said, stressing the 'you and I', without taking her eyes from his.

"I'm sure that we shall. I met my nieces yesterday afternoon, I joined my mother for tea, and Nanny Anson brought them along—they are charming and delightful creatures, you must be very proud of them, as I'm sure my brother was—Millicent has taken to me I believe, and I hope that we shall be seeing a little more of them over the festive period"

"Indeed, I am glad that you enjoyed their company, but I think that you should marry and have children of your own Richard"

"Oh no, I don't think that is going to happen anytime soon—you are as bad as my mother, trying to marry me off"

"Not at all, but you are a very eligible gentleman you know, I'm very surprised that you have not been captured already—you must have met many lovely young women on your travels?"

"I did indeed, I also met mama's who did their best to ensnare me, but to no avail—I'm afraid that I have no intention of marrying, as I have already told the Duchess, I suppose that I shall have to consider it at some point, but for me to offer for a young lady, she will have to be something extremely bewitching to capture my attention, and besides, all the young ladies I've ever met, talk of nothing but love, I don't believe in such nonsense—I'm sorry to disappoint you"

"On the contrary, I don't believe in love either—I thought we could spend some time together, we should get better acquainted, do you not agree? So I will hold you to our ride"

"I will ride with you one morning if you wish, it will be my pleasure"

"Good, then that's settled" she looked like the cat that got the cream—why did he feel so uneasy about it.

"Well, I must go—I shall see you later, if you will excuse me" said Richard, rising from the table. He stood and walked out of the door, closing it behind him. He left the house by the side door, and strode across the courtyard to the stables. After instructing one of the grooms to saddle a horse for him, he rode off down the main drive. He was going to see the most beautiful girl he had ever met he would never have agreed to having Maria accompany him when visiting Clara Penrose—already he could feel the excitement, welling up inside of him, just the thought of her induced him to this. He smiled as he rode away.

Richard rode down through the village, the wind had picked up a little, and the snow had started falling again—the wind was raw this morning, and he was glad to reach the rectory. He climbed down from his mount, tethering it to a post in a sheltered spot out of the wind and headed to the front door—he lifted the knocker—there was bustling inside before the door swung open and the maid, Daisy—he remembered her name, stood there.

"Good Morning, could you let your mistress know that Mr Richard Penleigh is here to visit Miss Penrose"

"Yes my Lord, please step inside" she held the door for him to walk past her, before closing it shut, and bustling off to find her master or mistress. Moments later, she returned

"Please my Lord, follow me" Richard followed her to the same room that he had carried Miss Penrose too last time he was here. He felt very excited and elated, at the prospect of seeing this lovely lady once again. He bowed on entering the drawing room Ada Penrose stood and bobbed a curtsey.

"Good morning ladies, I trust that I haven't called at an inopportune moment, but I wanted to be sure that Miss Penrose was feeling better than when I left her the other evening"

"Please sit down, it is very good of you to call my Lord" Ada Penrose ushered Richard onto one of the settee's, facing her daughter. He couldn't take his eyes from Clara, if anything, she was more beautiful than the last time he had seen her—and her smile melted his heart. She had a dress of rose muslin and decorated with tiny rosebuds, cut low at the bust, his heart was beating so fast he thought that the girl would surely notice.

"Thank you my Lord, I am feeling much better—my ankle was merely sprained, and although I have to rest it still, it is a lot less painful now" Clara spoke—her voice was soft and gentle and he could feel the shivers of pleasure dancing up and down his spine as she spoke to him.

"I am very glad to hear it" he said, giving her one of his lovely warm smiles.

"Perhaps you would care for some refreshment my Lord" Ada Penrose enquired

"Thank you, that would be splendid" he said, and inclined his head

Ada went to the fireplace, and rang the bell pull situated on the wall, before taking her seat once again. Within moments the door opened and Daisy entered.

"We would like some tea Daisy and perhaps some of cooks freshly baked biscuits"

"Yes ma'am" she bobbed a curtsey before leaving and closing the door behind her. Richard was finding this difficult, for as much as he was trying desperately hard not to keep his eyes fixed on Clara, he found himself drawn back to her lovely face, and to make matters worse, each time he allowed himself a glance in her direction, she was looking over at him. For the first time in his life he could feel the colour rising in his cheeks.

"I was very sorry to hear of your brother's death—he was a good man, well liked and respected in the village my Lord" said Ada Penrose, trying to make conversation

"Thank you ma'am—it was a terrible blow to us all, especially my mother— the Duchess has been devastated as you can imagine"

"And are you now planning to stay at Penleigh Court?"

"Indeed for the foreseeable future."

"You will miss London my lord?" this time Clara asked the question, this time he could not avoid looking directly at this beauty

"I miss my good friends, but I believe that I shall soon become accustomed to country ways again now of course, with the house in mourning, social occasions have been placed on hold"

"Yes of course" she lowered her head

At that moment the door opened and Daisy came in carrying a tray with three cups and saucers and a small plate of biscuits, fresh from the oven.

She placed the tray on a small table beside Ada Penrose, before bobbing a curtsey and leaving. Ada poured the tea and handed a cup to Clara and Richard, before lifting the third one to her lips and taking a sip. Then she offered one of the biscuits on the plate, Richard took one and started crunching his way through it.

"These biscuits are delicious ma'am" Richard said looking to Ada Penrose

"I'm glad that you like them, would you like another?" she picked up the plate and offered another biscuit

"Your very kind" he replied taking another biscuit off the plate

"It is unfortunate that my husband is not at home this morning, as I know that he would have liked to meet you my Lord, but his duties in the community can take him out at all hours of the day and night" Ada Penrose said

"Yes indeed, I am sure that we shall meet in the near future—I have spoken to Lincroft, and I shall be accompanying him to meet our tenants and the people of the village, so perhaps we shall be able to call on him then"

"I'm sure he would be pleased to see you my Lord, but perhaps he will meet you in church?" she asked, her attention once again resting on her tea cup.

"Church, of course" he hadn't given that much thought—as a child he and Edward had gone to church and sat in the family pew, every Sunday, but of late, he wasn't so in the habit of going. His mother and Nanny Grey would still go he presumed, as they had always in the past, although with the weather so bad, and his mother finding it harder to get out, it wasn't always possible. Perhaps this lovely young woman would be the incentive he needed

"So, we shall see you on Sunday morning?" Ada Penrose insisted

"You shall indeed—weather permitting, of course" he cast a glance at the window—the snow was still falling outside—he decided to change the subject

"How long have you lived here ma'am?" directing his question at Ada Penrose

"Only two years—not very long I'm afraid. My husband had lived in Cornwall as a child, although he had been near to Penzance, so when he saw that this church had just lost their old vicar, and that no-one from the estate had been appointed to fill the post, my dear husband had seen it advertised and made his decision to apply for the post—of course, the Duke was happy to offer my husband this appointment, he was the only applicant. The parish is a lot smaller than the one which he did have, but his heart was set on Cornwall, so this is where we have now settled".

"I see, a solution to suit everyone—when I left for London, the old vicar—I seem to have forgotten his name—anyway, he was getting rather old for the post, but I didn't realize that he had died until I met Miss Penrose, and she gave the Rectory as her address" he said this glancing across at Clara with a smile—which she returned

"Well, I must say that the old vicar did not have two such lovely ladies as clearly the new one has" he always knew how to win the ladies approval

"So kind my Lord" Ada Penrose said, colour flooding her cheeks, and flicking open her fan to wave before her reddened face

Richard had started to feel uncomfortable, his eyes were constantly straying back to sweet Clara, and the conversation was running thin. He had been here for a good hour already, it was about time to take his leave

"Well ladies, if you will excuse me, I shall be on my way now—I am pleased to see that you are on the mend Miss Penrose, I trust the ankle will be healed the next time we meet".

"Thank you my Lord" said Clara Penrose "and thank you for calling this morning, it was very kind of you sir"

"The pleasure is all mine" he stood up and went over to where she lie on another settee, now her cheeks had turned very pink, and she held out her hand to him—he held her hand and raised it to his lips, brushing her fingers with his mouth, before turning to Ada Penrose, and bowing to her.

"Good day to you both ladies—and thank you for the hospitality" before turning to the door. Once in the hall, Daisy ran to open the front door for him. Outside in the chill morning air the snow still falling, he claimed his horse, and headed back to Penleigh Court.

Richard sat astride his horse, with excitement racing through his veins—the morning was bitterly cold, though he could only feel the heat rushing through his body and his cheeks were warm and aglow. He had never felt like this before, in the whole of his life—all the pretty woman, many who would have thrown themselves into his arms, but never had he felt as he did about the lovely Clara Penrose. This would never do—she was not of the social standing that would make her a suitable choice for a wife, why was he even thinking like that—he had no intention of taking a wife right now, and being in mourning, he would not be in a position to offer for one at least for the next twelve months. Maybe that was his saving grace, she would surely have other offers before then, so that would solve his dilemma. No, beautiful she may be but she wasn't for him. He would put her right out of his head. He had done his duty and called to check that her ankle was healing nicely, so he wouldn't need to visit her again. But the more he tried to put her from his thoughts, the more he kept seeing her eyes, as he lifted her fingers to his lips, his eyes never once left hers, and the look in those lovely deep dark pools, drawing him in, the dimples in her cheeks as she smiled at him—he gave an involuntary shudder—as he brushed her fingers with his lips, he could only think of kissing those lovely pink rosebud lips. Had they met in London, at one of the balls or assemblies, he would have surely escorted her out to the terrace, and have stolen a kiss or two—he couldn't help himself, but they were not in London now, and she was not of that society. She was merely a vicar's daughter—though a fortunate one from what he could see of the matter, so many girls in her position were forced eventually to take up posts such as governesses and the like, at least this girl would probably never have to be forced to such. No, he had a much more important task ahead of him, looking into his brother's death—that would keep him and his mind occupied—he would put her to the back of his mind, and try to forget this beautiful young lady who made every nerve in his body tingle, with just one of her smiles, or even the very thought of her.

He had reached the stables at Penleight Court he climbed down from his mount and handed the reins to one of the grooms, who had come running out to meet him, before striding up the steps and into the house.

The door closed behind Richard Penleigh. Clara sat back against the settee, and closed her eyes. Her mother had left the room to go and speak to cook, though Clara thought that it was really because Mr Penleigh had made her blush—he was such a charmer. Clara was fighting to keep the smile from her lips. She opened her hand and looked at the fingers which he had brushed with his lips—she placed those fingers against her cheek. Never before had she met a man like this one—he was the perfect gentleman. She remembered that he was handsome beyond compare, from her last meeting with him, but when she saw him her heart had leapt in her chest, and she thought that the beating would be visible. In his dark blue riding coat, his strong, muscled legs taut in his buff breeches, with his polished hessians—his raven black curls softly touching his collar and his snowy cravat, with its diamond pin, she had never before seen such an Adonis, she could only imagine what it would feel like to entwine her fingers through those curls. Of course, having lived in London, he was bound sure to be a man of the world—he would no doubt have met numerous young ladies, far prettier than she, and such a man as he would have mistresses, that was known to be the fashionable thing. His father had a bad reputation, though he seemed such a pleasant gentleman, and his poor brother Edward, had been a very gentle and respectable young man—always very pleasant. She had heard that his mother too, was a lovely lady, and if rumour was to be believed, she had been such a beauty in her day, though the only times that Clara herself had seen the Duchess, was when she attended church with the old Nanny, who was now her companion, and she looked so small and frail, she had heard that her life had not been a happy one, and her appearance corroborated the gossip. When Richard smiled at her, she felt a tingling all around her body, she had never before experienced such feelings. She closed her eyes again, remembering now, how he had lifted her up and carried her into the house, just as if she were as light as a feather, a rag doll, how he had covered her in his coat, and how he had rested her against that great strong chest of his—she opened her eyes, her parents were getting eager now to see her married, her mother's family had been well to do, but she had married the second son of a Lord, and he had decided on the church as a vocation—his parents had been pleased and he had received a good allowance, and there had been a generous sum on his father's death, but the bulk of what would make up her dowry, which wasn't vast, would come from her mother's family—her grandfather had idolised her and had offered to set up a dowry for his only beloved granddaughter, so she would have a dowry, but she had no doubt that it would not be enough to entice a Duke—especially with a home to run as Penleigh Court, she had heard it said that it would take thousands, just in repairs alone, so Richard Penleigh would need to marry a very wealthy young lady indeed. Her heart sank, no, she would just have to take her mind off this man—he wasn't for her, however much she would wish it. At that moment her mother entered the room again

"It will soon be lunchtime Clara" then seeing her daughter looked sad and thoughtful "what's the matter dear is something wrong?"

"No mama, there is nothing wrong" she answered

"Then cheer up dear, I thought that Mr Penleigh's visit would cheer you, when he arrived you seemed very pleased to see him" her mother was very perceptive—and the fact that they were hoping she would shortly find a husband, made it even more poignant, Clara didn't answer her mother for fear of giving herself and her feelings away.

"Well, didn't you like the young man Clara?"

"Yes mama, he is truly a gentleman"

"And very handsome too didn't you think?"

"Yes, I suppose that he is"

"Then what is wrong with you girl? Perhaps he will call again—I could see that he was taken with you my dear, he couldn't take his eyes from you"

"Please mama, I am sure that you are wrong, he came only to enquire after my health—no more"

"We shall see, and remember dear, the family is in mourning at the moment, but afterwards, who can tell, he doesn't speak as if he is in any hurry to return to London, and stands to reason the Duke will be eager to marry him off—look how he found a wife for his other son—there aren't so many eligible young ladies around here you know, and you are as pretty a young lady as he's likely to meet, London or no"

"Please mama, Mr Penleigh, I am sure, has many young ladies to admire—why would he even notice me?"

"As I say, because he couldn't take his eyes from you—you see if I'm not right Clara, he will be calling again before long—you mark my words young lady—that young gentleman was not only here about your ankle, he was here to see you."

Clara didn't argue any further, it was no use, she wished that her mother was right, but it would never come to anything—gentlemen of his standing were looking for more than just a young ladies looks, and although everyone told her how pretty she was, she wasn't a vain girl, she would have to try and put Mr Penleigh from her mind, she couldn't spend her life hankering after something never destined to be hers, that would be foolish. With her mama's help, she stood up, but with only the good leg taking the best part of her weight, she walked gingerly, taking great care not to put too much pressure on her bad leg. Her mother helped her into the dining room for her lunch.

CHAPTER EIGHT

(*Christmas at Penleigh Court*)

Christmas was upon them, at last his valet had arrived, with the rest of his luggage—his trip had not been an easy one, and he supposed that he would never hear the last of that, but at least he was here now. Richard had spoken to his father and it had been agreed (if grudgingly), that the carol singers should still come to Penleigh Court on Christmas morning at eleven o'clock. The Duchess and Nanny Grey were to join the rest of the family and spend the day with them after they had attended church at nine o'clock. Maria too attended church on Christmas morning, taking Millicent with her, now that she was old enough, her aunt and uncle would be there, and would expect to see her—they usually returned with Maria to Penleigh Court for the carol service, and a chance to see her daughter and to exchange small gifts—they would also get to see the baby this year. Nanny Anson stayed at home with Rebecca, who was still too young, but she would be called down to bring her charge, to meet Maria's family on their return. Richard had decided to accompany the ladies—after all, the Duke had no intention of going, so he would at least represent his father. He also had it in mind that he had promised Mrs Penrose that they would see him in church, and the thought of seeing Clara, was too much of a temptation to miss.

The snow was lying thicker than ever, as it had snowed almost non-stop for the last two days. But it had stopped now, and the cold North wind had taken over, causing thick frost on top of an already white world. Richard had gone out early with Melvin Lincroft, as they were to supervise the cutting down of the Christmas tree. Maria was delighted on their return, the tree was huge, and Lincroft called for a large pot to stand it in, so that it could be placed in the great hall—there was holly, ivy and mistletoe, all covered in white frost, after the snow had been shaken from the boughs. Maria called for some of the servants to help her dress the tree with small trinkets and scarlet ribbons, and finishing off with small candles attached to the branches, which would be lit for the carol singers the next day. Beneath the tree, small well wrapped parcels were placed, these were gifts for the servants, which Maria herself had bought and wrapped, this was something which the Duchess had always taken care of in the past, but which now fell to Maria's duties. Holly with glossy red berries were hung around the house, and garlands of ivy and large red bows of ribbon were placed along the fireplace mantel—small bunches of mistletoe, with its small white berries, were strategically placed—Maria looked at them remembering last Christmas, a large ball had been held and the mistletoe was well used, Maria thought of better times, how she had to entice her husband under one of the clusters for a kiss—even Lincroft needed enticing, in fact, she smiled as she thought of how she had waited while he went into the library with the Duke, as he alighted, she had caught him and the way they had kissed there and then, if the Duke had seen them—but he hadn't, Lincroft had rushed off afterwards, like a scalded cat, nervous that they would be caught, but Maria liked playing dangerous games—it was all the more exciting.

Once the decorations were finished, Maria stood back, surveying it in all its glory. Richard strode into the hall

"Very pretty" he said to her, looking round all the decorations "My mother will be proud of such a work of art"

"I'm glad you approve"

"Indeed I do, it's a pity that there won't be a ball this year, but maybe next year, things will be different"

"I do hope so, but for now . . . ." She walked towards him and reached for his hand, tugging him towards her until she had him in place, right below a sprig of mistletoe, then she lifted her head, looked into his eyes, and throwing her arms about him, placed her lips hard on his—Richard pulled away,

"What's the matter" she whispered "After all, isn't it the custom to kiss under the mistletoe at Christmas?"

"I hardly think it appropriate under the circumstances Maria" Richard had not expected that

"Just a little fun Richard, surely there's no harm in that"

"You are my brother's wife, and this is a house of mourning, had you forgot?" why did he feel so angry

"Of course not, but I see no harm in a little festivity, a mere kiss" she had lifted her arm, smiling up at him, and with the palm of her hand, was gently stroking the soft velvet of his jacket, the gleam less than repentant in her eyes

"I'm sorry Maria, I have things to do" this time he pulled away from her, turning, he walked back through the entrance door and out into the white world beyond.

Maria stood still, watching him retreat—she hadn't expected that reaction, not from Richard, indeed she had hoped that he would have thrown his arms about her and kissed her back, perhaps he was more like her husband than she had anticipated—he certainly didn't act like the man of the world that she thought him to be. Besides, she had never loved Edward, why should Richard be so shocked—he must have known that, and all this fuss for merely a peck under the mistletoe. She would educate him, he would come round eventually, she would show him how much he really wanted her, he would come to her, begging her to marry him, declaring his undying love for her, she would make sure of that. She turned and went into the drawing room, ready for a cup of tea, with a huge smile on her lips.

⁂

Richard was furious, damn the woman, why would she think he was interested in her—and a mere kiss indeed, she had damn near eaten him alive. Well, she picked the wrong candidate in him—did she really believe it would be so easy to have her way with him, if so, she would very soon learn differently. He may be a known rake, but he had no intention of ever seducing her, not even for his father's sake. He had planned on looking in on the Duchess and Nanny Grey, but in this frame of mind, he best not—he needed a drink, he would take a short walk, round to the stables and order the carriage to take them all to church in the morning, then he would head for the library for a drink before preparing for dinner.

He had managed to enter the house without seeing Maria, he wasn't ready for that yet. He strode into the library, his temper had abated, but he was ready for that drink. He had wondered if his father would be in there, a good fire was burning in the grate, but the room was empty, though the lamp was burning. He went to the dresser, and poured himself a large glass of brandy, before taking the large leather studded chair, and seating himself, leaning back and throwing his long muscled legs up onto the desk. He ordered the carriage for eight thirty in the morning, the service would start at nine o clock, with the snow lying so deep, they would need to allow enough time to arrive safely. The service, which Mr Penrose would take, he closed his eyes, and Clara, the beautiful, sweet Clara. Just thinking about her made his heart lurch and he had a desperate need to see her again, it would be worth going to church just to see her face again. And afterward, they would be invited back to Penleigh Court, to partake of the carol singers, and the warm pies, and mulled wine, on offer. He couldn't wait for the morrow—his heart quickened as he dreamed of her lovely face. Had she kissed him the way that Maria had, he would have been on fire, could never have resisted her. Suddenly, raised voices intruded through his thoughts

"Your husband not cold in his grave Madam" that was his father's voice, loud and booming

"What has that to do with anything, a triviality, nothing more" the silky voice that he had come to recognise

"You will stay away—do you hear me—stay away, or leave this house"

"Please Your Grace there is no need to shout,"

"How dare you speak to me like that—I shall not tolerate this, do you hear? It was I who brought you here, I was the one who chose you for my son, though for the life of me I can't understand why, you have flouted my wishes at every turn, and you nor my son, neither of you did your duty by me—you are fortunate indeed to carry on living under my roof—you and your bastard brats—but you will obey me—I promise you that"

"There is no need to raise your voice sir, someone will hear, my girls are not bastards, Edward was their father, and now he is dead. I know that you have been disappointed that we could not give you a son and heir, but had Edward lived, I'm sure we would have made more attempts, and succeeded in the end, I'm sorry that things have gone so wrong, but we all have to live with it"

"I have eyes and ears Madam, do you think that I don't know what goes on in my own home, I know what you're up to,—I may not be as young as I used to be, but very little gets past me—you had better believe that, if you know what's good for you"

"Then you are mistaken sir, I am up to nothing"

"You have been warned, you will obey my wishes—you have led me to believe that you are something which you are not—I will not have you make a fool of me, do you understand—you will obey me" he was shouting now, for all the house to hear

Richard froze did his father really believe that he wished to take advantage of his sister in law? Why would he even think that? He had no interest in Maria whatsoever, and after this afternoon, he hoped that he had proved this to her. He jumped up and went into the hall, he would put an end to this nonsense—but both Maria and the Duke had gone. Richard decided that it was time to prepare for dinner.

⁊⁊⁊⁊⁊⁊⁊

Maria had given in—she had walked away from this awful old man—he was known as a tyrant, and he certainly lived up to that. She was in a dangerous position now, at least while Edward had been alive, there was the chance of providing him with a son and heir, but now that had gone. She never thought the Duke would have turned on her as he had, in the early days, when he had chosen her above all the other young women, he had been charming—she had even entered into a mild flirtation with him, as she desperately wanted the marriage to his son, to give her status and title, and she used her charms to gain just that. She had always been a good daughter in law, other than her little secret, which she was certain that he had no knowledge of, even now. If he knew, he would surely have turned his estate manager out of the Gate Lodge. There was the other business though, he could replace an estate manager, but someone to fulfil his other duties, would be far harder to find. He must never know of Melvin's relationship with her, not now, she had too much to lose as did her lover. She was angry that he believed his granddaughters were bastards, she had deliberately avoided Melvin each time that her and Edward had been trying for a baby, it was safer that way, and she had thought that by providing her husband with a legitimate heir, she would then be released from that duty. Nothing worked out the way it should. She did fear being thrown out—where could she go with two small children. Her aunt and uncle would want no part of it, she felt sure that once the Duke had finished, she would never be welcome in society again. He would make sure of that. She would of course have all her wonderful jewels, but they would do her no good, unless she was living abroad—and if the Duke carried out his threats, she would be left without a penny to her name—she had to keep a roof over their heads, whatever happened. Tomorrow was Christmas Day, the Duchess would be joining them for the day, that may ease the situation—she felt like sending for her dinner in her room tonight, but the Duke would see that as a sign of guilt on her part, and would use that to prove himself to have been right all along—she couldn't allow that, so she would wash and dress and go down to dinner as on any other night—she would speak only when spoken too, and excuse herself at the first possible moment. She must also make her peace with Richard—perhaps she had moved too quickly—she must give him time to realize that he really did want her too—after all, she had barely known him a week. He was fond of her daughters, she would encourage his relationship with them—they would look to him as a father figure, he could surely not disappoint them. Yes, that was the way to go. She dried the tears which were now coursing down her cheeks, before calling her maid to prepare her for dinner.

Christmas morning dawned cold and bright—the sky was clear, but the snow still lay like a white shroud covering the landscape. Breakfast was early, as there was so much going on today, even though this year the festivities were obviously quieter than normal. Sitting round the table, the only sounds that could be heard was the ticking of the clock—and the munching sounds from the three people seated there.

The lack of conversation was due to the uncomfortable atmosphere that had carried over from the previous day. Once breakfast was over, Richard excused himself and went outside to see if the carriage had been made ready—the coachman was just climbing into his seat, so Richard went through to the East wing to find his mother and Nanny Grey, he would help them to the carriage, which was to collect them all from the West wing front door. He stepped into the passageway and immediately met Gracie, who was waiting for the two ladies to finish their breakfast. Gracie would take Nanny Grey's arm and help her to the carriage, but with her arthritis, it was a long and painful trip for her, but she was determined to go. Richard offered his mother his arm—once at the carriage he helped the ladies into their seats, though he had to lift Nanny in and out, as she couldn't make the steps—a few moments later Maria joined them, holding the hand of Millicent, who was excited to be riding with her mama in the carriage. He helped Maria into the carriage, then he lifted Millicent up, and handed her up to her mother. This was the first acknowledgment which had passed between them since the previous day disagreement. Even Maria was not saying a great deal today, she lifted Millicent onto the seat beside her before Richard jumped up and sat on the other side of Millicent—the little girl had taken a liking to Richard, she kept looking up at him, until he turned to smile at her, then smiling back, she put up her hand to touch his sapphire pin. Richard leant down towards her, allowing her to touch the pin, her tiny fingers pressing it further into his cravat the carriage was very slowly trundling along through the deep slippery snow.

"You really should be thinking about a wife and children Richard" said the Duchess, smiling and watching her granddaughter and the way her son was playing with the child

"Please mother, not today—I shall get married when I'm ready, and in the meantime, I can enjoy my brother's offspring" he looked at Maria as he said this—he hoped that it would repair any unpleasantness that had arisen from their disagreement, he hated the atmosphere which had descended on the household. Maria looked at him and gave a watery smile.

"But you look so comfortable with little ones Richard, more so than your brother was, don't you agree Maria?" Maria ignored the statement, and looked at Richard

"My daughters will be only too pleased to let you practise on them, I'm sure" she replied

"You are joining us today are you not mother?" Richard asked, changing the subject

"We are, as long as your father is in agreement of course, I would not wish to be the cause of his anger on Christmas day" she knew what her husband could be like

"I am sure the Duke will not object—it is Christmas mama" he replied simply

They were nearing the church now—the coachman was going to halt as close to the gate as he could, as poor Nanny Grey found it difficult to walk, even with the use of her stick—Richard would help her, while the Duchess took Maria's arm. Once inside the church, they made their way to the Penleigh family pew. Richard waited until he was seated before allowing himself to look around the church. It didn't take long to locate the object of his affection—she was sat at the front, two seats back, her warm thick red cloak wrapped tightly round her, and her bonnet with matching red ribbons. His heart lurched, he could only imagine her face, as her back was to their pew, but he could see her in his mind, and a smile touched his lips. He had never before been so enticed to church. Her father, the vicar was stood in the pulpit, telling the nativity story, his voice loud and clear. His hair was greying and he had small features, and a turned up nose, Richard could see that this man was definitely Clara's father, she was so like him. Clara was sat with her mother, and several other women from the village, although Richard couldn't see her face, his eyes were drawn to the back of her head—his mother had turned and looked at him several times, and each time he had wrenched his eyes away from Clara in the hope that his mother wouldn't notice the girl he was watching so closely. Once the service was over, people stood up and started to file out of the church—Mr Penrose stood in the church porch, shaking hands with his flock, his wife and daughter stood at his side. Richard, holding Nanny Grey's arm, followed his mother and Maria down the aisle, and out into the bright sunlight, Maria still clutching her daughters hand—Maria and the Duchess were shaking hands and speaking to the vicar and his wife, while Clara stood slightly behind her mother—when she saw Richard, a smile sprang to her lips, and her eyes went straight to his. Still holding Nanny's arm, he gave Clara a bow and a wide smile—not once breaking the eye contact between them. Her cheeks were very pink, probably due to the cold, but her eyes sparkled gold and the dimples in her cheeks, melted his heart. The dark red cloak that she wore, was particularly becoming, for a few moments, he could not drag his eyes from hers, until he noticed that the vicar was shaking Nanny Grey's hand and speaking to her. He looked away, then back to the vicar, who had now taken Richard's outstretched hand to shake—"Good day to you my Lord, how pleased I am to welcome you on this Christmas morning"

"Good morning vicar, I am pleased to be here", then he looked up at Ada Penrose "Good morning ma'am and Miss Penrose, I'm pleased to see you again" Ada Penrose smiled and inclined her head and Clara gave another wide smile, then Ada Penrose spoke "this is Mr Penleigh my dear, the gentleman who saved our daughter when she twisted her ankle" Richard looked to make sure that his mother and Maria had moved away from them and the conversation that was now being held—he certainly had no desire for them to learn of his infatuation

"I am much obliged to you your Grace, for your kindness, I know that my wife and daughter also share that sentiment" vicar Penrose was now saying to him

"Not at all, the pleasure was all mine" then Richard remembered the carol singers "I was wondering, due to being a house in mourning, we cannot celebrate the usual festivities this year, but we are holding a carol service for the people on the estate, in an hour, and we would be honoured if you, your wife and daughter would join us at Penleigh Court" Richard glanced quickly in Clara's direction, she was looking straight at him smiling

"Thank you your Grace, I'm sure we would be delighted" and he gave a small bow "We shall join you directly" Mrs Penrose's face lit up, she was almost excited at the thought of visiting so distinguished a place as Penleigh Court

Richard inclined his head before taking a quick glance at Clara, who was also smiling and still had her eyes fixed on him, then turning to Nanny Grey, and offering her his arm to walk along the path to the gate, and waiting carriage. He couldn't help showing his pleasure as they rumbled and slid back along the ice covered road, through the village and on up to Penleigh Court.

After seating the two older ladies in comfortable chairs, which were moved into the hall for their benefit, Richard and Maria now went to meet and greet the carol singers who had now started to file into the hall, followed by the estate tenants and employees and a few of the local gentry, including Maria's aunt and uncle, who looked so proud of their niece—Richard watched when he saw Melvin Lincroft step through the doorway, but Maria, now talking with her aunt and uncle, showed no signs of favouritism as she greeted everyone flooding through the door. Melvin Lincroft on the other hand, hovered close to Maria's side, though no-one else seemed to notice, and Maria showed no signs of even knowing Melvin, Richard was rather amused by this—but there was only one person that he was interested in seeing, and he was becoming excited with the anticipation of that prospect. Just at that moment, vicar Penrose stepped through the doorway, immediately Richard's eyes went to his lovely Clara—she was such a picture to behold, Richard strode over and welcomed them, before finding a seat for the ladies. Seating had been arranged in a semi-circle around the dais, where the carol singers were stood. He noticed that Maria had now seated herself close to the Duchess, and Melvin Lincroft had positioned himself behind her chair—her aunt and uncle sat the other side of her, though they seemed not to notice their niece's lover. Then he noticed that Nanny Anson had been called to bring baby Rebecca down to join the party—Maria's aunt held the child in her arms, cuddling her tight to her chest, and her husband had picked up Millicent, and placed her on his knee—he felt warmed at the scene before him.

The carol service seemed to be a great success, for Richard it was a dream, he had remained standing, but in very close proximity to his dear Clara, he longed to touch her, he could smell her perfume, she smelt of lavender, heady and intoxicating, but that was out of the question, and he wasn't about to give his feelings away—he couldn't believe his own feelings in fact, he had never felt like this before, and he didn't know why this was happening now—he had met many lovely women, but none that he couldn't bear to be parted from before. This time it was different, but to add to the irony, this young lady wasn't even of the class which would be considered suitable by his parents—she was a vicar's daughter—he could never offer her his hand in marriage, for that reason alone. So, after the refreshments had been partaken, his guests said their goodbye's and left, including the Penrose family. Clara still gazing at Richard, and he, although trying to hide the fact, was stealing quick glances at her too. He kissed her hand, and that of her mother, and bowed to the vicar, before they took their leave along with the other guests—Richard made up his mind that he had to put the girl from his mind—they had only met three times, so it should be no real loss, he must concentrate on sorting out problems, closer to home. The Duke hadn't shown his face, but that was probably a good thing. Once the last of the people had left the servants were called in to be presented with their gifts—Richard found his father in the library, but he wanted no part in it and left the presentation to his son. The servants all assembled in a line, while Maria took each gift in turn handing them to Richard, giving him the name on the card, for him then to present to the individual, whose name was written on the label—the men shook hands, and the women all bobbed a curtsey, as they received their gift, before returning to their work. Lunch came and went, and after they had all eaten a hearty meal, they retired to the drawing room to exchange presents between themselves. Everyone seemed pleased with the gifts which Richard had brought from London with him, there was a bright blue shawl for Maria, he could not of chosen better, as it actually matched the colour of her eyes, a lovely brooch for his mama, set with tiny diamonds, a black wool shawl for Nanny Grey, a cuddly bear each for the two girls, and a bottle of port for his father. He had bought a gift for his brother, but that had been left in London, once he heard that Edward had died. Nanny Anson had joined the party a little later, so the girls had their gifts too—Millicent was so excited, though opening the parcels seemed more entertaining than what was inside. Richard sat her on his knee, and swung her round again, making her laugh and chuckle, which amused the whole company—Maria sat watching Richard with her eldest daughter, and thinking what a good father he would be for her two children, she really would have to work on that. Nanny Grey had fallen asleep in the chair, and was snoring heavily. The Duke had made his excuses early and retired to his library, he had no desire to be part of any of this family day.

Once Nanny Anson had taken the children back to the nursery, and they had finished their dinner, Richard saw the Duchess and Nanny Grey back to their rooms in the East wing—then he returned to the library where he had planned to have a glass of brandy, but as he neared, he noticed that the library door was open, and voices were coming from inside

"You know full well what I want" that was his father's voice, low and gruff

"I'm sorry, I cannot—please do not ask that of me" Maria, at odds with the Duke again, would it never end? What was going on between them, there was a great deal of bad feelings and anger, but this was ridiculous

"Come now Maria, we agreed only yesterday, that you will obey me— besides, I thought that you wished to carry on living on my charity with your—brat's—surely this is such a small thing to ask?"

"I'm sorry"

"Are you—don't be sorry Maria, I have no need for sorry, you will obey me, or you will go—I agreed to allow you to stay until we are out of mourning, but I could change my mind?"

"You ask too much my Lord"

"Then be prepared to face the consequences—I gave you what you have here, and I shall be the one to take it away—you shall see—we will not have this conversation again—do you hear?—you will pay for this—I swear that you will pay" his voice was rising as he spoke—this last sentence was a roar.

Richard had heard enough—he would confront his father with this—now. Maria was part of this family whether he liked it or not, and whatever he felt about her, she didn't deserve this treatment and bullying—and he wasn't prepared to live with the constant rows—it was unthinkable. He strode to the door, pushing it wide, and walked in

"You should knock before entering Richard—we were having a private conversation here" once again he was angry, Maria looked up as he entered, her steady gaze fixed on him

"Maria is part of this family sir, she was my brother's wife, her daughters are your flesh and blood, I will not stand by and watch you turn them out on the streets—how could you be so cruel? And what's more, if you have no wish to involve the household in your disagreements, then you should discuss them more quietly"

"It's alright Richard—you need not be involved in my affairs—I thank you, but ask that you leave things be—please" Maria's voice was pleading

"But I am involved—I cannot go on listening to this nonsense every day— can we not just live here in peace? Is that too much to ask? My brother not cold in his grave and his father and his wife are at odds the whole time"

"Be quiet boy, do not get involved in things which don't concern you—and do not interfere in my business" the Duke was furious, but his anger was now directed at Richard

"Go to bed Maria" Richard turned to her "It is for the best"

"But . . . ."

"Go to bed both of you—I have no wish to discuss this matter further— leave me in peace" the Duke screamed this out

"This matter needs to be settled sir" Richard wanted this conversation closed for good as much as anyone

"Do not defy me—go to bed I say, now—before I throw you both out" there was no reasoning with the Duke in this mood. He had become more of a tyrant than he had ever been

"Do as he says Maria, we will settle this another time" Richard said addressing Maria

"Yes, you are right. Good night your Grace, good night Richard" she said leaving the room, then turning back to Richard still standing in the doorway

"Thank you" with that she reached up and kissed him lightly on the cheek, before going up the stairs—Richard left the room and shut the door behind him, he had had enough, he would get to the bottom of all this, perhaps he would do better to speak to Maria in the morning—with that he climbed the stairs and retired for the night.

CHAPTER NINE

(*End of an Era*)

With the arrival of the New Year, came a great change in the weather. Richard awoke to a pale and watery sunshine, and much milder conditions. The snow, which had once lay thick on the ground, was now almost gone without a trace, apart from a few little mounds where the wind had whisked it up and piled it high. The wind had died, and the outdoor world was quiet and peaceful. Although there was still no real warmth in the sun, it was after all still winter the air was mild and pleasant.

New Year's day was a day made for the Duke—one of his favourite pastimes was a tradition which had run for hundreds of years through his ancestors, and to which he would never be the exception. He had always kept a good pheasantry, and New Year Day, was the biggest pheasant shoot that he offered to the local gentry and landowners, all over Cornwall. Of all the occasions which were put on hold, while the house was in mourning, the pheasant shoot was not one of them. Richard had never been as interested in this as Edward had been, but as he would now be expected to carry on the tradition once he became Duke, then it was also expected of him to join in this activity. Many of the estate workers were there, employed by the Duke, who even paid them over the odds, to act as beaters for his sport. Thirty or more men took to the back road from Penleigh Court, and then on to the field beyond, their guns slung over their shoulders, many with their dogs, Richard was amongst them even though he was more interested in the refreshments back at the Court, which would follow the day's events.

As Richard strode along the rutted road, along with the other gentlemen, his mind was elsewhere, things at Penleigh Court had been quiet all week—the Duke had been busy organising his pheasant shoot with Melvin Lincroft and Maria, she had been acting exceptionally strange. She had not attended any meals for several days, and when she had appeared, she had seemed very quiet and far away. Richard wondered if she was unhappy, as his father was keeping Melvin so busy, perhaps she was upset that her clandestine meetings had been kerbed for a while. She had barely spoken more than two words to Richard, so he thought that perhaps she was still angry with him, for re-buffing her advances. No doubt she would get over it in time. He had also been thinking about his sweet Clara, his Sweet Clara? Hardly that, and never destined to be so either. He had thought of calling on her one morning, but he had no good reason to do so—after all, there was no point encouraging her affection, or allowing her to believe that he would ever make her an offer, as that was not going to happen, not because he didn't want it, but the Duke wouldn't hear of it. So, he had spent his time riding round the estate each morning, he knew that there was no chance of talking Melvin into joining him while his time was taken up by the Duke, so he went out and about on his own, besides, there was always the chance of seeing Clara out walking, or riding, and he couldn't help secretly hoping for a chance to spend a little time with her. One day he had even rode down to the churchyard, and visited the family crypt, where Edward lay, but he saw no-one. He had made regular visits to see his dear mother though, she was delighted to see him, though Nanny Grey was still spending most of her time asleep, and when she did wake, she was still very confused as to his identity. He had also made a point of visiting the nursery each day—he was becoming good friends with little Millicent, and he had even held Rebecca in his arms, though he had felt uncomfortable with this, and had very soon handed her back to Nanny Anson. Millicent seemed so excited to see him, he would throw her in the air, and she would shrill with pleasure. He had even collected her one day, and took her in to see the Duchess, before Nanny Anson arrived with Rebecca. He had started to really love the little girl, he had already decided that once she was a little older, he would buy her a pony and teach her to ride—she already had a natural interest in animals—she loved Mr Tubby, the large ginger cat who lived in his mother's rooms—she would chase him round, until he ran and hid somewhere that she couldn't reach him. He had also taken her out to the stables one afternoon, to visit the horses there—she was fascinated with everything that was going on, but he had kept her in his arms all the time, to make sure that she came to no harm.

By now they had reached the field—the gentlemen were spreading out, and setting up their guns ready to fire. Then, there was a noise in the bushes and hedgerow behind them, and the birds had taken flight—there was squawking and flapping of wings, as the birds flew over their heads, the crack of the rifles, then the thud of the birds as they dropped to the ground. Several dogs were running forward to retrieve their master's game, more cracks as the men took aim and fired again, while their assistant re-loaded a rifle for them to take their next shot—then, all of a sudden, a shout to halt fire, before the gun cracks were silent—Richard looked round him, someone was laid face down on the grass, and men were running to his side—Melvin Lincroft was knelt down, inspecting the man lying on the ground. Richard, taking large strides, could only see a large group gathered now, and more gentlemen moving in the same direction, then he came upon the group gathered round and pushed his way through the crowd, then he stopped—he couldn't believe his eyes, the Duke was lying face down in the grass, and he wasn't moving. Melvin Lincroft was desperately trying to stem the flow of blood oozing from a wound in the centre of his back, Richard immediately kneeled beside him, but he could tell straight away that the Duke was dead. One of the men had already taken off toward Penleigh Court, he would go to the stables and have one of the grooms to go into the village and bring back doctor Sommerville. In less than an hour, the doctor had arrived, followed by two of the grooms, who had followed him in order to carry the body of their master home. The doctor announced that he had been shot, and that the bullet had gone straight through his heart. The men lifted his body on to a make shift stretcher, and carried him back to Penleigh Court. Richard was in a daze—this couldn't be happening—first his brother Edward had died of an accident by falling over the cliff above Devil's Point, and now his father, shot in the back—was this an accident? Surely it had to be—after all, the men with their guns had formed a line, and they were shooting into the air—how could any of them have shot him by accident or otherwise. The days shoot was over—the men collected the birds which they had shot, and made their way home. There would have to be an inquest of course, things like this didn't happen every day. He would have to tell his mother—she would be shocked but there had been nothing between them now, for years. They couldn't even organise his burial as the authorities would first have to decide whether someone would be charged with his murder, or not. Richard had that cold shivery feeling creeping all over him again, that terrible foreboding—who would want to kill him anyway? He was a tyrant, and there were more people who hated him than liked him, but to dislike the man was one thing, to murder him, quite another.

Richard ordered the men to have the curtains in the large dining hall closed, and the Duke be laid out on the table, until the authorities had been and arrangements could be made.

The next few days were just a blur, there was so much going on, the authorities arrived two days after the incident—they had spoken to the all the people who had attended the shoot, and also everyone living at Penleigh Court, by the fifth day, and a great deal of questions answered, they seemed satisfied that what had happened to the Duke, had indeed been just an awful accident. The Duke had been killed with a bullet from one of the rifles, and it was more likely that whoever had shot him, had no idea what they had done. So, that was the end of that—Richard couldn't help but think that they had got it wrong, but he said nothing, as he had no proof either way, and what was the point in contradicting their result, without a good reason to do so. After all, he now stood to inherit his father's estate and title, and that could easily be misconstrued as a reason to kill. Best to let sleeping dogs lie for now, though he promised himself to get to the root of all this.

Arrangements were to be made, and although at any other time, he would have welcomed a visit to the rectory, this wasn't the time—so he sent for vicar Penrose to visit him at Penleigh Court, to organise the funeral. It was to be a very quiet affair, although many of the local gentry would attend. The Duchess had also agreed to attend the funeral, that it would be her last duty, to a husband who had treated her with nothing but contempt for the last ten years, but she would carry out that duty—it would be expected of her, and though things were non-existent between them, she had never shirked her duty, not from the day she had married him—she had even shed a tear or two when she had first heard of his death—there had been a time when she had truly loved her husband, and although he had killed most of that in the last years, he had still been her husband, and the father of her two wonderful sons. Maria, on the other hand, had acted quite strange—he knew that there was no love lost between them, but he never did get to the bottom of all the rows and arguments—perhaps he never would now. Maria chose not to attend the funeral—Richard understood her reluctance, but still he felt that she should attend, it was expected of her, she was one of the family, and people would expect them to stand together as such. So one evening, after dinner, he invited her to the library, so he could speak to her about it. She had been very quiet for the last week, and when she had been told of the Duke's death, she had said nothing and walked away—he hadn't seen her again for a couple of days, and even then, she hardly spoke a word—but once the arrangements were made for the funeral, she had started appearing for dinner with Richard in the evenings, though she hardly spoke a word to him—Richard thought that she had been going out in the afternoons again, and guessed that she was with her lover, though that wasn't the case, Melvin's time had been taken with helping the authorities with their investigations, and later, helping to organise arrangements, he would have had no time for his secret assignations.

Richard retired to his library, it was his now—he poured himself a large glass of brandy, and sat down in the large studded chair. Only moments later a small tap came at the door

"Come in" Richard called gently Maria slipped inside and closed the door behind her

"Please, sit down" he said nodding to the chair opposite him "I wanted to talk to you, would you like a drink?" Maria shook her head, then took a seat, head held high—although still a very attractive woman, her face was looking rather strained, as if something was bothering her

"Are you alright?"

"Yes of course, why do you ask?"

"No particular reason, I only thought that you were very quiet of late, which under the circumstances is to be expected—first Edward's accident, and now the Duke"

"Yes, it has all been rather a shock"

"But that is not why I asked to speak to you—am I right in thinking that you have no intention of attending the Duke's funeral tomorrow?"

"Yes that is correct, as you know, the Duke and I were less than on friendly terms—in fact he was threatening to throw me and my daughters out on the streets without a penny, and all because Edward and I had not produced an heir for him—I have no wish to speak ill of the dead, but I am not a hypocrite, I realize that he was your father, and I've no wish to distress you further, but he was not a liked man—he was known as a tyrant, and he treated me and my children badly, so I will not be attending his funeral tomorrow" she spoke quietly, but firmly

"I understand your reasons, believe me, the Duchess has every reason to feel the same way, but we have a duty to this estate, and to the people, they will expect us to stand as a family in mourning, and together—I am sure that if my mother can do her duty and attend the funeral, then you can also do this—it will all soon be over, and once it is, I can assure you that I shall see to it that you and your girls are taken care of for as long as you wish it."

"Thank you Richard, for your kindness, but I see no reason why my presence is so important"

"As I said, you are part of this family, and it is expected of you—come now Maria, it is but one morning, surely that is not too much to ask of you?" Maria looked straight into Richard's eyes—the blue like a deep ocean, turning shades darker as he watched—both sat in silence, then she spoke very softly

"I will attend if you wish, but it will be because you have asked me too, not through any loyalty to the Duke" she said

"Of course, I understand. It is the right thing to do you know—and once this is all over, and my father's will has been disclosed, then we will have a further talk about a proper allowance for you and money set aside in trust for your girls"

"Dear Richard, you are so kind, I cannot tell you how I bless the day you returned home, already it feels like a weight has been lifted from me" she stood up and walked around the desk, planting a kiss on his cheek.

"Please Maria, there is no need for thanks, I only wish to do my duty by you, my brother would have expected it"

"And I am very grateful to you my Lord" with that, she turned and left the room, head held high.

Maria truly was a proud woman, and he would do his duty by her and her girls—he was already growing attached to the little ones, especially Millicent, who was so excited when he visited them in the nursery. He still had uneasy feelings when in close proximity to their mother—he had the distinct feeling that she had some sort of agenda, and she had already shown at Christmas, that she would welcome his attention—but in that she would be sorely disappointed, he had no desire for the woman at all, and besides, there was no reason that her affections for Melvin Lincroft, should not develop now—he would show no interference there.

⸙

The following day, the heavens opened, and the rain beat down—the coffin was to be transported to the church in a glass cased carriage with a team of four pure black horses with black feathered plumes. As the church was a little way out from the village, and the rain beating down in torrents, Richard had the Duke's carriage brought round, that the ladies could be transported in a modicum of comfort. The procession would travel at a very slow pace, through the village, over the bridge and on down the rutted road. Once beneath the shelter of the lych-gate, six of the estate workers were waiting to carry the Duke's coffin into the church, followed by Richard and the Duchess with Maria just behind. In the church many of the villagers, and estate workers, along with a handful of the local gentry, had all come to say their final goodbyes to the man known as the tyrant. Vicar Penrose had led the procession, before standing in the pulpit, and going over the life and times of this great man—fortunately, he had the good grace to omit the not so savoury side of his nature—but not having known the Duke hardly at all, he could only tell his congregation of the things which he had been told, and everyone knew that you should never speak ill of the dead. The Duchess walked straight, and upright, a black hat and veil covering her face, so that none could see the odd tear which spilled from those warm brown eyes. Maria also wore a black hat with a veil, she too walked tall and straight, but there were no tears falling from her eyes, though her face carried a strain that she was wearing like a cloak, she never once gave away anything which she was feeling. Once the short service was ended, the coffin was carried from the main door of the church, and round the path at the side, to the Penleigh family crypt, where it would reach its final resting place—Henry Penleigh would be set down on the opposite side of the cold damp crypt, to his son Edward. A few prayers were said, though only the family and vicar Penrose entered the crypt, then, everyone left, and walked through the pouring rain, back up the path, and into the waiting carriage, shaking the hand of the vicar, who had placed himself just inside the lych-gate. As the carriage rolled and jutted through the ruts and now large puddles, it had started to dawn on Richard exactly his position—he was the duke, and Penleigh Court was now his. He looked across at the two ladies sat on the opposite seat, before gazing out of the window. Nobody spoke—there was little to say. Once the carriage arrived, the door was opened by one of the footmen, and the steps pulled down—Richard jumped to the ground, ready to help his mother and sister in law to alight. They mounted the steps and into the front entrance, where tables had been laid with foods of all kinds, and wine ready to serve. Many of the villagers, and tenants arrived, along with a few of the gentry who were on good terms with the Duke, for a while the hall was a hive of activity, and a buzz of conversation. But it was all over soon enough, and Richard stood by the doors, thanking everyone for coming, before going to his library, and pouring a glass of brandy.

What a start to the New Year, his brother not yet cold in his grave, and now his father laid in the crypt opposite. Two accidents and both within two months of each other, whatever could be going on here—surely there had to be something more behind all this, none of it made any sense. Now all that was left was the reading of the will, his father's old solicitor Mr Truscott of Truscott and Penn, had been the family solicitor for as far back as he could remember—his father had refused to allow anyone else, to deal with his affairs. Of late, old Mr Truscott was dealing with less of the work load, he was finding it harder to manage, especially if it meant taking trips to places outside of Truro, his old bones were not what they were, so young Mr Penn, who had taken over from his father, would take on the travelling, and things which were more difficult. The Duke had refused to let Mr Penn have any dealings with his affairs, his mother had written in one of her letters that there had been some sort of dispute when Mr Penn had tried to come to Penleigh Court on behalf of his business partner, and his father had seen him off the property himself—the Duchess had been astounded, and Edward, who had been given the responsibility of the matter in hand, had felt a sense of guilt and embarrassment at the situation, that he had sent a letter of apology to Mr Penn, unbeknown to his father, to calm the situation down and so as not to induce his father's ire further. Another glass of brandy, and then to prepare for the will reading, he had already had instruction to gather all the servants together, so he would make sure that they were seated in the dining room for when Mr Truscott arrived at three o clock.

CHAPTER TEN

(The Will)

It had been years since he last saw Mr Truscott, he had remembered him as a little old man even then, but now he was indeed wizened, and frail looking—he walked with a stoop, his hair was snowy white, but his eyes were small black dots in his head, and they were very much alive and alert. Richard was eying the papers which he held in his hand, tied up with a blue ribbon. Richard led him through to the dining room, where everyone had been assembled, all of the staff had been instructed to attend, and Richard had duly made sure that they were all there. Richard led the little old man to the chair made ready for him, at the head of the table, before taking up his own seat on the man's left hand side, and next to the Duchess. The little old man's fingers tugged at the ribbon securing the papers, until it dropped to the table. Then he looked around at the sea of faces, over the top of his glasses, before casting his eye back to the paperwork before him. He cleared his throat, in a clear voice he started to read through all the legal jargon on the page in his hand.

"I will begin with the smaller bequeaths" he then went on to name the individuals, and the sum which the Duke was to settle on them, there was surprises all round, even the lowest servant of the household, was to receive a small sum, which had been totally unexpected, especially as the Duke had never been the easiest man, in his reign, he had frightened many of the lower servants, they lived in fear of his temper. The amount each one was to receive was relevant to their position in the house, though they were all assured that their position would carry on as before. There were but two exceptions, the Duke's valet was one, unfortunately his services were no longer required, but he was to receive a King's ransom of five hundred pounds for all his loyalty, and a roof over his head for six months, to allow him to find another post. There was also a letter with the Duke's own seal, which was a reference for his new employer, once employment had been settled for him, and Mr Truscott would be placing an advertisement to help him find the correct position. He had sighed with relief at this, then bowed his head in acknowledgement, a pleasant surprise no doubt, five hundred pound would set him up for a while. The other exception had been Melvin Lincroft, and he was the only person in the Duke's employ, who wasn't even mentioned. This was very strange—even the lowliest of servants had received a small sum, yet Melvin Lincroft had received not as much as a mention.

Once this had been completed, Mr Truscott turned to Richard and said

"That completes the smaller bequeaths your Grace, perhaps now the remainder should be discussed more privately?"

"Yes of course" he turned to his staff "you are all now free to go about your business—thank you for your time" and bowed his head as final. For several moments there was the clatter and noise as the servants left the dining room, the last one being the butler, who closed the door behind him.

"Can we proceed now?" he asked Mr Truscott—everyone had left apart from the Duchess, Maria and himself—they all sat eagerly awaiting to hear the remainder of the contents of this will. The old man continued

"To my creditors, a list held by Truscott and Penn solicitors, all debts to be repaid in full. For Miss Edwina Penrith, a house, forty six Tallow Road Truro also the sum of twenty thousand pounds, for services rendered—the house to be made over to her complete and in its entirety. For my wife Alice Elizabeth Penleigh, Penleigh Court shall remain her home for the rest of her days, or as long as she so chooses—her allowance to remain as before. The remainder is for my son and heir, Richard Henry Julian Penleigh, though he shall not receive the whole until he has married and provided a legitimate heir to my title and estate. His allowance is to be doubled, the title and my estate should be his immediately but the remainder of my estate is the sum of one million pound—which will be held in trust, until such time that his final duty to me has been fulfilled. Should he fail to fulfil his obligation, the money should then go to the next of my kin in line, who succeeds my son. This completes the last will and testimony of Henry Edward David Penleigh" the little man with the beady eyes, looked up at the faces watching him, "And that concludes the Duke's will" he stated, bowing his head.

"And what is to become of me?" Maria had spoken for the first time, her voice frantic "What am I to do, where should I go, with my two children, and nothing—was there nothing as to the allowance I receive—is that going to cease?" her voice was rising in hysteria

"I have given you the details of the Duke's will, I'm afraid that there was no mention of you or your children Madam, there has been no provision made" said Mr Truscott, in his matter of fact way

"He has left a house and a large sum of money to his mistress in Truro, yet his son's wife and his own flesh and blood, he sees fit to cast us aside as if we don't exist?" she was becoming hysterical now—Richard jumped up from his seat and went to her, putting an arm about her shoulders

"Please Maria, you must not worry yourself, I have already told you that you shall be taken care of, and I intend to keep my word" he said soothingly, but there was no reasoning with this woman

"And how do you propose to do that?" she stated looking straight at him "Tell me, you have inherited his title and estate, that which should have been my husband Edwards, but you will not receive the money until you have married and provided the estate with a son and heir, so I ask again Richard, how do you propose to take care of me and my family?"

Mr Truscott, having completed his duty, stood up, picking up the papers in front of him, and excused himself—he gave a small bow and left the room—clearly he could not and would not have any dealings with outbursts such as this. He had carried out his duty to the Duke, his job was now complete. Richard asked his mother to go to Maria, and followed him out into the hall

"Mr Truscott, may I ask you a question?"

"Certainly Your Grace" as he turned to cast those small black dots in Richard's direction, studying his face in anticipation of what the young Duke may ask

"I have to ask this, as it is very important, on the afternoon that my brother Edward died, I believe he paid you a visit, I should be interested to know the purpose of this visit?"

"I'm sorry Your Grace, but you are mistaken, you have been misinformed. I had not seen Mr Edward Penleigh for at least twelve months, and being the only one allowed to deal with Penleigh matters, I can assure you there was no such meeting with my partner, Mr Penn either." now the old man's beady little eyes were burning into his

"My family believed it to be so—but there has obviously been a mistake—I'm sorry to have troubled you—I shall be in touch shortly of course, I trust that your journey back to Truro will be a comfortable one"

"Indeed Your Grace, thank you" he gave a small incline of his head, before leaving through the front entrance, now opened wide by the butler. Once he had left, Richard went back into the dining room, where his mother was seated next to Maria, trying to calm her frantic sobs. He went over to her, and placed his arm about her shoulders once again "Please Maria, dry your tears, you need not fear for your future, I shall take care of you and your girls and that is an end to it" she turned to Richard and threw herself into his arms, pressing her head against his large hard chest. The Duchess stood up and left the room closing the door behind her. Maria clung to Richard until her tears had abated, before turning her head up, and looking into his eyes, yet still clinging to his body

"Oh Richard" she whispered softly, "you are so good to us, how could the Duke have cut off his own flesh and blood, without an allowance, I know that the allowance he gave me after Edward's death, was but a pittance, but with that cancelled, I have nothing at all—must I be expected to come to you, cap in hand for the most meagre purchases in future?"

"I promise you Maria, that we shall come to some arrangement to suit us both, please trust me, I shall not let you down, it is after all what Edward would have expected"

"He has given you his title and his estate, the responsibility of it all, but without the means to support it—you do know that you now have to marry

Richard, it is your only hope, you are required to provide a legitimate heir to your title. I could help you, you know, your father has cheated you from what is yours, it is the only way you will receive what's rightfully yours, and quickly—I could help you, marry me Richard, we could marry quietly, away from this place, no-one would have time to question it, when we returned married, I could already be carrying your heir—you would not have to wait to come out of mourning, please let me help you gain what is rightfully yours?" Richard could not believe what he was hearing did she think that he was desperate? He could never marry Maria, though he had no intention of saying so, and hurting her feelings.

"You need not worry on my account Maria, I would never ask you to sacrifice yourself to my cause" he said softly

"But it would be no hardship, I would gladly marry you, and give you a son and heir, two if you wish" she would do anything to have her way with him? Even the promise of a son and heir or more

"No Maria, I do not wish it. And you must stop worrying yourself needlessly, you will see, all will be well—I promise" he tried to be as firm as he could, without upsetting her further, but Maria persisted, she reached up and threw her arms about his neck, pressing her lips hard to his—he tried to pull away, but her hold tightened before she softly cupped her hand to his cheek, and she looked up into his eyes again

"It is the answer you know, or do you find me so repulsive?" Richard took hold of her wrist, pulling it away from his face, the black lace, edging the sleeves of her black taffeta gown fell back, and she winced—Richard's eyes went straight to her wrist, and he let her hand go immediately

"You are hurt, how did it happen?" he asked genuinely concerned

"It is nothing, merely clumsiness on my part—it will be better in a few days"

"I could call doctor Sommerville to take a look, maybe bandage it up for you"

"No, please Richard, there is no need—besides it is healing perfectly well by itself" she stood up, promptly covering her black and blue wrist, brushing the lace that had fallen away, back down over her injured wrist. The moment had gone Richard felt a great sense of relief

"I am very tired, I have a headache so I shall take my dinner in my room— thank you for your kindness my Lord" Maria had regained her pride, she opened the door and slipped out into the hall and up the stairs, leaving Richard sat alone, and now with more thoughts to fill his head.

Once alone in her room, Maria, after sending her maid away, and pleading a headache, she threw off her clothes, leaving them thrown over her chair. Then she went to her full length mirror and stood, wincing at the sight before her eyes. Large black and blue marks surrounding her wrists, there were others, some now purple, on her neck, across her breast, and down her thighs—she closed her eyes, trying to blot out the memories. Then there was Richard, handsome, supportive, caring Richard. She pulled on her cotton lawn nightshift, and climbed between the cool white sheets of her large comfortable bed, he was still denying her his love, but once her injuries had healed, she would do her utmost to encourage his affections, he had admitted himself that he would take care of her, she wanted that in more ways than one—she would give up everything for this one man. Her daughters, he was already bewitched with them, especially Millicent, she could not think of a better father for them than he—and they would be thrilled at the prospect of having him as their new father—he would love them as his own, after all, they carried the same blood in their veins. Yes, she would concentrate on having her wounds healed, then she would carefully work on Richard, she would show him that he couldn't be without her, she knew that she could win him round, given time, and with a house in mourning, where else would he look for a wife—there was to be no balls or assemblies in the near future, and even if there were, how many eligible young ladies were there in the local vicinity—she could think only of two, Jane Manson, she smiled to herself, poor Jane, she had never been a beauty—her mama had tried so hard to find a suitable husband for her, but had eventually given up, without success. Then there was Luella Compton, she was certainly more attractive than Jane, but her father had incurred many debts, and unlike herself, she had not been fortunate enough to have a relative to take her under their wing, once her father's estate was sold, on his death, and the creditors paid off, there was just enough money left for her mother and herself, to make a new life, living in a small cottage, with two servants only, and taking in sewing—to pay for their food and clothing. She may once have been a gentlewoman, but no longer, certainly not a suitable wife for a Duke, and definitely not for a man such as dear Richard, he was everything a gentleman should be, he would never marry beneath him. She lay back sinking her head into the pillow, yes, her plan now set in her mind, she had started to tire of Melvin, though he did make for a pleasant pastime, but Richard was her future, he would be her first priority now, she would give up everything for him, she closed her eyes contentedly and fell into a deep peaceful sleep.

Richard had eaten his dinner alone. His mind returning to Maria, he was glad that she had decided not to join him—she had offered herself to him this afternoon, and he couldn't deal with it—he felt sorry for her, his father had treated her very badly, but he had been known for his tyranny. No, he felt for her and wished only to show her comfort, but that was an end to it, and after all, if she needed a man's comfort, then surely she could go to Melvin, Richard would not interfere with her business, he would only wish her well—his only interest was to see that her and her children, had a roof over their heads and food in their bellies—he would see that her girls were given an education and eventually, found suitable husbands. He sat at the dinner table, long after finishing his meal, with only the fire and the light of one lamp, pondering on the events of this afternoon—so, he would have to marry, and sooner rather than later, Maria had been correct in that. His allowance had been doubled, but with Penleigh Court to support, and all the people in it, his new allowance would still not stretch that far, for too long. He could also sell off his father's town property in Bond Street, that would have to go before his own house in Mayfair, after all, his home was a modern town house, with all his home comforts, so the Bond Street house must go. He would have to decide how to proceed, but first he would have to speak to Melvin, once he had a clearer picture, he would then be able to go to old Truscott, and set the wheels in motion. The most baffling part of it all for him was the fact that his father had one million pound in money—looking about him at the state of the house, he felt sure that there was little or no money left in the coffers—his room alone screamed of this. There was also the tenants, he had seen the ledger of requests made for repairs, Melvin had told him that the Duke had no money to fulfil any of the requests made, unless the roof had caved in or something life threatening had happened, then a temporary job would be completed, just to keep the tenant happy. He had always enjoyed gambling, and had made heavy losses years before, or so his mother had told him, so much so that her dowry had been swallowed. Perhaps he had done better at the cards of late—but he would have to have done more than better to have accumulated that much money—and leaving his mistress not only a house, but twenty thousand pounds to live on—yet the Duchess had merely her small allowance, and Maria nothing. He would have to set up some sort of allowance for her and the children, though he wasn't sure how to do that, unless he sold the Bond Street house—it wasn't right that she must ask him for every penny she required, but before he could agree to that, he would surely have to discuss the best way forward—perhaps a meeting should be arranged with Melvin and Mr Truscott—they could then find the best way to proceed.

He had started to feel really tired he reached for the port decanter, only to find that he had emptied it. He loosened his cravat and stood up—he would go to bed. He climbed the stairs to his room, James was already in his dressing room, waiting for him, as soon as he entered James came through to greet him

"An early night Your Grace, and by the smell, a bottle of port" James, as usual, always something to say

"Is there something wrong with that?" Richard asked

"No, nothing at all Your Grace—just preparing for a sore head and a late rise in the morning"

"You should remember that you work for a Duke now James, and that there's a valet, not far from here, looking for a new post, I could as easily employ him in your place—perhaps you should prepare for that"

"But if you did that Your Grace, you would soon miss our stimulating conversation" Richard had to allow him that—as he was truly correct, he did enjoy their banter, though he would never let James get the better of him

"Yes, I'm sure that I would, but perhaps the quiet would suit me more, had you considered that?"

"No, we both know that you would be lost without me—you have to admit, that you would have to look a long way to find a man used to the way you like things done—after all, I'm well used to all your strange little ways now"

"I don't have a clue what you mean, I have no strange little ways, as you put it and you should watch your tongue"

"You think not, Your Grace?"

"you are an insolent oaf, and I should throw you out on the street without a penny to your name, but I couldn't be responsible for allowing you to harass another gentleman, so I suppose that I shall just have to keep you" Richard really did enjoy their little spats "but now, you can tidy my clothes and leave—I intend to have an early night"

"As you wish Your Grace, wouldn't dream of keeping you from your beauty sleep"

"Good night James" said Richard finally

"Good night Sir" James, with a huge grin on his face, went through the connecting door to the dressing room, closing it behind him and Richard knew that he would leave through the door directly from the dressing room to the passage.

Richard took off his clothes, and climbed between the sheets—old Truscott had told him that Edward had never visited their office in Truro, yet everyone seemed to think that was where he was headed. But if that wasn't the case, the question remained—what had induced him to go along that path and fall to his death. Furthermore, he was there when his father died, but he couldn't believe that one of the men there had shot him, it was almost impossible—the authorities surely hadn't thought it through properly—to have shot his father, and for it to have passed straight through his heart, would have meant that the person responsible would have had to point the gun level at his chest, and not in the air—there was definitely something wrong with all of this. But if he had been shot deliberately, then who would have gone to such lengths? Then there was Maria, and Melvin Lincroft—tis true that of late, there had been too much going on that was taking up Melvin's time, which in turn was curbing their pleasure, but was Maria so desperate that she would have him as her lover? And there was the bruises around her wrist, perhaps her and Melvin had argued, and he had treated her roughly, and bruised her arm, though if that were so it would show Melvin to be a violent man, he didn't like or trust him, but he had never considered him to be violent until now. Perhaps Melvin knew of his lover's attempts on him—and had become angry with her, perhaps he was angry with his new master too. It was a fact that they neither liked each other very much. Then there was the will, Melvin Lincroft was the only man who received nothing from his father's will—why had that been the case, had Melvin upset the old Duke, was that his reason for cutting him out of his will, yet he had housed him at the Gate Lodge—that was an act of favour. Then there was the rest of the will, nothing at all for Maria or the girls, his mother was only granted a home at Penleigh Court and the same allowance that she had already been receiving, so nothing extra at all—his mistress had been given twenty thousand pounds as well as the house she lived in already—surely the house alone would have been sufficient. And for himself—marriage—the one thing which he had determined to decide for himself. He knew very well, that he would have to find a wife, but with a year of mourning ahead, that wasn't likely in the short term, but to connect the money to not only his marriage, but depending on his producing a son and heir, was preposterous—how should he keep the estate running properly in the meantime, if he couldn't touch the bulk. It would help if he married an heiress, but this was all forcing his hand—taking away his choice in the matter. Well, he wouldn't be bullied into anything—he lay back on his pillow—his eyes drooping shut, there he was, back in the field down at the pheasantry, he was holding a pistol in his hand, the birds were flying overhead, squawking, he took aim, suddenly, as he squeezed the trigger, he was no longer aiming at the birds, but straight at his father—watching in slow motion as he fell to the ground—the authorities were after him, he was running and running, but they had caught up to him—then he was down at Gallows Cross—the crowd had him they were cheering and jeering him, he was being lifted up, and a rope was being placed about his neck—he tried to scream out but no noise came, he could feel the rope tightening about his neck—he couldn't breathe, then the crowd stood back—he opened his eyes, the beads of sweat were rolling down his face, and his breathing was coming in gasps—then he realized that it had all been a dream—he lay there still until his breathing had subsided and slowed to a normal rate, the feeling of foreboding had returned with a vengeance—his candle burned almost out, he snuffed it and turned over, hoping that this time his sleep would be peaceful.

CHAPTER ELEVEN

(The Decision)

For the next few weeks, Richard's life seemed to fall into a pattern. He would rise early, and breakfast alone, before joining Melvin Lincroft in the estate office. He spent hours mulling over the ledgers, trying to make sense of the way they read. He would then return to the house for lunch, which again he ate alone, then after lunch he would go for a ride before visiting his dear mama for tea, and spending an enjoyable hour or two in the company of his nieces. Maria joined him most nights for dinner, but there had been no reference to her outburst, and she had showed no more interest in him, for which he was very grateful. After dinner, he would retire to his library, where he could shut the door and be left with his port and his thoughts.

Melvin was very suspicious of his interests, though for what reason, Richard had no idea—it was surely natural for him to take an interest in the way his estate was run, and now even more important than before. The estate itself was making a small profit, but not enough to complete the repairs which his tenants had requested, and certainly not enough to show so much money in his father's coffers. There was nothing for it he would just have to sell one of the properties, belonging to his father. He would have Melvin arrange a meeting with Truscott, and the three of them would decide what to do next. Although Richard had no liking for Melvin, he had to admit that he was an astute business man, and that if kept on side, a good estate manager. He had also noticed that Melvin had taken to disappearing in the afternoons again, so he could only presume that this was the reason that Maria was kept so sweet—but that was none of his concern—as long as the work was taken care of, which on that score he had no complaints, what Melvin did in private should stay that way.

Richard had taken to going for a ride in the afternoon, this left his morning's free for estate business. He made a point of riding round the outlaying farms which were part of the estate and making himself known to any tenants who he had not met, though there were only two of them, all the others he had remembered from his childhood. He had planned to do this with Melvin, but he always seemed too busy for social calls and reluctant to take his young master, and besides, Richard's time was better filled examining the books—he needed to know exactly the situation, before his meeting with Truscott.

On his afternoon excursions, he had always hoped that he should meet the lovely Clara again, but so far, that had not happened. He had on several occasions been very tempted to call at the rectory, but he had no reason to do so, and he could think of no good reason to see Clara, even if he made an excuse to speak to her father. He had tried to forget her, put her out of his mind, but it was impossible, this young lady had really gotten into his head, and there was no getting her out, though in truth he wouldn't want too anyway. He knew that he must marry—that did bother him as there were no eligible young ladies in the local vicinity—unfortunately Maria had been right there, and he couldn't afford to wait a whole year to spend a season in London, he would be old himself before he could touch the family coffers, and by then the estate would have been sold off bit by bit. He would have to discuss this with the Duchess, she would offer him good advice, of that he was sure.

So, one afternoon, as he slipped through into the passage and into the East wing, he resolved to speak to his mother and seek her advice. As he entered the drawing room, he could hear Nanny Grey snoring, and knew that this would be an ideal opportunity—he walked over to his mother, who was laid back in her chair with her eyes closed, her needlework laid in her lap—but she wasn't asleep, as soon as he crept near, her eyes flicked open and she jumped up, startled

"Richard my dearest, I didn't hear you come in"

"Good afternoon mama—I need a chance to speak to you this afternoon" he was eager for her help

"Of course my darling, what is it that's troubling you?"

"As you know, I have been studying father's estate ledgers, and although the estate is making a small profit, there is not enough to do the repairs required, and certainly not enough to keep us going. I am confused to say the least, to know where all his money came from, but having that money frozen for the present time, I'm not sure how we shall go on, unless I marry of course, but how can I find a wife, when we are in mourning, it's not as if I can go to London for the season, and to make things worse, I cannot touch the money, until I have a son and heir. It is an impossible situation—what can I do?"

"My dearest, I have no idea to what your father was thinking, and I have little knowledge of business, but I can tell you that he was eager to see you married and settled with a family of your own, he would have been eager for your son and heir. But I see your predicament, with such a lack of young ladies perhaps I could help you there."

"I would welcome your suggestions mama"

"Have you considered Maria? She looks at you in such a way my dear, I think that she would welcome your attention—while I admit that I cannot trust her entirely, I fear your father never made things easy for her, and now, her situation is even more precarious than ever"

Richard was horrified—there was no way that he would consider marrying Maria—he could never keep a promise to spend the rest of his life with her, and he knew her to be less than honest, her dealings with Melvin were proof of that, not that he would worry his mother with the details

"No mama, and again no—I could never marry Maria, did you know that she had already propositioned me?"

"I did wonder, she is a beautiful woman Richard, though I could never ask you to marry someone that you obviously oppose so much"

"It's not that I oppose her, I shall willingly see that she has a home here with us, and I enjoy my nieces immensely, but I cannot marry her—I do not trust her mama, there is more to Maria than meets the eye, and something, I have no idea what exactly that is, but something is not quite right—Maria will never be my bride" he spoke with finality

"I have to agree with you there, it seems that we both feel the same—she is clearly not the answer to your problems, I'm sure we will find a solution" she spoke softly

"But what other options are there mama, I would go back to Mayfair, and spend the season there, looking for a bride, but we are in mourning, the ton would surely slight me for such an action"

"Of course you cannot do that the ton would make your life unbearable. I could always move back into the West wing if you like, we could close this wing down again, we cannot throw any balls or parties, but I see no reason why I should not hold some intimate afternoon teas, in your honour. I could invite some of the gentry, though there are none in the local vicinity, but there are a few, a little farther afield, who I know to have an eligible daughter, to take tea with me—at least you would then have a chance to meet some of the young ladies, that are on offer, and from their part, I'm certain that any of them would jump at the chance of marrying their daughter to the handsome, dashing new young Duke of Warren, I think that you would have more problems, warding them off" she smiled broadly, the lines around her eyes creased with amusement and love for her son and giving his arm a playful little tap with her fan

"I suppose you are right, that would be a solution, and for you and Nanny Grey to return to the West wing, would certainly save a little money—we can shut this wing again completely. Your place mama, as dowager Duchess, should be with me—and I think your idea splendid, that way I shall get to choose my own bride. I shall order the servants prepare your rooms and you shall return tomorrow.

"You shall find a wife my dearest, and one of your choosing—I would not wish it otherwise"

"I have to say that I'm not eager mama, but fathers will, has left me no choice, I think that I can make a few alterations to ease the situation for now, but the only long term solution is for me to marry, and produce an heir, and until I do, I shall have no lasting solution to this problem"

"I do understand—though what have you in mind when you say that you could ease the situation?"

"My intention is to sell the house in Bond Street—we have no further use of it, but I shall speak to Truscott, and see about finalising the details"

"But what of the servants You are not in a position to offer them anything—what is to become of them?"

"Have no fear mama, I shall do nothing to leave them homeless or penniless—I'm sure that Truscott, with the help of Melvin Lincroft, can come up with a way round this problem"

"So, we are to be left without a London home? Not that I'm likely to use it again, but my thoughts are for Maria, and for her girls, where would they stay if she wishes to go to London? She may wish to go for the season, once we are out of mourning, I'm sure that she will wish to find another husband eventually, after all, she is but a young woman still"

"There is always my town house in Mayfair, I would be more than happy for them to use it while in town, and besides, it's far more modern than Bond Street and much more fashionable"

"Yes, of course. Well, I shall call Gracie and make arrangements for her to move my things and those of Nanny Grey, back home, we shall settle in tomorrow"

"And I shall leave you now, so that I can make arrangements for your rooms to be aired and prepared for your return"

Alice reached out to her son, pulling him close to her, while he kissed her cheek. She was overjoyed at the prospect of being back where she belonged. The family would all be back together again—and her dear son had brought this about. She adored her son, and she would do whatever she could to find him a wife that suited his needs, and who was worthy of his affection. There would no doubt be a large amount of young ladies, who would be clamouring to be noticed by the Duke of Warren, and he such a handsome and charming man too. She would have to be careful of course, she could not allow her dear son to be completely thrown to the wolves. Her husband had been a tyrant and a bully, but for one thing at least, she was grateful to him, he had given her two sons to be proud of, and even though her poor dear Edward was now dead and gone, she still had Richard to cherish and be a comfort to her in her old age.

A few days later, Melvin had called for old Truscott to pay them a visit. Mr Truscott had sent word that he would be at Penleigh Court at three o clock that afternoon. Richard, still looking for more options, had spent the morning in the estate office, with Melvin glaring at him while he went over and over the different ledgers there. Although this new allowance which his father had granted him, helped a little, it wasn't enough to cover all the outgoings, and if something wasn't done very soon, he would find himself being forced to sell off parts of the estate, and he was determined that this shouldn't happen.

After lunch, Alice had asked to speak to him, she knew that the meeting was to go ahead, though she had news of her own plans which she felt sure he should know, but she was agitated when he found her in her small drawing room

"Are you alright mama?" Richard asked going to her and kissing her cheek

"Of course, I wanted to let you know that I have made arrangements for afternoon tea tomorrow afternoon at four o clock, Mrs Bonetti and her daughter Ellen are coming to tea—Ellen is a quiet girl, they live in Truro, but I know that they are eager to take her to London for her first season this time. I haven't seen the girl of course, but her mother would welcome her marriage to a Duke, and I understand that she has a very good dowry, but my darling, you must not offer for her just to suit Penleigh coffers, promise me Richard, that you will only marry to suit yourself—I am so afraid that you will feel pushed into a marriage of convenience and although your father gave me Edward and yourself, such blessings to my life, there was nothing more, my life has been filled with heartache and misery—I would not choose that for you."

"Of course mama, haven't I already told you, that I shall never marry just to set things right, even father's will would not induce me to marry unless I meet a young lady who really catches my eye, otherwise, I certainly will not be offering for her—you must not worry yourself about that"

"Richard, there is something else which I need to speak to you about—but I don't know where to start—I had thought to let this matter die with your father, but I feel that you should know the truth"

"What is it mama?" Richard was intrigued now

"Where can I start?" she was even more agitated now, winding her lace handkerchief between her long bony fingers

"Your father, he was less than honest Richard"

"My father was a tyrant mama, he was involved in most things frowned upon, but surely we are all aware of that"

"His dealings, he had some less than savoury associates" she was speaking slowly now, choosing her words carefully

"We all know of his mistress mama, but you shouldn't let that worry you, and he was a man that liked to gamble a great deal—that's what surprises me, that he had one million pound in the Penleigh coffers, I had expected there to be very little, or even debts which could not be met"

"Yes, well, it's the money which I refer too—your father, he ran the local band of smuggling. The authorities, they never caught him, oh he came close many times, and of course, of late he has not been able to play an active role, he was too old, but I'm sure that he was still involved with it all.

"No mama, I'm sure that you are wrong, Rufus Drummond, he was a regular visitor here at the time, when smuggling was at its height—father would always take him into his library and they would talk and drink brandy until late into the evening—he even came to dinner on occasions. He used to tell father what he suspected, even telling him the plans of the authorities, and when they were going out to catch the culprits—father couldn't possibly have had a hand in it"

"You are wrong—it has been going on since I first married your father, possibly before that—though I never knew about his dealing then, I followed him one night, not long after our marriage—I believed that he was meeting a mistress, so I followed him as I had to find out—he has caves down on the Smugglers Cove beach, caves that cannot be accessed at high tide, they are well hidden from view—he befriended Rufus Drummond years later, it was his plan to avoid the hangman's rope, that's the reason he was never caught—Rufus spoke openly of his intentions, and Henry used the information to his benefit. Richard, my darling, I fear that you will be dragged into this whole miserable affair, it is true, I promise you, I know that you will be discussing how to release this money from his coffers, and that is the reason why there is so much of it—it's all down to his underhand dealings. I fear that someone in this house is also involved, though I'm not sure who, you must be very careful Richard, give nothing away, if the authorities should ever suspect that we are in any way linked to this gang, our lives would be in danger—the crime carries a hanging sentence—I could not bear to lose you my dearest, it would be the death of me, but before you attend this meeting, I had to warn you" she reached out and hugged her son tightly "please be careful" she whispered in his ear

"You need not worry mother, I shall say nothing of this, but I can promise you that I have no intention of getting involved in such practises, and if I were to find that any of my employees or tenants were part of this affair, then I shall be forced to involve the authorities myself"

"Please Richard, do be careful—this matter is a very serious one, these people would kill if they felt threatened, I have no proof of course, but my husband and one of my sons are dead already—I cannot allow you to be next—please be careful my darling"

"Have no fear, think no more of it mother, it would explain all that money, but no-one will ever know the truth, your secret is safe with me, of that you can be sure. My father and brother have both gone to their graves, but if my father was involved with all this, it's hardly likely that he was killed for his part, and I can't believe Edward played any part at all, he was an honest, kind and gentle man, he would not have the stomach for something like this, so do not worry yourself any longer mama—my father is dead and gone, and his undercover affairs must die with him"

"Yes I suppose you are right—but you must be careful my darling, we have no idea the identity of your fathers associates, if there are any living under this roof, you could be in grave danger" He leaned forward and kissed his mother on the cheek.

"I shall be careful, but now I must go, Truscott will be arriving shortly and if I'm right, Melvin will be waiting for me by now"

"I won't keep you longer, but you won't forget to join us for tea tomorrow afternoon will you?"

"How could I forget, I couldn't possibly miss being there to vet my 'would be' future wife now could I?" Richard spoke in a playful tone, though his thoughts were far from that

"Go my dearest, your guests will be waiting for you—I have kept you too long already"

"I shall see you at dinner mama" he kissed her cheek and hurried from the room. He found it very difficult to believe that his father would be involved in such matters, with all his faults, but it would account for such a large amount of money in the Penleigh trust, and his mother would not have told him something like that if it were not true—indeed, she had risked her own life through it all, and had lived with her secret ever since, such a heavy burden for her to carry on her own. Like his mother's fear, he had to find out for sure now if all this was the cause of both his father's and his brother's deaths, and more importantly, if there was anyone living under his roof, who was still involved in all this—but whatever he did, he must, as his mother pointed out, be extremely careful, he couldn't be responsible for any more deaths.

Richard was striding up the passageway towards the large hall, his mind racing, and not with the details of the meeting, which he was about to attend. His father, a smuggler—all those times he and Edward had told horror stories in their childhood, frightening each other until they couldn't sleep at night and Nanny Grey had eventually become very annoyed with them both. They had had a fascination with the whole thing in those days. But never, had they imagined, in their wildest dreams, that their father was part of it all—indeed, if his mother was right, the leader of the smuggling ring. Then there was Rufus Drummond, he had always seemed as if he was on good terms with the Duke, old friends even, how could his father have possibly faced the man, knowing that he was the root cause of his problems, without Mr Drummond ever having known—and he couldn't have known, or he would surely have arrested the Duke, he was a blood hound of a man if nothing else. Then, suddenly he stopped dead, voices were drifting to him from the great hall, luckily he was still in the passageway, and well out of view

"Please Melvin, I can easily slip away tonight, after dinner, no-one would notice, we have seen so little of each other lately" Maria's soft lilt

"I'm sorry my dear, tonight is not possible—besides, we agreed that we should meet only in the afternoon—and that is the way it must be" who else but Melvin

"But who would know, I could stay all night"

"As one day you shall—one day, we shall be together all the time Maria, I promise" Maria heaved a great sigh

"Then I shall have to be patient, when may I come to you—let it be soon, I need you"

"Tomorrow afternoon my darling, come tomorrow—I shall be waiting for you—we will talk then"

"I have no mind to talk, I can think of better ways to occupy our afternoon" then they both laughed. Richard decided that this was the time to interrupt their little meeting. As he approached the hall, a knock came at the front door Newbridge was making his way across the hall to answer it, so Richard headed directly for the library, to take his seat, Melvin Lincroft arriving just ahead of him. There was a tap on the door and Newbridge showed Truscott in. Richard had already prepared seats for them Truscott bowed his head, then seated himself next to Melvin Lincroft.

"Can I get you a drink gentlemen?" Richard asked

"Yes, thank you" Melvin had never refused one yet

"No thank you" said Mr Truscott. Richard poured brandy from the crystal decanter into two glasses and handed one to Melvin, before seating himself back at his desk

"Right, let us get down to business gentlemen" Richard stated looking from one to the other

"Truscott, perhaps you have some good news for us?"

"I'm afraid not Your Grace, I have gone through all the papers and your only option as I see it, is for you to marry, and as soon as possible I would say—your new allowance is not going to last very long I'm afraid—it will give you twelve months at the most, and that's without any emergencies arising, one large set back, and you could be forced to start selling off your assets my lord"

"I see, then it's as I feared—Melvin, is there any way in which we could raise any more capital from the estate itself, or any way in which we can cut down on costs?"

"I don't believe so Your Grace, we are only just making a profit now, and I have a ledger, as you already know, of requests for repairs and things which desperately need attention, but there isn't enough money to meet those needs—again, if we had to spend any of the money which we have to meet any of these needs, then it would put us in a very dire situation"

"Yes, it's as I had suspected. Damn my father for this lunacy. As I see it gentlemen, I have no choice but to sell something, which would buy us a little time. If say, I was to sell the house in Bond Street in London, would that affect the situation enough to buy us more time Truscott?"

"Indeed it would Your Grace, but what of the servants—you would be expected to pay them off, and ensure their welfare, at least until they could find other posts, it would take a little time to organize, though, it could buy you another year or so, and allow you to complete the outstanding work requests of your tenants, but it would only be the means to buy you time, you would still be required to marry and produce an heir, before you could touch the bulk of the money"

"Yes, I do understand that. But as for selling Bond Street, that is something which I shall need you to put into progress immediately—there are only four servants kept as retainers there, the cook, the butler and two young maids—the cook and butler are a married couple. Is there no way in which we could sell the house, with the servants as part of the contract?" Richard was determined that he must do everything he could to see them taken care of

"It's possible, but most people would choose their own servants—it could cost you the early sale of the house Your Grace, and if you wish to sell, you surely would put no obstacles in the way?" Truscott did know his business

"Yes, of course—so you suggest that we give them notice? I cannot help thinking though, that a better course of action, would be to put it to the buyers, when they first survey the house, that the servants would remain as part of the contract, at least until the house is sold, that way if the new owners chose not to keep the servants, we could at least compensate them and furnish them with references"

"As you wish Your Grace, I could write to them I suppose, and explain the situation to them, and ask that they stay on until the new owners take up residence. Once the house is sold, we could perhaps offer them a little incentive anyway" Truscott agreed, looking straight at Richard for an answer.

"Indeed, an admirable suggestion Truscott. There is of course a cottage stood empty on this estate, if the couple particularly, had no desire to stay on and had nowhere to go, perhaps they could move here and take up residence in the cottage for a short period of time of course, just until further employment and a home had been secured for them—I am right in thinking that we have an empty cottage on the estate am I not Melvin?" Richard looked straight at Melvin for a reply

"A cottage"

"The cottage that belonged to your parents, it still stands empty does it not?"

"Oh yes, but how would they live?"

"As we have already said, as soon as the Bond Street house is sold, then they will be offered an incentive, the cottage could be part of that incentive"

"I suppose so" Melvin replied, but seemed very negative

"Then it's settled. Melvin, if you could get the cottage prepared for the couple, just in case they have need of it, though if all goes well, perhaps the new owners will in fact be glad to keep the servants on, and they will be happy to stay, we shall have to carry on paying their wages until everything is settled. And Truscott, if you could get on to the sale and all the things which we have discussed this afternoon, straight away—the sooner we get the wheels in motion, the better it will be"

"Certainly Your Grace, I shall get things underway first thing in the morning—I have to say that it's a good time of year to be selling in that area of London, with the season not far away, there should be plenty of buyers presenting themselves, you have made a wise decision. But, as to the other matter Forgive me Your Grace, I realize it's rather a delicate matter, but could I be so presumptuous as to ask if there are any signs of an early marriage?"

"That matter is shall we say also underway—I admit that marriage is not yet imminent, but my dear mother has plans in that direction for me, so you may rest assured, there will be no peace until I am safely married with an army of offspring" Richard said with a smile on his lips, Mr Truscott smiled too, but Melvin saw no humour

"Then I shall leave that little matter, with the Duchess to take good care of, I'm sure she is more well equipped than any of us in that direction, a good judge of character also I believe" said Truscott, bowing his head

"Indeed, I believe there is none better"

"Then, if there is nothing else, you will excuse me and I will be on my way—I shall get everything underway, and I will write to you regularly to keep you informed of how things are coming along—you have made a wise decision of that I am sure Your Grace, I'm certain that we can look forward to an early sale" said Mr Truscott

"I certainly hope so Truscott—thank you for coming" Richard pulled the bell pull, Newbridge had been there in a moment "Mr Truscott is leaving Newbridge—show him out"

"Yes Your Grace" Both gentlemen went out, closing the door behind them, Richard turned to Melvin "I believe that we have found the best solution for everyone Melvin, if the house in Bond Street sells quickly, as old Truscott believes it should, then it could put us in better stead for a while, at least until the other matters are settled"

"Perhaps—but the cottage, I didn't like to say anything while Truscott was here, but I'm not sure that it's suitable as a dwelling, at the moment"

"Why is that Melvin?"

"It's not in good repair—I believe it would cost too much to make it habitable Your Grace"

"I have ridden past it several times, and it doesn't look too bad to me—but if you think that it's not suitable to live in, then perhaps we should go and inspect it tomorrow"

"Tomorrow, I won't have time tomorrow" he hurriedly replied

"I could always take the key and have a look myself"

"No—no, leave it with me, after all, that's what you pay me for—I shall go and have a look Your Grace, I will see what can be done, I'm sure that I will be able to sort something out, besides, if the new owners of Bond Street decide to keep the servants on, then the need for the cottage will not exist, will it?" Melvin spoke with a touch of sarcasm

"Good, then that is settled" Richard was becoming tired of Melvin's belligerence, he had soon changed his mind when Richard had called his bluff—that must be the way to deal with him in future, he was sure that his father would not have put up with his nonsense and he was a fool to think that he would either, there were plenty of people out there, who would have jumped at the chance of his job, obviously his affair with Maria was going to his head, and he was getting above his station—Richard would soon cure that.

"Thank you for coming Melvin, I shall not keep you any longer, but I shall leave the cottage to you to look into, perhaps you would be good enough to keep me informed"

"Of course, Your Grace—good day" he stood up, gave a small nod, then turned and left.

So, Maria wasn't successful with her attempt to marry him, so she had once again transferred her affections back to the man who bought her presents—how fickle could women be—if he were to choose a bride, he would do well to be guided by his dear mama, she was a good judge of character, though after having been duped by her own husband, it would have made her more aware of such things. So, tomorrow the game would begin.

CHAPTER TWELVE

(Alice's First Tea Party)

March already, the old saying 'in like a lion, out like a lamb' was proving to be the opposite way round this year. The days were warm and balmy there wasn't even a great deal of wind, though there was a slight breeze which came off the sea.

It was Thursday afternoon, and Richard was preparing himself for his mother's first tea party. How he hated things such as this, but it seemed the only way in which to get to meet an eligible young lady while the house was still in mourning. Lady Bonetti and her daughter Ellen, were due to arrive at four o clock, and Richard had agreed to join them at four thirty—he didn't need to stay throughout the infernal chatter, but he did need to view the young lady, as this was the specific purpose after all.

Alice had taken her seat on a large settee in the drawing room, when she heard the knock at the front door—Newbridge opened the door and welcomed the two ladies, before taking them through to the drawing room and to be greeted by Alice.

"Good afternoon Mrs Bonetti, Miss Bonetti" said Alice, each giving a small curtsey

"What a pleasant room—it's so kind of you to invite my daughter and me to have tea with you My Lady—are we the only ones?" Mrs Bonetti was looking round the large room now

"Please, do take a seat" said Alice "We are not expecting anyone else today"

"I must offer you our sympathy on the sad loss of your son and your husband—your son was such a good man, it must have been such a shock"

"Yes indeed. It was a great shock to us all" Alice answered

"Your son's wife, she must be devastated, left with two young children I believe, whatever will the poor woman do"

"Maria will remain here with her children of course she is as much part of this family as any of us"

"Well that's all very well, but if she chooses to re-marry, after mourning of course, that would no doubt put a different light on things?"

"If Maria chooses to re-marry, we shall be very pleased for her, after all, she is but a young woman still, and how awful would it be, if her life was over as well as my dear son Edward"

"But you have another son do you not Lady Penleigh?"

"My younger son has now inherited his father's title and estate—yes that is correct—in fact, you will have a chance to meet the Duke, he will be joining us for tea shortly"

"Really, I had heard that you had two sons, but it was always thought that the younger son was living away?"

"He has been travelling in Europe for two years, he had only just returned when I had to inform him of his brother's death—and of course, he returned to Cornwall immediately"

"Where is his home?"

"He has a house in London—and had been there for three years, until he returned home to take up his position here"

"And is he married?"

"I'm afraid he is not—though he will be looking for a wife once we are no longer in mourning—it's most important now that he has inherited his father's title, he is expected, you understand, to settle down with a family of his own"

Alice watched the look between mother and daughter, the mother was certainly interested, even if the daughter wasn't, and she wasn't afraid of showing it openly either—Ellen Bonetti wasn't the most sociable girl, though she probably wouldn't have got a word in anyway, even if she had tried. She didn't come over as the most intelligent of girls, and she hadn't been at the front of the queue when beauty was handed out. Alice felt that this one was not going to turn out to be the future Duchess of Warren. At that moment the door opened and Richard entered what a sight to behold as he strode into the room—with a dark green jacket and buff coloured breeches, showing off the strength of his thighs, and a snowy white shirt and cravat, with an emerald pin which sparkled in the sunlight, streaming in through the window. Alice was so proud of him, she had loved Edward with a passion, but he could never cut the same dash as his brother. He went to his mother and leant down to kiss her cheek, before turning to their guests and making a bow. Mrs Bonetti was studying him with a smile on her face, obviously she approved of the Duke, he would make a good husband for her daughter

"How lovely to meet you ladies—Lady Bonetti and Miss Bonetti I believe"

"Charmed I'm sure Your Grace" said Mrs Bonetti, her cheeks turning pink and in a put on voice "this is my daughter Ellen" Ellen looked up and smiled, but seemed a little embarrassed by this stunning gentleman

"Shall I ring for tea now mother" he asked, turning to Alice

"Thank you Richard—I'm sure that we are ready" she said this turning to Mrs Bonetti

"Indeed, that would be lovely" she replied

"So, you live in London Your Grace?" asked Mrs Bonetti—considering Richard was supposed to be finding himself a wife, Mrs Bonetti was asking all the questions, it was certainly clear that she was looking for a suitable husband for her daughter, though Ellen seemed to be unconcerned

"Yes, that's right—I have a town house in Mayfair, but due to present circumstances, I shall be spending the foreseeable future here, on my estate"

"You have a house in Mayfair?" this had impressed her "a very fashionable place to live I believe"

"I am very fond of the house, and I do enjoy London and my lifestyle there, but now we are in mourning, I would not be able to attend the usual hectic season this year"

Just then a knock came at the door, and a maid followed Newbridge in, he had a tray with cups and saucers, tea, hot water jug, sugar and cream, and a pile of small plates the maid was carrying sandwiches and cakes— these were all placed on a small table close to Alice, who started to pour the tea, while Richard handed it round, followed by small plates and sandwiches. After tea had been taken, Richard looked through the large French windows and down to lawns, stretching out before him

"Perhaps Miss Bonetti would like to take a walk in the garden?" Richard asked, directing the question at Ellen. Shyly she looked up and said

"Thank you Sir" but before she had a chance to say any more, her mother spoke up for her "you would be delighted wouldn't you Ellen dear" The girl just looked at Richard and smiled, he could see that she wouldn't get a chance to speak to him unless he got her away from her mother, so he stood beside the settee which she was seated on, and held out his arm for her to take. Ellen stood up and took the arm offered to her, before they stepped out into the spring sunshine. Richard led the girl down the path, still in full view of the drawing room windows, and into the rose garden

"You live in Truro I believe Miss Bonetti?"

"Yes, that's right sir"

"I believe that you are to have your first season this year?" her face coloured. Had he said the wrong thing, it was difficult to talk to this girl who was so shy, yet really rather sweet. He felt sorry for her that she had such a bombastic mother—this certainly made her worse than she would have been otherwise. He looked at her face, she couldn't meet his eyes, she dropped her head but Richard was determined to take a good look at the young lady. Her hair was mousy, though certain strands seemed to pick up the sunlight, which made it appear much lighter than it was she had green eyes and soft little lashes which shaded her eyes. Her features were quite large she had a prominent nose that spread at the nostrils, and a large wide mouth, though her teeth were straight and even, as was proved when she smiled. She was no beauty, but there was something about her that had appeal. She wore a pale lemon silk dress, with frothy white lace at the bust, showing off her very slim figure, her bonnet was of straw, with a pale lemon ribbon adorning the brim, and tailed off down her back.

"My mother is hoping that I shall find a husband, she is eager for this season, although I am living in dread of it, I do so hate all the fuss and large quantities of people, I'm not even interested in being the height of fashion, you see, I'm rather a private person—that's boring I know, my mother despairs so of me—I'm afraid that I shall let her down, as I do not dance very well either sir"

"It's true that London will be a hive of activity, and the centre for the rich and fashionable. There will be balls and assemblies every evening, and I'm sure that it will take your breath away. Most young women that I know are unhappy to miss the busy town life, but you should not dread it Miss Bonetti—and you would have your choice of a husband—if for nothing else, you should be glad of that, be yourself, and find someone of your choice, that is what matters, and in doing so, you will also please your mother"

"But that's the point sir, you do not know my mother, she would give me no choice in a husband—she would decide and I would have to follow her instructions" Richard smiled

"I'm sure that she has your best interests at heart—you must not blame her, she must be eager to see you settled and happy"

"Of course, I didn't mean . . ." she recoiled, as if she had said too much

"I do understand what you mean, but try and enjoy the time you have there, I'm sure that everything will turn out for the best in the end" for a few minutes things went quiet before Richard said "perhaps we should return inside now—both your mother and mine will wonder where we have got too"

"Indeed—thank you for showing me your lovely garden sir"

"The pleasure is mine Miss Bonetti"

They returned back along the path from which they had come, in silence— Richard was finding it difficult to make a conversation with this young woman—she would have been a more suitable candidate for Edward than for him. This young lady would never win his affections, he could never offer her marriage, and he was more than certain she would never have accepted an offer from him anyway. As they walked back in silence, his mind went to the rectory—what he would give for a chance with Clara, how he longed to see her again—she was so beautiful, and he could never have taken her into the garden, for fear of being unable to restrain himself from kissing those luscious pink lips. The girl that he was destined to marry, would always be compared with her, he could not help himself—she was everything that he wanted in a wife, if only she were of his standing, not that it bothered him one bit, but he knew that it would cause problems with not only his family, but also the trustees of his money, they would not be amused were he to marry below him, sometimes he just hated his status, and was very tempted to just do as he pleased anyway, but his fear now that if he flouted the rules, would his trustees then refuse to release the money—and he really needed that if he were to have control of his estate and take care of his family and tenants. He owed it to them to do the right thing, which gave him no choice.

"Ellen dear, I'm glad you have returned as it's time we were leaving" said Mrs Bonetti as they stepped back into the drawing room

"Then we returned at just the right time, did we not?" said Richard smiling, Mrs Bonetti was looking at them, probably for a sign that he would be requesting a further meeting with her daughter—well, she would be sadly disappointed.

The ladies said their goodbyes and Richard bowed to the ladies before calling for Newbridge to show them to the door. Once they had left, Richard turned to his mother

"I'm afraid that Miss Bonetti will not be the future Duchess mother—she was sweet, but not for me"

"No, I'm afraid that I have to agree—her mother is rather forward too, a dreadful woman to be sure. So we must arrange another tea next week"

"I'm afraid so—if only there were another way, I'm not so sure that this is going to be the solution, though I am grateful for your help" he went to his mother and kissed her cheek

"Are there no young ladies whom you are already acquainted, who would be more suitable?" Richard longed to tell his mother of Miss Penrose, but could not do so, besides, he had no idea how Miss Penrose felt about him, she would probably refuse his advances anyway—no his chosen one was lost to him—he must not think of her now, he had to marry, and to someone suitable for a Duchess

"I have met many young ladies its true, but there are none that were more than an amusement for a short time—they were not ladies who I would choose to marry, or for that matter, who would choose me"

"Then we have no choice—you are in need of a wife, and as it is there can be no wedding until the end of the year, but it's essential that we find you a suitable bride, as soon as possible—young ladies expect to be courted, nothing is done overnight, so we must act now while we have a chance"

"Alright, I shall leave it to you, you are right as usual—I will do as you suggest, and I shall see you at dinner" with that he left the room and went to his library, he needed a drink.

He poured himself a brandy and sat down at his desk—this was insufferable, this whole situation was impossible. Edward and his father were both dead—accidents, or so it was believed, but he didn't believe that—certainly not any more. His brother had to call on his solicitor, yet he had never been there, and according to everyone else, there had been nothing to see a solicitor for. The large amount of money in his father's coffers, his mother confirming that he had been part of, indeed leader of the local smuggling gang, Maria, and her relationship with Melvin, and Melvin, un-cooperative and surly. All these thoughts going round and round in his head, all of this had to be connected, he was sure of it, but he must find the missing links. The other thing which had occurred to him while lying sleepless in his bed, was that so far each of the people connected to this Dukedom, were now dead, he was the next—was his life in danger too?

❧ ❧ ❧ ❧ ❧

Maria walked into the entrance hall, she had a smile on her face, this had been the first time in months that Melvin had had the time for her, she had been walking down to the Gate Lodge for the last couple of months, but not once found him at home—she had even called into the estate office several times, but he had always been elsewhere—she was beginning to think that he had lost his desire for her, but this afternoon had certainly proved that theory wrong—she guessed it had to be something to do with Richard. Ah Richard, she had kept her distance for a while—given him space and she hoped time to realize that she was the one he really wanted. There was of course an added complication now, she was certain that she was with child, there had been no monthly visitors for the past three months—not since that awful night, she still tried to bury that in the back of her mind. Then there was the fact that it couldn't possibly be Melvin's child, so the facts were unthinkable—luckily, Melvin hadn't noticed anything today, perhaps she could persuade him that the child was a little further developed than it was, so that she could convince him and everyone else that the child was his, but that really wasn't a good idea either, after all, no-one knew of their relationship, and it had to stay that way, especially if she was to win Richard's affections, there was no possible way she could make Richard the father, as much as she would like too, he had never laid a hand on her, that was a pity, she wanted so much to have his child. Perhaps she would be able to let people think that it was Edwards, after all, there had only been about ten days difference, she could always plead that the child was born late—yes, that's what she would do, babies were born two weeks late all of the time, babies arrive in their time—no-one would question that. She would tell Melvin tomorrow, that she was with child and that it was Edwards, that she must have conceived just prior to Edward's death, no-one need know that they had not even spent a night together—then she would have to work on Richard again, she had to win him over, she was determined to become the Duchess of Warren.

⁂

The three ladies sat in the drawing room after dinner—Richard had remained at the table with his decanter of port and an excellent piece of stilton and by all accounts, Rufus Drummond had joined him. Rufus Drummond had not visited Penleigh Court for a while—there had been rumours of smugglers cove being a hive of activity once again, and that the authorities were stepping up their plans to catch them in the act. Now that her husband was gone, Alice was no longer sure who may or may not be involved in all this, she did know that Mr Drummond would have been hard put, to pin anything on Henry—he made sure that he fell short of suspicion, so someone would be set up to carry the can. Alice shuddered—she had hoped and prayed that this house could now be left free of involvement. She had her needlework on her lap, and Nanny Grey, was as usual snoring by the fire, Maria seated herself beside Alice on the settee

"Are you alright Maria, we have seen little of you of late" Alice was trying to make conversation

"I'm in very good health, thank you" Maria replied

"I'm glad to hear it. I had expected you to join our little tea party this afternoon"

"Tea party, I had no idea that you were having one, I thought the house to be in mourning"

"Indeed we are, but times are hard Maria, Richard must find a wife, and as soon as possible—the estate will not survive unless he does, as we cannot throw a ball in his honour, I have suggested some small intimate tea parties instead, he will get to meet a few eligible young ladies, so perhaps he will find a wife"

136

"I see, and Richard, is he happy with this arrangement?"

"He likes it no better than I, but what choice do we have, he has to find a wife, once we are out of mourning, he will have to marry and produce an heir, the alternative does not bear thinking about Maria, he could lose everything"

"But surely, with so few eligible young ladies locally there will be so little choice"

"Nevertheless, Richard must find a wife, if we are to keep the estate intact, and we have to help him all we can"

"Of course, and you can rely on me Alice, I will do what I can to help"

"Good, between us I hope that we can find someone suitable" Alice now felt the need to retire—she had an overwhelming feeling of fatigue, she must be getting a little too old for all of this excitement, the sooner she could see her dearest boy settled, the better

"And now I believe it's time for myself and Nanny to retire, I am feeling rather tired" with that Alice laid her needlework aside, and stood up, tapping Nanny Grey on the arm to rouse her from her sleep, then helping her to her room.

Maria sat still for a while, she hadn't anticipated this happening. This meant that she would have to make another move and quickly, after all, she couldn't allow him to meet another woman, she had thought that she would have time to carry out her plan slowly but not anymore, she must act without delay, if she were to win her prize. She stood up, brushed her hands down her gown to straighten it, then went to her room, there was no time to lose, she must act without delay.

Richard sat in his library, laid back in his leather studded chair, with his long legs rested on the desk in front of him. His brandy glass half full beside him. He ended his day here every day, it was peaceful and he was

rarely disturbed. He wasn't happy about this afternoon's charade, but what else could they do. He started to ponder on what Drummond had said, they were getting closer now to the smuggling band, Drummond had stepped up the surveillance, and he was sure that they would make some arrests very soon—and when they did, they would hang, that was for sure—he wouldn't want to be stood in their shoes. The door latch clicked, Richard looked up, expecting to see Newbridge, but instead, there in the doorway stood Maria, she was dressed only in a velvet robe, tied at the waist. She stepped into the library and closed the door behind her, she walked over to the desk where Richard was sat

"I'm sorry to disturb you Richard, but I thought that I should fetch a book to help me sleep"

"Of course, help yourself, there are plenty to choose from" Richard replied

"I have spoken with the Duchess this evening she informs me that you are seeking a bride"

"Yes, that is true—my father's will as you know, has made it necessary now"

"So, the Duchess is to throw tea parties to attract young ladies on your behalf—a little drastic is it not?"

"Well, we cannot throw a ball while we're in mourning—that would never do, and the money tied into the estate will not be released until I have produced a legitimate heir, and to do that, I must first find a wife. The thing is that we have a year or so at the most, before we are in serious trouble, I cannot afford to wait until then, and if I'm fortunate enough, I could be married a year from now."

"I understand your reasons, but it seems rather drastic action to take—surely you would prefer to marry someone you are more used to?"

"Who have you in mind?" Richard asked, as soon as the question was out of his mouth, he knew that he shouldn't have asked. Maria walked around the desk, to where Richard was seated, she said nothing but she was gazing straight into his eyes, with a smile on her face—Richard wasn't sure what was going on, and he wasn't sure that he would like what she would do next. Then without more ado, Maria, still with unflinching eye contact, caught the tie of the robe, which was around her waist, and with one pull, the robe flew open and with a little shake of her arms, the robe fell to the floor in a heap around her ankles—Maria stood in front of him absolutely naked. Richard was stunned, he could not believe his eyes, they were fixed on the nakedness before him, he could not tear his gaze away, with no time to think, she had moved towards him, cupping his face in her hands, she stepped forward and lifted his face up to meet hers, placing her lips firmly on his, and pressing her body against him. Richard could feel the heat and the roundness of her body, and realizing what was happening, knew he must escape from her temptation. He tried to pull away, but she pressed harder to him. Richard kept pushing her away, but she didn't relent, then lifting his hands to her arms, he managed to push with enough force, to shove her body far enough to allow him to stand, her eyes were like ice, and her mouth in a tight line, her nostrils flaring with fury

"Please Maria—this is not right" he said gently

"Come Richard, do you not like what you see?" she was really purring now, trying to hide her anger

"I'm sorry, but I have already told you that this cannot happen, and I meant it" his voice a little firmer

"I am the solution to all your problems, why can you not see that—can you not see that I adore you? I would make you so happy, if you would just give me the chance—don't tell me that you are not tempted, I can see in your eyes that you want me, and I'm offering myself to you now, if you prefer, we can go to your room, or mine for that matter, we could consummate our love tonight" with that she moved back to him, throwing her arms tightly round his neck and pressing the full length of her body against his, while reaching for his lips again

"No Maria, I have said no and I meant it" this time he was really firm "I cannot marry you, besides I believe that your feelings are otherwise engaged", there, he had said it now this time it was her turn to jump back, she was obviously shocked that he knew

"What do you mean my feelings are otherwise engaged, haven't I already told you that I adore you, and only you?"

"You already have a lover in Melvin Lincroft do you not?"

"Who told you that—did he, he's a liar, you should not listen to his poison"

"No, he did not tell me, but it is true is it not? Besides, I could never marry you, I have already told you that—the woman I choose will be someone who I wish to spend the rest of my life with, and while I am fond of you as my sister in law, and am happy to keep you here and offer you a home for you and your girls, for my brother's sake, there will never be anything more between us, I do not love you, and never will, nor do you love me—now please, while you still have your pride, put on your wrap and leave" this time there was no room for manoeuvre.

"You, you are worse than your father—you say that you care about us, then you throw it back in my face—I was prepared to marry you, help you out of your predicament, and all you can do is insult me, I hate you Richard Penleigh, I hate and loathe you, you are no better than he"

"No better than who Maria" but she didn't answer that, she probably hadn't even heard the question properly

"I hope that you lose everything you have, you don't deserve a title or estates, indeed you are no gentleman—what young woman would want you, if they heard how you have treated me—I was your last hope—now you can rot—rot in hell for all I'm concerned, you shall have no help from me and you will pay for your treatment of me—you shall pay with your life, you mark my words Richard Penleigh, you shall pay with your life, I promise you that much" she clawed up her robe, wrapped it around her and left the library, slamming the door behind her.

Richard poured himself another brandy which he tossed down his throat in one go—she was angry, and he knew that she was hurt that he had spurned her attempts, but she had acted venomously, he had not expected that—he kept hearing her words rushing round in his head—"you will pay with your life" that's what she had said, she was hysterical, or even worse, her actions were those of madness, or lunacy, she was unstable—he could see her now, she had spat the words out at him, that was no action of a sane person—but he had gone cold, started to shiver, "you will pay with your life" she had certainly meant that—he would have to watch his step, he had no intention of following his brother or father to the grave—now he was certain that Maria had a hand in this evil web, somewhere. He would be very wary of the woman in future indeed he would not allow her to corner him alone again. He poured another brandy and once again threw it straight down—it warmed him a little and he had stopped shivering now—he was ready to retire—this incident had really shook his very being.

CHAPTER THIRTEEN

(Richard's Pleasure)

The weeks were passing quickly now. It was mid-June and the weather had turned from the balmy warm spring days, to heavy showers—although the sun made the odd appearance, the rain had taken its vengeance. Richard was still spending his mornings on estate business, he had hoped that as time went on Melvin would change his attitude towards his master, but this wasn't to be. He had no desire to have him around, and made no show of hiding the fact. His mother had set up many more tea parties, each following the same line, but none producing a young lady who he would choose for a wife. His mother was becoming tired of the whole thing, he could see that, but what else could he do. Maria had been keeping out of his way—he was very glad of that, after her last outburst, he had seriously considered calling Dr Sommerville to come and check her out, but he thought better of it, she wouldn't appreciate his concern, and it would have given her more reason to seek vengeance on him. He had noticed though, when he last saw her a few days before, that she had looked very pale and drawn, yet she had put on a little weight, especially about her stomach, he had thought to speak to his mother about it, but had entirely forgotten in his concerns for the rest of his life—he was still showing a great interest in his two nieces though, he had even taken Milly out one day, and took her for a ride around the field at a slow trot—she had been thrilled with it all, she had squealed with delight, and Richard was more than happy to spend time with her. He had decided that once he was able, he would buy a pony for the little girl, and he would teach her to ride himself. Rebecca too had started to take notice of things and people, she would smile when he walked into the nursery, and he would spend time talking to her, before taking her sister off in his arms. Drummond had become a regular visitor at Penleigh Court again, he certainly seemed to know what he was about, although he had been trying to catch the smugglers for years, and hadn't succeeded yet, but if his father had been involved, then it was hardly likely that he would have caught the ring leader, for his father would have made sure that he was well and truly safe. He had had a little success quite recently, he had even found the caves where the smugglers kept their ill-gotten gains when they first took them from the unsuspecting ships. The main problem was catching them in the act, by the time he arrived they had disappeared, and he was at a loss to know how, since he had carried out many all-night vigils along that piece of coast, yet never seen anything of great value to him—he believed there must be another entrance into the caves, something more in keeping with an underground tunnel, but if that were so, he had no idea where it led. Richard could not help him, he had no idea himself, though he did wonder if his father had known of one, and the thought had crossed his mind that Penleigh Court could be involved.

The more time went on, the more Richard thought about Clara, she was about the only thing which kept him going, though he had not set eyes on her since Christmas day. Six whole months had passed—he knew that he should have attended church, that way he would have got to see her, if only for a few moments, but what with everything that was happening, and the fact that he needed to concentrate on finding a wife, he had tried to put her to the back of his mind—the big problem being that he couldn't keep her there—she kept coming back to him, and when she did, he would feel a real desire and longing for the girl, he had never felt like this before, even the beauties who had amused him in Europe, had not given him a lasting desire as this one had—he was desperate to see her again. Although his mother had another young lady, along with her mother, lined up for tomorrow afternoon, he had no interest in meeting them anymore—she would never compare to his lovely Clara—of that he was sure. Perhaps he should take a ride over to the rectory this afternoon—she would probably already be engaged, but his need and desire were fervent inside of him, he must do something, and he could wait no longer.

Once he had eaten his lunch, he went to his room, after all, he must check that his appearance was in order, he couldn't possibly meet Clara looking untidy. James was in his dressing room when he entered

"Your Grace, have I mistook the day and time?" James asked

"I have no idea what you mean"

143

"I thought that today was Wednesday, not Thursday, and just after lunch, tea isn't for another few hours yet"

"I am well aware of the day and the time James, I am going out for a ride, and wish to look my best, is there any harm in that?"

"None at all, I'm sure your stallion will appreciate you looking your best"

"You are an insolent swine James, I should cast you out without a penny or a reference"

"But were you to do that, you would have no-one to spar with, would you Your Grace" said James lightly

"But I should have the luxury of a quiet life"

"And nothing to brighten your otherwise dull day"

"You think my life dull? I promise you that it's anything but that—I have more things to give my attention too, than I ever have before"

"And a young lady who has caught your eye perhaps"

"Perhaps—and that is your business because?"

"Because your business is my business" said James playfully

"Is that so, then perhaps you have a suggestion for me, considering you have suggestions for most things"

"You would have to pay me a great deal more than you do now if you want me to sort your problems for you as well as all my other duties"

"Ah, so that is it—you are after more money"

"That would be very welcome Your Grace—I always thought you to be a generous man"

"The answer is no James, there will be no raise in your pay—but I shall let you take these clothes and see that they are cleaned" handing him the shirt and jacket he had taken off

"I shall just have to settle for that then" Richard smiled at him before leaving the room.

❧

Richard ran down the stairs and out into the courtyard, the rain was still pouring down, but he didn't care about that at all, he was going to find his dearest Clara, and nothing would cloud his spirit today. He went into the stables and ordered his horse to be saddled—the head groom came forward, with the horse already prepared for him. He jumped up into the saddle, before riding out at a trot, down the hill and through the village, over the bridge and out onto the road toward the rectory. Once he arrived, he climbed down, and tied his horse to the same post that he had used the last time he was here. He strode to the door and lifted the knocker, within minutes Daisy the maid opened the door—Richard had started to become nervous now, he had no excuse for his call, that had seemed irrelevant earlier, when his only thoughts were for Clara, now he would have to think of a reason for this call

"Perhaps you would inform your mistress that Richard Penleigh is here to see her" Daisy bobbed a curtsey and smiled before going off at a trot to inform her mistress. Richard had started to think of all sorts of reasons why she would refuse to see him, and by the time she returned, he had started to lose his confidence

"The mistress will see you now sir"

"Thank you" Richard followed Daisy to the room that he had now become accustomed, thankful that she had not turned him away. She had introduced him as Richard Penleigh, most people now introduced him as the Duke of Warren, but he wasn't worried about that

"Come in Your Grace—what a pleasant surprise to see you" Mrs Penrose spoke without getting up

"Thank you Mrs Penrose, I was out for a ride, and thought how I had neglected you of late, so I called to check that you are all well" Richard had to make some lame excuse, and lame this was

"Yes we are all very well thank you, please take a seat, Your Grace. We are indeed honoured to have you this afternoon, I had expected to see you in church, but since Christmas you have not attended once" Richard was embarrassed, what could he say, he cast his eyes around but Clara was not there—the disappointment must have shown, he couldn't help it

"You are right of course, I fear that I have neglected many things since my father's death—I must make more effort in the future ma'am" he had been chastised—and rightly so, he had not even given church a second thought with everything which had been happening in his life—he would have to make more effort, though seeing Clara today, would have been an incentive to do that

"I shall call for some tea" she stood up and went to the pull cord, within minutes Daisy had returned

"Yes My Lady"

"Could you bring us some tea, and three cups please, Clara will be joining us shortly" Richard's heart had skipped a beat at the mention of her name—he had felt disappointed, when he could see that she wasn't in the drawing room and had feared that perhaps she was out somewhere, but now he was hopeful of seeing her once again

"So, Your Grace—tell me, how are you enjoying country life, I should think it a little quieter than you have been used too"

"Indeed, very different from London, though my time has been taken up with estate matters of late, leaving me little time for anything else"

"Then we shall consider ourselves honoured that you have found the time to visit this afternoon"

"And how is Miss Penrose, I trust that her ankle is fully recovered now"

"Clara is very well, her ankle was but a sprain, though she was fortunate that you chanced by when you did, or I would hate to think what may have become of her—she will always be grateful to you for your kindness sir" Richard felt waves of excitement flood through his body, just to be able to speak of Clara

"I was wondering if you would allow me to invite Miss Penrose to take a drive with me in my carriage one afternoon—it would give me great pleasure madam" Now he had stuck his head out—if her mother refused, what would he do then

"What an excellent idea Your Grace, Clara would be delighted I'm sure, and Daisy could act as her chaperone—Clara doesn't get out very much I'm afraid, I tell her frequently that she should meet other young people, but there are so few suitable friends for her locally. She does have a friend in Truro, but as you can imagine, it is rather a long distance to travel for just an hour or two"

"Indeed it is, then I shall look forward to it" at that moment the door opened and Daisy came in with the tea, followed closely by Clara. She looked like an angel, each time he had set eyes on her he was more bewitched by her. She was wearing a beautiful cream coloured gown, with white lace at the bust, her large dark eyes like inviting pools, which he would find impossible to resist. She looked straight at him, and a smile broke out on her lips

"Good afternoon Your Grace, how nice to see you again" she said, dropping a curtsey—her voice so soft, warm and inviting

"Ah Clara, there you are, I had wondered where you had got too—come and sit down dear, and join us for tea" Clara went to the settee opposite her mother and seated herself, Daisy had put down the tray on the little table beside Mrs Penrose, so that she could pour. Richard stood up and took the cup offered to him and handed it to Clara, before taking his own and sitting once again.

"His Grace has asked if you would like to go for a ride with him one afternoon Clara, I told him that you would be delighted"

"Indeed I would be delighted sir it's very kind of you to ask me" she said

"The pleasure would be all mine Miss Penrose" he had to pinch himself—this lovely woman had agreed to take a ride in his carriage, he couldn't be more happy

"Would Friday afternoon at two o clock suit you?" Richard asked in anticipation

"Oh dear, Friday I visit the old and sick of the parish sir, they rely on me to take food, I couldn't possibly let them down, perhaps another day instead?" Richard's heart leapt—another day—he cursed to himself that the following day he had another damned tea party

"Perhaps next week would be more convenient, whichever day suits you best?" Clara smiled, her cheeks growing very pink

"Friday is the only day that I have other duties—but any other day would suit me well"

"Then perhaps Monday afternoon at two o clock?" Richard replied quickly, he couldn't wait much longer, to see her again, especially now she had agreed

"I shall look forward to it sir" watching her face, he could see that she certainly looked delighted, he truly hoped that she was, though he doubted she could be as happy about it as he was

"Well I'm glad that is settled, now, I believe the rain has stopped and the sun is beginning to shine—perhaps you should show the Duke the garden, while you have a chance Clara" said Mrs Penrose. Richard's stomach lurched, it was easy for him taking the young ladies out for a short stroll when he had no real interest in them, but Clara was a totally different matter—he would have to fight to save himself from taking liberties—he couldn't afford to do that, not with her

"Yes of course, would you like to see the gardens sir?"

"Indeed I should" Richard stood up and went to the settee where Miss Penrose was sat, he held out his arm to her, she stood up, and took the arm he offered, the excitement flooded through him like a bolt of lightning, causing his whole body to tingle with pleasure. Clara led him into the garden through the French doors they stood on the wet patio before Clara led him down the steps and on to the path below, The roses were truly beautiful, the small beads of water settled on each one, and the fresh smell from the grass, was all that was left from the earlier rain.

"The gardens as you see are very pretty, though not as pretty as the gardens at Penleigh Court, I'm sure" Clara said

"Then I have to tell you that you would be quite wrong, I have travelled all over Europe, but the prettiest rose garden that I've ever had the good fortune of experiencing, is this one here at the rectory, I remember it from when my brother and I visited here as boys, and have very fond memories. I also remember that the vicar who was here at the time, had a cook called Mrs Preen, she made the most delicious biscuits I have ever tasted and she would always tempt us with a glass of lemonade and a biscuit freshly baked from the oven" Clara was looking up at him, taking in every word that he was saying

"You were very close to your brother Your Grace" Clara asked—Richard was trying hard not to look at her, as the temptation to take her in his arms was overwhelming

"As boys we were very close, but once I had finished at Eton, we started very different lives, my brother was the heir, so it was only right that he stayed here to learn about the running of the estate and the country life, I on the other hand, sought something a little more lively, my father encouraged me to spread my wings, so I went to London, bought a very nice town house, which I still have, before spending two years travelling Europe, I had only just returned when my mother wrote of Edward's death, as you can imagine it was a great shock to us all, and I decided that I should return home for a while."

"Do you plan to return to London?"

"Perhaps one day but not for the foreseeable future since my father's death, I have now inherited his title and estate, so there is too much to be dealt with here, and while we are in mourning, there would be little point being in London, I should not be welcome to attend any of the seasons balls or assemblies, so I am far better situated here."

"Of course, the country must seem very dull after the life you have been used too"

"There has been little time to contemplate I'm afraid, I am spending a great deal of my time attending to business, which has given me little time for anything else"

"It must be very difficult for you sir"

"But it has it's compensations—had I not returned to Cornwall when I did, I should never have met you, that would have been a terrible thing" they stopped walking for a moment and stood facing each other on the pathway. Clara's pink cheeks had now turned a definite shade of red

"You tease me Your Grace" she said, hardly a whisper

"On the contrary, I have never been more serious Miss Penrose" their eyes met and their gaze held, nothing else in the world was important in that moment, Richard was sorely tempted to take her in his arms and kiss her, but that would be too forward, he must restrain himself, instead, he took both her hands in his before raising first one, then the other to his lips and planting a light kiss on each

"Perhaps we should go back now sir, my mother will be wondering where we have got too" Clara stated gently, he hoped that he had done nothing to offend her

"Of course, forgive me" Richard suddenly realized the reality of the situation

"This afternoon has been very enjoyable, and I thank you for calling" Clara said softly

"Indeed you are right, but may I ask your permission to call again?" Richard was almost holding his breath

"I rather hope that you will, I should be very disappointed otherwise"

"And I should be very disappointed if you had refused me" they looked at each other and laughed—this young lady was miles above the rest, he could never meet anyone who made him feel quite like Clara Penrose did, and he got the distinct impression that she was not averse to him either

Once they reached the house they slipped back into the drawing room, Mrs Penrose was there waiting for their return

"Did you enjoy your walk?"

"Very much, thank you Mrs Penrose" said Richard "but now I think that it is time to take my leave, thank you both for your wonderful hospitality" he took Clara's hand in his and pressed it against his lips, before giving Mrs Penrose a small bow. Then turning he left the house. Riding back to Penleigh Court, Richard had not felt so happy in a very long time—his mind was on their eyes meeting in the gardens, and how she had allowed him to kiss her hands, she had seemed as delighted as he was. Tomorrow seemed one hundred years away, but for today, nothing would get him down.

Once he returned to Penleigh Court, he ran up the front steps and went straight to his library, poured himself a large brandy and seated himself at his desk, before he had chance to do anything, a tap came at the door, it was Newbridge

"This came for you this afternoon Your Grace"

"Thank you Newbridge" taking the note lying on the silver salver offered to him, he broke the seal and opened it up—it was from Truscott it read

Your Grace,

I am writing to let you know that a buyer has been found for your Bond Street house, they have agreed to our terms, and will keep the servants on, as long as they are happy with that arrangement, which I have already confirmed.

I'm afraid that the price, is less than we had first agreed, but not by very much, and it is the best offer which we have received to date.

I should be obliged for your early reply, in order to get this sale underway.

Yours sincerely

Edwin Truscott Esq

This was excellent news—so they had sold Bond Street, even if it was a little under the original price asked, it would buy him a little time. He would write to Truscott straight away and tell him to go ahead, one thing for sure at least he wouldn't have to worry for the servants at the house, not now they were being employed by the new owners. Things were probably turning out better there than he had anticipated.

He had had a glorious day, but he was still concerned about Clara, he was starting to think that he was falling in love—how ridiculous, but how could he explain what he was feeling for her—he had never thought he would ever meet the girl who he wished to spend the rest of his life with, until Clara, he couldn't imagine going through life without her. He would have to see tomorrow through, and his mother's tea party, but after that, he would have to speak to his mother, she would know what to do. As he sat in his library pondering everything that had happened, there was a knock at the door, Newbridge entered again

"Sorry to disturb you Your Grace, but Mr Drummond is here, and he wishes to speak to you immediately"

"Show him in Newbridge"

"Yes My Lord"

"How can I help you today Mr Drummond"

"I have some bad news for you Your Grace, as you know we have been following the leads which we have had for some time now, but this afternoon, our lead took us to a cottage on your estate—so we waited when we saw your estate manager, Melvin Lincroft enter, we closed in on him and searched the cottage, I'm afraid that we have reclaimed a large amount of smuggled goods, and we have arrested Melvin Lincroft—he will be sent to jail now until his trial, and if found guilty, he could hang." This took the wind from Richard's sails—he always knew that he didn't like or trust this man, but him, part of the smuggling gang that was something very different, he hadn't expected that.

"You are sure that this man is involved Mr Drummond?"

"No doubt about it Your Grace"

"And whose cottage was housing the contraband?"

"The cottage was empty my lord, but there is no doubt whatsoever that the goods were contraband, he went directly to them—no mistake—he knew they were there alright"

"I see, the empty cottage on the estate was once lived in by his family, in fact recently he was asked to clear the place out and prepare it in case it were needed to house a family."

"What family would that be?"

"Some servants, who are at present in our Bond Street house, we plan to sell the house, and had the new owners not wished to keep them, then we would offer them the cottage until they had found further employment— so I had given orders for Lincroft to prepare the cottage in case it was required"

"I see, well I have no doubt that the man wasn't there to do much but to retrieve his stolen property Your Grace, that's definitely what he was up too"

"Well, if there is anything I can do to help in any way, you have only to ask Drummond"

"Yes, thank you Your Grace, but I shall keep you informed of how things proceed—there is nothing else that you can do now. We shall be searching his house too—I believe that he lives in the Gate Lodge, here at Penleigh?"

"Yes that is correct"

"I shall let you know if we find anything else of interest Your Grace"

"Thank you. Can I offer you a brandy?"

"Nothing I should like more, but I must get along now—just wanted to let you know what has happened—maybe next time"

"Well thank you for keeping me informed"

"I can see myself out Your Grace—good afternoon to you"

"Good afternoon Drummond"

Richard sat back, he knew that there was something with Melvin, but he had never expected this, but thinking about it all, perhaps it made sense—and that would account for his father having let him live in the Gate Lodge, he was part of his smuggling gang, possibly the leading factor once his father could no longer play an active part. This would cause problems though, as now he would need to find a new estate manager, Melvin wouldn't be returning for at least a while, he would write to Truscott about it, and get him to put an advertisement out advertising for someone, that would be the best plan. So, he set about writing to Truscott and Penn, he would then have to wait until things were underway.

CHAPTER FOURTEEN

(Alice's Last Tea Party)

Thursday dawned fresh and bright—not a cloud in the sky and the sun, warm and inviting. Richard was still in a state of shock at losing his estate manager as a smuggler, but his memories of his rectory visit was the thing filling his mind. As he sat astride his horse, he breathed in the fresh warm day, and fought the longing to return to the rectory once again—but he must not—and besides, there was yet another boring tea party to attend—he had put off turning his horse and returning to Penleigh Court, but the time was getting on, and his mother was doing this for him, he would not let her down.

Once back at Penleigh Court, he threw the reins to the groom and took the steps two at a time—he had better go in and do his duty. As he entered the hall, he met Maria, they had not spoken a word since her last outburst, he had nothing to say to the woman, it was better that they avoid each other for everyone's sake, but now he could not ignore the sight before him—she was without a doubt with child. It must be Melvin's child, she must be devastated—her lover now arrested for smuggling, and if proved, he would surely hang. He must speak with her, after everything which went on before, he felt very sorry for her at this moment, after all he wasn't a monster

"Good afternoon Maria, you look tired"

"Tired? Why would that be Your Grace" she retorted in an offhand manner

"I am right am I not in thinking that you are with child?"

"I would have thought that obvious—I suppose that you are going to ask the name of the father"

"I had not intended asking that at all, although, I presume that Melvin Lincroft is the father?"

"You presume wrong—this child belongs to my husband—I must have conceived before he died, if you must know, yet you choose to insult me once again—what would I want with Melvin Lincroft—he means nothing to me, do you hear, nothing"

"I see, then, I must apologize for being so presumptuous. But if the baby is my brother, Edward's child, then you must allow me to see that you are both taken care of—it is the least that I can do now"

"We need nothing more from you" Maria came up very close to him and looked him straight in the eye, just a few inches from his face

"You could have helped me, and helped yourself at the same time—you could have given my family what they needed most, yet you chose to insult me and cast me aside, leaving me without a husband and my children without a father—this is your fault, therefore I want nothing more from you—do you hear me Richard" her voice had started to become more of a scream as it rose several pitches "you are the reason that I have nothing, now I want nothing more from you sir—I told you before you will pay for your behaviour, your ill treatment of me, and I meant it—I shall see you pay, and I shall not rest until you pay with your life—believe me, I shall take great pleasure in watching you hang—I hate you, do not come near me—I loathe the ground you stand on, do you hear me, do you hear me?" now she had turned hysterical once again—this was no good for her or her baby, he had best leave her well alone. She lived in his house, but he wanted no more to do with this mad woman. In the next moment Alice had left the drawing room, and came to see what all the screaming was for, when she saw that it was Maria, she placed an arm about her, and led her up the stairs, and to her room for a rest. Richard knew that Mrs Kirkby and her daughter Sarah were sat in the drawing room alone—damn, that they should have witnessed this outburst, he would not have had that happen, as he could well imagine what she would tell her friends in Truro when next she saw them, he only knew that it would be embroidered grossly, and the Penleigh's would be blamed for something unsavoury. Richard decided that he would have to go into the drawing room and try to calm the situation down, before it went any further.

"Good afternoon ladies—I'm sorry that my mother seems to have been called away for a while—perhaps you will allow me to ring for tea?" Mrs Kirkby looked at him in a strange way before agreeing

"Is the Duchess expected to return?" she asked

"Indeed, I am sure of it. I must apologize for the interruption, Maria is very upset you understand, not only has she lost my brother, but she also found herself with child, it has been a very stressful time for her" Richard tried to explain

"Yes, well, upset or not I have never heard a lady scream like that before, perhaps you should fetch the doctor" she suggested haughtily

"I believe that you are right, my mother, I am sure, will do so"

"Well, perhaps it would be better if we were to leave—don't you think Sarah?" addressing her daughter now

"It would be rude to leave before we have taken tea mother, and the Duke has explained the reason for the outburst, if Mrs Penleigh returns to find we have gone, without taking our leave, what would she think of us— surely we could take some refreshment, before we take our leave" she said this looking at Richard as she did so, giving him a warm smile. Richard smiled back, she was a sensible girl, unlike her mother he thought, she had blonde curls and large brown eyes, though nothing like his dear Clara's, she had large features, and a very winning way, had he not met Clara, he may have been tempted by this young lady, she was far from beautiful, but she had other qualities, as it was he could not see her as his wife, but she seemed the most enchanting of all the girls he had met so far, they could certainly have been friends.

"As you wish—I suppose half hour won't hurt" Richard went to the bell pull and rang for service, within minutes Newbridge entered

"Could you bring the tea now Newbridge, and you had better allow for the Duchess, as she will probably be joining us shortly"

"Yes Your Grace, right away" he left closing the door behind him

"I apologize for the upheaval—perhaps I could persuade you to allow me to accompany you both to take a stroll in the garden, the roses are all in bloom and quite a picture at the moment" said Richard, trying to make conversation

"Oh please mama lets—I would dearly love to see the roses" said Sarah, though looking at her mother's face, it was less than accommodating, she truly looked more likely to have swallowed a wasp, than taking a stroll

"I suppose that we could—not that the roses here are any different to the ones we have at home"

"Thank you mama" Sarah was eager for she had already stood up, waiting to go. Richard strode over to her and offered his arm, which she took willingly, then the door clicked open and his mother had entered

"Ah mama, I have ordered the tea, but first we are going to take a stroll in the garden"

"Yes of course, you go, I shall stay here and wait for the tea" said Alice

"And if you have no objection Lady Penleigh, I shall stay with you—I have no desire to walk about outside looking at roses" what a miserable woman she was—Richard was beginning to feel sorry for her daughter and her husband, he could imagine that she didn't make for an easy going wife. He thought of his own dear mama, she would have been an ideal wife for the Duke had he given her the chance, yet someone like this woman, who had it all, could be so obnoxious. Richard opened the French doors, and led Sarah Kirkby out on to the patio, the sun was bright, but her bonnet shielded her skin from the direct sunlight

"This is an enchanting garden sir, it is little wonder you wished to show it off"

"But you also have a lovely garden, do you not?" Richard asked

"Yes we do, but ours is nothing so large or grand as this" they looked at each other and smiled—she had a very pleasing smile, her teeth were very straight, although the two front upper teeth protruded slightly. Then there was a noise, it came from one of the upper windows—Richard glanced up to see where the sound had come from—Maria was stood there, she was watching him with Miss Kirkby—she did not avert her gaze at all, she was just staring at them, strolling in the garden, a shiver went down Richard's spine—that feeling of foreboding back again. He quickly regained his composure and concentrated on the young woman who's company he was enjoying

"I would have thought that you would be in London now for the season, I'm surprised that you are still here in Cornwall at this time of year Miss Kirkby"

"My mother would gladly go, but my father has no desire to go to town at all, so I don't believe that I shall ever get my season—I shall probably end up an old maid"

"I hardly think so, though in London you would undoubtedly be snapped up in no time I'm sure"

"That's very kind of you to say so, though I know only too well that I'm not very pretty—and I seem to choose all the wrong colours to suit me—mama despairs of me"

"Well I believe that you are entirely wrong—you are a very attractive young woman, and if your gown is to go by, you have very good fashion sense" she was wearing a gown of rose coloured satin, with ivory lace. The dress was cut low, showing off a large bosom, and a very curvy figure—this young lady wasn't without a certain charm—his good friend Jasper would have been very interested in Sarah Kirkby, though it would probably have been for the wrong reasons, knowing him.

"You are very kind to say so sir. You have attended the balls and assemblies then?" now she was turning the conversation to him

"Yes indeed—but for the last two years I travelled Europe—it was very enjoyable"

"I too would love to travel, but I don't think that will ever happen, where did you stay when you went to London, do you have a family home there?"

"I have my own home there—I have a modern town house in Mayfair, which is my pride and joy I have to admit" she laughed now

"And rightly so, Mayfair I hear is the height of fashion, you are very fortunate Your Grace"

Richard enjoyed speaking with this young lady, she wasn't Clara of course, no one could compare with her, but this young lady had something appealing about her—he hoped that she would find a good husband, who would care for her sometime soon. There was a noise, someone calling, and they both turned towards the house, Mrs Kirkby was stood in the open doorway, calling to them to return for their tea. As they reached the doorway, Mrs Kirkby spoke

"Come along, tea has been here for ages, I can't think what the two of you have found to keep you out for so long"

"I'm sorry Mrs Kirkby, we were chatting and lost all sense of time" Richard answered, hoping to save her daughter the need to find an excuse—Sarah glanced at Richard and gave him a warm smile

"Yes, well, we must have tea, and then take our leave" she was a miserable woman, how did she ever manage to produce such a friendly daughter

Richard said little more, he was listening to his mother's conversation with Mrs Kirkby, his mother seemed to be handling the woman with care and diplomacy, though there was something very untrusting about her—every few minutes she would glance from Sarah to him and back, this really was uncanny. Richard was rather relieved when they took their leave, or rather when the mother did.

"What an awful woman mother, and yet her daughter wasn't so bad"

"Indeed, so you took a liking for Sarah?" his mother asked amused

"She was very pleasant—who would not have enjoyed her company"

"Perhaps we have succeeded at last?" his mother was now living in hopes

"I wouldn't go quite that far—she was a very pleasant girl, no beauty tis true, yet there is something very fetching about her, but I'm sure that she is very marriageable, that's if the mother is kept out of the equation of course, she would dowse any young suitor's ardour—do you not agree?"

"Flora Kirkby has always been somewhat overpowering—but her husband and Sarah are very charming, her husband is quite suited to her you know—she has her own way, and he does as she says, I agree that it's a shame that Sarah has been so burdened though" she was smiling now

"But Miss Kirkby told me that the reason she hasn't had a season is because her father has no desire to go to London?"

"She has failed to tell her daughter then, that they are going to Bath, Flora has managed to secure a house there for the two of them and they leave this weekend"

"Then I'm very pleased for her" his mother looked at him thoughtfully

"But where does that leave you my dear?" now she was looking out for him again

"I want an end to these damned tea parties—they have been less than useful, and I fear that they are tiring you too much also mama, you are looking tired and pale of late"

"But you have to find a wife Richard we cannot forget that—the need is becoming greater all the time"

"The house in Bond Street has sold—Truscott wrote to me yesterday, that will give us a little more time—they have agreed to keep the servants on, so that is a weight off my mind. But we no longer have an estate manager"

"Why, where is Melvin Lincroft?"

"He has been arrested for smuggling, he was caught with the goods in his father's old cottage on the estate—it seems that is where he has been stashing it all, at least of late"

"I cannot say that I'm surprised—clearly he was your father's right hand man in more ways than we realized—if he is convicted he will be hung, should we not try and do something Richard?"

"What would you have me do?"

"I don't know, but we can't let it happen and do nothing"

"There is nothing that we can do mama—Mr Drummond assures me he is guilty, his fate is in his own hands, there is nothing we can do, it now all rests with the authorities—I like it no more than you mother"

"What will you do about an estate manager now? You cannot be expected to manage without one, you must do something quickly"

"I have asked old Truscott to find a new estate manager for us—I thought that he would be able to find a suitable person to take up the post, and with so many things to deal with, I have no desire to contend with that as well"

"Very wise my dear—very wise. But in the meantime, what will you do about a wife, if we stop the tea parties you won't even get to meet a suitable young lady"

"I'm sure that something will turn up" he replied, with a wry smile on his lips

Alice said nothing, Richard had had enough of wife seeking and she had had enough of tea parties for young ladies. She wasn't sure what he would decide to do, but she would be glad of some respite.

"And how is Maria, should we call Dr Somerville do you think mama?" Richard asked, changing the subject

"I think that she will be alright now but she is incensed with you Richard, whatever did you say to her?"

"I have said nothing to her mama—some weeks ago she suggested that I marry her, and I turned her down, that incident threw her into a frenzy, since then I have kept my distance, I thought it better that way, this afternoon I merely asked if she were alright, as I could clearly see that she is with child, and thought that she looked tired, that's when she flew into another rage, I thought she might strike me, so I have learnt a lesson, I shall say nothing more to her, I cannot then be accused of upsetting her in any way"

"I persuaded her to have a lie down and rest, perhaps she has had too much sun, she must be careful, now that she is with child again—though I cannot help but think that it's strange that she should find herself with Edward's child, so long after his death"

"I too thought it very strange but I suppose it's a possibility, though I know very little of these things"

"I think that we should keep an eye on her, she is very low and in poor spirits, I suppose that is natural, finding herself with yet another child, when her husband is dead and gone"

"Yes, I suppose so" Richard could think of a good reason that would have upset her—the child was more likely Melvin's child, and now it looked as if he would never get to see it, that made more sense to him, she had lost her husband, and now she was about to lose her lover too, but if the child was Lincroft's, it would end up a bastard, she wouldn't want anyone to know if that were the case—obviously his mother didn't know of her clandestine meetings, and for now, he wasn't going to tell her.

CHAPTER FIFTEEN

(A Perfect Afternoon)

Richard made his way to the stables, he needed to speak to the head groom, he would request that the landau be cleaned and made ready, as he would require it brought round to the front door, by one thirty this afternoon. Today was a very important day indeed. His first outing with the lovely Clara—everything had to be tip top for that young lady. Once he was satisfied, he went back into the house—he was excited, he couldn't concentrate to do any work—his only concern was falling for someone not of a similar social status as himself, but he had already decided that he wouldn't allow that to stand in his way anymore. Had he not met all those eligible young ladies, in hopes of finding a suitable wife, and what had he found—not one to compare to his beautiful Clara. He slipped into the house and came face to face with Maria—he gave her a nod of the head as he passed her in the hallway—she looked very pale and strained, and in a way, he still felt a little sorry for her, after all, her lover was facing the gallows, leaving her with his bastard—little wonder that she was looking ill—perhaps he should pity her.

"You are preparing for an outing?" she spoke to him today, that was quite a shock, he hadn't expected that and he wasn't sure that he welcomed her friendly manner, though he had no intention of being frank with her

"I shall be going out in the landau this afternoon, yes—was there something you wanted?"

"No, not at all, I just wondered, you were looking dressed for an outing"

"How are you Maria?" He would keep things simple he had no desire for another screaming, demented bout from her, not today of all days

"I am well thank you" she was certainly making the effort to be civil, just at that moment the Duchess walked into the hallway

"Ah Richard, there you are" then noticing Maria there too "Maria, too, will you both be joining me for lunch?"

"I shall be lunching in, yes" replied Richard

"You look as if you are going somewhere my dearest?" said his mother, taking in his appearance, why did he look so different today, of all days, he had taken particular notice of his toilette this morning, but he hadn't thought it to be so obvious

"He is taking the landau this afternoon Alice" said Maria, breaking in on their conversation

"Where are you going then Richard?" Alice was smiling, had they both guessed what he was up too, surely not

"I shall be going out for a while—nothing that should worry either of you ladies, I can assure you" he said smiling, he didn't intend to tell them about Clara, at least not yet

"I see, but taking the landau, could a young lady be involved in your venture?" his mother was very astute, or perhaps she was just wishful thinking "Perhaps you have decided to take Miss Kirkby for a drive?"

"Why ever would you think that mother?"

"You have that look on your face, as you did as a boy when you were determined about something, but the landau, that is only used when driving for pleasure so if you are taking Miss Kirkby out, then I shall be very pleased for you" she said watching him carefully with a smile on her old face

"I'm sorry to disappoint you mother, but I am not taking Miss Kirkby for a ride this afternoon" he replied

"Then perhaps we should go into lunch" she said, giving up on her sons secrecy

They all went into the dining room and seated themselves around the large table. Alice led the conversation as Richard had too many things going on in his mind

"How are you Maria, you look very tired dear" she said softly

"I am quite well thank you Alice, in fact, the weather is so pleasant today I thought that I should take a stroll after lunch" she replied

"You must be careful Maria, you must not overtire yourself"

"I'm sure that I shall be alright, just a stroll down the drive and back that should not overtire me"

"I'm sure you are right. So Richard, will you not tell us where you are going this afternoon?" his mother was certainly persistent—he would have to give her that

"It is nothing for you to worry yourself about—it's just business, I do not intend to bore you with the details" he replied, he had to tell her something, but he knew his mother, she would not let it rest for long

"I can see that you are determined not to say—I do know you my darling, well enough to know that you are planning something of which you are determined to keep a secret"

Maria was listening to the conversation, though she said nothing—but Richard noticed that her gaze, although guarded, kept resting on him, it was unsettling to receive her attention once again, he was telling no-one his secret, and if things turned out well, in the future perhaps, then would be soon enough to discuss the matter with his mama.

Lunch was almost at an end when the dining room door opened and Newbridge entered, in honesty Richard was glad of his interruption as he was becoming tired of the questioning

"Yes Newbridge" said Richard

"Mr Drummond is here to see you Your Grace—he says that it's urgent, and he wishes to speak with you now"

"Show him into the library, I shall come and speak to him"

Maria looked up she sat still and silent, her back straight and her face blank, giving none of her feelings away

"If you will excuse me ladies" Richard got up and strode into the library, where Rufus Drummond sat, patiently awaiting him

"Mr Drummond, how can I help you" Richard asked seating himself in the chair which Newbridge had drawn up for him

"I'm sorry to bother you Your Grace, but we have reason to believe that there are goods stashed in the Gate Lodge—it was Lincroft's home I believe?"

"I see, I will ask Newbridge to find the spare key for you, of course"

"Thank you. Can you tell me for what reason your father chose to give his estate manager the Gate Lodge, surely it would have been more fitting for a member of the family perhaps?"

"I have no idea Drummond, of my father's dealings, he never discussed them with me, and having only arrived back here just a week before his death"

"Yes, I see" he sounded satisfied, but it was a question which he had asked many times himself

"There is no doubt that Melvin Lincroft is one of the smuggling gang then?" Richard ventured

"No doubt whatsoever—I'm afraid you will need to find another estate manager, as this one won't have a need to work where he's going"

"I have already instructed old Truscott to find someone to take up that position"

"Then you are very wise Your Grace—this one will hang as sure as night follows day" Richard said no more—what could he say, this man had worked for his father, and had his father lived, he would have possibly been facing the hangman's noose, too, although he would have been too clever for that—that was the whole point of employing someone to take his punishment, but he wanted nothing to do with it—he had no desire to be involved in such things, and he more than enough on his plate than to worry about it now.

"Well Mr Drummond, if that is all" Richard asked, he had noticed that it was almost one thirty, the time he had ordered the landau to be brought round, he had no intention of keeping Miss Penrose waiting.

"Yes of course Your Grace, I'm sorry to keep you, I realize that you're a very busy man" with that he got up, Richard called Newbridge and instructed him to find the spare key for the Gate Lodge. Newbridge returned a few minutes later

"I'm very sorry Your Grace, but the key seems to have disappeared" he stated

"What do you mean Newbridge, how can it of disappeared?" Richard couldn't understand that

"I have looked in the usual place, and the key has gone Your Grace—I can't think who would have wanted it" the old man was becoming a little flustered now, he feared being blamed for the disappearance

"The key must be there—where could it have gone. Perhaps you would take Mr Drummond and have another look, I have business to take care of and I assume the landau is at the front door ready?"

"Yes Your Grace, I will have another look" he turned on his heels and left the library—Rufus Drummond following closely behind him.

Richard closed the library door and stepped outside into the warm sunshine—his landau was waiting, a footman had already opened the door and pulled the steps down, though Richard jumped up into the landau, without using the steps, and took his seat, already forgetting his interview with Drummond and the lost key. The excitement was almost unbearable, he even found himself to be a little nervous—but he had a great deal to lose—even if Penleigh Court went he knew now, that he couldn't stand to lose this young lady—he had not even kissed her, but he knew that he was in love with her—there was no other explanation for it. They pulled away at a steady trot—his horses hooves, and the tweet of the birds song, the only sound as they clip clopped down the hill and into the village. Once he arrived at the rectory, he jumped down and knocked at the door—Daisy came rushing to the door, opening it, and ushering Richard inside

"The mistress is ready and expecting you sir"

"Thank you Daisy" as he spoke to Daisy, Clara came through to the entrance, Daisy handed her her bonnet, which she tied onto her head, then Daisy picked up her own bonnet and tied it in place, before they all walked out into the afternoon sunshine. The landau door was open ready Richard offered his hand to first Clara, helping her in, then to Daisy, before jumping up into the landau and taking the seat opposite the young ladies. He was transfixed—he couldn't take his eyes off of her, she was lovelier in reality than she could ever be in his dreams.

"This is de je vu sir, except the last time we were inside an enclosed carriage" she said softly "I can still remember the night that you saved my life, and drove me home, I shall always be grateful" Richard laughed

"That was a little different though I think—you had hurt your ankle, and the night was bitterly cold—I prefer the sunshine and to see you in good health" they laughed together—Daisy sat beside her mistress watching the countryside go by, she had never ridden in such a fashionable way before, an open landau, it was all so exciting

"It was very kind of you to ask me to go with you for a drive today, and in such style too—I have never been in such a fashionable contraption as this, in fact, I rarely go very far—my father has to keep the carriage close at hand, in his profession, he can be called to attend one of his congregation much further afield, and at any time"

"Then I'm very glad to be able to give you such a treat" Richard could not take his eyes from her, she was bewitching, adorable

"I do hope that I haven't kept you from your work Your Grace, I know that you must be very busy, with the estate and I hear that you have recently lost your estate manager"

"Yes, I'm afraid that you have heard right—Melvin Lincroft was a good estate manager, although his other more sinister activities have now cost him a great deal, but I have no intention of letting his unhappy situation spoil our afternoon" he smiled at her again

Clara tried to study the man sat in front of her, she had dreamed of kissing those lips, and curling his dark locks round her fingers, she wanted to look at him properly, but that would be wrong, she had been taught never to be caught staring at a gentleman, it was rude, and frowned upon, so the best she could hope for was small glances in his direction

"I thought that on such a beautiful afternoon, we should have a picnic tea—although I have no idea what food you enjoy, I have brought a selection of things in a basket, and we have a blanket so that we may sit on the grass—if that would suit you?" Clara's face lit up, she couldn't remember the last time she had gone on a picnic

"Where are we going Your Grace?"

"Well, I thought that we could go to the lake on my estate—it's quiet there and we should not be disturbed, but we can sit on the bank and enjoy our picnic, and perhaps take a stroll in the sunshine, and of course, to feed the ducks"

"That sounds lovely sir"

"Please, call me Richard, after all we are friends are we not?" her face was better than a picture—her lovely pink kissable lips, and rosy cheeks—it was so hard for him to bear, he wanted too much to touch that glorious ivory skin, so clear and without a single blemish

"I would like to think we are Richard" she replied, trying his name out

"But if I am to call you Richard, then you must call me Clara—after all, it is only right and proper do you not agree?"

"Indeed I do Clara" her name gave a nice ring on his lips, he had used it many times, to himself, but never to her face. He looked at Daisy, she was still sat taking in the scenery—how he wished that they were alone—but, at least he was here with his beloved—he had not thought to see this day. The landau came to a halt, they were turning in at the large iron gates, by the Gate House—Richard could see no sign of life, and wondered if they had found the spare keys. They rumbled on, though instead of taking the main drive, they had turned off, and were now heading towards the trees—there was a pathway which took them through the wooded area, then out on to the back road which no-one used these days. As the landau rumbled onto the back road, it slowed right down, to almost a walking pace—Richard called to the coachman

"Why have we slowed down Perry?"

"I'm sorry Your Grace, but there is someone on the road just ahead, I didn't spot her until we came out of the trees"

"And who is it?"

"I believe it's the Lady Maria Your Grace, she's on her own" Richard might of guessed, the last person he wanted to see right now—but it was too late to change his mind, still the landau carried on at a walking pace, as they passed Maria, she had stepped back into the grassy verge, out of the way of the passing vehicle, but her eyes were taking in the occupants of the open top vehicle. Her face was like thunder—so she had seen him with dear Clara—he would never have wished for that to happen, he was sure that she would be angry, but there was nothing which he could do, and besides, she would have to know one day, when they married. The landau went a little further, then pulled up and stopped. The footman opened the door and pulled down the steps for them to alight. Richard jumped down first, before offering his hand to Clara, and finally to Daisy. They started walking across the grass, toward the lake, Clara taking Richard's arm and Daisy following behind—then behind them, the footman carrying the blanket and the basket of food and wine. Once they had chosen the place, the footman was ordered to lay out the blanket and the contents of the basket, before they sat down and started to eat—Daisy sat on the grass a little away from the couple. There were pies and cheese and freshly baked bread, and strawberry's and raspberry's, fresh from the gardens, and a bottle of wine—Richard poured some into each of the two glasses before him and passed one to Clara—she was delighted, what a wonderful venture, but the company was best of all

"This is all lovely Richard, you really are spoiling me you know" she said

"I'm glad that you approve—I thought it an ideal opportunity to make the most of such a lovely day, and with such charming company"

"Indeed it is" she was looking into his eyes, they were dark pools of desire, she wanted so much for him to kiss her, but knew that would be unlikely, he was taking her out, but they were only friends after all, hadn't he said so himself, and besides, Daisy was there to make sure that things like that would not happen. It must be the wine which had gone to her head, giving her such wild thoughts

"Would you care to take a short stroll, perhaps down to that cluster of trees, around the water?" Richard asked once they had finished eating "we can take the remainder of the bread for the ducks"

"Indeed I should" she replied, then he lowered his voice and whispered

"I thought that we could go alone—Daisy can still see us from here, and she may like something to eat while we are gone" Clara laughed out loud

"I will suggest it to her" she replied

"Daisy?" she called, Daisy stood up and went over to the couple on the blanket

"Yes Miss?"

"Are you hungry Daisy?"

"No Miss, I am quite alright thank you Miss"

"Then perhaps you would like to rest on the blanket for a little while, as Mr Penleigh and I wish to take a stroll down to the cluster of trees, just down there" she said, pointing to the trees "we are going to feed the ducks" though she secretly longed for his kiss

"But Miss" Daisy started to say, Clara raised her hand and silenced her

"It's alright Daisy, you can still watch us from here—and my mother will never know anyway, will she?"

"No Miss" said Daisy, an uncertain look on her face

"We won't be long Daisy, we just wish to stretch our legs, that is all"

"Yes Miss, I shall wait for you here then Miss"

"Thank you Daisy"

Richard stood up, holding out his hand for Clara to take, keeping his eyes on Clara he said to Daisy

"Help yourself to the remainder of the food, while we're gone Daisy, I'm sure you like raspberry's and strawberry's do you not?"

"Thank you sir, that's very kind" she still had an apprehensive look on her face

Richard helped Clara to her feet, then gave her his arm—they took a steady walk down towards the trees—once they arrived, and Clara had broken the last crumbs of bread and thrown them to the ducks swimming on the water, Richard turned to Clara, checking that they were just out of view, he took both Clara's hands in his, before pulling her closer to him, wrapping his arms around her tightly

"Dearest Clara" he whispered, smelling her wonderful lavender perfume "I have waited for so long for this moment" Clara, looking into his eyes was mesmerised by this charming man, he was holding her so close she could hear his breathing and feel the beating of his heart, but she could not pull away from him, he lowered his head, brushing her lips as he did so, then placing his lips on hers, this time a little firmer, the kiss growing more feverish as it continued—no-one had ever kissed her like this before, she wrapped her arms about his neck and leaned her body into his, her feverish need as great as his. Then Richard stood back a little, he must calm his yearning, he would not compromise this lady for anything, besides standing back gave him the chance to drink in her beauty, suddenly a voice behind them startled them, and horrified Richard

"Oh Richard, I had not expected to see you here" the voice was Maria's. Richard pulled away from Clara and turned to look at Maria now

"Maria, you decided to take a walk after all" he couldn't help but feign surprised, she ignored Richard and looked straight to his companion

"Miss Penrose, how nice—are you enjoying your afternoon?" Maria keeping her gaze steady, her blue eyes sharp and cold, and the smile on her lips was less than pleasant

"Yes, indeed I am Your Lady" said Clara bobbing a small curtsey

"Good, obviously Richard is looking after you"

"Yes, we have had a picnic" said Clara innocently

"Have you?, how very quaint" Richard noticed that Maria's tone was not as civil as she sounded, and he was beginning to think that there could be trouble, he had best end this conversation before things had a chance to get out of hand. Clara on the other hand was looking at Maria's stomach, and taking in the fact that she was with child, although she no longer had a husband

"Well, if you would excuse us Maria, we should be on our way, I believe Clara's mother will worry where we have got too"

"Of course, I wouldn't want to interrupt—good day Miss Penrose" she said without a glance at Richard, then she started making her way back toward the road. Richard felt a cold shiver run down his spine, he must be wary of this woman, he would not have her spoil anything with Clara, she was so sweet and innocent, and he wouldn't have her avenge her spite on the beauty before him

"I'm sorry about Maria, she is not herself at the moment—you must not take any notice of her abrupt manner" Richard said to her, taking her once again in his arms, and pulling her to him, he stroked her hair and kissed her lips, those lovely luscious lips, they were indeed as sweet as he had hoped. Clara was so happy, she thought that her heart would burst—this gentleman was the one she dreamed about at night, and he had kissed her until her knees felt like collapsing under her—her happiness could not be greater. Finally Richard pulled away from her—he had to force himself to do so, as he could have stayed there with her in his arms all night. He took both her hands in his, one at a time, and opening her hand, planted kisses on both of her wrists, the point of her pulse and in both her palms. Clara was breathless, her heart beating wildly, she was desperately trying to keep her composure, but she could see how easy it would be to allow herself to be compromised, she was experiencing feelings and emotions she had never known existed

"You are the most beautiful woman I have ever met Clara" he whispered

"I'm sure that cannot be, you have travelled to many places, and you have attended many high society occasions, you must meet lots of beautiful women, I couldn't hope to compete with them"

"You have no need to compete, I realized that I had feelings for you the very first time I saw you, but I know that you are far lovelier than any other woman I've ever met"

"I too, wanted to know you better, but I should not have allowed you to kiss me like that sir—after all, I am not of your society, our worlds are far apart, and I have shown nothing but wanton recklessness" she must draw back now, while she still could

"Nonsense, our upbringing may have been worlds apart, but I have never met anyone who thrills me as you do" he raised his hand to her cheek, stroking it gently with his thumb

"Perhaps we should return now—I have enjoyed your company this afternoon, but I think that we should go" she was nervous, he had no desire to make her feel uncomfortable—perhaps he had said too much too soon, but he was finding it difficult to keep his feelings hidden

"As you wish, perhaps you would allow me to drive you out another day, or, do you ride Clara?"

"Indeed I do, I haven't ridden very much of late, my father used to ride with me, but he no longer has the time, and my parents are not eager for me to ride alone, so I rarely have the pleasure these days"

"Then I shall accompany you—if you would allow me too"

"Yes Richard, I should enjoy that very much" Richard was relieved—he thought for a moment that he may have gone too far, but she had agreed to their meeting again

"Splendid, I shall come to the rectory at ten o clock on Wednesday,"

"Thank you, I shall look forward to it sir" Richard took one last long look into those great pools of pleasure, before offering his arm to Clara to return to Daisy, and their waiting landau. They were both very happy, as he held her hand and helped her into the landau, before helping her maid in next, then Richard climbed up and sat opposite the two ladies. The footman had already packed up the remains of the picnic and packed it back into the basket, and collected and folded the blanket. Then they made their way back to the rectory. Once they arrived, Richard helped the two ladies out of the landau, before taking Clara's hand and kissing her fingers, just light as a whisper, then watched as she disappeared into the house behind

Daisy, but not before she turned to allow him one last smile, before he headed back home.

⁂

"Did you have a good afternoon my dear?" Clara smiled thinking about all that had happened, she should never have allowed a gentleman to have kissed her like that, though she had enjoyed every moment, too much, and she couldn't shake it from her mind, she should not have encouraged him so

"It was a very pleasant afternoon mama, His Grace took a picnic, and we went to the lake at Penleigh Court, where we enjoyed our picnic and took a stroll by the lake" she was being guarded as to the information she would impart—her mother would not have approved of her allowing him such kisses

"It is time that you started enjoying a little social pleasure my dear, a girl of your age should have friends, and meeting people, you spend your life shut in this house with your father and me—it's not right. If it had only been possible, your father and I would have given you a season you know, I hate that we cannot do this for you, and although your father was determined to set aside a good sum for your dowry, there is little left for much else" her mother had a faraway look in her eye

"Please mama, I enjoy my life here with you and papa, I have no complaints, and I do meet people socially, when we go to church each Sunday, and also when I visit the old and sick—I do not crave for a season, and things which are not possible, I'm happy as I am—truly I am" she had never felt less than content with her lot

"I know Clara, but you should meet with other young people your own age—there are so few young ladies who you can share a friendship with, and I despair of that—we want you to find a gentleman who will care for you, and who will take care of you—our dearest wish Clara is to see you settled, your father is as concerned as I. The Duke is taken with you, I saw it in his eyes, that first night he brought you home—he will be a good friend to you Clara, and I believe that twinkle in your eyes tells me that you are not averse to him either" her mother had noticed, she could feel the heat rise in her cheeks

"But it would not be wise to set my heart on the Duke, he could never offer me marriage, he was born into gentry, he has travelled and he is a man of the world, and all I know is my family and my home—I could never be enough for him, though I enjoy his company very much"

"Enjoy his company my dear, the rest we shall see, just because he is more skilled in worldly ways does not mean that he would choose someone worldly to marry—some gentlemen prefer a simpler, more natural bride, and if my intuition is correct, I believe that this gentleman's intentions for you are most honourable—you mark my words Clara" her mother said smiling.

Richard had been open about his feelings, though she could say nothing of that, but she knew that she felt alive and happy in his presence, and he made her feel so special—just the sight of him made her very nerves tingle, right through her body

"We are going riding together on Wednesday morning mama, if you have no objections" said Clara

"Of course you must go Clara, it's time that you enjoy yourself—perhaps you would like to ask the Duke to stay for lunch afterwards?" Clara smiled, there was nothing she would like more

"I shall invite him when he arrives, thank you mama" Clara went to her mother and kissed her cheek, she may not be gentry, but she could not of wished for better parents, she knew that she was very fortunate—she would never have to take up a governess post or anything so horrifying, as many other young girls in her position were forced to do—yes, she really was a fortunate young lady.

Richard left the rectory feeling happier than he could ever remember, he hadn't dare hope that Clara felt as he did, and for a moment he was worried

that he had shown too much of his feelings, a little too soon perhaps, but now she had agreed to go riding with him in a couple of days, he was sure that she wanted him as much as he wanted her, his mind was full of this lovely lady. It was later than he had anticipated, when he jumped from the phaeton, and handed the reins to his groom—he took the steps to the front entrance, two at a time and strode into the hall with a smile on his face

"Did you have an enjoyable afternoon?" the voice behind him pulled him up sharp—it was soft and low and he knew that he now had to face Maria—she would be angry, she saw him with Clara, she would have seen how they were locked in a warm embrace, he should prepare for another outburst

"I did, very much thank you" he replied levelly

"Spending time with the vicars daughter, really Richard, I thought that you had more sense, do you think for a moment that you will be allowed to marry a mere vicar's daughter—she is better suited to a governess, than a Duchess" Richard could feel the anger mounting inside of him, but he must keep his temper checked, he had no desire for a another screaming session

"I took Miss Penrose out for a drive, we had a very enjoyable afternoon, that is all" he said, trying to keep the anger from his voice—why should he have to answer to this woman—he was the master here

"I noticed, you seemed very cosy" so she had seen them kissing, he had thought as much—his cheeks started to burn all the same, but it still had nothing to do with her

"Miss Penrose is a delightful creature, I thought to give her a pleasant afternoon, I don't believe that she has so many of those"

"I'm sure you did that—she was obviously enjoying your attentions" she said sarcastically

"And I enjoyed hers, now if you will excuse me Maria, I have things to attend too" Richard said walking away from the woman

"You will never marry her Richard" her voice was raised and she was beginning to shout now "I will never allow it—never" Richard carried on walking away down the corridor, and to his library, he had no intention of having another hysterical outburst with this woman. He was beginning to regret promising her a home. He went into his library and shut the door, going to the dresser he picked up the crystal decanter and poured a large measure of brandy into a glass, then he tossed it down in one. She really was an impossible woman.

CHAPTER SIXTEEN

(Love Realised)

Two days later Richard woke with a spring in his step, he was going riding with Clara this morning. He had received a letter the previous day, from Truscott, informing him that the sale of the Bond Street house was now imminent—what a relief, he could at least breathe easy for a while—as soon as a new estate manager had been installed, he would instruct him to get the repairs for the tenants underway. There was a list of things which required attention at Penleigh Court, but that would have to wait, there was nothing that urgent.

Richard had breakfast alone no one else seemed to be around. Maria had gone back to her none talking mode, and he was relieved that she had, he really had had enough of her and her comments—it was bad enough having James, who was also giving him a hard time, though his valet wasn't privy to his plans—but Maria was something else—she was a woman scorned, and he was apprehensive how she would react when she learnt the truth about him and Clara—supposing that Clara would eventually agree to be his wife—he would need to get his mother on his side, she was adamant that his happiness came first, and Clara was his happiness, but he was still unsure whether she would approve of his choice. The only thing which he knew for sure now, was that he couldn't think of life without her anymore.

Once breakfast was over, Richard slipped out of the side door and across the yard to the stables—he shouted to the groom to saddle his stallion, before jumping up on to his back and digging his heels in his flank, to encourage his speed. The sun was still warm, and although the sky was not cloudless, the clouds that were hanging there, were light and fluffy, without the threat of rain. Once Richard reached the rectory, he went to the front door and rapped the knocker—Daisy answered the door.

"Daisy, I have come to call for Miss Penrose, we are going riding this morning"

"Good morning sir, I shall see if Miss Penrose is ready" she smiled and bobbed a curtsey, before going off to find her mistress. While he was stood in the hall, where he had been ushered by Daisy, Mrs Penrose had heard the door and guessing that it was the Duke, had come to greet him

"Good morning Your Grace, how lovely to see you again" she said

"Good morning Mrs Penrose, another lovely day. I have come to collect Miss Penrose we are going for a ride, with your permission of course"

"You certainly have my permission, Clara had a very pleasant afternoon on Monday, the picnic did her the world of good—I'm afraid that she doesn't get out half as much as she should for a young girl of her age—there are so few young ladies in the local area, and I know that makes things difficult for her, but I know that she so much enjoyed your outing the other day, and that she is looking forward to your ride this morning"

"And I am very pleased that she is happy to spend time in my company—living in the country can be rather confining, and I admit that I miss my friends, who I spend a great deal of time with in London"

"I expect your life in town is very hectic?" she asked

"Indeed it is, but not always for the best, and I have to say that when I went off to travel Europe, I was relieved to get away from the ton and all the mama's intent on landing their daughters with a good marriage—at that time I had no intention of settling down"

"And now are you still determined not to marry?" Damn, how did he get on to this subject, and with Clara's mother, he would have to be very careful how he answered

"I realize that I am now expected to take a wife, and produce an heir, but as I have already told my mother, I have no intention of marrying for convenience, I would sooner not marry at all"

"You are a very wise man—then I hope that you will find the right young lady to fulfil your plan, and the Duchess, she agrees with you?

"Yes, indeed she does" he would have to steer her away from this conversation, it was becoming rather uncomfortable. As if reading his thoughts, Clara came down the stairs at that moment, which saved him from more questioning

"Miss Penrose, how delightful you look" she did look a picture, in her dark green velvet riding habit, and black hat, with a black net attached, and her black gloves—her pale skin, and large brown eyes, he was so bewitched by her, she may not be of his standing, but she was more a lady than some of the ladies that he knew

"Thank you" she replied smiling, Richard offered her his arm, and Clara took it then they stepped outside into the sunlight, a few seconds later Mrs Penrose called out from the doorway

"I'm sorry Your Grace, I nearly forgot—would you care to join us for a bite of lunch on your return—we eat at twelve thirty" Richard turned round and strode back to where she was standing

"Thank you Mrs Penrose, that is very kind of you, I should be delighted to join you"

"Excellent—I shall tell cook to prepare for an extra person—enjoy your ride"

"Thank you, we most certainly will" he replied and went back to join Clara, who was stood waiting for him. They rounded the side of the house, to where there was one large stable, with several different stalls—unlike the stables at Penleigh Court, which were abuzz with activity, here there was only one groom, who doubled as coachman when required, and one stable boy. There were two bay mares, which pulled the vicar's carriage and two other horses besides—Clara asked that the grey should be saddled and made ready for her. Once this was done, Richard lifted Clara up onto the horse's back, before mounting his own. They rode off up toward the next village—past the drive to Penleigh Court, and on up to the top of the hill—the view up there was stunning, as they reached the peak of the hill, Richard suggested that they dismount to take in the view, right down to the sea. Clara had been to this spot with her father once, the view was breathtaking, and the sun shining on the water below, made the water sparkle in its rays, a ship out on the horizon, with its white sails, was moving lazily across the expanse of water, was soon lost in the shimmering light—such a beautiful sight to behold

"This is such a beautiful spot, don't you think Richard?" Clara couldn't remember when she had been this happy or content

"Yes indeed it is" he said just as content as his companion

"Who would think that the rocks below, at Devil's Point, are so treacherous, when here all you can see is such beauty?" she was thinking of his poor dear brother, how sad that with so much beauty comes so much sorrow

"It is all part of the charm of Cornwall—is it not?" Richard replied

"I'm sure it is" she replied, still looking down at the beauty before her. Richard moved closer to her laying his arm about her waist before turning her towards him, Clara knew that he would kiss her, and as much as she knew that she shouldn't allow him, she knew that she couldn't stop him— she welcomed his kisses. Richard moved as close to her as he could get, before lifting her veil from her face, then wrapping his arms about her, and placing his lips on hers—until Monday, she had never experienced anything like this—but now, she longed for it, when she laid in bed at night, her thoughts were all for Richard and his kisses. His handsome face and firm, hard body which excited her and black curling hair, which she could at last fulfil her desire now to twist her fingers in the curls lying on the collar of his jacket. The kiss lasted for ages, and when they parted, her breath was coming in gasps, she was left feeling weak and shaken at the effect this man had on her

"You are so beautiful Clara" her knees had started shaking, no-one had ever spoken to her in this fashion before, she took a few moments to steady and recompose herself before replying

"Do you tell all the young ladies you meet this?" she asked, now calmed and with her thoughts collected again. Richard looked into her eyes

"I may have complimented the odd young lady on her appearance, but I have never met anyone as beautiful as you, and that I have never said to anyone ever before"

"And how many young ladies have you kissed in such a way as this?" Richard knew that she was unsure of him, but he would not lie to her

"I have kissed many woman, that is true, but none who I've enjoyed as much as you—I know that you must be feeling unsure of me, and I have been to lots of places and met many young ladies but believe me Clara, there is no-one I would rather be with, not now or ever, you are the first young lady who has affected me like this, I have no desire for anyone but you "

"And I enjoy your company Richard, though I'm not sure that I should allow you to kiss me in this way—it's not that I don't enjoy it, but I'm not sure that it's right—I must seem rather wanton and forward to you, yet that isn't at all the way I really am"

"I don't care who or what you are, I love you Clara, just the way you are, my feelings for you are true, and my intentions are honourable. I cannot offer you marriage at the moment, as we are still in mourning, but if you feel as I do, then I shall request an interview with your father, to ask for your hand once I am in a position to do so" Clara was surprised, lost for words, she felt faint—she wanted this man, more than any other she had ever met, though there had not been anyone serious in her life before. She just kept gazing at Richard and saying nothing—the tears started to prick her eyes

"Clara, my dearest, I have upset you—I would not have done so for anything in the world—please forgive me dearest" Richard looked anxious, before removing his handkerchief and offering it to her, he still wasn't sure why women cried at the most inopportune moments

"I love you too Richard, but you can never marry me—you are a Duke, and I'm purely a vicar's daughter, I'm so aware of the great differences between us—your family would never accept me"

"You think I care for that? You know very little of me, but I intend to speak with my mother, I know that she will be delighted for me, but only if you wish it—if you feel the same about me"

"I do feel the same Richard" she whispered through her tears

Richard pulled her close once again, kissing the tears from her eyes, before kissing her lips hard and with longing—then still holding her tight, he said

"Then you will marry me?" Clara looked up into his eyes again

"Yes of course" she said this in a whisper Richard had never thought to be so happy, now he was kissing her mouth, her hair, her eyes, her cheeks, and also her neck. This was what love was all about—he had never felt like this before, and doubted he ever would again, and knowing that Clara loved him too, was a dream come true—they held each other tight, without any words to interrupt their thoughts, before saying

"I must speak to your father, ask his permission—but I cannot do that for now, he would not take kindly to me asking for your hand, while we are still in mourning—but soon—I promise that at the first opportunity, I shall ask for your hand"

"It doesn't matter Richard, I will wait for you, however long it takes, I could never love another, you have no fear of that"

"But there is no reason that we shouldn't enjoy each other's company in the meantime, is there?" he asked

"None at all, though I do worry about your family, you say that you will speak to your mother, I am still very worried that she will not accept me, and as your wife I would become a Duchess, what would you expect of me, and what would be my duties, I have no idea"

"I shall speak to my mother soon—I'm sure that she will want to invite you to Penleigh Court for tea—she is eager to see me married, although at present I'm unable to do so, but I'm sure she will be eager to meet you, and I promise that you have nothing to fear" Richard kissed her again, squeezing her hard against his body. Neither of them ever having felt the love, joy or happiness, that they were now both experiencing.

Eventually Richard pulled away and stated that it was time for them to return to the rectory—he was to have lunch with the Penrose family, and he couldn't be happier. They rode back in silence, but a warm and contented silence. Once back at the rectory they had lunch, before Richard took his leave, but with the promise that he would call again soon. Richard knew that Mrs Penrose had soon caught on to her daughter's new found happiness, and he guessed that she would be questioned, once he had taken his leave, but nothing would stem the happiness that he was experiencing—all the women he had ever known, even his mistresses—but not one of them made him feel the way Clara did—now, at last, he was understanding just what all these women were frequently babbling on about all the time—perhaps they knew more than men believed they did. The ride home was glorious, and his mood mirrored the day.

As Richard stepped into Penleigh Court, his mother was waiting in the drawing room for him, she wished to see him—Newbridge had met him with the instruction. Richard entered the drawing room to find his mother, Nanny Grey and Maria all sat quietly together. Nanny Grey was sleeping as usual, though she wasn't making that awful snoring noise at the moment, Maria sat by the window looking out into the garden and his mother sat with her embroidery

"Richard, you are back, I was so worried about you, you went off on your horse, and you said nothing about where you were going, or when you were to return, and when you didn't show up for lunch, I was preparing to send out a search party for you—please don't frighten me so. I have been so worried about you"

"I'm so sorry mama, I didn't think", in his new found joy, he had not given a thought for his mother's concern—he felt so guilty now

"I really am sorry mama, but you must not worry about me—I am quite able to look after myself and I do not intend to have any untimely accidents—of that I promise you" he went to her and kissed her forehead

"I know, I am sorry to cause a fuss my dearest, but you do understand my concern, since your dear brother went out and didn't come home—I couldn't bear to lose you as well" she said, trying to explain the obvious

"You will not lose me mama, I should have thought—in future I shall have a message sent to you—it was thoughtless of me, but I promise not to worry you again"

"And now, come and tell me what kept you" he knew that this was coming—he wanted to talk to his mama about Clara but not in front of Maria

"There is nothing to tell mama, I went for a ride with a friend this morning, and I was invited to join them for lunch, nothing more than that" his mother was smiling, he knew that look, she wasn't going to let it go at that

"Come now Richard, will you not tell your mama of your new acquaintance?" Maria was going to do her bit now damn the woman, why should she involve herself in his business—he threw her a sharp glance, she had a smile on her lips, she obviously hoped to cause a problem, but by now his mother had picked up on her words

"You have a new acquaintance? Am I to understand that it's a young lady perhaps?" his mother may be getting older, but there was nothing wrong with her faculties

"I merely offered to go riding with Miss Penrose, the vicar's daughter, I hear that she has few friends, and doesn't get out a great deal—I thought that she may like some company, so we went for a ride this morning, and Mrs Penrose offered me lunch, which I was delighted to accept, that is all, there is no great secret" he hoped to leave his explanation at that until he could get his mother alone, but with Maria there, and vastly jealous, her eyes told him that, he would not have the chance to change the subject

"I see, I had no idea that you even knew Miss Penrose, she is rather a beauty is she not?, though I know her only from church, I know that she helps her father with the old and sick of the village, and visits them with gifts of food, each week—but more than that I have little knowledge of the girl" Alice remarked

"She is indeed a very attractive young lady and a very pleasant companion" he stated, looking in Maria's direction as he said it, but it didn't take long for her retort

"Indeed, she must be a very pleasant companion, to induce you to spend two days with her already this week" her smile and gaze were both fixed on him and this had also roused his mother's interest as she had raised her eyes to him also

"Two days, that is rather an exaggeration—merely a few hours on Monday afternoon and we went for a ride this morning—we are friends, that is all" he hoped that Maria would say no more, but unfortunately she would have her say

"Friends" Maria almost spat the word out "forgive me if I misread the situation, but I have never known friends to embrace the way that you and Miss Penrose were embracing by the lake on Monday afternoon— though perhaps after living in London, things are done very differently in high society these days" now Richard was becoming very angry—but he must keep his temper, this was no time for another outburst, it was none of Maria's business, yet she was determined to upset his mama before he could speak to her. The situation was delicate enough, without having her make things worse, but he had made an enemy of her—that had not been a wise move

"We are friends, very good friends, and I can assure you that nothing improper has passed between us" he said sharply. His mother was still looking in his direction, this time it was her turn to speak

"So you have shared this young woman's company before today? You must be careful my dearest, you see how easily your good nature can be misconstrued" dear mama, she was determined to defend him in her way

"I thank you for your concern mama, but misconstrued or not, Miss Penrose and I are friends, and I shall not ignore her to suit the opinions of others" Maria's jealousy was detestable, but he would never give Clara up, not even for his mother.

Richard did not wait to hear more, he turned on his heels and left the room—Maria, damn the jealous, spiteful woman, she was now trying to turn his mother against him—he wouldn't allow her to do this—he would have a word with his mother in private, the sooner the better now—but he intended to marry Clara and nothing would stop him.

Richard went upstairs, and straight to the nursery, he would go and regain his composure with his dear little niece Milly, although she was Maria's daughter, she was a sweet and mesmerising little creature. As he entered Nanny Anson met him,

"Good afternoon You Grace" she said, bobbing a curtsey "you have caught us just in time, we were about to take a walk in the garden"

"What a splendid idea, perhaps you would allow me to join you" Nanny Anson looked surprised, but he paid her wages, if that's what he wanted, then she had no objection—in fact, she almost welcomed the idea, Miss Millicent always seemed to behave better when the master was around—if there was one thing which Nanny Anson knew, it was that the master had taken to the girls, as if they were his own—in her opinion, he should be looking for a wife himself—he would make an excellent father, though what would happen to her little wards then, she dreaded to think—their own mother had been nowhere near them for over a week, and the last time she had popped her head into the nursery, she had been left, with a very unhappy child—Millicent had thrown a tantrum as she wanted to go with her mama, and it had taken Nanny Anson all of an hour to calm her down again—they still visited their grandmother each day, at least the Dowager Duchess had time and lots of love for them—she would always make sure that they were cared for—Nanny Anson only hoped that she would live long enough to see that they had the education they needed and a season, and eventually, found good husbands—their mother didn't seem to care either way. She had seen so much of this sort of thing before, and it never ended well. Suddenly Nanny realised that the master was awaiting an answer

"Of course Your Grace, Miss Millicent would find it a pleasure I'm sure"

"Good—then that's settled" he stated firmly. By now Millicent had heard her uncle and had come running to see him, eyes alight and squealing with pleasure, Richard swung her up in his arms, she had thrown her little podgy arms around his neck, and clung to him like he would disappear before her eyes

"Now Milly, you have to be good, we are going outside in the garden, with Nanny Anson and your little sister Becky" her eyes were big and round with excitement, and she scrambled down, running to her toy box, and taking a ball, which she then ran back and handed to Richard.

"So, you want to play ball, then I had better carry it for you, had I not"

"Ball, ball" Milly said excitedly

"That's right, it is a ball, and we will have a game in the garden if you like" her face was a picture, she was a lovely child, with her curls bobbing and those large eyes and long lashes. It had crossed his mind that he hoped to have a child very like this one, of his own—but she would of course look exactly like her mother. This little girl resembled his brother with her dark curls, and although her little sister, still had very fine hair, it had at last started to grow, she was proving to be just like her mother, very blonde, though he hoped that she wouldn't end up with her mother's ways, he was beginning to dislike Maria, though for the sake of these two little girls, he could never throw her out of his home

"There Your Grace, we are all ready to go now" said Nanny Anson, tying the ribbons of Millicent's bonnet

"Then shall we go?" asked Richard, looking at little Milly as he spoke. The little girl ran back to him lifting her arms for him to carry her, which he did, with her in one arm, and her arm thrown about his neck with the ball lodged between them, they all left the nursery and headed for the gardens.

Richard so enjoyed spending time with these children, he had grown to love them, and couldn't imagine not having them living in his house. Once they had reached the lawn, they headed for a large sycamore tree which was the only shade from the elements Nanny had a folded blanket under her arm, to lay baby Rebecca on. Richard took the blanket from Nanny Anson, and spread it out beneath the shade of the tree, for Nanny and Rebecca, before picking up the ball, and throwing it gently to Millicent. The little girl ran after the ball, she was very steady on her legs now—she had learned to walk quite early, in fact, she was a very bright little girl. They played ball in the sunshine for a while, Milly squealing with laughter, and chuckling all the time, and Richard smiling and laughing with her. Once she had grown tired of playing, Richard decided that they should have a glass of lemonade and one of cooks freshly baked biscuits, and he thought that Nanny would be glad of one too, so he took Milly's hand, and told Nanny that they would be back soon, and led Milly up the garden and into the house, through the French doors (which had been opened already). Once inside he called for Newbridge, who came a moment later

"Ah Newbridge, there you are"

"Your Grace?"

"Could you arrange for a large pitcher of lemonade and some of cook's freshly baked biscuits to be brought out on to the lawn, there are three of us, are there not Milly, and we are sat beneath the tree" he said looking down at the little girl as he spoke

"Yes Your Grace" Newbridge was looking at them together, smiling and thinking how good it was to see the master enjoying the company of his little niece

"Lemonade I like" said the little girl

"And you shall have some Milly, just as soon as Newbridge has arranged it"

Newbridge went off to see to his task, smiling to himself as he went and Richard bent down to gather up the little girl in his arms, and placing a kiss upon her little cheek, before striding back the way he had come, to wait for the refreshments.

They didn't have to wait long one of the maids came down the lawn carrying a tray, with a large jug full of lemonade and a small plate of biscuits, and placed them on the blanket beside Richard. He took the lace doily from the top of the jug and poured out some of the lemonade into three glasses—which they took sips of the cold refreshing drink, then they tucked into the biscuits—Milly ate three biscuits, devouring them one after the other. Once they were finished, Nanny Anson got up

"I think that we had better go now Your Grace, it's been a lovely afternoon"

"It has indeed Nanny, and we must do it again must we not Milly?" he said, looking at the little girl

"We must go now, as the children are to visit their grandmother" she said, apologetically

"Of course, mama will be wondering where they have got too"

"Carry, uncle Ritch" said little Millicent, holding up her arms once again

"This time, you are going to have to walk young lady, as I have to bring the tray back inside—I shall follow you though my sweet Milly" then looking up at Nanny "use the path and go into the drawing room through the open French doors, it will be quicker than going all the way round and through the house" Nanny looked relieved, with both the children for company

"Thank you Your Grace" Nanny bent down to fold the blanket, but Richard, moving the tray, lifted Becky and handed her to Nanny to hold, while he bent down and folded the blanket, before handing it to Nanny again. Although Milly took Nanny's hand, she was watching her uncle she didn't take her eyes from him as he picked up the tray with the empty receptacles on it

"You go on ahead with Nanny sweet thing, I shall follow, and we will all go and visit grandma together" he told her, this seemed to pacify her, and

193

she trotted along at Nanny's heels, but still throwing the odd glance to make sure that Richard was indeed following them

Richard followed them into the drawing room, and called for Newbridge to take the tray back to the kitchen—Alice was now seated next to Nanny Grey, both awake—that was a surprise, as Nanny Grey spent more time asleep than awake these days, Alice had already rung for tea—as soon as the tray had been taken from him, he took a seat on a stool near to his mother—though it took no time at all for Milly to scrabble back onto his knee. Alice laughed at the little girl, and the way in which she adored Richard

"I believe that children like you Richard" she said smiling

"I believe this one does, don't you Milly" he said giving the little child a tickle—she giggled and squealed at him in delight

"Children suit you my dear" she proclaimed

"These are rather delightful are they not mama?" He asked

"And yours will be too, when you get round to it" oh no—not back to this again—at least Maria wasn't in attendance anymore

"I'm sure they will be mama" he replied trying to end this conversation before it started. Alice held out her arms to take the little girl, who was now trying to scrabble onto her grandmother's knee, once there, she wanted to play with Alice's necklace

"I see that she is as all women, susceptible to jewellery" Richard remarked smiling

"Then you had better save plenty of money my dearest, for you will have two adopted daughters to furnish" Alice said smiling and looking at her son as she did

"So I see, though hopefully they will have rich husbands that will do that for them" he answered smiling. The afternoon was a pleasant one, once

Milly had sat with his mother for a while, she went back to Richard, and climbed back on his knee, while Nanny Anson handed the baby to Alice. An hour later Nanny Anson stood up and stated that it was time to take the children back to the nursery, and after kisses and hugs all round, even Nanny Grey joined in this, Nanny Anson disappeared closing the door behind her. Richard decided that this was the time to speak to his mother, apart from Nanny Grey, who was falling asleep once again, there was no-one to interrupt their conversation

"Mama, I need to speak with you" he started

"Of course my dearest, what is it?"

"It's about Miss Penrose mama, I have fallen in love with her—and I have asked her to marry me" it had all come out—he had said it. Alice studied him under her fixed gaze, before simply saying

"I see" there was silence, he was trying to work out what she was thinking, but she gave nothing away, then after a few moments of thought she replied

"I have to say that I'm surprised, I had never considered her as a suitable wife for my son, but I know very little about her" Alice said steadily

"She is lovely mama, she has such a sweet nature, and she truly cares for me in return, I had always thought love to be a nonsense, but not anymore, since meeting Clara mama, I could never marry anyone else, I have never met a woman yet, who charms me more" he was looking for a flicker or sign of her thoughts

"Then we had better get to know this young lady better, hadn't we?" Alice held his gaze and she spoke slow and steady

"Yes mama, I know that you will love her as I do, if you were to meet her" now he spoke in anticipation

"We shall see—I will invite her and her mother to tea, perhaps tomorrow, if you have nothing else arranged?"

"Tomorrow would be perfect mama" he jumped to his feet, leaning over to kiss his mother's cheek "thank you mama".

Maria came down the stairs, she had intended making her way to the drawing room—she was feeling pleased with herself—if Richard thought that he could flout her for a vicar's daughter, then he was very mistaken—she had no intention of being pushed out for the likes of that little peasant. She had spoiled his little secret—Alice wouldn't stand for it—there was no doubt about that, and if he thought that she would he would soon learn differently. This damn child which she was carrying, she would be glad to be rid of it, she never wanted this to happen—but she had managed to convince everyone that it was Edward's child—although there had been talk and speculation in the beginning, but it seemed generally accepted now. Then there was Melvin, she would always think of him with a smile—tis true he had been the perfect lover, and the gifts he had bestowed on her, but he was a fool—he had been caught as a smuggler, and was soon due to hang—she would have to find someone else to replace him, she had even agreed to go away with him, until Richard had appeared on the scene. Why had Richard been so opposed to her, hadn't she done everything she could think of to entice him into her bed, even standing stark naked in front of him, and still that had not been enough—although, she was sure that she saw a spark of interest in his eyes, though he wouldn't admit it—they could have married and she would have done everything to make him happy—but instead he would have none of it, and then, as if to tantalise her, she caught him in a compromising situation with that chit. He would have to pay for that—she had meant it, by God had she meant it. She would rather see him die than see him with that Penrose girl, she had already decided what she would do if it came to that. She approached the door to the drawing room, and quietly lifted the latch, there was no-one around at the moment, so she stood still there in the passage, listening to the voices floating through to her where she stood. Richard, he was talking to Alice about the chit—he loved her, and she was to be invited to tea the following day—had Alice lost her mind—surely she wouldn't entertain this match for her son. She quietly closed the door once again, and returned to her room—she had to think of a plan to rid herself of them both—time to repay his treatment of her.

CHAPTER SEVENTEEN

(Alice's Revelation)

Richard awoke full of excitement—his mother had sent a note to Mrs Penrose, requesting that she and Clara join her for tea. She had written the note before dinner the previous evening and had one of the servants take it to the rectory. As yet, there had been no reply, though he supposed that Mrs Penrose would reply this morning.

After breakfast, he decided to go to his library, there were a few things which he needed to attend too, including a note which had arrived which he had instructed Newbridge to place on his desk. After seating himself at his desk, he broke the seal and read the note—it was from old Truscott, he had found a new estate manager for them, that was good news, the man, a Mr Mark Chandler, would be arriving on Monday next, to take up the position. Richard would have to prepare for his arrival, and although the obvious place to have him stay was the little cottage, standing empty on the estate, it had not been lived in for some time now, at least a couple of years, so it would probably need attention, which Melvin had already told him before he was arrested. So, he had better take a look at it and check it all out, before deciding, but first he would pen a letter to Truscott thanking him for his help. Once he had finished, he went out to the stables and had the groom saddle his horse, before taking a ride down to the village, and to the cottage in question. The cottage was a little stone building, it was one of two cottages, perched on a ledge, and cut into the hill, at the top of a small lane, the entrance to the lane was shielded by hedgerows on either side, making it difficult to find, clearly it had become very overgrown as the lane wasn't used very much of late. The lane ran parallel back along the brook, before reaching the end, where the brook turned abruptly and went off in a different direction—the two cottages were nestled in the dip, before the hills rose away steeply behind them. It was a pretty little place, though very solitary, the other cottage housed only by an old man who once worked on the land, but now too old and frail to do so anymore—he was the man, Richard realized, who his precious Clara had visited when she fell and hurt her ankle on the briars at the entrance, the day he arrived here. It was understandable then that Melvin Lincroft had used this place to house his smugglers bounty, it was the perfect hideaway. Richard dismounted and tethered his horse to a post, and walked through the little wooden gate, which was set in a little picket fence, once painted and quaint, but now uncared for and dilapidated, and up the path—there was what once had been a lovely flower garden either side of the path, though it was now no more than a wilderness. The old wooden door had a small wooden porch with a roof, giving shelter to any visitor calling at the cottage, though several of the roof slats were now rotted and half hanging out. Richard opened the latch, the door swung in, Richard stepped inside. The cottage was dark and damp and uninviting, and where the brambles had grown, they had covered the windows taking a great deal of the daylight with them, the damp and musty smell did nothing to alleviate the problems either, it was in quite a poor state, there was evidence of water having come through the roof, leaving walls with thick brown stains and the floorboards creaked and moved when Richard stood on them—a few were broken, so he had to pick his way carefully. When Melvin had been arrested and Drummond had told him that this cottage had been the hideaway for their contraband, Richard had thought that had been the reason for Melvin's opposition to offering the servants from the Bond Street house, a home for a while—now he could see that the place was in fact unliveable. So, this would have to be another repair to add to the already long list, except this one was now probably the most urgent of them all.

Richard made his way back up the lane, keeping his horse to a slow walk he didn't want any injuries today. He would have to decide where to house this new estate manager—the best thing for the time being, would probably be the Gate Lodge—he had hoped to avoid that, but there was little choice, he could have put him above the stables, there was several rooms there, two of which were stood empty, but they were built for the stable staff, not for his estate manager. He would go back to the house, and find the key to the Gate Lodge, he knew that would be suitable, on the proviso that he should move to the cottage as soon as it had been made habitable for him. He went to his library, and rang the bell pull, within a few moments Newbridge opened the door and entered

"Ah Newbridge, I need the key to the Gate Lodge, could you fetch it for me please?" Newbridge looked uncomfortable before saying

"I'm sorry Your Grace but I no longer have the key"

"What do you mean Newbridge, you keep all the spare keys in your office"

"Yes Your Grace, but if you remember, Mr Drummond came for it the other week, and I searched for it then, but it was never found" Newbridge looked to Richard now for an answer

"But where can it have gone, who would want that key Newbridge?" Richard asked carelessly

"I don't know Your Grace, but it definitely isn't with the others" he waited again

"Alright Newbridge, I shall have to take a ride into Truro, and speak to old Truscott, we need to get this sorted out as our new estate manager should be arriving on Monday, and at the moment, we have nowhere to put him" Richard was looking at the opened note in front of him "Thank you Newbridge, could you please inform my mother that I have gone out, it cannot be helped, tell her that I've gone to Truro to see Truscott on business and will be back as soon as possible"

"Yes Your Grace, I shall tell her straight away"

"Thank you Newbridge" with that Richard jumped up from his seat and went back to the stables—he reclaimed his horse, before setting out toward Truro.

The day was warm again, that was a blessing, he was disappointed that he had to go today of all days, but this matter needed sorting out immediately, he couldn't afford to wait. He arrived just over an hour later, it was lunchtime, so he went to the Wheat Sheaf, left his horse at the hostelry there and slipped inside the taproom for a large piece of freshly baked pie, and a glass of cider. Once done, he made his way down the high street, until he reached the offices of Truscott and Penn, where he climbed the steps and slipped inside. Mr Truscott saw him enter straight away and went to him

"What a lovely surprise Your Grace, come through, please" Richard followed the old man into a stuffy little room with a large desk that filled it. Mr Truscott sat down in his chair and pointed to the other chair for Richard—the walls were lined with books of all descriptions, which made the room even more stuffy and untidy, and his desk was piled high with papers all tied up with ribbons—Richard was surprised the old man could find anything in this state.

"Now Your Grace, how can I help you?" asked the little old man looking over the rim of his spectacles

"Mr Chandler—he is due to arrive on Monday, but I am a little concerned about where to house him temporarily until I can get the cottage done up for him—so, the ideal place has to be the Gate Lodge, just until the repairs are completed of course, but there seems to be no spare key to the Gate Lodge, or it seems to have disappeared."

"I see—perhaps I should inform you then that the Gate Lodge no longer belongs to your estate Your Grace, your father had it made over twelve months ago" said the old man

"I'm sorry—you misunderstand me—I am talking about the Gate Lodge at Penleigh Court, it is all part of the estate"

"As I say, it has been signed over to another owner, twelve months ago"

"Signed over, then who is this new owner?" Richard asked unbelievably

"It's Melvin Lincroft Your Grace" Richard was speechless, when he finally did speak he said

"For what reason was this transaction reached" Richard thought it must be through his father's gambling, there could be no other reason for it, he must have lost heavily, and therefore signed the Gate Lodge away, yet that didn't make sense, not with so much money in his coffers

"Your father never gave a reason, he just requested that I draw up the appropriate paperwork, which is what I did Your Grace"

"Melvin Lincroft was arrested as you know, he has been found guilty and he is awaiting his sentence, but we all know that the sentence will be hanging, is there no way that perhaps he could be persuaded to return the building to the estate now"

"I'm afraid not Your Grace, the Gate Lodge belongs to Mr Lincroft, he is entitled to pass it to whomever he chooses, there is nothing that anyone can do about it"

"Has Lincroft left a will?"

"I'm sorry Your Grace I'm not at liberty to disclose that, you do understand"

"What I understand is that my father must have lost his sanity—he has given away part of the estate, and chose not to tell his family, the property is now owned by a common offender, who is to hang for his deeds, and yet I have no jurisdiction to claim it back, that what should never have been given away in the first place—this is an outrage Truscott, and I want you to find out why my father should do such a preposterous thing"

"I'm sorry Your Grace, but it is all legally binding, and there is nothing that can be done about it now—everything depends on Mr Lincroft"

"Then I have no choice but to wait and see who he leaves it too"

"I'm afraid that's about the long and short of the matter—but I think that you should be prepared Your Grace, to give up any claim that you thought you had on the place—I'm sorry that this has happened, but I'm sure that your father did what he did for a very good reason"

"Perhaps he had lost his senses, or had you not considered that?"

"I wish I could say that was a consideration, but I cannot—your father was as sane as you or I, there is no doubt of that"

"Then there is little else to say—and now I have to find a temporary alternative home for Mr Chandler when he arrives"

"I'm really very sorry Your Grace I cannot be of more help to you"

Richard stood and gave a bow Mr Truscott did the same,

"Good day to you Truscott" Richard said

"Good day Your Grace"

Richard left the building deep in thought—why would his father have done this, and more to the point, what was he to do now?

Richard arrived back at Penleigh Court at just after five o clock in the afternoon—he had pondered every possible reason why his father would have done such a thing, giving away a part of his estate—it was unheard of. He had completely forgotten about Clara, this was the first time in a long time that his mind had been occupied totally elsewhere. As he rode up the drive, he noticed the carriage waiting at the entrance, of course, it was Clara and her mother, come to tea—how could he have forgotten that—he had wanted to get home before now, his mother would not be happy with him. He went round to the stables and handed the reins to the groom, before rushing back to the entrance and climbing the steps two at a time and striding to the drawing room. He stopped outside the door, to try and regain some calm, at present the anger was still bubbling up inside of him. He opened the door and stepped inside, Clara, as lovely as ever, sat straight and composed opposite his mother on the settee, Mrs Penrose by her side

"Richard, here you are at last, whatever kept you, had you forgotten that we have guests for tea?" his mother spoke very calm and with a smile, but he knew that underneath she was wasn't very happy with him

"I must apologise to you all, I'm afraid it was an urgent business matter which needed attention, and with no estate manager at this present time, I had no choice but to deal with the matter myself" Richard looked at Clara and smiled, she smiled back at him

"Yes, well you had better sit down and I shall call for a fresh pot of tea—I'm afraid we have had ours earlier" Alice was still angry with him, though he could see that she was relenting a little

"I'm sure there is no need to apologize, Your Grace, we understand that you are a busy man" Mrs Penrose spoke this time

"Thank you madam, you are very kind" Richard pulled Nanny Grey's usual chair round and took a seat—Alice pulled the bell pull and ordered another pot of tea

"So, tell me, all that I have missed in my absence" Richard said on a lighter note

"I have been telling Miss Penrose that you have lived in London for the past three years and that for two of those, you have been travelling Europe" Alice said, looking him straight in the eye

"It must have been lovely to be able to travel, all the sights there are to be seen, or so I've been led to understand—I should love to travel myself, but unfortunately, I have never had the chance to do so" Clara spoke now, her voice like a bell, tinkling sweet and soft, while her mother sat next to her, colour rising in her cheeks—he knew that she felt guilty that she could not give her daughter these luxuries

"Indeed I have been very fortunate, I had no intention of being away from home for so long, but there seemed so much to see and do, that I extended my stay" he said, looking straight at Clara, though he wasn't going to disclose that Druscilla Maltby had been instrumental in keeping him away so long. He was looking at those lovely pink enticing lips, and thinking that one thousand Druscilla's would not make up for one Clara, however pleasant the time he had shared with her—he had missed his chance to take Clara for a walk in the gardens, to hold her in his arms, and to kiss those enchanting lips, that would have to wait for another time—he felt a little disappointed and frustrated at the thought

"You must have met many interesting people too" said Clara—dear Clara, she was still unsure of him

"There were a few interesting people, but no more than anywhere else" Alice shot him a glance and Clara was watching him closely

"I suppose that you find yourself extremely busy, now that you have returned to your estate, it must be difficult to enjoy your time here the same?" this time Mrs Penrose asked the question

"There is plenty to occupy me now of course, but I am quite content to enjoy the country life—indeed, I look forward to being able to perhaps hold a ball, though that won't be for a while, as the house is still in mourning—but the country has certain charms" his eyes strayed to Clara as he said this—he would be happy anywhere that she was

"I am very glad to hear it Your Grace" at that moment the tea arrived and fresh cups and saucers for everyone—Alice poured the tea and Richard handed it around before seating himself back down with his own cup

"Tell me Mrs Penrose, have you considered giving your daughter a season?" Alice had asked

"Considered it yes, but unfortunately that won't be possible" she replied, once again lowering her head, colour spreading through her cheeks

"I see, what a pity, I feel that she would do very well were she introduced in town"

"Thank you Your Grace, it is very kind of you to say so" said Mrs Penrose, proud of her lovely daughter

"Well I see no reason for Miss Penrose to feel cheated, because she has had no season in town—she is not in need of being paraded in front of all the young bucks, just to find a husband, I'm sure that she is lovely enough and quite able to find a suitable match, without all that" Richard couldn't help himself—Alice shot him another of her looks, Ada Penrose smiled at him, thankful for his kind words, and Clara sat, her eyes fixed on his face, and a smile touching her lips—she loved him so much, she felt she would burst

"Well, I think that it's time that Clara and I take our leave, my husband will be wondering what has kept us for so long" Mrs Penrose directed this to Alice

"You must blame my son for his tardiness" Alice said quickly

"Thank you for inviting us to tea Your Grace, it has been a most pleasant afternoon, both Clara and I have enjoyed it immensely" said Ada Penrose

"It was my pleasure—to be able to become better acquainted with both yourself and your daughter—I hope that our paths will cross again soon"

Richard rose to his feet—then he went to hold his hand out to first Mrs Penrose and then Clara, helping them both to their feet. He placed a whisper kiss on Ada Penrose's hand, before placing a firm and elongated kiss on Clara's fingers, gently stroking her palm with his thumb, and looking into her eyes and holding her gaze all the time. Alice stayed where she was, but inclined her head, the two ladies bobbed curtsey's, before Richard saw them to their carriage. He helped them step up inside, before returning to the steps, and watching as their carriage rattled away down the drive, then returning into the house. He strode back to the drawing room, he needed to speak with his mother while she was still alone—he had no intention of discussing his father's lunacy in front of anyone else.

As he entered the drawing room again, Alice looked up at him straight away

"So, what kept you? I invited the Penrose's for tea, on behalf of you, and you desert me" Alice was still angry with him

"I'm sorry mama, I would never have let you down deliberately, and I was eager to see my dear Clara" Richard replied

"So, what business kept you away so long?" Richard seated himself next to his mother once again before telling her about his new discovery

"Our new estate manager is to arrive on Monday, and we have nowhere to house him"

"Why ever not, surely he will go into the cottage which has been stood empty for the last few years" she suggested

"That was my first thought too, but I'm afraid it desperately needs attention before anyone can live there"

"Then I suppose you will have to put him in the Gate Lodge, only temporary mind, but just while the work on his cottage is being completed"

"But that's where we have a problem mama, I couldn't find the spare keys to the Gate Lodge, and after Newbridge confirmed that they have been missing for a while, I thought that I should go to Truro and speak to Truscott about it, only to be told that my father must have lost his mind—he only made the Gate Lodge over to Lincroft, so it is no longer part of this estate" his mother's face showed an expression of horror

"That surely can't be" she said, her face growing paler

"I'm afraid it's true—and there is nothing that we are able to do about it"

"This is not to be endured—your father could not do this to us surely, I know that he had a great liking for Lincroft, but that is no reason to give him part of this estate—my boy's inheritance"

"Nevertheless, that's what he has done—but more to the point, once he hangs, who will the new owner be?" Alice put her hands to her cheeks

"He must have found out" she said, faraway, talking to herself as much as him

"Found out what mama?" asked Richard, now intrigued

"Melvin Lincroft was your father's bastard—he was born to Esther Lincroft's sister Henrietta Sterling, she had been staying at the Lincroft's for a while, then one day she was gone—it was before you were born I had only just given birth to Edward at the time, your father had a visit from Lincroft, he came to the house one night while we were at dinner, there was a terrible row, we all thought that it was some estate business, your father was shouting and raving, like I had never seen him before, but I became suspicious as this started to happen often—one night, I stood by the library door and listened, I know that I shouldn't have done that, but I was eager to know what it was all about, I had never witnessed your father's temper so bad as it was after Lincroft's evening visits, so I opened the door a crack and listened hard—Lincroft accused your father of having raped his wife's sister, and that she was with child, I was frozen to the spot, while your father ranted and raved, I tried to come to terms with what had passed between them, yet in the whole of the conversation which took place, your father didn't once deny his part in the affair—I knew then, Lincroft would never have lied, he and your father were as close as a Duke could be to his estate manager, and Lincroft was such a sweet, unobtrusive old man, but after this, there had always been a rift which had never healed. I learnt later that the girl had been pregnant, and died giving birth to her son, the Lincroft's took the child as their own, though her parents paid for an education for him and he spent many years living with them, but he was always led to believe that the Lincroft's were his real parents. I believe that your father was coerced into paying for his sins, by taking care of the Lincroft's well until they died, in return for them keeping his evil little secret, and afterward, well, I can only assume that old Lincroft told him about his real parentage before he died. Once Melvin took up the post of estate manager, and helped your father with his more underhand dealings, your father became attached to the man, that's when he was moved into the Gate Lodge, where your father left all his dealings in Melvin's hands, I believe that he told your father that he knew his secret. That can be the only reason he would have done what he did—and now, who will get the Gate Lodge, once he is gone, your guess is as good as mine—but it frightens me Richard, no good can come of all this, it is nothing less than a web of evil and I fear what is to become of us all" Alice had broken off suddenly, then she bowed her head, watching her bony fingers twist and turn round her lace handkerchief.

Richard sat speechless his father had raped a girl, and left her to give birth to his child, in which she lost her life. He was shocked and outraged at his father's transgressions—he knew that his father was less than scrupulous in his dealings, but this was horrific, and his treatment of his own mother, his dear sweet mother, the torture that he had put her through, how could he have done such a thing—she had a small child of her own, and after all this he had gone back to her bed, where eventually he had been conceived, there could be no doubt that he was never conceived in love, and not even in happiness. His own conception had been little more than rape. It was so difficult to take it all in. He had met less than savoury characters in his life, but his own father, he was the worst of any of them. He may have been known as a tyrant, but that was nothing compared with his evil behaviour.

"How could you have stayed true to him mama, how could you have carried on as though nothing had happened, allowed him to come to your bed or even been associated in any way?"

"What could I do? He would have killed me had I gone against him—and worst of all, I believed that I loved him—I had married him for love, I know that is very difficult for you to believe—once he was a dashing, gallant man, all the young ladies were seeking his favours—he was the handsomest man I had ever had the fortune to meet, and he had eyes for no-one but me, or so I thought then" she was talking, but her mind was faraway, back to her courting days "I knew that I had a very favourable dowry, but I truly believed that he cared for me as I did for him

"How did things become so bad mama?"

"Soon after our marriage, I found out that he was visiting his mistress of that time, it had almost broken my heart as I believed that our marriage was a good one, and this was the proof that so soon into our marriage, he didn't feel the same way for me. At first I tried everything I knew to regain his favour, but as time went on, he spent more time out, and less time at home, we became like strangers, he would only share my bed in order to gain a son and heir, the minute that I was with child, he no longer showed me any interest, let alone anything more. Once Edward was born, he did come to see me several times, and he bought me a diamond necklace, to show his appreciation, I thought that perhaps we could start again then, and for a while, it seemed that way, until the visits with old Lincroft— each time he visited, the next few days were awful, he threw things at Newbridge and at the maids, he once threw my maid to the floor, just because she didn't leave my bed chamber when he entered. I knew that something was terribly wrong, yet he would talk to me of none of it—all I knew, I found out for myself. After you were born, I was relieved—I had given him two sons, and he was as happy as anyone could expect at that time, he bought me more diamonds, earrings this time, but soon after he went his own way, my job was done, my only duties were to play hostess, when he threw balls and dinners, otherwise, he ignored me. He even brought his mistresses into this house, when you were still very small—he had broken my heart, eventually I could stand no more—certainly not to be civil to his women coming and going freely, yet he expected me to dance to their tune—it was unbearable, they had the run of this house, and I was treated as less than a servant, I, the Duchess of Warren, but he was my husband, and I had to get on with it. That's when I chose to move to the East wing—I should not have to bear it any longer, and Nanny Grey, who was getting too old and frail by then, came with me, and Gracie, who I had shortly before taken on as my maid, agreed to come with us and take care of the two of us. Your father was angry at first, and he had threatened to throw me out, I was neither use nor ornament was his exact words, but eventually he agreed that I could live where I chose, and Nanny Grey could be my companion, with Gracie to care for us, at least it gave him a free reign to do as he pleased, though he had by then found a new mistress and had installed her in her house in Truro, he spent most of his time there with her, gambling, drinking, and parties—and when he returned home, he was master of his own domain—your brother suffered his torment, then there was the marriage, he found Maria and had plans for her as a mistress, but first he had to install her here in this house, so Edward was ordered to marry her, which he did, but by all accounts, Maria would have none of his nonsense, and when they failed to produce a son and heir, your father turned against them both. That Maria didn't give him his pleasure, was no real misfortune for him, he had his mistress in Truro, to fulfil his needs, though your father has always preferred variety, certainly in his women. After Edward was found dead, things became frightening, your father was forever in Truro, and Melvin Lincroft had the run of this place, when I wrote to you asking you to come home, it was because I was afraid what might happen next, your father was happy for Melvin to carry on like nothing had happened, but Melvin wanted everything, he was your father's son in that much, he wanted what was rightfully yours, and he would have easily taken it from you with your father's consent, I feared that he would not stop at murder to get his own way—I couldn't allow that to happen, that's why I was desperate for you to return home, to take up your rightful place and position here. I expect your father was less happy at your return—that is really all there is to know my darling," The tears were rolling down her cheeks and she dabbed at them with her handkerchief, then she got up and kissed her son, before leaving the drawing room without another word.

Richard went to the library, poured himself a large brandy and seated himself at his desk. There was just too much to take in, he knew that there had to be more to all this, yet he would never have guessed, in his wildest dreams, just how bad things had been. He remembered, when he and Edward were but children, the young ladies who stayed at the house from time to time, and one in particular who's face was plastered with powder and paint, and he had thought then, and even remarked on one occasion to his brother, that the girl would look much better without destroying her looks so, and Edward had agreed—though they had never known that the girls were there for his father's benefit, and his poor mother, she had been hurt and humiliated, having to accept them and treat them like family—how could she have born that, even for a day. It was little wonder that she had retired to the East wing it was her only way of escape. And Melvin Lincroft—his father's son, after having raped his mother, perhaps Melvin should have been pitied—little wonder that he had been given a cold reception, when he arrived, maybe Melvin thought that had he not returned to Cornwall, he would take on the estate—with his own father's blessing, though he could never have taken his father's title—he shivered, maybe that's why Edward had been murdered, he had always been a thorn in his father's side, he was too much like his mother, who his father evidently held in nothing less than contempt. So many things were clearer now, if Melvin murdered his brother Edward so that he could take over the estate, then maybe he killed his father too—Richard's mind went back to the day of his father's death, Melvin Lincroft had been next to his father, loading his gun for him, he couldn't possibly have killed him, he was far too close. But Richard felt that foreboding feeling overtaking him again, there was more to all this than he had at first thought—he could never have foreseen or even guessed at the revelations of today. Richard poured himself another brandy and tossed it down his throat before going to his room to prepare himself for dinner.

CHAPTER EIGHTEEN

(Mark Chandler arrives)

Monday morning descended, and with it a change in the weather. Although still very warm, thundery outbursts pelted on the ground and beat off again. Richard had hoped for at least a dry day, as he had planned to take Mark Chandler out around the estate on his arrival. Though the cottage had still not been touched, that would be Mr Chandler's first project, it had been agreed that he would be given a room in the house, there were several in the servants quarters, and although he would eat with the family, it seemed the best solution for the time being.

Maria was well and truly keeping out of the way, in fact, she was rarely seen—even Richard wasn't sure where she might be hiding, though he refrained from mentioning it to anyone, as he had no intention of facing any more battles with her for the present—his mother had returned to her normal self, yet Richard wanted to reach out to her, every time he saw her, as it brought back the terrible memories of what she had told him about her life with his father, and each time he thought about it his anger would rise anew.

Richard ate his breakfast alone, that was becoming quite a habit these days, but with so much on his mind, perhaps it was for the best. Although nearly eight thirty, the room was almost dark—the rain, beating against the window pane, with such a force it almost broke the glass. Once he had finished, he took an umbrella from the hall stand, and slipped out of the side door, and across the yard to the estate office—he wanted to check that everything was in order, and that the ledgers were all straight and up to date—if the rain didn't stop, he wouldn't venture around the estate today, but they could go through the ledgers first, so he would have everything ready for Mr Chandler's arrival. Once he had everything prepared, he ventured back out into the rain, and back to the house.

He had planned to go to his library, and wait for his new estate manager to arrive, but his mother was just on her way to the drawing room, with Maria not far behind

"Ah Richard, before the estate manager arrives, could I have a quick word with you please?"

"If you wish mama, I'm all ears" he replied noticing Maria over her shoulder—now she was showing interest too

"You are certain that Mr Chandler is not married with a family, we have agreed that he should have a room here for the time being, but have you considered that if he were married, we would need to reconsider"

"So, a new estate manager is expected—then you have written the old one off already" this time Maria asked the question

"Melvin Lincroft has been found guilty of smuggling, I think there is little chance that he will be freed any time soon—and the estate will not run itself" he replied curtly

"Clearly—so who is to be the new estate manager now?" she asked

"Mr Chandler, who will be arriving shortly" Richard replied flatly, then looking to his mother

"I am quite certain mama, that Truscott would have mentioned it, had he been a married man"

"I do hope that you are right"

"I'm certain of it mama—you need not worry about things like that" he said, trying to set her mind at rest. Just at that moment a knock came on the door—Newbridge strode across the hall to answer it, Richard turned to his mother and his sister in law

"If you ladies will excuse me" and he went off in the direction of the entrance hall.

Newbridge showed a very wet and sodden young man into the hall—taking his overcoat, and shaking the raindrops from it before hanging it on the stand, he then took Mark Chandler's hat and gloves and placed them on the hall table, before Richard moved forward

"Thank you Newbridge" then turning to the young man in front of him "Mr Chandler I believe, I fear that you have had a very wet and miserable journey this morning"

"I'm afraid so, I had hoped to arrive sooner, but the weather has slowed me considerably Your Grace"

"You had better come inside" Richard turned and led the young man into his library, where he closed the door and poured two glasses of brandy from the decanter sat there

"Please, take a seat" Richard cast his hand in the direction of the chair, which he had pulled up in readiness

"Thank you Your Grace"

"Now, I had planned to take you out on a ride around the estate this morning, but due to the filthy weather, I think we shall leave that for another time—finish your brandy, and then we will go to the estate office, so that you can inspect the ledgers, and we can discuss the most urgent requirements there"

"Good, I am eager to get started" he replied

"Splendid, I believe that we shall get along fine" Richard felt a real infinity with this man. He liked him from the moment that he saw him, there was something about his manner, so open and amicable. Mark Chandler was a young man, of a similar age to himself, he had dark brown hair, and eyes that matched. He was small of stature, with delicate features, although these were partially hidden behind his dark moustache and beard. Though not as handsome as Richard, he was certainly not unattractive and when he smiled his even white teeth seemed to stand out and shine through his facial hair. Richard immediately felt comfortable with this gentleman, indeed, had they been young bucks together in London they could have been good friends, Richard hoped that this arrangement would work out well for both of them. He waited until Mr Chandler had finished his brandy, then he stood up

"Shall we go?" he asked

"Indeed—lead the way Your Grace"

"We have a bit of a problem at the moment, there is a cottage for you eventually, but it is in need of rather a great deal of repair, which in fact will be your first major project—once this damned rain stops, we will have a ride over, and we can assess the cost then I shall leave it to you to have the repairs undertaken. But in the meantime, we thought that you would be a little more comfortable in one of the attic rooms here, and you will of course take your meals with us until you are settled"

"I'm very grateful to you My Lord I have no wish to put you to any trouble"

"It's no trouble at all—in fact, I shall be glad of the company, what with my mother and sister in law, I tend to be lacking in male companionship" Richard was being honest, he missed his companions in town, and this man would give him a little relief from the females under his roof

"Thank you—I'm most grateful My Lord. My trunk will follow I'm afraid, I have managed to hire a carrier to deliver it, but it won't be here until tomorrow"

"Then I shall instruct Newbridge to see that it is taken to your room, once it arrives."

Richard led Mr Chandler to the side door and through to the courtyard— the rain had slowed down significantly, though it was still enough to soak them to the skin, were they to go out without an umbrella. Richard took Mark Chandler to the estate office, and they spent the morning going through ledgers, before taking their lunch with the ladies in the dining room. Richard introduced his mother and Maria, who had joined them, to their new estate manager, although he noticed that Maria was very quiet, he could see her throwing glances across the table at the new man—did she now have designs on him too?

Once lunch was over, and the rain had stopped, Richard suggested that they should perhaps go down to the village and inspect the cottage—Mark Chandler, eager to see his future home, had agreed whole heartedly. So, they went to the stables, where Richard ordered the groom to saddle two horses, before they rode down the hill to the village. They reached West Lane, but one of the first jobs would have to be taking care of the brambles which were infringing the opening to the track—if they were not cut back very soon, the lane would not be accessible at all.

"As you can see Chandler, this will have to be dealt with immediately, perhaps you could get two of the men to start work here tomorrow morning, and get this all cleared"

"I shall get onto it this afternoon My Lord" They walked their horses carefully up the lane until they reached the cottages, again there was work enough here to keep his workers busy for a month or more, without starting on the cottage itself

"As you can see, everything is very much run down and out of hand, and in desperate need of attention, but once the work has been carried out, I think that you will find the cottage sufficient to your needs"

"I'm sure I shall My Lord, does anyone live next door?" they both glanced over to the adjoining cottage, with its dingy windows, and dirty curtains, and the paint nearly worn completely from the front door, it could be almost as dilapidated as the empty one

"There is an old gentleman who lives next door, Mr Hogan used to work on the estate for my father, but he has now retired—his cottage also needs attention, as you see, so perhaps you could look to doing the repairs for his cottage also—I shall speak to my mother, and see if we can't get some of the décor and soft furnishings replaced for him, as he is too old to be able to care himself"

"That would make good sense, as they are adjoining—I should be grateful if you would introduce me to your men My Lord, perhaps when we have finished here, then I shall get them started first thing tomorrow morning"

"Very well, I shall call them together and make the introductions, and then I shall leave it in your capable hands" Richard felt sure that this would be the case, the man was eager to get started and to get on with the work needing so much attention—he really felt that he could trust this young man, Truscott had chosen well.

They spent the next hour trawling the rooms of the cottage, with Mr Chandler logging all the repairs required, and in what order they would need to be attended—he was certainly very efficient. Once they had finished, Richard thought that they should call on old Mr Hogan, to warn him of the work which was imminent. They left the cottage closing the door behind them, they were pleased to be outside once again, as the dark and damp of the cottage seemed to seep into their very bones, and having to watch every step, for fear of falling through the wooden boards underfoot. Instead of following down the path to the gate, they used the little pathway, which linked the two cottages and rapped at Mr Hogan's front door, there was a slow shuffling noise from inside, before the door was thrown open, and Mr Hogan stood before them, he looked as if he had been sleeping and his clothes were old, and in tatters, and he walked leant over his walking stick, he eyed the two gentlemen stood on his doorstep, he knew neither of them, though one he had seen on a previous occasion, or at least he thought that he had, only the other day the man had visited next door, and he had thought to ask Miss Penrose, when she had visited him, who it could be and what he was doing in the lost and forgotten cottage, but it clean went out of his head—he would ask them to introduce themselves, after all, he didn't get many visitors, and the only one he saw next door as a rule was that one he didn't like—who ruled the Duke's estates with no respect for his tenants. He wasn't sure what two young gentlemen wanted with him, he was no longer able to do very much at all

"What is it you want" the old gentleman asked looking from one to the other of the gentlemen before him

"Mr Hogan, may we come in?" Richard asked

"I don't allow strangers into my home" the old man replied

"It's alright Mr Hogan, I am the Duke of Warren, and this is my new estate manager, Mr Chandler—we would like a word with you if we may" Richard looked to Mark Chandler, as if for support

"The Duke you say, I heard that the old one had an accident and died— and good riddance too I say, he was a devil and that's for sure—are you the same as him, cause if you are, you can leave right now?" the old man certainly believed in speaking his mind

"So, you did not like my father?" Richard asked smiling

"I did not, nor did anyone around here—you ask any of them, they will tell you, and all those comings and goings in the middle of the night, devil's work I tell you—what man with nothing to hide does that, ah? I thought that things like that had all stopped, haven't had any of those goings on for two month or more—and now you want to poke about here all over again" Richard felt only sorrow for this old chap—no doubt he had been privy to all the underhand dealings going on, and if his cottage was anything to go by, something should have been done a long time ago

"Perhaps if you would just allow us to come inside for a few moments, we could sort this all out with you Mr Hogan" Richard said gently. He stood watching the old man, still looking from one to the other of them, warily deciding whether or not he should allow them into his home

"Well" he said still very wary of them "I suppose that you had better come in then" slowly turning backwards, allowing them entry into his small dingy little living room. Closing the door behind them, he slowly hobbled across the room to take up his chair beside the small fireplace, before taking his stick and pointing at an old and worn settee under the window

"You best sit down then"

"Thank you" said Richard perching himself on the edge of the settee, his associate following suit. Richard's eyes wandered round the room—it was dark and dingy, though not as bad as the cottage next door, the furnishings were old and worn, they should have been thrown out years ago, there were also several holes in the curtains, and the furniture was old, what little there was—in the centre was a very basic wooden table, with two chairs tucked beneath, and there was the old wooden armchair, with dirty cushions, which was clearly Mr Hogan's favourite chair as he had made his way directly to it, after closing the door, then there was the settee—that had once been quite a luxurious piece of furniture, but age had left it worn and threadbare, and as Richard and Mark seated themselves on to the seat, the dust puffed out like a puff of smoke from the fire, causing a tickle in Richard's throat, making him cough and splutter. Mr Hogan never took his eye from the gentleman for a single second, he was wary to say the least, and maybe a little frightened what they had come to say to him, especially after his father had treated this poor old man so badly. Once Richard had regained his composure, he looked at the old man and spoke clearly

"I am Richard Penleigh as I have said, Duke of Warren, and this is my estate manager, Mr Chandler—now Mr Chandler is going to be taking care of getting work done to your cottage and the one next door—in fact, once the cottage next door has been completed, you will have a new neighbour, and Mr Chandler will be your neighbour"

"Work done, to my cottage, what work do you want to do here—it's not enough for you to mess with that place next door, now you want to turn me out of me own home—I worked hard for your father, for years, and what thanks did I get—he never left me in peace, day or night—and just when I thought that I had some peace and quiet, you come round with your fancy man here—trying to upset me all over again"

"My dear man, I have no intention of upsetting you, would you not like to have me sort your cottage out, give you a little more comfort in your old age, surely you would allow me that, after all the years you have worked to serve my family, see it as my turn to serve you" Richard would have to go carefully, he could see that this old man needed some gentle handling. Then he thought, Mr Hogan trusted Miss Penrose, perhaps he could mention her, it may help his cause, the old man said nothing, but he was studying Richard until he felt uncomfortable under the older ones gaze

"I believe that Miss Penrose comes to visit you on Friday's, she brings you some food and some company?"

"Miss Penrose, you mean Miss Clara, the vicar's girl, now there's a young lady who really cares, she's a good girl, better than the likes of you, she comes here, every week without fail, and she sits with me, and talks to me, and she brings me something to eat, but what's that to do with you?"

"I too know Miss Penrose, and you are right, she is a lovely young lady, I'm sure she would be very pleased to know that we were going to make you a little more comfortable"

"And how are you going to do that" he looked straight into Richards eyes, his own beady little old eyes, black and intense

"Well, we are going to tidy your garden, and look to make any repairs needed to this cottage, and we could give your house a lick of paint, the door certainly needs a coat of paint, and perhaps we could find you a new rug for your floor, and some curtains, these are looking a little old, are they not, some new ones would be better for the winter, they would keep you warmer, Mr Chandler here will do anything he can to make things better for you, but perhaps you have ideas that would make things better for you yourself? If you have, I'm sure Mr Chandler would love to hear them" Richard so wanted to help make this man's life a little better, but old people get set in their ways, and are very reluctant to accept help. His father had obviously shown no concern for his old retired workers—he would have probably moved the old man into the workhouse, if he had dared. The old man was now thinking over what he had suggested, there was silence for what seemed a long time, before he looked up and said

"I suppose that my old bones could do with a bit more warmth in the winter—and there are a few things which I just can't do anymore" Richard cut in quickly before he had chance to change his mind

"Splendid, then we shall do our best to see that you are better taken care of from now on—and if there is anything which you want, just let Mr Chandler know, you will be seeing a good deal more of him from now on" Mark Chandler smiled at the old man

"Indeed, I shall pop in and see you again shortly, after all, we shall soon be neighbours, I shall need your advice, you have worked on the estate for so many years, I'm sure you could give me some ideas which will be useful"

"Well, I suppose that if I could help, then it will be alright" the old man said slowly

"Good, and now we will leave you in peace, if you need anything Mr Hogan, just speak to Mr Chandler, and he will do whatever he can for you" with that Richard stood up, followed by Mark Chandler, before saying

"Good afternoon Mr Hogan, it's been a pleasure to meet you" Richard said, bowing his head, the old man was struggling to stand up, Richard felt sorry for the old chap

"Please don't get up, we can see ourselves out"

"Right you are—you're more of a gentleman than that other devil aren't you?" he said, comparing him to his tyrannical father. Richard smiled as they left the cottage, latching the door behind them. Once away up the lane, Richard turned to Mr Chandler

"I'm afraid my father was not well liked, I think that you will find this man's sentiments concurred throughout the tenants—perhaps I should apologize now, for his behaviour"

"I'm sure there is no reason to apologize my Lord, what is done is done, but you seem to have the situation in hand, I'm sure the tenants will soon recognize your concern for their welfare"

"Yes, well I hope so" said Richard, he certainly didn't want to be cast in the same mould as his father, especially after learning the things that he had

"May I ask you something Your Grace?" Mark asked his master

"Certainly, is there something bothering you?"

"Not really bothering me, I had heard of the Dukes death, which was only a short time ago, but I wondered about the former estate manager, did he leave when your father died Your Grace?"

"Ah Mr Lincroft—no, I'm afraid that he left only a couple of months ago, or rather, he was forced to leave"

"I see, perhaps then I should not ask anything further"

"Melvin Lincroft was arrested for smuggling, and has since been found guilty apparently he was the leader of the local smugglers gang down in Smugglers Cove, just outside the village, so we can only presume that he will hang"

"A smuggler, that is preposterous, and you were not aware that it was going on under your nose Your Grace?"

"No, I had no notion of his involvement at all, though I have only been back in Cornwall since December, when my brother Edward died—I moved to London soon after finishing at Eton, and I've spent two years travelling Europe, so coming home has been quite a shock to my system, as you can well imagine"

"I'm sure it was, but I hope to be able to take at least some of the burden from your shoulders from now on My Lord—I hope that will be of some use to you"

"Indeed, it will take a great deal of the worry off my shoulders—and once the cottages have been brought up to date, then there is a whole ledger of things requiring attention"

"Plenty to be going on with then My Lord, that's good, I enjoy being kept busy" said Mark Chandler smiling

"I think that you and I are going to get along very well Mr Chandler"

"I believe we shall Your Grace" they smiled at each other before digging their heels into their horse's flanks, urging them to a canter.

After returning to Penleigh Court, Richard decided it easier to take his new estate manager round to all his estate workers and introduce each one to him, before returning to the estate office to allow Mark Chandler to reorganise his staff to do the work required. He would draw up a work rota, with Richard's help, so that work could get underway the very next day. It was early into the evening before the two men left the office and went to their rooms to prepare for dinner, although Mr Chandler's trunk would not follow until the next day, so he would just have to wash and freshen up, for this evening.

Mark Chandler had been the third son of a businessman, his two brothers had both gone into the family business which amounted to a hardware shop in Truro, but Mark had shown an aptitude for figures and management, and as both his brothers were more than able to take over from their father, Mark had decided to look for a managerial post elsewhere. Once his training was complete, he had been taken on by a friend of his father who owned the hostelry in town, but the work there wasn't really what he had been seeking, it was more laborious work than he had anticipated, but he had worked hard there for ten years, until he saw this advertisement for estate manager's post, he had waited a long time for a post like this to arise, so when it did, he immediately applied to Truscott and Penn, and was given an interview—his training had finally paid off, he took all his paperwork with him, and even old Truscott had been impressed, he could see it on the old man's face, his little black beady eyes had gazed at him over the top of his glasses, and Mark had squirmed under his perusal, but he had obviously thought him a suitable candidate for the post, and within two days, had offered him the job. Mark had been delighted, now he would surely get a chance to prove his capability, and he wasn't going to let the Duke down—he had heard lots of stories, he had heard that the old Duke had been a tyrant, and his accident had been the talk of Truro, he remembered having seen the Duke on many occasions, such a proud and arrogant man, he was glad that he wasn't going to be working for him, and his eldest son, he had been such a fine man, totally different to the father, but also unfortunate enough to have died before his time. The new Duke though, he knew nothing of—although similar of age to himself, there had been little known of him, he lived in London, and it was reported that he was something of a fashionable rake, but that is all he had heard, but now here he was, at Penleigh Court, taking up the post which he had spent the first half of his life working for—he would show them all that he was the best estate manager that they could hope for, indeed, after meeting Richard Penleigh his concerns faded—for they were not only of an age, but they thought alike—he had learnt that in the first morning, so he could look forward to his post with encouragement and hope. Then he thought of his beloved Angela Moreton, she was such a beautiful young woman, how sad it was that she had been forced to work for that awful Mrs Flora Kirky, she was at present trying to find a husband for her daughter, but in his mind, the only way the poor girl would find a decent match would be without the mother to blight it all. She was cruel to her servants, and she had constantly boxed Angela's ears, sometimes she would have great black and blue bruises all up her arms, and even marks on her face and neck—Mark wanted to do something about it, but Angela pleaded that it was down to her stupidity, and she couldn't afford to lose her job there. He had desperately wanted to offer her marriage, but until he could find a job, which would pay enough money to keep a wife, he must keep his plans to himself—but now, not only had he found the very employment that he had been seeking, but there was a cottage with it, he had never hoped for that generosity, so, once the cottage was ready to move into, he would be able to ask Angela to be his wife, and he would no longer have to worry for her safety. Perhaps if he spoke with the Duke, he would be able to suggest some charity work that she could offer on the estate to the tenants, at least she would have something other to think about and that would be right up Angie's street. He felt suddenly excited by all his prospects coming realities—he would serve the Duke well.

Dinner was a quiet and intimate affair, although all four attendees had met for lunch, it had been for merely half hour, before the two gentlemen went back to work, but dinner was a different matter. They all assembled in the drawing room, to wait for Newbridge to let them know that dinner was served, at least this way Mark Chandler would have a chance to be introduced properly, before they ate.

"Ah, Mr Chandler, join us please" said Richard as Mark entered the room

"Thank you Your Grace" he said inclining his head, first to Richard and then the two ladies sat the other side

"I trust that your room is sufficient to your needs, though it is only temporary" Richard enquired

"Thank you Your Grace, it will be very comfortable, I'm sure"

"You remember my mother, The Dowager Duchess, and my sister in law Maria Penleigh" Mark moved forward and acknowledged each one in turn

"So Mr Chandler, have you come far?" Alice asked him with a smile

"No My Lady, not far at all, I was born and bred in Truro" he replied

"Indeed, and your father is?" she persisted

"Harold Chandler, of Chandler and Sons, the hardware store, My Lady" he replied

"Ah yes, though clearly you are not one of the sons in the business"

"No My Lady, I was more interested in taking up an estate post, and my father already had my two elder brothers in the business with him"

"I see, then I hope that you will enjoy your place here with us"

"I am very sure that I shall My Lady—I look forward to serving you well"

"Good. I see that you are not married Mr Chandler, have you no young lady at all?"

"Mother, don't embarrass Mr Chandler, I'm sure he is quite able to find himself a wife when he is good and ready" Richard said turning to his estate manager "She has probably had enough of encouraging me, that she has now turned her attention on you" both men smiled at each other amused

"But I have to admit My Lady, and I have been wondering, there is in fact, a young lady whom I intend to ask for her hand, although until the cottage is ready, it will have to wait, though I wondered if perhaps you could suggest some charity work or something that she could devote her time with locally once we are married of course" that was his chance to broach the subject and the Dowager Duchess would be more informed of these things than the Duke

"Well, that is good news Mr Chandler, but would the young lady as your wife, not devote her time to you? she asked

"Of course, but she is also keen to do something to help in the community, and I believe that you are a better judge than I, of things which would be of help here My Lady" he replied

"Well, I am little able to advise you these days, but perhaps you could suggest that your young lady go to the rectory and speak with Miss Penrose, I am sure she will be glad of some help in this parish" Alice turned her gaze to her son, as she mentioned Miss Penrose's name, Richard threw his mother a glance

"Thank you My Lady, I shall indeed do that"

As he finished speaking, the door opened and Newbridge stated that dinner was served, so they all followed him to the dining room. Once seated, Maria spoke for the first time, though she was still avoiding Richard at present, which he was grateful for

"So, Mr Chandler, you are hoping to marry" Richard thought this conversation had already been covered, but thought better of saying so

"I am hoping so, My Lady" he said

"I see, and where does your young lady live Mr Chandler?"

"She is living in Truro My Lady"

"And by whom is she employed currently?" Richard was becoming annoyed now, what had it got to do with Maria, he had seen her vengeful ways.

"I'm sure that is no business of ours Maria, Mr Chandler is eating here as our guest, not to answer personal questions" Richard couldn't help himself, not even at the chance of inducing her anger, she fixed her gaze on Richard, staring straight into his eyes without as much as smile on her lips, before looking back at Mr Chandler again

"You are right of course Richard, forgive me Mr Chandler, I had no intention of embarrassing you"

"That is quite alright My Lady—I take no offence" Mark Chandler looked directly at her and gave a warm smile, she in return, smiled back at him, and Richard noticed a deepening pink growing in her cheeks.

"I thought after dinner, we could perhaps go to my library, there are a few things that we still need to discuss Chandler, and I thought it more civil to do so over a brandy" said Richard

"That certainly sounds very civil to me too—I shall look forward to it"

Once dinner was finished, Newbridge brought in a good plate of cheese and a decanter of best port, and placed it on the table between the two gentlemen, Mark Chandler thought that he could very soon get used to this living. The ladies retired to the drawing room, and left the men alone. Once they had enjoyed their fill, Mark Chandler followed Richard to his library, where they both seated themselves, with the decanter of brandy on the desk, between them.

"I'm afraid Chandler, that you must forgive my sister in law, she has had quite a trying time with the death of her husband, and now, finding herself with child, which must have been conceived only just before Edward's death, I fear that so many shocks have all had their effect on her" Richard had to try and apologize for her, he didn't want her getting her claws into this estate manager too

"I understand, but you need have no fear on that score, I'm sure she meant no harm Your Grace"

"Please, I think that we should dispense with some of the formality, my name is Richard so I would prefer you use my name—and I shall call you Mark from now on, if that suits you" Richard said, feeling as if he had known the man for years already

"As you wish Richard" Mark felt a little awkward calling his master by his name, but he was sure that he would get used to it eventually

"Good. Now, I have some paperwork here, which I would be glad of your opinion on Mark, it is about Highcliffe Farm, I know that your priority will be to get the cottages sorted out first, but this has become a problem in the last couple of weeks, and your urgent attention would be much appreciated" Richard said, handing a sheaf of papers, tied up with green ribbon.

"Of course Richard, leave it to me, I shall go through it tonight—would it be possible to have the use of this room, for now?" Mark asked

"Certainly, I would prefer it if you did, but first, let's have another brandy before I am bound to join the ladies" said Richard smiling

"That sounds like a very good idea Richard—thank you"

Richard drank his brandy, then left Mark to deal with the paperwork alone—he went to the drawing room to join the ladies for a little while—his mother always expected it, and Nanny Grey would have joined them by now.

<hr/>

Richard sat himself on the settee in the drawing room, Maria sat quietly, saying very little while Nanny Grey was snoring, as usual and his dear mama was sat with her needlework in her lap. They talked of Mr Chandler, Alice thought him a very nice young man, and Maria didn't comment either way, Richard knew that he was going to bless the day he employed him. After a little while, Maria rose from her chair and declared that she was ready for bed—with that she left the room.

Maria's thoughts were on the young man, sat in the library, he was nothing like Richard, and he was definitely not as handsome, though he was very appealing in his way, his smile was delightful, but she thought him very amicable and friendly, and goodness knew that she could do with some of that of late. She crept as quietly as she could, to the library door and opened it slowly, trying not to make a noise—she stood in the doorway, looking at the young man, sat at Richard's desk, his head bent over the papers in his hand, he hadn't heard her open the door, she stood for a moment, watching him, she could do a lot worse.

"I hope that I'm not interrupting anything Mr Chandler" she spoke softly, Mark lifted his head with a start

"My Lady, I apologize, I didn't hear you come in" Mark tried to jump to his feet

"Please, Mr Chandler, Mark? There is no need to get up, I hadn't meant to disturb you" her voice so soft and smooth and enticing

"You were deep in thought" she pushed the door too with a click, before turning the key in the lock, unbeknown to her companion—after all, she wanted no interruption from the Duke

"You have not yet been here one whole day, and you let Richard bully you into working all evening—you are too enthusiastic sir" she said sweetly

"Not at all My Lady, I am happy to fill my time" he replied

"You shouldn't work so hard you know, Richard will not thank you for it. You are a very handsome young man, you should spend time with your young lady instead" she was so plausible and sweet

"That wouldn't be possible, even if I were not working, Angela only has a half day off a fortnight, on a Sunday, so it would not be possible to spend any more time with her"

"What a pity—such a handsome young man as yourself, must be very popular with the young ladies, I'm sure that there are many who would make you happy if you would let them—you shouldn't waste your time on one you only get to see once a fortnight" her words soft and low and enticing, she walked round the desk to where he was standing and perched on the edge of the desk, with him watching her every move

"Am I not right?" she whispered

"My Lady, there is only one lady who appeals to me" he replied, the colour rising in his cheeks, his eyes settling on the bump of her stomach. Maria gazed into his eyes, before reaching out and placing her hand around his cheek and stroking his beard with her thumb, then taking his hand and placing it on the roundness of her belly

"Then why does your young woman leave you alone for so long?" her voice was no more than a whisper—Mark had never found himself in a position such as this before—he wasn't sure what he should do now, but he left his hand placed upon her stomach—he had never had much to do with ladies as it was, he had never taken mistresses and it had taken him six months to approach his dear Angela, this behaviour was something new, and he wasn't sure what to do or say though he found her touch soothing and extremely pleasant, it was also stirring feelings deep within him that he had not experienced before, and he was becoming a little embarrassed about that too

"I—I don't know" he said simply, almost forgetting the question she had asked—Maria stood up, and moved closer to his chair, then as close as she could get to him before throwing her arms about his neck, and placing her lips on his—the kiss had started off as a whisper, but her lips parted, encouraging a deeper more passionate kiss the longer it went on. Her lips were indeed warm and inviting and he could not help but to taste them with his tongue, the way she was teaching him too, and enjoying the experience. His heart beat as it had never done before. He had of course kissed Angie, but only a gentle quick kiss, touching her lips with his, nothing like this. When she broke away from him, his face, what she could see of it, had turned scarlet—she was enjoying every minute of this, giving him such a warm exciting smile—the pleasure seemed to make him melt into her

"You see" she whispered "you did enjoy it didn't you?" she was watching him closely now "didn't you?" she whispered again to prompt him, he was in a trance he mumbled still staring into those bright blue sparkling eyes, like an ocean he could get lost in

"Yes" he hardly breathed

"I know you did, you should never deny yourself pleasure in life you know" she said and in a moment she had sat on his knee, thrown her arms around his neck and started kissing him again—she knew that she could take this man any time she wished, he was a novice, perhaps even a virgin, she would teach him, at least she would have a good time teaching him, now that her dear Melvin had gone, and Richard had blatantly shunned her advances, she would have to take what she could get, and she wasn't unhappy with Mark, he was proving to be a quick learner.

He had been nervous and found this a completely new experience, in fact, he was definitely not experienced in these matters, perhaps she was right, perhaps it would be better for both him and Angela, if he knew a little more before marriage, after all, this woman was with child, and he would never have thought her the right person to teach him, but she was more than willing and eager, he would have to fight her off to stop her now, and he didn't think that would do the baby any good, and it would certainly not do him any good either, besides, he didn't want to stop her now, she was making him feel senses and emotions that he'd never felt before, and that he never knew existed, perhaps he should go along with whatever it was she wanted of him, and explore the unknown, the feelings inside him were craving for more. She released her kiss, but still holding him close, she turned around on his knee and had him undo her buttons at the back of her gown—his fingers fumbled with them, they were so tiny all the way down her back, but he was eager to carry on—then she stood up and faced him, allowing her gown to fall around her feet—Mark didn't know where to look, he had never seen a woman like this before, he could never have imagined it either—next she slipped out of her chemise, the top of her body naked before him, her bump prominent now, encouraging him to kiss her naked body—she carried on, stepping out of her white lace bloomers, until she stood before him completely naked, then turning her attention on him, she relieved him of his clothing too, until like her he stood before her naked as well—she taught him how to make love to her, there on the floor of the library before finally, both seemingly happy and content, Maria pushed him away and stood up and started to dress, Mark having experienced human delights for the first time, had no desire for it to end, taking her in his arms and kissing her again and again and touching her body, as she had taught him to do—she had certainly made a man of him, and she couldn't be more happy, and in Richard's library too, that was the best part for her—he had blown his chance, though she could never forgive him for turning her away, she knew that Mark would be more than happy to carry on their liaison now, he had well and truly tasted the fruit, and he would definitely be eager for more—he had been a novice, just as she had surmised, and she had been his teacher, she had plenty more to teach him yet, and she fully intended to make the most of that.

"I must go now my dear Mark" she stuttered between kisses "I don't think Richard would be happy to find us thus"

"No, I should not like him to know" he said, realizing it for the first time

"You need not fear my darling, I shall tell no-one, after all, we wouldn't want to spoil our little relationship would we?" she whispered

"I'm so sorry My Lady, I should not of taken advantage of you—it was very wrong of me, it must never happen again, I promise you" Mark was suddenly horrified at the thought of what he had done, and worse still, at the pleasure which he had experienced from it—he could understand now why men took mistresses, but with a Lady like Lady Maria, no man would have need of anyone else

"On the contrary my darling, you and I are now officially lovers, I have no intention of ending that before it's started—there is much more for us both to experience and enjoy, and I will teach you everything—after all, this was your first time was it not?" she stated this more firmly. The colour flew to Mark's cheeks yet again, it had indeed been his first time ever, but he hadn't wanted this woman to know that

"But I love Angela, I'm sorry My Lady, there is no future for us" said Mark

"Really Mark, I don't need your love, your body is enough for me" she said smiling, then before he had chance to answer she said "But I must go now my darling, next time we will meet at my house, not far from here, it will have to be our secret of course, I don't think anyone here would understand, but you and I are now lovers, and I shall look forward to the next time when we can be together, I know that you enjoyed it as much as me, you cannot deny that you know, unlike you I am experienced in these things" then she went to him and threw her arms about his neck and kissed him hard on the lips

"A little reminder until we meet again—I shall let you know when we can meet, don't let me down sweet Mark, I should be very upset if you did, and when I get upset, I'm not a pleasant person, you understand" with that she walked to the door and opened it, but she turned and blew him a kiss before leaving and shutting the door behind her.

Mark stood still he couldn't work out what had just happened, or how he had just allowed it. Never in his wildest dreams would he ever have thought that he would have been seduced on his first night in his new job, by a Lady no less, and a very attractive one at that. He had never experienced that before, and he hadn't expected to learn that way either. He had always thought that he and his dear Angela would learn together, but he found Lady Maria impossible to refuse. In a way he was pleased that he had experienced it before his wedding night, as he would not have wanted his wife to think him a total novice, as this woman had. But she was expecting them to carry on being lovers—how could he do that, not now he had Angela, and if he did, would she still want him after he and Angela were married—that was unthinkable. He couldn't deny that he had found it most pleasurable, and now he knew why men took mistresses, and held so much store by them, but he had to find a way of breaking it off. He would have to meet her at least one more time, and then he would find a way to put a stop to it, he was still stunned that his first experience was with a women, fairly heavy with child—the whole incident made him feel strange, as if someone had taken over his body, and used it for some obscene purpose. He would meet Lady Maria, and experience their pleasure once more, and then he would find a way to let her down, without upsetting her too much—that was the last thing he wanted to do, and he wasn't going to risk his job for anything—he was happy to be here and he had waited for this chance for a very long time. He went to the sideboard, lifted the decanter and helped himself to another brandy, he needed something for the shock, then he tossed it back down his throat before blowing out the candle and closing the door behind him, and climbing the stairs to his room.

CHAPTER NINETEEN

(Maria's House)

S ummer was now at an end, Richard had blessed the day that he had met Mark, he was proving to be not only an exceptional estate manager, but a good friend and faithful servant. It was now the last days of September, and the cottages were almost finished, Richard had high hopes of seeing the roofing jobs and outside repairs, on the rest of the estate, complete before the winter set in.

Richard had become a regular visitor at the rectory—his relationship with Clara was developing to both their liking, and as for Mrs Penrose, she was almost sat with baited breath, waiting for Richard to request an interview with vicar Penrose, Richard too was hoping that another month and they could at least set plans in motion. His mother had invited Clara and her mother to Penleigh once more, and things had seemingly gone very well, this time Richard had made sure that he would be there to walk his lovely Clara through the gardens, and down the path leading to the cliffs below. Their passion for each other was growing rapidly, and although at times he had to fight to keep himself from seducing her, he would never do that to this young lady, she had high principles, and he would do whatever he had to do, to contain his love until they were married. He wanted to speak to vicar Penrose as much as Clara's mother waited in hopes, but there seemed little point until they could set the date.

Maria hadn't changed toward Richard at all—fortunately he didn't have to see much of her, but when he did, she could not offer him a civil word, so he chose to avoid her if possible, he had meant her no harm, but he had no desire to anger her further. Her two daughters though, they were a completely different matter, Richard had become a staple figure in their lives, even little Becky would put out her little plump arms to be held, and he would take them off for an hour, in the garden, or to the stables, or sometimes to see their grandmother and they would get spoiled with biscuits and lemonade, and other little treats. Becky was truly very different from her sister, she was as fair as Milly was dark, and definitely more like her mother than Edward. Both Richard and Alice were disappointed though, as Maria still had little time for her daughters, she visited the nursery on the odd occasion, but due to long absences, when no-one seemed to know where she had disappeared too, she was only seen around now and then, although she always appeared for dinner—her stomach had grown large and round and the midwife had been put on standby, the child should be born any day. Richard had called Maria in to his library one morning, as he had spoken with old Truscott, and it had been agreed that he was now in a position to offer her and her children a satisfactory monthly allowance, it wasn't a fortune, but more than enough to cover her dressmakers bill, and clothe the children and to pay for any little trinkets she desired. Richard had been shocked then, when she had turned to him and told him that he should keep his money, she would not be bought for such a pittance—he had thought to do her a kindness, not to insult her in any way, he could only think that she was still angry that he refused to make her his wife, and his Duchess—but that was one thing which he would never be able to offer her, so he ignored her words, and went ahead with his plans anyway—since that interview, she had said no more on the matter, but he felt sure that she was pleased to have the allowance, even though she would never admit to it.

Alice could see now, why her son was so enchanted by this young lady, she was fresh and young with an innocence which reminded her of herself at that age, she too had been young and innocent when she had first set eyes on Henry—she had believed that he would always love her, the way she fell in love with him, but that had ended almost before it began—soon after they got married, she had learned that her dreams would never come true, but she knew her son, he was different to his father, she watched him with Clara, and knew that he really truly loved the girl, and she truly loved him, it was written all over their faces—he could certainly do a lot worse for himself than Clara, and she would welcome the girl with open arms, if she could make her only living son as happy always, as he was now.

Maria wandered round her new home—this was all hers now, Melvin had been hung for his sins, but she smiled, thinking how Mr Penn had met her here, in this house, two weeks later and informed her that the Gate Lodge now belonged to her, she had stood rooted to the spot, this was indeed justice, she had been coming here ever since Melvin's arrest, to remove all the goods which remained in this house, she had even thought of this place as hers, she had entertained Mark here on numerous occasions, but just a week ago, she learnt that this was hers—Melvin had willed it to her and Richard had been cheated of part of his estate—it was all hers, if he had married her, then he could have gained it back—she still wanted him so badly that it hurt physically. She would give anything for the baby she was carrying to have been Richard's baby, she still looked at him with such longing, and dreams of what she could have had with him, if only he had agreed. This wretched baby was due, she just wanted it gone now—it was becoming cumbersome and she longed for it to be born, and join the girls in the nursery, then she could forget about it and try again to make Richard see how he could benefit from making her his wife. She had heard that he was becoming fond of that vicar's daughter, but she was nothing, little more than a servant, surely the Duke would have more sense than to cast her aside again, for the sake of a servant, a mealy mouthed little thing at that—she had high hopes of winning him round this time. There was Mark now of course, dear Mark, he was a very pleasant companion and he wouldn't hurt her she knew that, but he was only an interlude, he kept telling her that their relationship could not go on, but he kept coming back for more—he couldn't get enough of her, but as pleasant as it was, he had nothing to really offer her—not like Melvin, dear dear Melvin, he should have been more careful, he had been Henry's true son, and she would have settled for him, had she not met Richard—at least Melvin left her this house, dear sweet man, and she had cleared the place out and filled her trunk, before the authorities could steal his goods—they all belonged to her, and no-one, but no-one would have one penny of any of it—it was all for her, Melvin would have wanted her to have it all, after all, he loved her, really loved her, but for Richard she would have been so happy with Melvin. She would give Mark his freedom, he could marry the girl he always kept on about, with pleasure, but only in exchange for Richard, until she had Richard she would hold onto Mark, she needed someone— once this damned child was born, she would have her body back again, then she would do all she could to win Richard for herself—he had given her a small allowance, perhaps he could be convinced that she was worth much more, she would convince him, she had too—she would not accept second best, not for anyone—if he didn't, then she would see that he paid for his rejection of her, but it wouldn't come to that, she was sure of it.

Mark had settled in nicely—he fully enjoyed his work, he was happy to spend long days, and sometimes evenings, keeping himself busy with the cottages and also arranging for some of the very urgent requests from the tenants, the outside work had to be completed before the winter, and some of the jobs were taking longer than he had first expected. His master, Richard, Duke of Warren, he was a good man Mark liked and admired him very much. He would often come to see Mark and ask how things were coming along and he felt that they were friends rather than master and servant, and he was being paid more than he had ever earned before, once the cottage was ready, which as things went, would be by the end of the month, he would be able to ask his beloved Angela to become his wife. He longed to have her here with him, although, he would have to do something about Lady Maria. He had become quite fond of the woman, she was a beauty, there was no doubting that, but she was a lady, and he loved his dear Angie. He had told her that he would invite her over once the cottage was ready, to see her new home, then he would marry her and bring her home here—he couldn't wait for that, but before he could do that, he had to break things off with Maria, she had taught him so much that he had never known, and he felt confident now to teach his lovely Angie once they were wed. But each time he had gone to her, she would insist that they meet again and again, and he was not strong enough to refuse her, but he must be strong with her—after all, there was no way that he could carry on enjoying Maria at the same time as his wife—that was unthinkable, and he would never do that—he couldn't live with himself. He had also met Miss Penrose, the vicar's daughter, she was the one who the Dowager Duchess had suggested Angela should speak too about help in the parish, she was a pretty girl, and with such a sweet disposition, he felt sure that Angela and Miss Penrose would become firm friends. He had his suspicions that the Duke was very fond of Miss Penrose too, he had seen his face when her name was mentioned, and he had frequently seen his horse tethered outside the vicarage, and on one occasion, he had seen them out riding together—they certainly made a handsome couple, the way they looked at each other told him that they were close. Mark had certainly become content with his lot, even his family seemed to be happy for him, his mother certainly was, she was looking forward to him getting wed, he would be the first of all his brothers to do so, and his father had to admit that his learning had not all been for nothing—just because he wasn't in the family business didn't mean that he was a failure, as he had first been led to believe. So, he had started to think that he was the luckiest man alive, he had everything he wanted from life and more, nothing and no-one would dampen his spirits now.

Richard left Penleigh Court, he was headed for the rectory—in his pocket was a little black velvet box, and inside, lying on its cushion, a solitaire diamond ring. It had cost him an obscene amount of money, but nothing was too good for his wonderful Clara. He slipped his hand into his pocket and wrapped it against the soft plush lying there—he knew that she would be as happy as he was, and the time had come for him to go to vicar Penrose and request his daughters hand in marriage. He had been to a jeweller in Truro for the ring, but because he could not offer anything like the Duke had wanted for his betrothed, the jeweller had sent to London for the diamond, which the jeweller had set himself, when it arrived—Richard was delighted with the finished product, though he had paid dearly for it, but that was of no account for his future wife. He took a steady trot down through the village and arrived at the rectory, this time, he would request an interview with vicar Penrose, he would surprise his sweet Clara, she would be so happy. He tethered his horse, then rapped at the front door, Daisy opened the door to him

"Your Grace, I will inform Miss Clara that you are here" she said turning to go

"No, no Daisy, I would first request an interview with vicar Penrose, if you please, and I should be grateful if you would not let Miss Clara know that I am here at the moment" Richard wanted this to be such a surprise, Daisy stopped and turned back to Richard, before a wide grin crossed her face

"Of course You Grace, I shall inform the master you wish to see him immediately" she replied, there was a smile on her lips and a twinkle in her eye

"Thank you Daisy" he said smiling back. Daisy went off, but returned a minute or two later

"The vicar will see you now Your Grace"

"Thank you Daisy" he followed her to the vicar's study, vicar Penrose spent most of his time there, Daisy opened the door for him and Richard stepped inside

"Good afternoon Your Grace" the vicar rose from his chair, and walked around his desk to greet Richard

"Good afternoon vicar" he said with a bow

"Please, won't you sit down?" the vicar asked pointing to a green leather bound chair

"I would prefer to stand if you don't mind" Richard was now finding this more difficult than he had imagined, after all, he had to convince this man that he wanted his daughter, the most precious thing in his life, so with that in mind, he could hardly think straight. Vicar Penrose returned to his chair behind the desk and seated himself once again

"So, My Lord, how can I help you?"

"I have come to ask for the hand of your lovely daughter Clara in marriage sir, I have loved her since the first time I set eyes on her, and I believe that she feels the same about me. I would like to assure you sir, that I shall love and cherish her as she deserves, she will want for nothing, of that you can be sure. She will of course inherit the title of Duchess of Warren, and I can promise you that I shall feel it my personal duty to care for her with my life sir, so I have come for your permission to ask her to marry me" he had finished, his nerves were getting the better of him, he hadn't contemplated that, but everything rested on this man's reply, his whole life and happiness, so it was vital to get this right. Vicar Penrose never spoke for a moment, which was a little disconcerting, then he cleared his throat before saying

"So you wish to marry Clara, and she wishes to marry you?" It was a question, it needed a reply

"I believe so sir, we love each other very much sir" Richard had started gabbling now, he wasn't normally prone to doing that

"I see, well, you have my permission and my blessing young man. There is also the matter of a dowry of course, I can tell you that although we are not wealthy, we have managed to set a sum aside for a dowry for our daughter, it is not a fortune, by any means, but twenty thousand pounds is the sum which I have in mind Your Grace" Richard was elated, at last he was to marry the girl that he loved, and as a bonus, there would be a dowry, what more could he ask—he would make certain that she would never have to experience any part of what his mother had been through, and even if she failed to provide him a son and heir, he would never blame her, he loved her and that's all that mattered now.

"Thank you sir, that is indeed a surprise, but I would have chosen Clara without a dowry, though the money will help to make things a little more comfortable I'm sure, so thank you for making me the happiest man alive" Richard said—vicar Penrose had stood up and came round the desk, holding out his hand, which Richard took and shook it with enthusiasm, they were both smiling now

"I have to say, that I think that Mrs Penrose will be as delighted as Clara, she has seen this moment coming for some time" he said, relaxing a little

"I have wanted this for a long time, but due to our family in mourning, I have been forced to wait longer than I would have wished, but I could wait no longer—of course, we won't be able to set the date until the new year, when the family is completely free of mourning, but a few more months are not so bad"

"Indeed, then I suggest that you go now and speak with Clara, I am very happy to welcome you into our family Your Grace" the vicar could not help showing his pleasure

"Please call me Richard, now that I am to be your son in law" Richard replied

"When you marry Clara, I shall consider it, in private of course, but until then, and in company I would prefer to address you by your rightful title Your Grace" he said firmly

"As you wish, I understand" Richard turned on his heel saying "If you will excuse me, I shall go now and find Clara as I am most eager to impart the good news"

"I'm sure that you are—she will be in the drawing room with her mother"

"Thank you sir" with that he left the library. His face was aglow, he had never felt so happy and elated as he did at this moment, he tucked his hand into his pocket and took hold of the little black velvet box, he couldn't wait to place its contents on Clara's finger. He opened the drawing room door, and stepped inside, the two women both looked up at the same time—smiles spreading across both faces.

"Good afternoon ladies" he said bowing his head, then he strode over to where they were sitting, first taking Mrs Penrose's hand and lightly kissing it, before taking her daughters, and bowing low while lifting it gently to his lips, and placing a firmer kiss there

"I thought it a glorious afternoon, and wondered if you would care to take a walk with me Clara, I thought we should make the most of this clement weather, as it will soon be on the turn" he looked straight at her smiling as he spoke

"Of course, I should love to walk with you" her heart was turning the usual somersaults he always managed to do that to her, even after all this time, his smile was enough to set her heart racing. She stood up, and took Richard's hand, and allowed him to lead her out into the garden. They walked down the path and across the lawn, Richard urged her on, over the style and into the churchyard at the bottom

"Why are we heading for the churchyard Richard?" she asked

"I thought that we could go into the field beyond, and down to the stream, unless you object of course?"

"No, I have no objections, you know that I should walk with you anywhere" she said softly. They walked on in silence, through the churchyard, with its gravestones grey and eerie in the pale afternoon sunshine, before reaching

241

the gate at the bottom, and through to the field that led down to the brook. Once they reached the flow of water, Richard turned to face Clara

"Clara, my darling, you know that I love you don't you?" he said, looking into her eyes

"Of course Richard, why what is wrong?" she asked. Without another word, Richard fell to one knee and lifting his head up to her he said "I love you Clara, and want to be with you for the rest of my life, I can't live without you, I want you to be my wife, and Duchess of Warren" he took her hands and kissed both her wrists, where her pulse thrummed, tenderly before looking back into her face

"I love you too Richard, I would gladly marry you, though you would need to speak to my father before I can consent" she said smiling at him

"Then you will marry me? I have already spoken to your father before I came to you this afternoon, and he has given his consent, our happiness is now down to you my love" he looked into her eyes, waiting for her reply, "Then of course I shall marry you Richard" she said in a whisper, he jumped to his feet and took her in his arms and swung her round, the way that he did with Milly, she was as excited as the little child and shouted out with joy, Richard stood her back on her feet again, and pulled her tightly to him, kissing her lips over and over. Then, breathlessly, he reached his hand into his pocket and pulled out the little velvet black box, taking her hand, and making her close her eyes, he took the ring lying on its soft cushion, and snapped it shut again, before placing the ring on the third finger of her left hand. The ring was a very good fit, he had gauged it very well

"You may open your eyes now" he said, placing a kiss on her hand, the diamond twinkling on her finger. Clara looked down at her finger, her face lit up, she was speechless, she couldn't take her eyes from the large sparkling treasure, her eyes went from the ring to Richard's face, tears sprang to her eyes and spilled down her cheek, Richard wiped them away with his finger

"Oh Richard, you have thought of it all, I love you so much but the ring, I have never possessed such a jewel before, it's more beautiful than anything that I've ever seen, I never ever thought that I should wear such a thing on my finger"

"You are more beautiful than any jewellery my love, and the ring is dull by comparison" he was kissing her lips again, her eyes, her nose, her neck before going back to her lips.

"Perhaps we should be getting back now—I am so eager to tell mother that we are betrothed, she will be so pleased as she has been waiting for you to ask my father for my hand—she will be so thrilled"

"And I shall tell my mother at dinner this evening—she too will be pleased for us, I'm sure" They started walking back to the rectory

"Are you sure that your mother will be happy for us" Clara asked, after a few moments, she had met Alice on several occasions, but she wasn't sure that the dowager approved of a vicar's daughter for her son

"Of course she will my darling, my mother wishes only to see us happy, and she is well aware of my feelings for you, there has never been any doubt of that"

They walked back in silent ecstasy. Once back in the drawing room, Clara could not wait to show her mama her new jewel

"Oh Clara" she said, clapping her hands over her mouth "It's beautiful, I'm so happy for you both" she stood up and hugged first Clara, and then the Duke "My daughter Duchess of Warren—I cannot take it in, I am so happy—and what of your mother Your Grace, have you told her of your good news" Ada Penrose too was sceptical as to her daughter's acceptance, as she was well aware of their class differences

"My mother is well aware of my feelings for Clara, but I shall inform her of our betrothal this evening at dinner, I wanted to make things official before saying more, after all, Clara may have turned me down" he was smiling as he said this, and looking straight at his beautiful bride to be, who smiled back at him, it was so obvious that she adored him as he adored her, there was very little chance that she would have refused his hand

"Will you stay for some tea My Lord?" asked Ada Penrose

"I had better not, as I have promised to visit Mark Chandler on a business matter, once I leave here, but I shall call again very soon, you can be sure of that—perhaps the next time I call we can set a date for the wedding, although I'm afraid it will have to wait until the new year, when my family are out of mourning"

"Of course My Lord, and besides, I want my daughter to have a wedding to be proud of, it will take time to arrange" said Ada excitedly. Richard went to Ada and kissed her hand, and bowed to her, while Clara rose and accompanied her betrothed to the door, Ada was too happy and excited to remark at all, she would have so much to prepare now, this wedding would be the happiest day in her life as well as her daughters, and to think that she had managed to end up a Duchess, she had never in her wildest dreams imagined that.

"I shall call again very soon my love, but I should think that my mother will invite you to Penleigh Court, she will not wish to be left out of the wedding arrangements" Richard said pulling Clara to him

"As long as your family will be happy at our match, I promise I will not let you down"

"I have no doubt about it" Richard said, kissing her lips "But I really have to go now" he pulled away, and opened the door, turning to blow her a kiss "Goodbye my love" before closing the door behind him. He felt like the happiest man alive, to think that becoming a married man could make him feel like this, after fighting it for so long.

<hr />

He reached the estate office and stepped inside, still happily aglow from his afternoon's venture he looked over to where his estate manager and now good friend was seated at his desk.

"Mark, how is everything with you today?"

"Very well I believe—the cottages are now completed and I thought that you would care to inspect them before I move in—and I wanted to ask your permission to marry my Angela and bring her to live with me in the cottage" Mark was looking at Richard, he noticed that he looked very happy

"You most certainly may, you whole heartedly have my permission my friend—I hope that you will be as happy as Clara has made me this very afternoon" the truth dawned on Mark then

"So you have asked Miss Penrose to marry you?"

"I have indeed, and she has consented, making me the happiest man alive"

"Then I should like to offer my congratulations" Mark said smiling

"Thank you and I shall wish you the same" said Richard happily "And now, if you like, we will ride down to West Lane and inspect the cottages" They both went off, chatting gaily as they mounted their horses and rode down to the village. The cottages looked totally different, even the lane had been trimmed back so that you could see the lane opening from the road. They first went to call on Mr Hogan, who was now happy with the work done for him. The door was freshly painted, and the garden was clear of both weeds and brambles, letting in so much more light, the windows had been cleaned and the cottage in general had been cleaned and tidied, there was new thick warm curtains hung at the windows, and even the settee had been cleaned. There were new cushions, and a warm blanket hung over the back of the old man's chair—and one of the women from the cottages had been persuaded to make a hot meal for the old gentleman each day, Mark had told the woman that it would only be temporary, until his wife was installed, she would then see to his care. Richard was delighted that Mark had made so much difference in so little time. Then they went to the abandoned cottage, this was delightful, better than he had ever known it to be. The roof had been re-done, as there was so many holes it was worse than a sieve, the picket fence had been mended and the roof to the porch, given new slats which had all ended up re-painted so that they looked shiny and new. The floors inside had new wood slats, and the stone floor in the kitchen had been scrubbed. There were rugs on the floor, which helped to make the place warm and cosy, and new curtains hanging from the windows. The walls were no longer brown, but painted white and with the windows cleaned and the garden cleared, the cottage was bright and light and airy. Furniture had been installed too, making it homely and welcoming a place for Mark to bring his bride.

"I can't believe what you have done my friend, in the short time you have been with us, what would we do without you?"

"I'm glad that you approve Richard, the furniture I have managed to get enough money together to buy, I wanted it to look nice for my Angela"

"And you have certainly done that—she is a very lucky young woman to have you"

"I believe that I'm the lucky one, I am now in a position to do the very thing which I have been waiting for so long to do—rescue the girl from her dreadful employer"

"And who is her employer?" Richard asked now listening to what his friend had to say

"It's a Mrs Flora Kirkby, she is a horrible woman, she has a daughter who she is trying to marry off, but the poor girl doesn't stand a chance of finding a husband with a mother like that continually at her. The woman is cruel and vicious, do you know, she has beat Angela, black and blue, I tried to persuade her to leave the woman's employ, but she just says that it must be her fault, even though she has done nothing—she is too sweet and kind for her own good. So, I shall be glad to take her away from all that and offer her a home of her own"

"Flora Kirkby, does she have a daughter called Sarah?" asked Richard, remembering the awful woman and her daughter who was actually not too bad, coming to Alice' tea party

"That's right—you have met her then" said Mark

"I have indeed, the daughter was rather an appealing girl, not a beauty of course, but had it not been for my dear Clara, I may have been tempted, and I have to agree with you, the mother was certainly a draw-back though I would never have guessed that she could be so cruel to her staff, you should get her away as soon as possible you know" Richard was looking straight at his friend now

"Yes, well, as soon as we possibly can" he answered, though his face, with its far-away look, told Richard that there was something else on his mind

"Is something the matter Mark?" Mark suddenly seemed to return to the conversation

"No, nothing at all—I shall speak to Angela on Sunday" he looked at Richard and smiled

Mark had now received permission to marry, and would have done all he could to arrange it by special licence, a few months ago he would have ridden over to Truro and collected Angie himself, but not now, he had to put an end to his new found pleasures with Maria before he could consider bringing Angie here—she must never know that they had been lovers, she would never forgive him for that, he was certain. He wasn't proud of it himself, but he had allowed himself to get caught up in the pleasure of it all, and had put off bringing it to an end, but now he had no choice. He would visit Maria very soon, and make her understand that it had to stop, he had to admit that she was like a drug, the more he had the more that he wanted, but he was to marry, he would have his dear sweet Angela to share all his experiences, Maria would not be needed anymore. They rode back to Penleigh Court in silent contentment, before going to their rooms to prepare for dinner.

Dinner was to be a fairly quiet affair, as it had come to be every night. Maria had been joining the family every night since Mark Chandler had arrived, and Richard believed that she had designs on him, but unlike Melvin, he wasn't disappearing through the day, or not that he had noticed, and he had never caught her in the estate office so he didn't see any need to speak with him on the matter, in any case, Mark was a sensible man, he surely being a man of the world, would not allow her to manipulate him. Richard had decided to inform his mother of his good news, while they ate, at least they would then all be aware of the situation. He waited until the main course had been served before broaching the subject.

"Mama, I should like to give you my good news, you have for a very long time now, urged me to marry and provide you with another grandchild, well, your wish is to be fulfilled—I have asked Miss Penrose for her hand in marriage, this very afternoon, and she has agreed, making me the happiest man alive, so you can make all your plans now" he said looking at his mother as he told her. For several moments she didn't speak, then she spoke softly

"Indeed, then if you are happy my dearest, I too am happy for you" she said, very calmly

"What is the matter mama, you were aware of my feelings for Clara, how we felt about each other" he said

"But I hadn't expected you to act on this so soon—it's quite a shock Richard" said Alice in a matter of fact tone

"You don't object to me marrying, so it must be my choice of bride?" he was getting angry now

"I like the girl alright, she is very sweet and very pretty, but I had expected the new Duchess of Warren to be a lady" she said simply

"You were aware mama that I have intended for some time to make Clara my wife, so I shall expect you to accept her as such, and help her if needs be, but that is an end to the matter" Richard wasn't going to argue about it he would choose his bride

"Of course Richard, I suppose the girl is young, and I shall assist her in any way I can."

"Good, then I think that we should invite them for dinner one evening—it would be the polite thing to do, would it not?" Richard asked her

"I shall write tomorrow morning, and invite them to dine on Saturday week" she said

"Splendid—perhaps then we may set a date for the wedding" said Richard, satisfied

"Are we not still in mourning?" asked Maria, who had been taken in the conversation, but without a word until now

"We are still in mourning at present, but I'm sure Richard doesn't plan to marry until our mourning is over" said Alice

"Of course, God forbid we flout propriety Maria" said Richard now aiming his remarks directly at her

"And to marry below your station, even your brother did not commit such a travesty—I had thought better of you Richard" she said

"But I shall marry for love, not because I have been forced into a loveless match" he knew he shouldn't have risen to her sarcasm, but he could not help himself—she wouldn't have said anything had he chosen to have married her, in fact, she wouldn't have said very much if he had agreed to take her as his mistress, but those things were better left unsaid

"Love, such nonsense—I would have thought that duty were more important—you owe it to Alice to marry and produce an heir, and to choose a wife of good breeding, isn't that your duty?" she asked, her voice rising

"And I intend too, Miss Penrose can hardly be considered unsuitably bred—I'm sure Maria, that you should not concern yourself with my affairs, it cannot be good for you or your child to become so agitated" Richard answered

Eliza Laval

"How dare you sir, speak to me of what I should or shouldn't do—you are impertinent" she was shouting now. Alice looked at Maria sharply

"Maria, calm yourself my dear, do not let my son rile you so—I would far sooner he marry for love than suffer the life I did, I would not wish that for him, you yourself was not happy with your marriage, so surely you too can understand his reasoning" Alice was trying to calm the situation down, though she had not seen the venom in Maria before. Suddenly the door opened, and Newbridge entered

"Yes Newbridge—what is it?"

"I'm sorry to interrupt Your Grace, but Mr Drummond is in the hall, he wishes to speak with you and he says it's urgent"

"Show him in Newbridge, I'm sure he will be glad to join us for cheese and port"

"Yes Your Grace" said the old man, shuffling through the door. A few seconds later Rufus Drummond entered the dining room

"I'm sorry Your Grace, My Lady, for interrupting your dinner, but I wondered if you found anything else when you cleared out the cottage in the village, and we also need access to the Gate Lodge and wondered if the key had come to light yet" he asked

"Ah Drummond, take a seat man, it's good to see you again. So, you are still on the hunt for the smugglers contraband I see" Richard asked

"Indeed we are Your Grace, but there's been little headway since I last saw you, and now that Lincroft has been hung, we seem to have come to a dead end, though there's been no new cases since he was captured, but it doesn't account for what was taken before"

"Well, as for the Gate Lodge, I am as in the dark as you are Drummond, apparently, it no longer belongs to the estate—I spoke to Truscott our solicitors in Truro, and have been told that the place was made over to Melvin Lincroft, and once he hung, he had willed it to a person of his

250

choice, but no-one seems to know who that person is—you could of course speak with him, Truscott and Penn, in the centre of Truro, you can't miss his office. As for the cottage, then you would do well to ask our new estate manager, Mr Chandler" he directed him to the gentleman sat at the table "in fact, if you ladies have now finished, perhaps you could leave us to talk business" he suggested, looking at his mother as he spoke

"Of course, Maria shall we?" Alice said pushing her chair back and standing, Maria did not speak but followed Alice out of the room. Once they had gone closing the door behind them Richard ushered Rufus Drummond to be seated—the door opened and Newbridge entered with a large platter of cheese and fruit and a decanter of good port. Once he had placed it in the centre of the table he left closing the door behind him

"Well Mark, perhaps you could help Drummond, did you find anything which may have equated to the kind of goods which he is seeking?" he asked looking straight at Mark

"I'm afraid not Mr Drummond, the cottage was empty—in fact, it was in a very poor state, and I'm surprised that it was used at all—the roof leaked and the goods would have been damaged had they been stored there for very long"

"I shall just have to go to Truro and speak to your solicitor I still need to get into the Gate Lodge, after all it was Lincroft's home, so chances are, we shall find something there—when he was arrested, he wouldn't have had time to do much about anything, so he couldn't have shifted it in the time"

"Good, then that is settled, and perhaps if you find out who is the new owner of my Gate Lodge, you will be able to let me know too, for I have no idea of the new owner, and I am eager to see if we can't buy the property back, after all, I am not happy having strangers on my estate"

"So, you've seen no-one going in there then Your Grace" said Drummond, Mark had gone quiet, he was saying very little, and he was bowing his head as if in thought—Richard was wondering what he was trying to hide

"Well Drummond, have some more cheese, a little drop more port?" Drummonds face lit up and he cut himself a hunk of stilton and an apple which he sliced with his knife—Richard topped up his glass of port

"So you say that there have been no other acts of smuggling since the demise of Lincroft?" asked Richard

"No Your Grace, he was obviously the leader, once he was caught, then rest of the gang fell apart, must have been too frightened to act without Lincroft, besides, Lincroft must have had his buyers, and without them, where would peasants go to sell their spoils—no, it were a good night's work the night we caught that one, I reckon as we put paid to it and stamped it out from round these parts for now" he had a satisfied look on his face

"Then we are forever grateful to you and your men Drummond" Richard said

"Well, I mustn't keep you any longer, many thanks for the hospitality Your Grace, you're a good man, as your father before you, folk around here didn't think much of him I know, but I tell you, he was a good man, and very co-operative too" he said pushing back his chair and rising to his feet, Richard wasn't so sure, after all, he knew that his father had been as much part of all this as Lincroft, more so perhaps, but he would say nothing—no good would come of raking up the past now

"And you can rely on us to help where we can" said Richard ringing for Newbridge to show Rufus Drummond out. Newbridge opened the door

"Newbridge, Mr Drummond is leaving" Richard said cutting another lump of stilton, and refilling his glass

Once Rufus Drummond had gone, Richard looked at Mark, who was still sat quietly, saying nothing. Richard knew that there was indeed something wrong, something was bothering him

"Mark, some more port perhaps?" he asked

"Thank you" he said forcing a smile

"Tell me Mark, what is bothering you is it something which Drummond said perhaps?"

"I'm not sure Richard, I didn't want to say anything, I'm a little embarrassed actually" Richard was watching him closely now

"Go on, you have no need be embarrassed with me—we are both men of the world are we not, and I like to think friends too?" Mark looked him in the eye

"Of course Richard, it's just a little delicate that's all" he said, obviously trying to think how to say what was on his mind

"Then it concern's a woman?" Richard enquired—delicate matters normally meant a woman of some sort

"I believe that I know the identity of the new owner of the Gate Lodge" he said

"You do? Then you know a great deal more than I, and who is the new owner, for I have been past the place dozens of times in the last few months, but never seen a soul at the Lodge"

"The new owner is your sister in law, Lady Maria" Richard heaved a sigh of clarification—of course, who else—Lincroft had left the Gate Lodge to her, after all she was his mistress—it all made sense now, but how would Mark Chandler know this

"Whatever makes you think that?" Richard asked, a shiver running down his spine—he believed that he already knew the answer

"I—I well I" he stammered—Richard didn't need to be told more, he could guess exactly how Mark knew that, so, Maria was up to her old tricks again was she, now she was finding her pleasure with Mark Chandler, and for all his plans to marry, he had fallen for her charms

"It's alright Mark, I understand, in a word, Maria has managed to seduce you, am I right?" the colour rising in his cheeks, now had to admit his downfall

"I cannot blame her, after all there is no excuse for my behaviour" he said quietly

"My dear friend, you are free to choose your own mistresses, but I would urge you to end the dalliance if you are to marry, you are looking forward to bringing your new wife here, and I don't think that Maria would take too kindly to that"

"Yes, yes of course, I fully intend to end what was no more than a brief affair, but Maria is a very persuasive woman" he said

"You must be firm with her, take no nonsense, and my advice is the sooner the better, it really is the best way" Richard felt shaken, he thought that Mark would have avoided something like this that could cause a scandal, but he knew exactly how persuasive Maria could be, had she not tested his patience? He could have easily fallen for her tricks, but thankfully he hadn't

"Thank you Richard, I shall take your advice—I'm afraid that although Maria is a beautiful woman, I could never love her or anything like that—but I do love Angie, more than anything in the world, and I won't have anything jeopardize my marriage to her"

"And rightly so" Richard said in a final tone "Now, let's have another drink, and thank you for being so honest with me—at least I now know who we are up against" Richard smiled to himself, perhaps he could persuade her to sell the Gate Lodge back to him, she was a woman who enjoyed money, and he would offer a good price. He could afford to now, he had learned that Miss Penrose came with a good dowry—not that it had interested him very much before, but it would be useful now, if only to help regain what was rightfully his own.

So, Rufus Drummond was still looking for her reward—Maria sat in her room, smiling to herself—she would not allow him to take what was hers—Melvin had left those things, so they were hers and she wouldn't part with them, not for anything in the world. And Richard, sat there at dinner, proclaiming to the world that he was to marry that vicar's daughter, how could he even entertain it, he had cast her aside for a nothing more than a peasant—some mealy mouthed simpering idiot, who would jump to his every whim, he needed a proper woman, one that would enhance his life, he would not dare shun her this time, she would not have any of it, she would give him one more chance, and she would get rid of that chit, that wouldn't be difficult, she wanted Richard more than she wanted anything else in her life—Mark had been a pleasant interlude, but Richard was her prize, she had some plans now, forming in her head, suddenly the pieces fit into place, once this child was born, she would set her plans into action. Suddenly, pain racked through her body, making her gasp for breath—it had begun, it would soon be over now and she would be free to find a new happiness. Another pain, she screamed out, as the pain wracked through her body, she waited until it had passed, then she made her way to the bell pull. Her maid arrived, and Maria ordered that the midwife should be called immediately the baby was on its way.

CHAPTER TWENTY

(The Hidden Cave)

The following morning, Maria had given birth to a boy, he was a large baby the midwife had feared for Maria's life, she didn't think her capable to giving birth to such a child, but the baby boy was born. Alice was thrilled, now she had a grandson, her joy was complete, Henry had missed the very thing which he had longed for all those years, it seemed ironic then that she should have a son, nine months after the death of both her husband and the Duke. Maria had laid in her bed that morning, wanting nothing to do with the child—she had no interest in even looking at him, until she had given things a great deal of thought— then it came to her in a flash, this child, being the product of her husband, would be next in line to the Dukedom, he would come before Richard— her son, and she smiled to herself—things were starting to look up and she would make the most of her newfound luck. She would name him Edward Richard, and she would see that her son was given his due recognition.

Richard was told of the birth of his nephew, he was delighted at the prospect, and he too realized that he may need to relinquish the title to the child, once he came of age—Richard would be more than happy to do so, but he wanted to have the estate in order before he took over, it was only right and fair that he do so. Richard had never before seen such a new born child, so he requested that he be allowed to visit—Maria was happy for him to visit at his own request, she wondered if this was the beginning of him relenting towards her—after all, she had got a son now.

Alice too was eager to visit, and sat beside Maria, nursing the child—he certainly could scream—Alice remarked that he was not like his father for that—Edward had been such a quiet child, as he was a quiet man, but he had a shock of black hair on the top of his head, so it was thought that he would take after his father's side of the family.

The baby seemed to be taking over everything at the house, Alice had decided to wait for a week or two, before inviting the Penrose family to dine—after all, Maria should be given time to heal first, and as part of the family, she would be expected to attend the dinner.

Mark had got his tenants busy working on the most urgent repairs first, even though they had expected to have them all completed before winter set in. He had been giving a great deal of thought to his conversation with Richard, he had felt so embarrassed having to admit that he had fallen for Maria's charms, not to mention that he had betrayed her as owner of the Gate Lodge, but at the end of the day, Richard was his master, and that's where his loyalty lay. He had also started thinking about his dear sweet Angie, the thought of sharing the pleasures which Maria had taught him with Angie, was filling him with a new longing—but he wouldn't wait long, he had thought to broach the subject when he met her this weekend, but now that he wouldn't have a chance to see Maria for a couple of weeks, he had better leave it until he had ended things with her first, and this time he would not leave until he had made her realize that it was truly over between them.

❧ ⁂ ☙

Maria had grown tired of lying in bed, so after a few days she got up, and persuaded her maid to help her dress, she had started to show an interest in Edward, and went to the nursery each day to visit him. The girls were thrilled with their tiny brother, and the wet nurse had now arrived too. Richard also visited the nursery regularly, taking the girls off of Nanny Anson's hands for a while. Maria had started to be civil once again toward Richard, and although it made him question why, he was glad of it, as he wished to speak to her about the Gate Lodge—he wanted to offer to buy it from her if he could get her to agree, but he would wait until she was fully recovered from the birth first. Maria had seen Mark a few times also, though she had grown cool towards him, giving him no encouragement of any kind, he was pleased about this as although he missed the fun they shared, he had to break it off with her, and this way was preferable to hurting her or causing a scene about it.

Clara had seen a little of Richard, and was also thrilled at the news of the Maria's baby, she would have dearly loved to have seen him, she loved babies and children, and they seemed to love her, but Richard thought it best for her to wait until they were married, he knew only too well what Maria could be like. They had talked a great deal of their marriage, and it had been agreed that they should wed on fifth of January, straight after the new year celebrations. Richard had thought this ideal, as there could be no ball again for Christmas, due to his father's death, so they would hold a ball on twelfth of January, in order for Richard to introduce his new wife to the local gentry. Things were working out very well—by next year they could be due to have a child themselves at this rate—Richard was happier than he had ever been.

One afternoon, a little later, Richard had spent the afternoon with Clara, they had been out for a ride, the leaves were really falling, their rich colours making a multi coloured carpet covering the ground. They had ridden away from the village and down past Gallows Cross gibbet, then turning right and down towards Smugglers Cove, Richard hadn't planned to go in that direction particularly, but they were riding and talking, and they had just headed off in that direction. They made their way down to the beach at Smugglers Cove and after dismounting, and tethering their horses, they took the path leading down to the beach. The path was not an easy one to navigate, and Richard held tightly to Clara's hand, so that she would not fall to the beach below, the path being narrow and the pebbles slipping under foot, made it hard going for them both, at the bottom, Richard jumped down, as there was a large void in which he would jump down to the sand below, before reaching his arms up, and placing them around Clara's waist and lifting her down the rest of the way, eventually they reached their destination. As they walked along the beach, Richard spotted an opening of which he had never noticed before, it was covered with brambles, but the afternoon light had shown the darkness of an opening behind, he instructed Clara to wait on the beach, while he looked inside—the mouth of the cave was set back in the rocks, and he crept inside, it was dark and damp but just inside the opening was a ledge, high up by his head, being tall it was at eye level for him, that was the only reason he saw it, on the ledge tucked a little further back, was a lantern and tinder, Richard lit the lantern and cast his eye around the small chamber, there was very little to see inside, the chamber was empty, then as if drawn as a moth to a flame, Richard spotted a wooden trap door in the ceiling of the cave, a shorter man would never have spotted it, he went over to it, and pushed the slats—they moved immediately, without his using any force, the first slat lifted and fell away into his hand, he then did the same with the other two, now there was a hole large enough to climb through—then tumbling down at him—was a small wooden ladder, Richard set the ladder in place, leant against the inside of the hole, then climbed up to investigate with the lantern in his hand—he could not believe what he reached up his hand to the inside of the gaping hole and then he jumped back quick, something came into view—kegs of liquor, stood on each other, small bundles of packed water-skins which held tobacco and bags of tea, waiting to be transferred into smaller bags, so this was what Rufus Drummond was looking for—and he had stumbled on it—he guessed that the upper chamber must also lead off somewhere, due to a passage across the far side, leading off into darkness—he would bring Mark and they must find out exactly where this came out, then he would inform Drummond where to find the contraband. He stepped back down the ladder, and pushed it back up in the hole, then he returned the three slats, until they had covered the hole, before extinguishing the lantern and placing it back on the ledge beside the tinder, and stepping out into the last rays of late afternoon autumn sunshine. He could not let Clara know what he had found, he didn't want her involved in any way, he needed to find out more about what was going on and in particular where the passageway from the upper chamber went.

"What was it, inside the rock? You were gone quite some minutes" Clara had enquired

"Just an old cave, nothing to worry about—it was empty and I should imagine at high tide, will be filled with water"

"I see, I thought that you might have found some contraband goods, and I should hate for you to get into trouble, or get mixed up with smugglers, you could have been in danger, it frightened me"

"No need to worry my dear, I should never do anything to cause you such worry" he said, taking her in his arms and kissing her

They started to make their way back to the single track pathway, it took much longer to climb back up, than it did to come down, and Richard had to help Clara to make it at all. Once they reached the spot that they had tethered their horses, Richard lifted Clara back into her saddle before mounting his own, ready to ride back to the rectory, they were just turning toward the village, when a lone rider was heading toward them at a great speed—Richard and Clara pulled their horses to a standstill, and waited for the rider to pass, but as the rider approached, Richard could hardly believe his eyes, the rider was one of his two best friends, it was Jasper Trent, Jasper pulled his horse to a halt

"Penleigh, or should I say Warren my dear friend—how good to see you" he shouted

"Whatever brings you to Cornwall Trent, I thought you would be enjoying London with Hinton"

"And when are you going to introduce me to this delectable creature" he asked his gaze resting on Clara

"This beautiful young lady, is Miss Clara Penrose, and she is my future wife, so she is unavailable to you Trent" Richard said with a smile

"Your future wife eh coming from the man who was a sworn bachelor—then I should offer my congratulations, I must say, you are indeed a very fortunate man" his gaze still on Clara

"This my love, is one of my good friends from London, Jasper Trent, who is needless to say, a born rake, no woman is safe where Jasper is" said Richard to his lovely fiancée

"Good afternoon Mr Trent, I am very pleased to meet any friend of Richard's" said Clara sweetly

"And I am exceedingly pleased to meet you, I can't believe that he kept you so quiet" he said, Clara smiled this man was very charming, though nothing in comparison to her dearest Richard

"So, what are you doing here Trent" asked Richard

"I came to look you up of course, what else would I be doing in Cornwall, so far away from civil society" he replied

"So you will be staying as my guest I presume?" Richard asked

"Of course, I've come to help you drink your port and brandy" he said laughing

"Have you no luggage?"

"My luggage will be arriving tomorrow—my man will be riding in the carriage with it" said Jasper

"Then you had better ride back with us now, you will have to wait while I return Clara home, then we shall go and have a room prepared for you—I must say it's good to see you, and what of Hinton, I've not heard from him either"

"The fellow has also got himself betrothed, he is to marry the delightful Miss Clarissa Martin, I expect we shall both receive an invitation, though the wedding is not to take place before next summer"

"Then we shall be married before Hinton, will we not my darling?" he turned to Clara

"Indeed, we are to marry on fifth of January, I do hope that you will be able to attend the wedding sir" Clara said to Jasper

"Please sweet Clara, call me Jasper, after all we are going to be friends now are we not, and I would not miss your wedding for anything" Clara laughed, if nothing else, this man was highly amusing

They walked their horses to the rectory, where Richard saw Clara home, then he joined Jasper and they carried on up the hill to Penleigh Court.

Richard was thrilled to have his dear friend staying with them—Jasper and Mark had also become good friends and in a very short time. A few days after Jasper's arrival, Richard was sat in his library one evening with his two friends, and relayed to them what he had found down at Smugglers Cove—it was agreed that they should go the very next day, as long as the tide allowed, and they would look into the passageway leading from the cove and where it emerges. Once they knew the answer to this, they could then bring in Drummond and have him seize the goods. After several glasses of brandy Mark and Jasper retired for the night, leaving Richard alone to ponder on their decision. By now the autumn had really set in, the nights were getting much longer, and the days shorter and much cooler than of late. As Richard sat with his brandy, the library door opened, and Maria slipped inside

"Maria, how are you?" he hadn't spoken very much to her since the baby had been born, there were other things on his mind

"I am very well Richard, I think that we should have a talk" she said

"What do you wish to discuss with me?" Richard asked

"You do know that now I have a son, he will inherit the Dukedom when he is old enough, I'm sorry that it has not turned out so well for you, but there it is, we must be adult about this and decide the best way to proceed I think" she said, this was all too sweetly, he couldn't trust her anymore

"I agree with you entirely, and of course your son should inherit, I would not have it any other way"

"Then we are agreed for once" she said smiling

"We are indeed. And while we are talking civilly, I believe that you are the new owner of the Gate Lodge, it is such a pity, especially now, that young Edward should inherit the estate and title, that the Gate Lodge has been separated from the remainder of the estate—so, I thought perhaps you would be prepared to sell it back to the estate, for a good price of course, it would give you a nice nest egg, and it would mean that the estate would be intact once more—do you not agree?"

"I see no reason to sell the Gate Lodge back to the estate, after all, it's part of it, my son is to inherit it all, so there is little point in selling it for money—but if you are set on this course, I'm sure that we could come to an arrangement" she was smiling as she walked around the desk—she perched on the edge as close to him as possible "and what do you have in mind?" he was beginning to think that he should never have asked. Maria lifted her hand to his face, stroking his cheek with her finger

"If we were to marry, then there would be no need to do anything, the house would automatically be part of our estate, and we could look after it together until Edward is old enough to take over himself" Richard should have known it would be something like this—would he never learn

"Maria, you know that I am betrothed, I am to marry Clara in the new year, and do you really think that it is the answer, you and I, we would never be suited, I would make you unhappy, and I don't want to do that"

"But how do you know that, we should at least try, should we not? Surely for the sake of the children, you love those children, and we could have more—I would do anything you asked of me Richard, I would make you happy, if you would just let me" she was beginning to annoy him now, her voice was no longer sweet, but grating. He took her hand and moved it away from his face

"No Maria, I'm so sorry, but it cannot be, I am going to marry Miss Penrose, and there will be no union between the two of us, but I am still more than happy to give you a good sum for the Gate Lodge" She pulled her hand free and jumped to her feet

"Then you shall never own the Gate Lodge again, and what's more, you will never marry the insipid vicar's daughter—I shall see you ruined Richard Penleigh, do you hear me? You have just made the biggest mistake of your life, you will rot in hell before I have finished with you" with that, she turned and walked out, slamming the door behind her.

Why was he surprised, she would not let go so easily—she was a woman scorned and everyone knew that there was nothing worse. He had really lost his chance of regaining the Gate Lodge now, but he would at least be able to point Drummond to the owner. He poured himself another glass of brandy, before retiring for the night.

The following morning dawned clear and bright—Richard leaped out of bed and dressed quickly, before going down to meet his two friends for breakfast. They were both already seated when he arrived, a large plate of eggs, ham and devilled kidneys on both their plates. Richard helped himself to some food, and took his seat along with them.

"So gentlemen, are you ready for our little escapade?" Richard was becoming quite excited by it all, he had even wondered whether or not he would learn anything about his father or Edward's death, he was certain that there was a link here somewhere.

"I can hardly contain my interest, I am more than inquisitive to find where this passageway leads, I have a distinct feeling that it will lead to this house, though I've no idea why" said Richard

"I have to agree with you Richard, these large old houses all seem to have secret passages in them, or so it's rumoured, it certainly seems likely that this one is no exception, and it is situated fairly close to the beach" said Mark

"Well, we shall soon find out" said Richard

"Pity that you can't keep the goods Warren, barrels of rum sound just up my street" stated Jasper

"That is not the point Trent, you do realize that being caught with these sort of goods, would carry the death sentence, and I hate to say that I value my neck too much for that"

"Perhaps you are right—I too have become accustomed to my neck also" repeated Jasper with amusement

The door opened and Alice entered

"Good morning gentlemen" she said walking to the sideboard and serving herself with a portion of the eggs from a side dish, then replacing the lid

"Good morning mama" said Richard "You are early this morning, have you plans for today?"

"I do have a few things to do—I shall write a note this morning, I thought that it was about time we invited the Penrose family to dine with us, I thought Saturday evening, if you have nothing else planned" she said

"Saturday evening will be splendid, thank you mama"

"Good, then that is settled, you two gentlemen will be joining us also will you not?" now she was speaking to Richard's good friends

"Indeed I shall be delighted madam" said Jasper

"And you too Mr Chandler?"

"Thank you madam, that is very kind of you"

"Now gentlemen, if you are ready, I think we should be off, if you will excuse us mama" he said speaking to his mother "We have much to do today

"Of course, but you sound as if you have some important business to take care of" she looked at her son

"We have that, we shall see you at dinner mama, I doubt that we shall make it back for lunch today" Alice couldn't help wondering what they were up too—she could remember the days when her two sons were boys, going off on adventures, and keeping it all a great secret, she sighed with a smile

"I will let cook know—good day gentlemen" she replied as they left the room

The three gentlemen went to the stables and were soon mounted, and riding out of the main gates. They rode, laughing and talking amongst themselves like young bucks hitting the town together—it was amazing the way that their personalities gelled, even Mark, although not a gentleman, no-one would ever have believed it. They rode on through the village and over the bridge, past the rectory, and the church, then on down to Gallows Cross and its gibbet, then they turned right and headed downhill, following the track down towards the beach. Once at the end of the main track they tethered their horses as they could take them no further, the small path tapered down and was very steep, which led down on to the beach, and in certain weather, would have been almost impossible to navigate, exactly like the cliff path above Devil's Cove. The young men followed Richard in single file, with each step the shingle beneath their feet slid and they had to pick their way carefully, then just before they reached the bottom there was a gap, and they had to jump from the pathway to the sand below. They tramped across the sand, to find the large hidden opening, Richard led the way, they were soon inside the lower chamber, and lighting the lantern from the ledge

"I can understand why this man who's looking for smugglers, couldn't find this place, I'm surprised that you found it Warren" said Jasper

"Indeed, I admit that I found it quite by chance the other afternoon, when I was walking with Clara along the beach" Richard said "The breeze from the sea was quite gusty and blew the brambles away from the cave—or I would never have guessed there were anything there at all"

Richard handed the lantern to Mark to hold up to the roof of the chamber, so that he could locate and remove the boards, marking the entrance to the upper chamber, he soon found it, he reached inside and pulled down the ladder which was hiding there, pulling it down to allow them to climb into the small space left in the upper chamber, there was only room for one of them at a time, and Richard being a large man, could not stand up at all, so he had to lean over and bend his head, reaching down to take the lantern from Mark, to allow him to see his way to the passage, like a black hole at the back of the upper chamber. Richard hooked the lamp to the top of the ladder, and moved slowly to the passage at the back, once he had found his way round the contraband, and reached the opening of the passage, it had opened up, allowing him to stand straight, then he called for Jasper to follow next, he climbed the ladder from the light of the lantern, which was enough to see his way up into the upper chamber, and to shine on the contraband stacked inside. Richard called to him, and he followed his way round to find his friend. Then finally, Richard called for Mark to join them, he climbed the ladder, before unhooking the lantern, and pulling the latter in through the gap, and placing the three wooden planks carefully back over the entrance, all signs of their entry now well and truly covered. Mark took the lantern and followed his friends the passage was much larger than Richard could have imagined it to be. Taking the lantern from Mark, Richard led the other two through the passageway stepping slowly and carefully. The passageway was a hole cut into the rocks themselves, and it was sloping upwards steeply—if the other end did actually take them to Penleigh Court, then he would expect the passage to become a great deal steeper than it already was, it would not have been a simple job for the smugglers, carrying all their rewards, to make their way along this passage to the other end. They followed the passage on, and on, they were beginning to think that there was no end to it all they climbed at a very steep rate for some time then suddenly, without further warning, they had reached another chamber, like a cave but much larger than either of the chambers they had entered from the beach. At one end of this chamber, was stacked hundreds of barrels, from floor to ceiling, besides the water-skin packages of tobacco and the large bags of tea, Richard stood still, casting his eye around, unable to take in all the goods he was seeing, Jasper and Mark soon falling in behind him.

"It is little wonder that Drummond is eager to find this stash, I'm surprised that he hasn't succeeded already" Richard mused—Jasper let out a low whistle

"This lot would fetch a fortune—this would solve all your money problems Warren—you could sell it from right under their noses" trust Jasper, he was always full of bright ideas

"Perhaps, but only if you succeeded—I would prefer to hand this to the authorities, and keep my life thank you Trent"

"I have never seen anything like this—we always knew that smuggling had been going on here for as long as we can remember, but I've never seen anything like this first hand before" said Mark bewildered by it all

"Indeed, and to think that a member of my own family is responsible for much of this" Richard was thinking about his father, but speaking his thoughts out loud

"A member of your family Warren" asked Jasper,

"Yes, my father, I found out from my mother that he was involved with all of this, he probably set it all up in fact"

"But I thought that your father was dead" Jasper persisted

"Yes, he is but my mother has since told me of his involvement—but our family shall not be tainted with such dealings again—of that I am sure" his thoughts had gone, his mind was back with his two friends again

"Now, we must get on, we have to find some way out of here, but we have to take good care, as we don't know where this will lead us" Richard took the lantern, and walked to the other side of the cave, he was looking for anything which might lead them out of this chamber, he cast his eye, by the light from the lantern round the wall, walking slowly looking for something which could lead to their way out. Richard searched for what seemed like hours, his two friends, following him round—three pairs of eyes must be better than one—then Richard stepped forward, as he did so, he caught his leg on something sharp, it had ripped through his breeches and into his flesh, and blood was now trickling from the wound, he shouted out in pain, but by the light of the lantern, he could see a small sharp piece of rock jutting out from the rest, surely this could not be what he was looking for, something told him to take hold of the rock, he would need to be careful as one side was very sharp, he placed his hand on the top of the rock, opposite the sharp side, and pushed down, immediately, taking the lantern, he bent back, he could hear the grinding as the mass of rocks in front of him had started to move—Jasper and Mark had now stepped forward to join him, and they watched in wonderment as an entrance had started to appear from the rock formation—there was a large heavy wooden door, Richard lifted the latch and it swung back on its hinges, revealing a long wooden staircase rising steeply with another large wooden door at the top, the steps had a wooden handrail, although it looked worn and in bad repair, they would surely need to take care when climbing the stairs. Richard went first, followed by the other two men, at the top on the wall beside the doorway, was a large wooden handle, Richard pulled down on the handle, and suddenly the door began to swing slowly outward, without a sound—the three gentlemen stood silently watching as the door reached its widest capacity, then Richard moved forward, taking the final steps up and stepping through the opening, and into the room before him. The other two close on his heels. They stood in silence, gazing round the room, this wasn't a room that Richard had ever seen in his life before, leaving the cave entrance open wide, he gingerly stepped to the window, to look out—below him was a lawn and well-tended flower beds, and beyond that were trees, and cliffs, though he could not see further, he knew that the sea was rushing in and hitting the rocks, throwing up a white frothy foam below. He had never been in this room before, but he now knew where he was, they were standing in an upper room in Maria's new house, he wasn't sure whether she was there or not, but they would have to be careful, he trusted her even less now than he had before, was this why Lincroft had left the house to her, because of the secret it held. Perhaps she was as involved in it all, as Lincroft and her father, was that why they had disagreed so much before his death, so many questions, yet no answers—he wondered if his mother was aware of this place, though why should she be, for though she had known about the goings on in her family, she had not been involved in her husband's underhand activities. He turned to his two friends, and whispered quietly

"I know where we are gentlemen, but we now have to be careful that my sister in law isn't here at present" Mark's face fell, the colour drained from his cheeks

"This is the Gate Lodge isn't it" he asked Richard

"Yes, I'm afraid it is, but we cannot be found here by my sister in law, if she were to find out that we knew about this, then we would all be in serious trouble, for they would immediately believe that we were involved and I think we are all aware of what that would mean"

"I will go" Mark whispered to Richard "If Maria is here then I could draw her attention to me, which would allow you gentlemen to escape"

"No Mark, I cannot let you do this" said Richard deep in thought while Jasper was trying to understand what he had meant before it dawned on him, a large grin spread across his face

"Are you telling us that the Lady Maria is your lover Chandler" he whispered softly—the colour rose in Mark's cheeks, but he didn't reply, he just threw him a glance

"You are, your lack of words is confirmation enough—I must applaud you for your taste sir" said Jasper with amusement

"Shh—not now Trent, our lives could depend on this" said Richard firmly "There will be time enough later for such jest"

"I'm sorry Richard, but if we are caught here like this, we are in trouble, but if you were to let me go and investigate, even if she is here, I could say that I was eager to see her, and that I had come here in the hopes of winning her favours, she would believe me I'm certain, and I have the perfect way in which to keep her amused while you get free of this place—it makes sense, it's the only way" Mark had thought this all through

"No Chandler, you are to marry in a few days, I cannot allow you to do this, it isn't right" Richard said

"But what is the alternative Richard, have you any ideas" Mark asked logically

"I would gladly ravish the lady, if that is what's required, after all, living here there is rather a shortage of the fairer sex is there not?" Jasper still thought this a jest, could he not be serious

Richard thought for a moment, ignoring his friends quips, he couldn't be caught here that was for sure, after last night's little discussion, he could of course go against all his resolve and give her what she wanted, but he wasn't even sure that he would be up to it, Maria did nothing for him, and even if he did, he would then never be free of her again, and he couldn't take that chance—no, Mark's suggestion did make sense, though Richard could not be held accountable for his friend sacrificing himself to save their necks—literally

"Please Richard, she may not be here, in which case, we will escape before we are found" Mark was sure, it was the most sensible solution, and if he was right they would escape without further ado

"Alright Chandler, I am in no position to argue, we shall wait for a quarter of an hour, if she is here, you will have that long to persuade her of your loyalty, and to gain her attention, we will then quietly slip down the stairs and through the front door" said Richard

"Good, then I shall go, if the coast is clear, I shall call you immediately" he promised as he slipped out of the room and down the stairs.

Richard and Jasper waited by the door, listening to every little sound, and waiting to see if Mark should call to them, but there was not a sound—then Maria was indeed in the house, they must proceed with the greatest care. Richard took out his pocket watch, and they watched the seconds ticking by as they stood in silence. Then, Richard slowly opened the door, listening all the time—the door opened out on to a small landing, with two other doors leading to the same place, with baited breath and in silence, they crept down the stairs, several of the steps creaking beneath their weight, then down to another much larger landing with several more doors leading from it, until finally, they were creeping down the main front staircase, across the hall and to the front door, they heard not a sound, as Richard opened the front door, and stepped outside into the fast sinking pale sunlight. Once out on the road, they could breathe again—they had made it, poor Mark, Richard had made up his mind to do everything he could to help him be free of Maria, but for now he was glad of his influence on her. The two men went directly to the stables where Richard ordered the groom to take one of the stable boys and collect the horses, still tethered to a post above Smugglers Cove, before retiring to the house for a well—earned brandy.

Mark had volunteered to be the scapegoat—he had crept down the stairs, to the main first floor passage, and headed directly for the main bedroom, Maria had been spending money to have a few little luxuries adorn it of late, he had spent several nights here with her in his arms, before her child had been born. They had crept out of the house, but not together, and down to the Gate Lodge, she would go as soon as she had retired, so that by the time he had arrived, she was ready and waiting for his arrival, laid in bed, her golden hair spread out on the pillows, he had to admit she looked like an angel, it had been easy to make love to this appealing women, though he could never love her, he knew that, she was a pastime, one of which he would forever be grateful, but nothing more—he would slip between the cool white sheets and they would spend the night together, in each other's arms but before sunrise, he would return to the house, to prepare for the new day, and no-one had ever known of their relationship, until Richard. But, now he was to marry his beloved Angie, he had to break this habit with Maria, he wanted to start as he meant to go on, true only to the woman he loved, this would break his resolve and Richard had not wanted him to do this, but what alternative was there, the thought of Maria catching them there could have devastating repercussions and he couldn't allow himself to even think of that. This had to be the best way. He opened the door to Maria's bedroom, and crept inside Maria wasn't there, so he walked as noisily as he could to the top of the main staircase and softly called her name, she must have heard the noise and came from the drawing room to see who was responsible

"Who's there" she shouted as she stood in the hall below, Mark stood hidden from view by the wall at the top of the stairs, he must attract her attention, and get her to the bedroom and very quickly, he hadn't much time

"It is I Maria my darling, I'm waiting for you" he replied. Within seconds he heard her footsteps on the stairs and he knew that he had managed to succeed in his task—he slipped back into the bedroom and closed the door, quickly removing his jacket and cravat, he must look as if he meant it, the handle of the door moved and the door flew open wide—she stood for a moment in the doorway, looking straight at him, and he was looking at her

"What are you doing here today" she asked, slipping inside and closing the door behind her "And how did you get in?"

"I had to see you sweet Maria, I needed to feel your lips on mine, and your body laid in my arms, is that so wrong of me?" Suddenly a smile broke out on her face and she moved towards him as elegant as a swan on water

"And how did you get in?" she asked again, cupping his face in her hands

"I came through the front door, how else?" he only hoped that she hadn't locked it the minute she had entered—he held his breath for a few seconds, before her face softened, he was safe

"So, you have come to me, I knew that you would you know, you have been eager to finish our relationship, but you cannot do without me can you?"

"It looks like it" he replied in a whisper, throwing his arms around her and pressing his lips hard to hers, then she broke away from him "In thinking that you would not share my bed again, it seems to have made you more eager than ever, you had better relieve me of my clothing if you are to share my pleasure"

Mark sighed, it was a sigh of relief, though Maria must have thought it a sigh because he hadn't stuck to his resolve, she was going to allow him to carry out his plan, he would take her to bed as long as he had returned to the house in time for dinner, he would have done what he promised to do, and kept his good friends safe—he now had the problem of breaking it off with her, but that would have to keep for another day—besides, once he was married she would know that it was no longer possible to keep assignations with her anymore.

Very soon they had slid between the sheets, and made love for the first time in weeks, then locked in each other's embrace, Maria was relaxed and content she had won in her mind, only Mark knew that this was not strictly the case.

Richard was relieved when Mark descended the stairs and joined them in the drawing room before dinner. He had feared for his friend, there were a thousand things which could have gone wrong, and he knew Maria's anger and spite, he had tasted that for himself. But he looked happy and unscathed, and for that Richard sighed with relief. He would be ever grateful for his sacrifice, and he would make damned certain that the man was not made to suffer at Maria's hand for his part.

Once seated around the table, Alice had news for her son

"I have sent an invitation to the Penrose family, requesting that they join us for dinner next Saturday, and they have now accepted the invitation" she said very formerly

"That is excellent news mama, thank you" he said, then turning to Mark he went on "And Mr Chandler will be moving into the cottage on Wednesday, is that not so Mark? I for one will be sorry to see you move out of my house, but you must bring your wife and eat with us sometimes, in fact, I should be glad if you would both join us Saturday week, I would very much like you to meet my bride to be"

"I would not wish to intrude Richard" he said, bowing his head

"Intrude—nonsense, not at all man, you must come, I insist" Richard persisted, Mark looked up and looked to Alice, though she said nothing, before he rested his gaze on his friend and master

"My wife and I would be delighted I'm sure, thank you"

"We shall be rather a gay party then, you are to be married on Thursday next I believe Mr Chandler" Alice asked, she too had taken to this young man—he was indeed a gem, he did a particularly good job, and like her son, she would welcome him as one of the family

"I am indeed My Lady" he said smiling

"And where is the wedding to be held Mr Chandler?"

"At the church down in the village, My Lady, Angela has no parents you see, so she was happy to allow me to arrange everything for her" he replied nervously, glancing at Maria now and again

"I see, and have you taken care of a wedding gown and wedding breakfast too?" Alice was looking straight at Mark Chandler now

"I believe that she has a Sunday best gown and bonnet My Lady, I'm sure she will do nicely thank you, and we shall just go straight back to the cottage afterwards, there will be so few people to attend, I have asked if vicar Penrose will bring his family along as witnesses, and of course, if anyone from here would be kind enough to come, we should be very grateful My Lady" Alice had thought as much, she knew how fond her son was of his new estate manager, he had told her often enough, and she had to admit that he was a vast improvement on the last one, the least they could do would be to give them a wedding day to remember. Her dressmaker always kept a few gowns already made up, and if the girl came to Penleigh Court for a few days as her guest, Alice would make sure that she was looked after properly

"Mr Chandler, you are visiting your young lady this weekend?" said Alice, Richard looked at his mother, as he had no idea what was going on in her mind now

"Yes My Lady, Sunday after lunch" he replied

"Then you will take the carriage, and you will bring the young lady back with you, you must send word to her immediately after dinner tonight, telling her to pack her trunk and be ready to leave when you arrive, then you will bring the young lady back here and she will be a guest of mine, until you are married" she said. Richard had started to guess what was going on his mother's mind, she had never had a daughter to look after, so Mark's bride was to receive the royal treatment—he was delighted, if for nothing else, for the things which Mark had done already since taking over this post—he was more than just an estate manager, he was a good friend, who Richard would trust with his life

"What an excellent idea mama—I should have thought of it myself" he said

"I don't know what to say My Lady, it is so very kind of you, and I have to say that I do so worry about the girl, her employer is brutal at times, I have wanted for so long to rescue her from the woman's cruelty, though she has had a little reprieve of late, as the lady in question has been in Bath for a few months, giving her daughter a short season, but she returned only two weeks ago" he remarked

"Who is her employer?" Alice asked

"A Mrs Flora Kirkby My Lady" Alice's mind focused on the memory of that awful woman, who tried to overpower her daughter

"Ah, I know the women—she is not well liked I think, then you must bring your young lady here on Sunday, and she will then be in my care until the day of her wedding"

"Thank you My Lady" then turning to Richard "Your Grace"

Richard had been paying attention to Maria during the conversation Mark was having with his mother, she had definitely been taking it all on board but he only hoped now that she had no sinister ideas of her own, he would need to watch for her spite, the poor man had no idea of her reprisals yet, and Richard would rather that he didn't have to witness them. He must be on his guard.

CHAPTER TWENTY ONE

(Chandler's Wedding)

Alice had given orders to prepare a room for her guest who would be arriving on Sunday afternoon. Sundays was the day that many of the servants had time off, so they would dine at lunchtime and as only two maids would be in attendance at tea time, there would be sandwiches and cake left in the pantry, for them to serve to the family. Alice was looking forward to putting her plans into action, she had no daughters of her own, and it would be a very long time before her granddaughters would be ready for marriage, and they would have their mother to make the arrangements for them, so she was determined to splash out, and make this wedding for Mr Chandler and his bride, a day to remember and cherish. As well as giving the orders to make a room ready for the girl, she had also spoken with the cook, she would be responsible for the catering, though the menu for the wedding feast, could not be finalised until the girl had arrived, they would have to act very quickly once she had settled in, as there was much to be done, and a visit to Truro, to her own dressmaker to see that the girl was suitably attired. Alice had a little money set aside, as she needed so little herself, that there would certainly be sufficient to cover the cost of a new gown and all the things she would require for her trousseau. Alice was very excited at the prospect—she had also spoken to Richard and suggested that he have the landau made ready, although it wasn't used through the winter months, due to its openess and unsuitability to inclement weather, but as long as it stayed fine, the landau, dressed with flowers and ribbons, would be a special treat for them, and Richard would also be tasked with giving the girl away, well, there was no-one else to perform that task. Mr Chandler had already asked his brother to be his best man, and apart from his family, and the vicar's family, Alice's family would be the only other guests in attendance.

Maria sat alone in her room, she couldn't help but smile at the thought of Mark. He had spent so much time with her before the birth of Edward, yet every time he went to her he insisted that their relationship must end, but each time she had asked him to meet her, he was always there—the few weeks after her son's birth, she had been in no condition to entertain a gentleman. She had begun to think that he really wasn't interested any more, he was to be married, how many times had he told her that—and then, suddenly out of the blue he had sneaked into her house, in fact, her bedroom to be precise—he had gone to the trouble of enticing her there to join him, and finally to spend the afternoon in his arms, he had needed her so badly, she hadn't expected that, but it proved to her that he would never do without her, this wife of his, if she had any experience in these matters, wouldn't she have taught him, but he was definitely a virgin when she seduced him, he had no idea whatsoever of such pleasures, she had taught him all he knew, and she would soon have him knocking her door down to spend a night in her bed. He couldn't resist her, and she intended to make sure of it, wife or not. Then there was Richard—she had given him more chances than she would ever have given anyone else, yet still he shunned her advances, did he really believe that mealy mouthed simpering chit from the rectory could satisfy his desires, well, she would make sure that not only would she not marry him, but that she would never wish to as much as look at him again, by the time she had finished. He would rue the day he cast her aside, and she would take pleasure in watching him suffer, and she knew exactly what she would do—she had it all planned out—she wanted to finish him for once and for all. He would be sorry he crossed her, she would make him pay with his life. She would have to play her cards close to her chest now, she had her son Edward, he would take the title and estate, as soon as he was old enough, and he would take good care of his dear mama, but in the future, Mark would carry on serving her well, and she would make sure of that.

Sunday afternoon, was always a quiet day, but today Alice couldn't help herself, as she sat, her needlework in her lap, and Nanny Grey snoring opposite her, every little while she would look at the clock on the mantelpiece, it really wasn't moving very fast today, it was as if there were a gremlin in the works making it stand still every time she glanced away. The weather had turned out cloudy and there was a stiff chill in the air, the fires had been lit early, and the lamps too. The autumnal feeling seemed to get into the very soul. Maria had disappeared after lunch, as did Richard and his friend—she supposed that they had gone riding—that would be their usual pursuit these days. She was a little worried as Richard didn't seem to be paying so much attention to Miss Penrose of late she hoped that nothing was amiss there. Suddenly, she heard a noise from the hall, it must be Mr Chandler and his bride arrived, she jumped from her seat, she must go and greet her guest.

As she reached the hall, Mark had entered, with a very thin, pale faced girl next to him. She had rich auburn hair and tiny features, Mark came forward to introduce her to Alice, when she turned her eyes to look up, she had the most beautiful vivid green eyes that Alice had ever before seen, fringed with fair lashes. Mark certainly knew how to choose a beauty.

"This is Angela Moreton My Lady, soon to be Mrs Chandler" Mark said, bowing his head to Alice. Alice smiled at the young lady before her, and the girl bobbed a curtsey

"Very pleased to meet you My Lady" she said, casting her eyes down as her former mistress had ordered too

"Welcome to Penleigh Court my dear" Alice was paying attention to the girls old and worn clothing, and wondered if this was her Sunday best dress, that Mark had already told her of, if that were the case, then she was only too glad to take her under her wing, it was beginning to look as if she would need a great deal more than she had at first thought, she was no more than a child, but she was alone and forlorn in the world, and she was someone Alice could take under her wing, a project which she could focus on, the daughter she never had, although her heart went out to the girl in front of her, she felt a sense of excitement at the prospect of schooling this young miss for the role that she was to become—the wife of a highly respected employee—yes, Alice was certainly going to make the most of this young lady

"Come my dear, let's go through to the drawing room, there's a fire in there it will be warmer and I shall ring for one of the maids to bring us some tea, and you can tell me all about yourself" Angela looked up into Mark's face, and he nodded his head at her, to follow Alice, the poor girl seemed afraid. Mark followed them into the drawing room and Alice pulled the bell pull

"Sit down my dear, we will have some tea, and a chat, and then I shall have someone show you to your room"

"Thank you madam" once again, she cast her eyes to the floor

"So, tell me you have been working for Mrs Kirkby I hear, how long have you been in her employ?"

"Three years madam" again, her eyes went straight to the floor

"Is there something wrong my dear, you look a little nervous" Alice ventured—Mark had seen Alice's reason for asking this and had rushed to her defence

"Angela has been trained that she should not look her betters in the eye My Lady, she was taught to look to the ground unless spoken too directly, as her employer Mrs Kirkby would box her ears if she failed to look at her toes" Alice drew a sharp intake of breath in horror—how could anyone have been treated this way. She stood up and went to the girl, and lifted her face to look at her

"I would not have you look down when you speak to me Angela, it is preposterous—you are here as my guest my dear, and you shall stay here until you are married. Tomorrow we will plan your wedding, and we are going to visit Truro in the afternoon, and I am going to buy you some suitable clothing, you are soon to be the wife of a our estate manager, who also happens to be a very good friend, so you will never be treated badly ever again, and I shall personally see to it that you are not" Alice wrapped an arm around the girl, and the tears streamed down her cheeks—then she sobbed loud and hard into Alice's shoulder. Alice saw the bruises on her neck she was shocked, stunned, she couldn't believe that anyone could serve another human being so, this cruelty was every bit as bad as Henry's—she was beginning to think that Richard was right not to have chosen the Kirkby girl, though by all accounts she was not much better treated by her mother, a tear trickled from Alice's eye, she would not see this poor frightened child before her harmed ever again. The maid entered then, Alice patted the girls back, then pulled away, Angela looked up to see the young maid, a girl of barely her own age, stood smiling in the doorway

"Ah Lucy, could you please bring tea for us, my son is not yet back I suppose?"

"Yes My Lady, the Duke and Mr Trent have just arrived My Lady"

"Then you had better bring tea for all of us"

"Yes My Lady" then she left, closing the door behind her

Mark seated himself on the settee next to Angela, before the door opened to the loud guffaw from the two gentlemen as they had returned from their ride, followed closely by Maria. Mark introduced Angela to everyone, though she said little, entwining her fingers nervously and tried to break her habit of bowing her head in the company of her betters. Jasper spent the rest of the afternoon, casting glances at Angela, although not of his class, he had to admit that Mark had made a good choice for a bride, she truly was a beauty, with a few alterations she would be just the thing. Richard suggested that Angela should meet his fiancée, as they were about the same age, and he thought that they may get along very well, indeed, he hoped that they would be friends. Maria was the only one not involved in the conversation—she sat apart from the rest, listening to the voices which were buzzing, and planning—she wasn't at all impressed with the chit, and Mark had thought that this skinny wench, with the dowdy old worn out clothing, could take her place in his bed, it was laughable. Tis true she had a certain attraction she supposed—all that pretty hair and those large green eyes, but she was nothing but a chit, and Maria wasn't about to allow herself and her pleasure to be pushed aside for a chit, she would never satisfy his needs as Maria had and intended carrying on doing, the girl would surely burst into tears at the very thought of keeping her husband happy—she would have to speak to him, and the sooner the better, they must carry on as before, and if he refused, then she would have to ensure that he didn't. As she sat planning, her lip curled in a mean and monstrous way, though her eyes were starting to shine with a secret pleasure of her own. She looked around the people gathered there—she already had a plan for Richard—what a pity he had chosen his own fate, but there it is, now she had the perfect plan for Mark too, if he didn't comply of course.

To everyone's pleasure, the day of the wedding was dry and bright, and there was a warmth which was balmy in the air—the drive was a carpet of beautiful colours, reds, golds, russets, and browns, the perfect day to get wed. Alice stood at her window, very tired, she had done so much to make this wedding memorable for the young couple—and she was bubbling with pleasure and pride at the thought of it all. Cook had made all sorts of delights in the kitchen for this wonderful wedding breakfast, including taking pride in making the finest cake, that would have made a true daughter of Alice's proud. The servants had been up since the break of dawn, preparing the great hall, where the feast was to take place. There would be no dancing, as they still had another month or so to go until they were out of mourning, but there had been a blessing in disguise, Tuesday morning a young friend of Angela's had turned up at the front door, it was Sarah Kirkby, although she was a lady, she had always been kind to Angela, and they had secretly become good friends, due to their common fear of Sarah's awful parent. Flora Kirkby would never have allowed her daughter to mix with the likes of Angela, she hated her having any friends at all, and ruled Sarah's life until she couldn't move without her mama. On learning that Angela had gone, Flora Kirkby had said good riddance, but Sarah had been devastated, her only friend had left, and she was left without a soul she could talk too, she had hoped that she would receive an offer of marriage herself, but her mama managed to frighten all the eligible young men away, before she had as much as a chance. So, she had packed a small bag herself, she didn't want the maid alerting her mama, and she had gone to the stables and ordered a horse saddled, then she had rode out of Truro, on her own, and made her way to Penleigh Court, where she had once been for tea with her mama, she had heard that's where her dear friend had gone. On arrival, Alice had invited her to take tea with them, and she had told them how she felt a prisoner in her own home and that she had come to find her only friend, Alice, although having to tread carefully in this matter, she couldn't be seen to be enticing the girl away from her home after all, but nor could she send her back to that awful woman—so she had sent word to Flora Kirkby that her daughter had been invited to stay, as her guest for a few weeks, at Penleigh Court, and requested that a trunk could be packed for her and Alice would send their carriage over the very next day to collect it. Sarah had been thrilled and excited, this way she need not raise her mother's suspicions or anger, and as she was a wonderful pianist, and had a beautiful voice, she had offered to play the piano and sing some songs, so the wedding wouldn't be totally without entertainment, Alice was delighted as was Angela—she was very fond of such entertainment, and had Sarah sing and play for them often, Maria had never offered anything such as this, which Alice thought to be a great pity, but most of all, Alice loved having these young ladies around her, it gave her a real sense of pleasure and excitement, and something she could take a pride in again. Neither of the girls had ever had such attention before, and they were both revelling in their newfound freedom. Angela, having had the life of a lowly servant, was now starting to enjoy being treated as a lady, she would never be able to repay Alice for such kindness, she was like the mother she had never known. Alice had decided that she would choose a navy gown, with a white lace collar for the day's activity—she had mourned enough the son she adored and the cruel man who had made her life so miserable. She thought back over the last few days, and all the hard work she had put herself too, to make this day a success for the dear young lady, who was so grateful she had wept so much, Alice thought that there could be no tears left inside her, though this time they were tears of joy and not of misery. Alice had taken the girl to visit her dressmaker on Monday afternoon, Priscilla Dawson was a very adept seamstress and could turn her hand to almost anything. The old lady had valued her for many years, Priscilla took one look at Angela and was horrified, on Alice's instruction Priscilla had gone to her rack of already made up gowns—luckily this girl was very thin, and of average height so there was a good choice which would not take too much alteration. Alice chose three gowns for Angela to try on, which she did with glee, she had never stepped in to such lovely things, let alone own them before, each of the gowns were tried in turn, the ivory satin was the most suitable, it was fairly low cut, with a band of tiny pearls set under the bust, then falling away to the ankle, it had long sleeves which were cut to a point over the hands, with little clusters of flowers made up of embroidery and pearls at the points and all around the hem, it had no train but that was for the best, it could then be altered for an evening gown at a later date, or even kept to be cut into a christening gown for their first child, it had frothy lace at the bust, to retain her modesty, yet it showed off her slight figure beautifully, and this particular gown needed no alterations. Alice agreed with Priscilla, that this gown may have been made especially for the girl. Alice also chose a beautiful ivory lace veil, made of the finest lace, which complimented the gown perfectly—Angela stood before the mirror, unable to remove her gaze—the girl looking back at her was someone she had never seen before, this woman was beautiful, it couldn't be her. Alice had also purchased three pretty sets of underwear, including stockings and two shawls also a small string of pearls to entwine in her hair, which she would have Gracie dress for her. Then, to Angela's surprise, Alice had told Priscilla to dispose of the rags which the girl had taken off, and she had chosen two more gowns from the rail, these were day gowns and she had Priscilla measure the girl for four more—she also had her measured for two Sunday best gowns and a ball gown, as she knew that Richard had planned a ball at the beginning of the new year, the girl would need something to wear for that. Each of the gowns which were chosen were the colours of the ocean—greens and blue's and turquoise, all the colours which suited the girl and brought out the colour of her eyes, they had also chosen several pairs of shoes, and purses matching, which blended with the gowns, and ribbons for her hair. There was also three nightgowns, one of which was so beautiful, Angela kept running her hand over it, it was of a soft cotton, which was almost transparent, with lovely little embroidered flowers around the neckline and sleeves—this one was for her wedding night, Alice had told her. Once their purchases were complete, she had instructed that they be packed and her footmen would collect them before they left for home. They had another visit to make before leaving, and that was a visit to the milliner's, Angela had often stood looking through the window at all the fashionable hats on show, and wondered what it would be like to be able to step inside and make a purchase—her bonnet was something which she had attained as a cast off, when she went for her interview with Mrs Kirkby—now she was to have a brand new one of her very own. They stepped inside the shop, Alice chose two bonnets for her protégé, one with ivory ribbons, the other with ribbons in different shades of blue and green, it would suit any one of her gowns a treat. They left the shop again after Alice had promised to send one of her footmen to collect the goods. Finally, Alice had noticed the small jewellery shop, a few steps from where their carriage was awaiting them, Angela had thought that they were finished with their purchases although she was in a world of her own, a place of excited bliss that she had never visited before, in the whole of her life. She kept thinking about the way she would look for her dearest Mark, she loved him so much it hurt. When he had found this job at Penleigh Court she had been devastated—she knew that he wanted an estate manager post, hell he deserved it, but she had thought that she would never see him again, he would meet someone new and she would be forgotten, left to the horror of the awful Mrs Kirkby, but he had still visited her on her days off, he never faltered, and when he told her that they could be married she had thought she would burst with excited delight, she had never thought that she would be treated as a Lady, never in her wildest dreams. Alice had instructed her to wait in the carriage, she wouldn't be long, before informing the footmen that their packages needed collecting, then she took the few steps into the jeweller's shop. She wanted to give the girl something to treasure, to remind her of the most wonderful day of her life, she had suffered so much, but no more—Alice had already started to see her as the daughter she had never had. Standing at the counter, the little old jeweller, came to her asking how he could help—he knew who she was, and he had served their family many times throughout his working life, but never before had he served the Dowager Duchess, it was usually her husband, even her two sons, but he was happy to do business with this little, now ageing and frail lady. She had asked for a string of pearls, the jeweller reached for a black velvet case, and clicked the catch, opening it to reveal the goods inside. Alice looked at them, they were beautiful, each one of similar size, though not too large, and creamy in colour, they were perfect—this was exactly what she had been looking for, and she knew that the girl would treasure these with her life. She asked the jeweller to wrap the box, while she made the purchase, then slipping the package inside her reticule, she left the shop, happy with all her purchases. She would wait until Angela was dressed and ready for the church, then she would present them to her, to set off her gown. The door opened, which startled her back to the present

Gracie entered, she had been very busy this morning, she had taken her time in helping Alice with her toilette.

"How is Miss Angela this morning Gracie?" Alice asked smiling

"She is very nervous My Lady, but she seems very happy—Miss Kirkby is with her at the moment, I shall go back and help her to dress in a little while"

"Good, once she is dressed, I would like to see her, before she goes to the church"

"Of course My Lady, I shall let you know when she is ready"

"Thank you Gracie"

Alice allowed Gracie to help her bath and then to dress in the navy and white gown—she had spent enough time in black, she couldn't change the past, but she could play her part in the future, and she was determined that she would. Once dressed and ready, Gracie left her, to go and help Miss Angela into her lovely gown.

Angela was excited and so very happy, but so nervous she was afraid that she would do or say something wrong. Alice, dear Alice, she had been so good to her that she could never have dreamt of her good fortune, not in her wildest of dreams—she had always thought that she would be on the receiving end of slaps and even on a couple of occasions a kick. She had bathed, her dear friend Sarah had helped her—though her and Sarah were of very different background, Sarah was as isolated in her way, as she was herself—perhaps that was why they had become so close. Sarah had told her that her mama hated her because of her beauty—with her lovely colour hair and green eyes, Flora Kirkby had complained regularly that she was too pretty for her own good, and needed to learn a few lessons. But today was about her happiness, her's and Mark's—she had not believed her good fortune that Sunday afternoon that he had noticed her, taking a walk through the park, and when he had asked if he could walk with her, she had almost fainted with joy, such a handsome man, and he had actually noticed her. He had been well dressed and she was in her usual old worn clothes, holes darned, until there was very little left to darn. They had soon discovered that they enjoyed the same things, so when he told her that he had got the job of his dreams, she had been distraught, though she had never showed her feelings to him. Gracie had returned, and was holding the beautiful gown for her to step into, before buttoning the tiny pearl buttons at the back

"You look beautiful miss, Mr Chandler will not recognize you" said Gracie, with a smile on her face

"Thank you so much Gracie—it's so very kind of you to help me"

"Don't be daft miss, my mistress has taken to you and that's for sure, but it's easy to see why, you are so pretty, I wish that I looked as you do"

Angela turned around and threw her arms about Gracie, as tears rolled down her cheeks

"Don't cry miss, you mustn't cry today—you don't want to spoil your new dress now do you?" Angela gave her a watery smile

"You had better sit down, madam has instructed me to style your hair miss, and she's given me these pearls to weave in it—they will look lovely miss"

"Thank you Gracie" Angela did as she was told, and sat on an upright chair, which Gracie had pulled out from the writing desk in the corner of her room, and of which she would never use, as she was unable to read and write, being of the working class. Gracie pulled and styled her hair with a bone comb, which Alice had found for her use, until she had piled the auburn gold mass on the top of her head, allowing the curls to cascade down like a waterfall falling over rocks in its path, then taking the curls and weaving the tiny seed pearl garland, in and out until it had all been woven in delicate patterns around her head. Next the veil over the top and floating down to the ground its dainty lace softly circling that pretty face. Gracie told Angela she could now look into the mirror—she caught her breath—the face looking back at her was stunning—it could never be the face of Angela Moreton looking back at her, even the bruises on her neck had been covered with powder—Gracie had made such a good job of the disguise. Gracie had a tear in her eye, so she went to the window to hide it

"Look at the sunshine miss, you know what they say, happy is the bride that the sun shines on" Sarah entered the room again, she too was feeling very happy and pleased with herself, she too looked beautiful in a pink satin dress, gathered under the bust, it suited her very well—the Dukes friend had been taking particular notice of her the last few days, and she thought him a very handsome man, perhaps, without her mama to spoil her chances, she would find a man for herself, and she would be more than happy if it could be the dashing Mr Trent.

"Oh Angie, you look wonderful, Mark is a very lucky man" she said, noticing her friend she carefully threw her arms around Angie and kissed her cheek "I am so pleased that we are friends, we must always remain so"

"I have never had a friend before, no-one else had ever noticed me even"

"Nor I, my mother would never allow it" she stepped back "You look like a princess, but will I do?" she asked, thinking about Jasper

"You look lovely Sarah, but you always do" she replied

"I do hope so, or at least I hope the Mr Trent will think so" Sarah said laughing

"I think he's noticed you already, he doesn't take his eyes off you, let alone having to stand by your chair and rushing to open the door—I'd say he was smitten"

"Really Angie" she said tartly "I don't know what you mean" both girls looked at each and laughed

Gracie left the room smiling at the two and their banter, she had been ordered to fetch her mistress once she was ready, and she looked a picture and no mistake. Alice followed Gracie to Angela's room, Gracie opened the door and allowed her mistress to enter first. Alice was holding a package in her hand, wrapped in paper and tied with a bright red bow of ribbon, she stopped dead in the doorway, the sight before her was breath-taking, she had chosen a very worthy young lady to bestow her kindness on.

"Angela my dear, you are absolutely delightful, you look radiant, you will make for a beautiful blushing bride, and Mark is one very lucky young man" Alice told her

"Thank you so much My Lady, I feel like a princess—and I owe it all to you My Lady"

"You owe me nothing my dear, I am happy to help you you have allowed me in my old age, to enjoy the pleasures of a daughter who I never had—so

I thank you for allowing me this. And you must call me Alice, I want you to know that you can always come to me for anything my dear, anything at all, you have only to ask, but now, I have a little wedding gift for you, to finish off your appearance"

"My Lady, I mean Alice, you have spoilt me too much already"

"Nonsense, it has been my pleasure" she said, walking into the room and handing the wrapped package to Angela, the girl's eyes sparkled bright and she looked from the package to Alice's face and back to the package

"Are you not going to open it?" Alice asked, Angela looked at Alice and smiled, then tugging the ribbon which fell loose in her hand, she peeled back the paper, to see an oval black velvet box, she glanced up at Alice before lifting the lid, there, lying on the soft black plush, was a beautiful pearl necklace, the creamy stones small and even, with its little gold clasp, Angela stood staring at this delicate trinket, she had never owned such a beautiful thing, in fact, she had never owned a single piece of jewellery in her life, she would treasure this all her days, the tears spilled from her eyes once again, she had never known such kindness as this

"Let me fasten it for you Angie" said her friend, standing next to her. Sarah carefully fastened the necklace in place, before leading the girl back to see her reflection in the mirror

"How can I thank you for so much" she said, still fingering the small ivory gems at her throat, Alice could only smile at the girls reflection looking at her from the mirror

"But it's time to go, I'm afraid my son will be waiting to accompany you to the church, and he is rather impatient, we must not keep him waiting" said Alice "come Miss Kirkby, we shall leave first, and you can follow in five minutes, our carriage is already waiting for us. Alice took Sarah's arm as they descended the stairs to the hallway below, Richard was indeed waiting in the hall looking his usual immaculate self. He watched as the two ladies reached him

"You ladies are both looking very lovely" he remarked smiling. Sarah kept her gaze fixed on him, he was such a handsome man, she wished that she had been to his liking, but that was not to be, still, Mr Trent seemed taken with her, she was indeed impressed with him.

"You can help us to the carriage my dearest" Alice said to her son, who was already holding out his arm to his mother" they stepped outside, and Richard helped first his mother, and then Miss Kirkby into the carriage, the footman closed the door and lifted the steps as Richard stepped back into the hall to wait for the bride. He didn't have long, for as he looked up she was coming down the stairs, Gracie behind her holding up the young woman's veil. Richard was stunned, he just stared at this beauty coming down the stairs, his friend was certainly a very lucky man and his mama had done wonders for the girl. As she reached the bottom of the stairs, Richard went over and handed her his arm

"You look delightful Miss Moreton—your husband will be stunned with your beauty"

"I do hope so, I do love Mark very much sir, I hope that he will be pleased"

"How could he fail to be mesmerised"

"Thank you sir" she said, looking up and smiling at him

"Please call me Richard we are all to be friends are we not?"

"Yes sir, Richard" and they both smiled

Richard led her out into the sunshine, and into the waiting landau—it was all so beautiful, the carriage had been decorated with ivory ribbons and bows which were now flowing in the breeze, Angela could not believe that this was all happening to her, not after only a few short days ago, she had been slapped and beaten. If Flora Kirkby could only see her now, she would be shocked, Angela smiled to herself at that thought, as the Duke helped her into the carriage, and seated himself opposite her on the way through the village and on to the church.

The service was lovely, all the people sat in the church, but the most important one to her, was her dearest Mark, as Richard armed her up the aisle, the heads were turning and gasps of breath were heard, and when she reached her groom and he looked down into her face, he was almost struck dumb, his smile was warm and bright, and he was glowing by the time they alighted into the sunlight once again. At the lych gate the guests were throwing grains of rice at the happy couple, as they climbed into the landau and made their way back to Penleigh Court for the wedding breakfast—Mark certainly believed himself a very lucky man, in that moment he made up his mind that Maria was a thing of the past—why would he want anyone else, when he had the most beautiful girl in the world. He owed so much to Alice, what a wonderful woman she was, to do this for them and to turn his beautiful wife into a princess. On the way back, he just couldn't let go of her hand, clasping it tightly and kissing it, every few moments. Jasper would not leave Sarah's side and was there every time she turned round, though she was really enjoying the attention. Richard had smiled to himself, so Trent wasn't as resilient as he had always professed to be, though he would have to speak to him as he had a habit of flouting society, and he wanted no scandal here in Cornwall, like there had been in London. The only face that wasn't smiling and happy, and the only one who had not offered words of happiness and joy for the couple, was Maria—Richard had watched her throughout the day, noticing that she was not happy at all—what with the celebrations, and the beauty of the bride, and her new husbands pride in her—her face was set like a mask, of anger and contempt—she obviously knew that her time with her lover was well and truly over.

By mid-afternoon the guests had started to leave, Sarah was playing the piano and serenading everyone, while her shadow Jasper Trent, stood beside her turning the pages of the music for her. Mark with his bride, were talking to his family—they were talking and laughing together and Richard was happy that there was a family bond there. As the people said their goodbyes and wished the bride and groom happiness and a long marriage, Richard noticed one of the servants handing something to Mark, a note he turned away from his family to take a quiet minute to read it. Richard watched as a frown creased his brow, then excusing himself from his family, he walked down the corridor and into Richard's library. Richard had made a promise to himself, that he would look after his friend, and how strange that he should leave his guests to hide away in the library on the day of his wedding—he knew that there was more to it than that so he slipped away and stood by the library door, it was shut, he opened it gently, quietly without a sound, just enough to be able to hear the conversation taking place inside

"I'm sorry Maria, but now I'm a married man, you know that I can't meet you anymore"

"So you think that you can use me and dispose of me so easily?"

"No, of course not, but I had warned you that once I was married, our relationship would have to stop, you knew this months ago, I'm sorry—I shall always remember our times together with great fondness, but it has to be all over now, I have a wife and she must never know"

"Really, then all the more reason to keep me happy, don't you think?"

"Please Maria, this is my wedding day, my wife and my guests are awaiting me, I really must go"

"You are very eager to leave, I agree, you should not dessert your guests, so I shall expect to see you at my house, tonight?"

"No Maria, I shall be sharing my wife's bed tonight, and every night from now on, there will be no more nights spent with you at the Gate Lodge—it cannot be" this time he was speaking firmly

"Then perhaps I should have a few words with your bride, see if she thinks that you are being fair to be ignoring me, just because you have put a ring on her finger, and after you broke into my house to seduce me, just a week ago, I don't believe that she will be happy with your behaviour, do you?"

"You wouldn't be so cruel—I don't believe that you could be so vengeful"

"You will call me Lady Maria, when you speak to me—I am your better, and I have given you an order, you are no more than a servant—for all your finery and pretence today—I taught you what you know, and you will now do as I say, if you don't want your pretty little chit running off and leaving you"

"Please Lady Maria, it doesn't have to be like this, I am happy to have our pleasurable memories in my mind forever, no-one could ever doubt your beauty or your attraction, but I cannot keep any more assignations with you again"

"I don't care for memories, I have already told you before, it's your body that I crave, not your mind, and I shall have my way, believe me, you will not thwart me on this—be at my house tonight, or I may just have to pay your chit a call, and I will, in case you think to cross me in this"

"I cannot stay all night, please do not ask it of me"

"Lady Maria—you forgot to address me properly" she prompted

"I'm sorry Lady Maria, please do not ask me to stay all night"

"So, you will come? I can look forward to seeing you for at least a couple of hours—tell the chit what you like, but I shall expect you, and I shall wait for you, do not let me down"

"I will come Lady Maria" he relented

"Then I must go to prepare for you—don't keep me waiting too long"

Richard listening to the conversation, his stomach lurching, she was evil— just like his father, Richard knew that he must speak to Mark, they must find a way out of this situation, he should never have agreed for him to have gone to Maria like he did, they could have found another way out. Everything had gone quiet, he must move away, he couldn't chance being seen. He stepped along the corridor and into the empty drawing room, where he waited for a short while—their conversation should have finished by now, then he strode back to the library and opened the door. His friend was sat in a chair, his head in his hands—he looked up as Richard entered, trying to put a smile on his face

"It's alright my friend" Richard said to him, going to the sideboard, and pouring brandy from the decanter into two glasses

"I'm alright" he said

"No, you are not" Richard said firmly "I'm sorry for eavesdropping into your conversation, but I heard what went on"

"What am I to do Richard—today has been the happiest day of my life— you and Alice have given Angela and myself more than we could ever have hoped for, now Maria is threatening to ruin everything, I cannot allow her do so, I love Angie, she would never understand, I know that I have done wrong, allowing Lady Maria to become my mistress in the first place, but I had thought that she would understand, now that I'm a married man"

"Maria, I'm afraid to say is a parasite, she feeds on the misery of other people—I only wish that I could have stopped you becoming involved with her in the first place"

"I was a fool, allowing her to seduce me—but she was so tempting"

"Indeed, I have witnessed her attempts at seduction—I have had mistresses in the past, but I'm glad to say that I did not allow her to succeed with me—though she has threatened me also—but her reasoning with me is because I wouldn't seduce her, so I'm afraid, had you not fallen for her charms, you would still not be safe from her threats—we are both living to see what happens next" Richard slapped his friend on the back

"You are not to go near her tonight I shall go in your place"

"But she won't settle for that I'm sure" said Mark lifting his head and looking at Richard "I can't take any chances, I know that you mean well, but if she was to tell Angie of our meetings, it would be the end of my marriage before it began"

"But if you go tonight, not only have you got to lie to your bride, but you have to find excuses to leave her on your wedding night—surely no reason on this earth would justify that—it certainly wouldn't for me anyway"

"I know that you are right, but what will you say to her to convince her"

"I shall think of something. Have another brandy, and then join your bride, enjoy the rest of your day and leave everything else with me"

"Are you sure Richard?"

"Quite sure" he poured them both another drink, then Mark composed himself and went out to carry on the celebrations, although, Richard noticed, his spirits had been dampened, he wore bright smile on his lips, but he had a haunted look on his face.

Richard opened the door of the Gate Lodge and walked into the hallway, there was no lights on and everything was in darkness, he thought for a moment that he was alone here. Just as he had given up and was about to step outside again, he saw the flicker of a candle at the top of the stairs.

"So you decided to come my dear, I'm ready and waiting for you" said Maria in that soft lazy voice, Richard didn't answer as he knew that she would know he wasn't Mark straight away, he felt his way in the darkness to the stairs, and then watching his step, he climbed the stairs in silence

"Don't stand outside my bedroom teasing me, come inside and enjoy the delights I have in store for you tonight—and hurry, we haven't got all night or have we?"

Richard could see around the dim bedroom, from the light of the candle, as he stepped into the room—Maria was laid naked on the bed, stroking the eiderdown she was laid on, once she realized that it was Richard and not Mark she shot up

"What are you doing here" she said climbing off the bed and walking round to where he stood "I am expecting company, so perhaps you should go"

"That's exactly why I'm here Maria, your gentleman friend is otherwise occupied tonight, and cannot possibly keep his assignation"

"So you have come in his place?" she asked her voice soft and silky once more "I can forgive his neglect this once, now that you are here instead" she moved like a cat, ready to pounce, she threw her arms around his neck and pressed her body to his, then pressing her lips hard on his lips, while her hand was working its way inside his shirt—that was enough, he grabbed her arm and pushed it away from his body

"I am not here for your pleasure Maria, I am here to tell you that Mark is not coming, and he will not be coming again—I heard your conversation with him this afternoon, and I will not tolerate your behaviour towards my staff—do you hear me Maria? You live under my roof because I allow it, you have an allowance which I insisted you should have, but I can just as easily withdraw my kindness to you. You will stay away from Mark and his wife—and if you are looking for a lover, then go to Truro, and find a gentleman who is interested in your charms, but stay away from my family and my staff—is that understood?" Maria had never seen Richard's temper before, but today she had really tested his patience to the limit, Maria too was furious, she slapped his face with her full force, he grabbed her arm before she could repeat the action, glaring at her with a fixed gaze

"Get out—get out of my house" she shrieked

"Willingly madam" Richard retorted letting go of her arm

"But beware, you have crossed me once too often—I will finish you sir, believe me when I say I will take great pleasure in watching you hang from the gibbet at Gallows Cross, I will see you dead, and as for that weak virgin you employ, he will wish that he hadn't crossed me either—do you hear me" she was screeching like a witch "he will pay too" Richard found his way down the stairs, and across to the front door, his eyes had become accustomed to the darkness now, his face still stinging from the force of Maria's temper, he opened the door and strode outside, into the cool night air—he would take no more from this woman, he wanted nothing more to do with her, but if she dared to meddle in his life, or the life of his estate manager just once more, he would throw her out on the street—starve or not, he was at the end of his patience, and he would stand no more.

CHAPTER TWENTY TWO

(The Arrest)

Richard returned from his afternoon ride, he went directly to the library and poured himself a large glass of brandy he had been so looking forward to this evening, when the Penrose family were joining them for dinner. He kept thinking of Clara and how wonderful she had looked on Mark's wedding day, he had almost imagined it to be their wedding day, at least he wished it could have been. He had not seen so much of Clara lately, but he would make it up to her—they had already set the date for the wedding, and it was already the beginning of December—by the end of this month he would have been here a whole year, where had the time gone, and by next year at this time, he could potentially be a father—that would please his mother, she would be delighted, and if he were honest, so would he, at least he would have the full extent of his money at his disposal. He loved the girls dearly, and he knew that they had come to love and depend on him, but having his own child, with sweet Clara, would just be fulfilment of all his dreams and he could safely say that Ada Penrose would be overjoyed too. Tonight would be special for him, he wanted to show Clara off and it would give her a chance to get to meet the other young ladies who he was now acquainted with. Jasper was really taken with Miss Kirkby, he was still following her around like a shadow, though he believed that she welcomed his advances, just so long as that's all it was, he didn't want him taking advantage of her like he had so many others. Mark and Angela seemed happy and settled, Mark was still coming into work each morning, though Richard had persuaded him to spend his afternoons in the company of his bride, at least for a few days. Alice had insisted that Miss Kirkby stay on at Penleigh Court as her guest, although Angela had invited her to stay at the cottage, but Alice thought that it would be better for the young happy couple, to have the time to themselves, having a guest so early in their marriage was not right, they needed their privacy, and besides, Miss Kirkby seemed more than happy to be near to Trent. The only one who hadn't shown her face in any way or form, since the night of the wedding, was Maria, Richard could only be thankful that she was keeping well out of everyone's way—he would have liked to think that she had packed her bags and left, but that was too much to ask—so he would just have to settle for her absence.

Richard woke that morning, feeling that awful foreboding once again—though why and where it came from he just didn't know. The wind had been howling, blowing the leaves around everywhere and whistling through the house, the rain had been beating against the window panes, and cold had started to seep into the house. He had gone to the estate office to join Mark for a while, but he couldn't settle to do anything, what with his feeling of dread and excitement, he wasn't sure how he did feel. Eventually, he excused himself from the office, promising Mark that he would send the carriage for them at seven o clock that evening, before heading back to the house. After lunch, the weather seemed to abate for a while, allowing him to go out for his daily ride, though he didn't venture far, or for long, as the storms returned in force as he turned up the drive.

Alice was in a state of hectic joy, she had always loved occasions, be it a ball or dinner, or any other entertainment she decided to hold. She would organize the staff and have the table laid according to her instructions. There would be ten for dinner that evening, so quite an auspicious occasion, Alice would never have thirteen people for dinner, it was supposed to be extremely unlucky and the family had had more than their fair share of that over the years. There would be five courses, starting with a homemade soup, then a fish course which on this occasion would be trout, followed by a large joint of roast beef, rhubarb charlotte and finally cheese and fruit, and port for the gentlemen—Alice could be relied upon to offer a good table, and Richard had some excellent port. The table had been laid with the best crystal glasses and two large candelabras which Alice's parents had presented to her and Henry on their wedding day. Everything would be perfect and as the period of mourning was almost up, it was decided that they should not wear black. The guests were due to arrive at seven thirty, ready to eat at eight o clock.

By six o clock, Alice was happy with the arrangements, and was about to go upstairs to change, when she suddenly realized that she hadn't seen Maria for the last few days. Richard was still sat at his desk in the library so she popped her head around the door

"Richard, have you seen Maria lately, I haven't seen her in days, not since the wedding in fact" she asked

"No, I haven't seen her either, she will no doubt turn up"

"I'm sure that she will, but she is expected to join us for dinner tonight— she hasn't said that she won't be there"

"Then you should stop worrying mama, Maria can take care of herself, she will turn up once our guests arrive this evening"

"Yes, I expect you are right. I'm going to get changed now, and I think that you should do the same Richard, our guests are due to arrive in just over an hour, and we must be ready to greet them"

"I am on my way mama" Richard got up with a sigh, and followed his mother up the stairs.

It was exactly ten minutes past seven when Richard descended the stairs to the hall, he still had not managed to shake off that awful feeling of dread and foreboding, which had lingered with him since that morning. Just enough time for another brandy before their guests were due to arrive, Jasper was already there, helping himself from the decanter. Alice had already seated herself in the drawing room, along with Miss Kirkby— Nanny Grey was to be looked after by Gracie for the evening, she would only sleep in the chair anyway. It was twenty minutes past seven when Richard heard Newbridge walk across the hall to the front door, within minutes Alice had popped her head round the open door to the library, to tell her son that their first guests had arrived, Jasper followed him out and went to take up his position in the drawing room with the lovely Miss Kirkby.

Newbridge was showing Mark and Angela into the hall, as Richard and his mother arrived. Alice kissed Angela warmly before Richard took her hand and kissed it, complimenting her on her lovely gown, one of rich deep green, which matched her beautiful eyes, and wearing the lovely pearls that had been her wedding present from Alice. Before they had time to move on to the drawing room, there was another knock at the door, at last the moment that Richard had been waiting for. Newbridge opened the door, and as he did so, the gust of wind had blown a cluster of leaves into the hall—the rain was once again beating down, and it had turned degrees colder. Newbridge ushered the guests into the hall, where Alice welcomed them warmly, before Richard took first Ada Penrose's hand and kissed it, then his sweet Clara's. Newbridge took their cloaks and vicar Penrose's overcoat and hat which he hung the cloaks and coat on the stand in the hall, and placed the vicar's hat on the hall table. Richard took one look at Clara and caught his breath, she had a gown of ivory velvet, it was a simple cut, but most becoming, she was stunning—every time he saw the girl she looked more beautiful than the time before.

Alice led the way to the drawing room where introductions were made all round. A few moments later Newbridge came through and stated that dinner was served, and they followed Alice on the vicar's arm, with Richard and Ada Penrose to follow, the young people falling in behind.

Dinner was a noisy affair, there were several conversations going on around the table, but there was one place which had not been filled. Maria still had not shown. Alice was getting more concerned that she was alright, but Richard assured her that she would be fine he promised that if she had not shown by the following morning, he would send out a search party to find her, though secretly he believed that she was down at the Gate Lodge licking her wounds. The dinner was going famously everyone seemed to be getting on with one another, the three young ladies becoming acquainted with each other to Richard's pleasure. Clara had agreed that she would welcome some help in the parish, and both Angela and Sarah jumped at the chance of helping. With Christmas just around the corner, there would be plenty to do, and the elderly relied so much on Clara's help, even the more mobile ones could not get out of their homes when the weather was so bad, and some of them needed someone to offer them a hot meal, or even a cup of tea. They had just started on the main course of roast beef, when Newbridge entered the dining room he went straight to Richard and whispered in his ear

"Excuse me for interrupting your meal Your Grace, but Mr Drummond and his men are in the hall, he is insisting on speaking with you right away My Lord" Richard sighed—of all the times that Drummond should call he chose now to arrive

"Can he not wait until we have finished eating Newbridge"

"I'm afraid that he wishes to speak with you urgently, My Lord" he persisted. Richard turned to his guests

"I'm so sorry, please excuse me ladies and gentlemen, it seems that I am urgently required, but I shall return shortly" everyone round the table voiced their assent and Richard stood up and strode from the room. Drummond and several of his men were in the hall waiting to speak with him

"Drummond, my dear fellow, we have not seen you for some time, I would ask you to join us, but we have guests this evening, so perhaps next time"

"Good evening Your Grace, I'm very sorry to disturb you, but I am here on official business"

"Official business, that sounds rather serious—I have some information for you in fact, when you called last time you asked me about the Gate Lodge, well I have since learned that my sister in law Maria is the new owner, and I believe that the goods you have been seeking are in caves which you can access from one of the servants rooms at the top of the Gate Lodge—was that what you were looking for?"

"Not exactly, but thank you for the information My Lord, I shall have that looked into straight away. No, I'm afraid I'm here because we have been informed that there are items of contraband, here in this very house. I received a note this afternoon, advising me to bring men to search one of your bedchambers here My Lord—I don't expect that we shall find anything, not for one minute, but I have to follow every lead you understand"

"That is ridiculous Drummond, I don't believe that anyone living here has anything to do with that band of thieves—but, you are more than welcome to search all you wish"

"Thank you My Lord, we shall be as quick as we can, then we shall leave you in peace, but in the meantime, perhaps you wouldn't mind accompanying us to the room concerned"

"Who informed you of all this anyway, and where do you wish to search?"

"If you will, My Lord, I would ask you to accompany us, the informant was anonymous, I received a note with no signature—the room is the third room along the first floor passage to the right"

"Then you must have it all wrong, that room is my own, it hadn't been used in a long time, until I returned to occupy it—I don't believe that it was used all the time that I was away in London in fact"

"Nevertheless My Lord, I am bound to act on any information which comes my way. We shall soon see Your Grace, we shall soon see"

Richard led them to his bed chamber and held the door for them all to enter—once inside, Rufus Drummond went straight to the washstand with a small draw underneath, he opened the draw and pulled out a large padlock key, he held it out to Richard to show him what he had found, and to look for recognition—Richard showed none

"What have you found?" he asked

"A padlock key My Lord, just as the note had stated—in the washstand draw"

"I have no idea I have never seen the key before, though I don't think that I've opened the draw more than twice since my return"

"So, you have no idea to the whereabouts of the padlock which this key fits?"

"None at all—could you tell me what exactly are you looking for?

"No, but we shall know when we find it won't we My Lord" without further ado, Drummond made his way to the large solid oak chest with the blue plush lid, which sat at the bottom of Richard's large bed, he lifted the padlock and slid the key into the hole, the padlock sprang open— Drummond stepped back and glanced up at Richard, before slipping the padlock free and lifting the lid of the chest—there was huge intakes of breath, including Richard himself, for inside, almost full to the top, was gold and plush boxes of different sizes, also jewels, like he had never seen before—Drummond lifted one of the boxes out, and opened the lid, inside laid a beautiful sapphire and diamond necklace, sparkling in the light from the candle

"No, no—this cannot be—I have never seen any of this before" Richard said shaking his head, looking from one to the other of the faces gathered round in the candlelight

"Do you deny that you locked these gold and jewels away here in your room My Lord?"

"Yes Drummond, I do strongly deny it—I have never seen any of it ever before"

"I'm sorry Your Grace, but this isn't goods taken by smugglers, these goods are those of highway raids—jewels and gold My Lord, taken from Lords and Ladies when travelling at night, Oliver Townsend was hung last November, he was caught a man of the road so to speak, but the other one—he had gone—got away, and the stolen goods, went with him they were never recovered—because here they are" said Drummond now fixing Richard with his unflinching gaze

"This is nonsense, I know nothing of highway men, any more than smugglers—you must believe me Drummond, you know that I am not a party to any of such underhand goings on"

"I'm sorry My Lord, all I know is that we were informed that we would find goods stolen by the smugglers here in this room, with a key that would be found in the washstand draw, that would fit a padlock of a large oak chest covered with a blue velvet seat—and everything is just as the note said—so My Lord, I'm afraid that I'm going to arrest you for the second highwayman, the one who dodged the noose—last time round, I'm afraid you won't dodge it again" he then turned to his men "Go on then, get on with it—arrest this man, he's going to Newgate gaol, where he will be tried for highway robbery, and if found guilty, he will hang, as the highwayman Oliver Townsend his associate did last November.

"No Drummond, I cannot allow you to do this—you are making a grave mistake—I'm an innocent man—would you hang an innocent man?" Richard was shouting now, his mind in a panic, how could he have known what was in that trunk, or where it had come from

"Take him away men" Drummonds men grabbed him roughly and marched him down the staircase, and out of the front door and into the waiting prison cart. Richard was struggling and fighting to free himself but there were too many of them. He was finished he was to go to his death for something that he knew nothing of.

On seeing the commotion, Alice had left the dining table and gone into the hall to see what all the fuss was about, followed closely by Mark and Jasper. Rufus Drummond was stood at the bottom of the stairs, with a solemn look on his face

"I'm sorry My Lady, but I have no choice but to take the Duke in" he said, as she rushed towards him

"What do you mean Mr Drummond? Whatever is happening?" asked Alice confused

"I'm afraid the situation is very grave My Lady, the Duke has been arrested, for his part in highway robbery" he said

"That's nonsense, my son would never do any such thing, you cannot do this, I beg of you"

"I'm sorry My Lady, but it's true, the charges against him are very serious, and likely he will hang for his crime" Alice threw the palms of her hands to her face

"No, please Mr Drummond, you are wrong, I know my son"

"What evidence do you have against the Duke Drummond?" asked Mark, putting an arm about Alice's shoulders

"I'm afraid we have all the evidence that's needed to see him swing—there's no mistake" at that moment two of Drummonds men came down the stairs heaving with them the wooden trunk, Drummond looked over at them

"This is all the evidence we need Mr Chandler—I apologize for interrupting your evening, we will be about our business now, I shall wish you goodnight" said Drummond, turning to follow his two men with the trunk, out of the front door

Alice dropped to the floor—she had fainted, Mark lifted her up and carried her upstairs, and Newbridge scuttled off to find Gracie to take care of her mistress. Jasper returned to the dining room, where the other guests were finishing their meal. Vicar Penrose looked to Jasper for an explanation—Jasper took his seat at the table, knowing that the guests were waiting to hear what had just taken place, but he couldn't speak for the moment, he too was suffering from shock. Mark returned to the dining room, to take charge of the situation

"I'm sorry for the disturbance this evening, but I'm afraid we are going to have to cancel the remainder of the evening" he said

"Is there anything which we can do?" asked vicar Penrose

"No, I'm afraid there is not very much any of us can do, I fear"

"Is someone ill?" the vicar persisted

"No—no-one is ill. Actually, I believe a great mistake has just been made"

"May I ask what sort of a mistake Mr Chandler, is there nothing that I can do to help, is the Dowager Duchess alright?" vicar Penrose was very determined

"I'm afraid that Mr Drummond and his authorities have arrested the Duke on a charge of highway robbery, which we all know to be an utter nonsense, so much so that his poor mother has taken ill from the shock" said Mark. There were several sharp intakes of breath, and Clara was sat stunned, tears spilling down her cheek

"I see, what evidence does Mr Drummond have for his accusations?" asked the vicar

"Apparently, goods have been found in this house" replied Mark, deep in disbelief

"Then it doesn't bode well for the Duke I'm afraid" the vicar announced gravely

"I shall leave tomorrow morning and ride to London, our good friend Hinton will help me, we have to prove what nonsense this whole matter is—I trust I can rely on you Chandler to run things here, and see what you can discover, while we are away?" asked Jasper

"Of course, I shall do whatever I can, perhaps you would keep me informed of any new developments" Mark asked Jasper

"Indeed, I shall" he replied

"I'm going with you sir" Clara spoke now "I have to go to him—I cannot sit here and do nothing, when my future husband is sat in a cell, waiting for them to hang him" and she burst into tears—Angela went to her, putting her arms about her and trying to pacify the poor girl

"I'm sorry Miss Penrose, but I cannot take you with me, for one thing I must ride hard and fast, and cannot allow anything to hold me up, and in all honesty, Warren will not wish you to visit him in such an awful place— he would hold me accountable were I to take you there, and besides, were you to go, you would need a chaperone, you must stay here Miss Penrose, and have faith in Hinton and myself" Jasper said firmly

"Of course you cannot go Clara, whatever are you thinking my dear" said Ada Penrose to her daughter

"We must stay here and pray for him my dear" said the vicar to his daughter "perhaps we should be on our way" then turning to Mark he said "If there is anything which we can do to help Mr Chandler, you know where to find us, I'm certain that things will work out for the best—should Lady Alice wish me to call, you only need send word"

"Thank you vicar, I shall do that" the vicar stood up "Then I believe that it's time to go my dears" he said to his wife and daughter. The two ladies also stood and followed him from the room—Mark went with them to the front door, and Newbridge hurried to open the door for them—the weather had not ceased it's fury—Mark took an umbrella from the stand to shield the women on their way to the carriage, but the wind had taken it as soon as he had stepped out. The coachman opened the door and pulled down the steps, and Mark helped the ladies inside—before the vicar climbed in behind them. Mark returned to the other guests still seated in the dining room

"I think it's time that we took our leave also Angela my dear" Mark said to his wife "I wish you God's speed on your journey tomorrow Trent—and pray that you may find a way to free the Duke quickly" he said to Jasper

"Indeed, I know my friend, he is definitely not guilty of this crime, we have been friends since we were at Eton together, we have been known to do some fool hardy things, as all young men do—I fear that my crimes have been far worse than Warren's but this is totally ridiculous" he said

"Well my dear" Mark turned to his wife "we must be on our way now" then turning back to Jasper "I shall look forward to receiving good news from you Chandler" then he turned to Miss Kirkby, taking her hand and lifting it to his lips "Good evening Miss Kirkby, I shall check on Lady Alice in the morning, I trust that you will keep an eye to her for me" Sarah looked at him with a faraway look "Of course Mr Chandler, I shall be glad to be of help" then Angela went to Sarah and threw her arms about her friend—they clung together for a long moment before Angela spoke

"Dear Sarah, thank goodness that you are here, we must take care of both Lady Alice and Clara, they are both beside themselves"

"Yes of course we must, you can rely on me to help" agreed Sarah

Mark gave a bow, and taking his wife by the hand, left for their cottage.

Everyone had gone, leaving Jasper and Sarah alone. Jasper went to Sarah and took her hands in his

"My dear Miss Kirkby, what an awful evening this turned out to be—and now I must go back to London first thing in the morning, I am loathe to go and leave you here—I had hoped to get to know you better" he raised her hands to his lips and kissed them both, the kiss lingering longer than necessary. Sarah spoke breathlessly savouring each moment

"I too had hoped that we could become better acquainted sir"

"You need not despair lovely lady, I shall return, but I have to try and save my dear friend from this dreadful predicament, you do understand don't you?"

"Of course I understand sir, and I wish you well in your efforts, but you will not forget me will you, once you are back in London, amongst all the pretty young ladies there, I fear you will forget that I exist" her eyes were pleading

"Never, there was a time that I enjoyed the company of many pretty girls, I had even found myself in difficult circumstances once or twice, but not anymore—I am too old for such pleasures and games, this last week or so has made me realize that my happiness is with you"

"Then I shall wait for you, as long as it takes" she was looking straight into his eyes, before he wrapped his arms about her and pulled her to him, pressing his lips to hers and lingering there.

"You had better go to bed sweet Sarah, the temptation of you is too much for me, I have found myself in a compromising situation before, I have no intention of doing so again" he released Sarah and moved away "when I return, we will look to further our relationship, if you still want too of course, you may have tired of me by then"

"I shall never do that" she whispered

"I am leaving at dawn tomorrow, so I won't see you again before I go—take care dear girl, I will write to you while I'm away, but now you should retire" he said turning away from her—in the past he had carried on without further thought of the consequences, but this time was different—this young lady was worth more than that to him, and he wasn't going to blow the best chance he had ever had

"Goodnight then sir, I shall pray that you are safe, until we meet again" she said, turning on her heels and leaving the room.

Once she had gone, Jasper stood for a while, thinking about his situation with Sarah, with saving his friend, so many things to consider, but before he could devote himself to perhaps his future wife, he must see his good friend set free—and Hinton would be much more effective in doing that than he, so he would need to enrol his services too. Jasper left the dining room and went to the library, pouring a large glass of brandy, and swirling it round in his glass, before tossing it down his throat in one go.

CHAPTER TWENTY THREE

(Maria's Plans)

Jasper Trent had returned to London and sought out his good friend Russell Hinton, to try and get help to save their dear friend from the hangman's noose. Jasper had gone to his house, and explained the grave situation to him, Russell Hinton was horrified, he knew that their good friend would never be a party to anything so dreadful. They had gone directly to Newgate gaol, and were relieved that they had managed to speak to Richard, but Newgate gaol was not the most savoury place in the world. It was damp and cold, and the smell was appalling, the two gentlemen didn't know how Richard could put up with it—to say the conditions were horrific was an understatement, and most of the inmates were shouting abuse as they passed by each cell, most of them being hardened ruffians and criminals, not gentlemen. Richard, always a man so clean and particular in appearance, had become worse than a tramp, and they had noticed that the poor fellow stank, though they would never point that out to him. It was a cold wet day that they visited him, and they were only given a short length of time but they tried to fit as much as they could into the time that they had. The guard had pointed them in the right direction and they had stood by his cell, speaking to him through the bars, though it wasn't easy with all the shouting and jeering coming from the other cells in the area. As soon as Richard saw them he jumped from his wooden hard bunk, to rush to the bars

"Trent, Hinton, what brings you here my friends"

"We had to come Warren we are looking for a way to get you out of here"

"Then I fear you have wasted your time—as if what they found in my bedchamber wasn't damning enough, there was also the fact that I told Drummond of the underground passage to the caves, where the contraband was hidden—instead of them believing me to be a helpful citizen, they are seeing it as another sign of my guilt"

"But that is ridiculous—what did they find in your bedchamber?"

"A trunk, one that I had never set eyes on before returning to Penleigh Court, and it was full of gold and jewels—it wasn't even contraband—I have to say that I was totally shocked beyond belief"

"But surely it doesn't prove that it was yours?"

"It's hardly likely to be anyone else's in my room, is it?"

"Who told the authorities about it?"

"I wish that I knew, they received an anonymous note, it even told them where the key to the trunk was"

"But who would have done such a thing—I would not have thought you to have made enemies"

"I think that I know who's responsible—but I don't know how to prove it"

"And who do you believe to be responsible Richard?"

"I have my suspicions, but how can I accuse the person, without proof?"

"If you would tell us who you suspect, then could we not look into the matter?"

"And if I am wrong?"

"If we are to help you my friend, you have to trust us"

"I wish you luck, for I see no way out of this predicament, Drummond found the goods, where his informant had told him they would be, and due to them having been found in my bedchamber, I see no way out of this"

"Well you must have hope my dear fellow, we are going to do everything we can to get you out of here, that I can promise you—even if we have to return to Cornwall to seek the truth" said Russell

"Please be careful Hinton, if my suspicions are correct, then I fear your task could be dangerous"

"Don't worry yourself about us, or your estate, Chandler is looking after things there, and he is also looking for proof of your innocence"

"You must urge Mark to take great care, he is also in a dangerous position and I fear for his welfare—please warn him that he must step carefully"

"Can you not be more precise?"

"No, I'm sorry, I cannot speculate—it would be wrong for me to cast blame without proof—I shall leave it with you"

"We shall of course do our best for you—of that I can promise you Warren" said Russell

"I do not doubt it, have you news of my mother, and of Clara—dare I ask of their welfare?"

"Lady Alice has taken it very hard, though the girls are devoting their time to caring for her, as for Clara, she was intent in coming here to visit you, but I have managed to deter her—I didn't think that you would want to see her like this, besides, I'm not sure that she would be able to cope with it, this is no place for a lady" said Jasper

"You are right, I have no wish to see her, or anyone while I'm here—if she or my mother were to come, I should refuse to see them"

"I thought as much. We will do everything we can, and we will return in a few days to let you know how things go"

"Thank you gentlemen, I'm obliged to you, though I don't hold out much hope"

Jasper and Russell left, they had their work cut out now to prove that Richard wasn't the highwayman that he was accused of being.

Alice had taken things extremely badly, she had taken to her bed, and was refusing to get up, she was also refusing to eat—Gracie called for Dr Somerville to attend to her, but he couldn't persuade her. Sarah and Angela spent a great deal of time at Penleigh Court, trying to coax her into being strong for her son, and encouraging her with the news of Jasper and his friend Russell, and the task they had set for themselves. Jasper had written to Mark, and kept him informed of any progress, though there was little enough of that. Clara too was distraught, she had good and bad days, but she had started to look pale and wan, she was not a good eater at the best of times, but of late, was only able to eat small amounts of food. Sarah was missing Jasper, although he had written to her a couple of times, and she had managed to write back to him, but she was missing his company.

One afternoon when Angela and Sarah had gone to Truro, Clara decided to go and visit Alice, she so wanted to speak with her, she felt that they had so much in common, which in fact they did, and Richard was that binding factor between them. She had ridden over to Penleigh Court, as her father was using the carriage that afternoon—she took her horse to the stables, and left it with the groom there to take care of, then she walked round to the front door and knocked the knocker—the door swung open and Newbridge ushered the young lady inside

"I have come to see your mistress if you please" she said

"I'm afraid my mistress is not seeing anyone at the moment Miss, I could send her a message or tell her that you called"

"Could you not enquire, I think that she may see me"

"I'm afraid not Miss, she has insisted that she will see no one at this present time—I'm very sorry"

Maria had just come down the stairs and heard every word that had been said

"It's alright Newbridge—leave this with me"

"Yes My Lady" he replied, closing the door and going off about his duties

"Miss Penrose, how lovely to see you, please let's go and have some tea, I should welcome the company" Clara gave her a half smile, it wasn't what she had intended, but now that she was here, perhaps Lady Maria was as distraught as everyone else and needed her company

"Thank you Lady Maria" Maria led her into the drawing room where she pulled the bell pull to order tea. Within minutes a maid opened the door and bobbed a curtsey

"Tea for two Emily and look sharp about it" Maria said, in a rough tone "Yes My Lady", Emily bobbed another curtsey and left the room closing the door behind her

"Please sit down Miss Penrose" Maria said, pointing to the settee next to the fire, before seating herself in the armchair opposite

"I'm afraid Alice is indisposed my dear, she has told Newbridge that she will see no-one—this business with Richard has shook her up a great deal"

"It is to be expected, such a terrible time for her, what with losing her husband and one of her sons, and now facing the possibility of losing the other one" the door opened and Emily entered with a tray, which she placed on a small table next to Maria, then she bobbed a curtsey and left, closing the door behind her. Maria poured the tea and handed one to Clara, before taking her own

"You are right, not one of them having been of use to her, have they Miss Penrose?"

"I'm sorry, I don't understand" said Clara, looking at Maria confused at her words

"Well, everyone knew that her husband was rather a beastly man—very cruel, his reputation was renown, and his sons, well my husband was thought to be well liked, but he was a weak man, and now Richard—he has been arrested for highway robbery, so I hardly think that either of them to be ideal"

"But it's a lie Lady Maria, Richard is no more a highway robber, than I"

"I'm sorry my dear, but he was caught red handed so to speak, there is no getting away from it"

"But it isn't true—I know that it isn't true, someone has made it look as if it was him, but I know him to be innocent"

"Of course my dear, you would believe that, after all you love him don't you?"

"Yes, I do love him, and he loves me"

"My dear Miss Penrose, you are very young and innocent, you have no knowledge of the ways of men, or the world, you have been brought up with a sheltered background, I know that he has probably said some very pretty things to you, but it means very little, men have many secrets, you have a lot to learn, I'm sure Richard is no exception to that rule"

"You are wrong about Richard, I may have had a sheltered background, but I have got to know him so well of late, we are to be married next month" then realizing what she had said, she looked at the rock shimmering on her finger before bursting into tears. Maria went to her and wrapped her arm around the girl

"Please do not cry, men are not worth your tears my dear. I know that you expected to marry next month, but that was never going to happen I'm afraid"

"But it was" she sobbed

"Now now, let me tell you something, I believe that you deserve the truth, my brother in law has lied to you long enough—Richard has lived in London for several years, besides travelling Europe, which you probably already know—he has mixed with young ladies from very high backgrounds, beautiful young ladies, and you must realize that he has had many love affairs, he has had mistresses all over, and I would suspect still does, men of his standing will always do so. I don't say that he didn't enjoy your companionship, though it was cruel of him to lead you into believing that he would make you his wife, but you can surely see, that he couldn't seriously contemplate marrying you, after all, you are unfortunately far inferior to him, he must marry someone of similar birth my dear, you should think no more of him, he has given you a very pretty trinket" said Maria looking at the ring on her finger "obviously in payment for his appreciation of you"

"You are wrong Lady Maria, he wanted to marry me—I questioned him when he asked me, but he promised me that he wanted me for his wife, and he's never once led me to believe otherwise, in fact he has done everything to convince me of his love for me—I know that he loves me"

"I'm sorry my dear, I will be bluntly honest with you now, you must forgive me for I had not planned to tell you this but, Richard and I have been lovers since he came here a year ago, his father was threatening to throw me and my children out on the street, yet Richard would have none of it—so he made me his mistress, until mourning was over, you understand, and we could marry—he loves my children as his own, and as time went on, he wanted to give them a father again, the girls will have a Penleigh father of the same blood, and as for my son, well most people believe him to be Edward's child, but he is in fact Richard's boy—so you see my dear, he had no intention of marrying you at all." Clara lifted her eyes, heavy with tears to Maria's face, she had stopped sobbing now, and was studying Maria's gaze

"No, it's not true, he wouldn't—he loves me, he was going to marry me, that's why we came for dinner the night he was arrested, to mark our engagement and to plan our wedding, he could never have promised to marry you, I'm sorry but you are quite wrong" then she burst into fits of sobbing again

"Miss Penrose, I am telling you the truth—if anyone has a lot to lose by Richard's arrest, it is I, my children will be without a father again, and my son will remain illegitimate—would I lie about something as serious as that?" Clara stood up and taking one last long look at Maria, she fled from the room and the house collecting her horse from the stables she cantered all the way home, locking herself in her room, and not wishing to come out for anyone. If Richard had lied to her, she didn't want to live anymore—if he was to hang, then she would want to die too. Her parents tried to coax her, and to find out what was wrong, but she wouldn't tell a soul—she would never love again, or consider marriage.

❦

Maria sat on the settee where she had been seated when Miss Penrose left in a hurry—a smile crossing her lips—she had warned him, he had scorned her for the last time, so she had blackened his name, and was more than happy to see him hang, she had been fair and warned him had she not—she would have given him anything he wanted had he married her, but still he chose that pathetic chit over her, she was a Lady after all, and he still chose a chit. Well, she would do it all again. Now she would have to find Mark—after all, he was all that was left for her now—with Richard gone she had little choice, but she would ensure that he would do her bidding. She stood up, stepping into the hall, she took her cloak from the stand in the hall where she had hung it when the vicar's daughter had shown up and wrapped it around her—Mark would be in the estate office, so she would get a chance to speak with him before he left for home. She stepped out of the side door and slipped across the yard, it had stopped raining though the wind was still blowing a gale, then round the corner and into the estate office.

"Mark, you are still here then" she said, a huge smile crossing her lips, Mark looked up as she went in

"Maria, how can I help you?" he asked sceptically

"I thought that you had forgotten me, you have not called by the Lodge recently" she stepped over to the desk and walked round to where he was sat, and perched on the edge of the desk, staring at him, gaze never faltering

"I—I have been rather busy Maria" he answered flatly

"But surely you can make time for me" she said softly, placing her hand to his cheek"

"I'm sorry Maria, I thought that we had discussed this over a week ago, I am a married man now, I cannot see you anymore"

"That's rubbish, there is no cannot about it, are you saying that you will not?"

"If that is it, then yes, I'm afraid I cannot and will not—you are a lovely woman Maria, you should be looking for a husband of your own again soon—I'm certain there would be no shortage of gentleman suitors" and he smiled as he said it

"But I don't want gentleman suitors Mark, what do I need with them when I have you?

"But you don't have me Maria, not anymore—I love my wife, she is beautiful and adorable, and I have no intention of hurting her"

"Ha, you have no intention of hurting, so you think that it wouldn't hurt her to know that you were in my bed only days before your wedding?"

"Yes, well that was a mistake—I don't know what came over me"

"It was no mistake Mark, you were hungry for me, you even crept inside my bedroom and laid in wait of me—you need me as I do you, so do not deny it—you will come to me tonight Mark, we will make love, and you will stay all night, I demand it this time"

"No Maria, not any more—my wife is all that counts to me now—so perhaps you should go" that horrible curl of the lip, as she pondered on her next move, then she slipped off the desk and moved in close to him, sliding her fingers inside his shirt and flicking the buttons open, before leaning forward and kissing his chest. He had to admit that he found her so difficult to resist, but he would never tell her that—he took her hand from inside his shirt, and pushed her back against the desk once more—he could see the ice in her eyes as she looked into his

"You will be sorry for that—I promise you, just like he is, you shall be next"

"I have no idea what you are talking about Maria—but you don't frighten me—please leave my office"

"Gladly, but don't say I have not warned you" she turned on her heels and left, slamming the door nearly off its hinges as she left. Richard sat down in his seat, dropped his head in his hands and tried to regain his composure, she had made a statement about 'being sorry, just like he is—what did she mean by those words—had she been responsible for his good friends demise, she knew how to get to him, he hated that as much as anything, but he would not allow her to seduce him again, he must not, he loved Angie, and as much as he enjoyed the pleasure they shared, he wasn't going to risk his marriage because of it.

Maria slipped back into the house, as she entered the hall she met Sarah—so they had returned from Truro, she looked at the clock, it was three thirty—time enough to do what she knew she must. Without removing her cloak, she slipped back outside the side door and across the yard to the stables—the carriage had only just arrived back, so it was perfect timing, she shouted to the coachman, who was still sat atop, that she wished to go out for a little while, and the footman helped her inside. She told them where she was going, it was only down in the village, it wouldn't take long. The horses slowed, and turned sharp right, into West Lane, they would learn one day, and then it would be too late. She smiled to herself as the carried jolted along through the ruts, then it came to a halt. As the footman helped her alight, she told them to wait for her, her business here wouldn't take long. She opened the freshly painted gate and followed the path to the front door, it was a little more sheltered here, and although the wind ripped at her cloak, she pulled it tightly around her, pulling the hood lower over her face. She lifted her hand and rapped on the wood, there was shuffling of footsteps inside, before the door flew back, to reveal Mark's new wife in the doorway, as soon as Angela saw who was stood on her doorstep, she immediately bobbed a curtsey

"Mrs Chandler, how nice to see you again" said Maria gaily

"Good afternoon My Lady, I'm afraid that my husband isn't home yet"

"That's excellent, as it's you I have come to see"

"Me?" Angela said blankly, whatever could Lady Maria want with her, she had hardly said two words to her while she had been staying with Alice, now she had come to the cottage to see her

"Indeed my dear—will you not invite me inside?"

"Yes, of course, forgive my manners" Angela stood back, holding the door wide to admit Lady Maria, then closing the door behind her, she offered her a seat on the new settee which her husband had so lovingly bought. Maria pushed back her hood, and released the catch of her cloak, looking around the small freshly re-decorated room

"What a quaint room, a little small, but quaint all the same" she remarked

"It's lovely My Lady, I had never thought to have such a place of my own" Maria forced a smile

"No, I suppose not" then looking directly at the young girl in front of her "And how are you finding married life my dear"

"We are very happy thank you My Lady"

"Yes, well—it must be very difficult with your husband spending so much of his time at work do you not get a little lonely here, all by yourself?"

"Not at all My Lady—I understand that my husband has his duties, and with the Duke not around at the moment, my husband's time is even more taken up, but that doesn't matter, once the Duke comes home it will all sort itself out again"

"You are a very understanding young lady, but it doesn't look likely that Richard will be returning home—he was arrested for highway robbery, and as we all know, the sentence for that crime is hanging"

"But he isn't guilty—we all know that he isn't My Lady—there has been an awful mistake, and it will only be a matter of time before he comes home again"

"Yes, well we shall see, but in the meantime, I should be glad if you could ask Mark, your husband" she had slipped that in deliberately, and noticed that the girl had returned her gaze as soon as the remark had left her lips—she had the desired affect "if he would be so good as to come over to Penleigh Court when he arrives home—I'm afraid that there is something which needs doing urgently, though I warn you, it may well be a long job, but you have told me that you are happy that his duties are fulfilled, so I'm sure that you won't mind me taking his time, will you?" she was watching the girls face closely now, but there was no sign of her disappointment—she wouldn't miss Mark for one night, and her need was the greater at the moment.

"Of course My Lady, I will gladly pass on the message when he returns"

"And you should not tell him that I was here, Lady Alice is the one wishing for the work to be carried out, not I" she said to the girl, not taking her eyes from her face "please tell him that Lady Alice has sent word that he should meet with her tonight"

"Yes My Lady, as you wish" Maria dropped her gaze

"Thank you my dear, and now I shall go and leave you in peace, good afternoon Mrs Chandler" Angela bobbed the lady another curtsey, before showing her to the door

"Good evening My Lady"

Angie didn't really understand, her husband was in his office and Alice wasn't leaving her bedchamber, yet Lady Maria had come all the way to his cottage to ask him to visit Lady Alice tonight—it didn't make sense at all—Angie had a strange feeling that something was not quite right with all of this, but she didn't know why.

Maria climbed back into the carriage, and ordered the coachman to drive her back to Penleigh Court. She would have her way, this very night—she saw the desire in his eyes this afternoon, and she knew that it wouldn't take a great deal to persuade him into her bed. She laughed out loud—she was determined to ensure this night would not be the last time—she would need to think of a plan in which he would never be allowed to be free of her, as long as she chose to have him in her bed—and if he did, she would go to his wife with the evidence. The carriage jolted to a stop, the footman helped her out. She ascended the steps to the door, with a new spring in her step and a happy and excited beat of the heart.

Once inside her room, she had ordered a bath, with rose petals to scent the water. Then she stepped out and let her maid dry her with a towel, and ordered the bath be taken away. After sending her maid off, stating that she was going to have an early night, and didn't wish to be disturbed again, she went to her cupboard and opened the door, she chose a pretty satin robe, which was almost transparent, in a beautiful peach colour and edged with ivory lace—it clung nicely to her body, emphasizing all of her womanly curves—this would be enough to persuade Mark—with her hair brushed out and left without adornment, she took a glimpse in the mirror, she was more than happy with her appearance, and she knew that Mark would never be able to resist her now. Then she padded softly down the stairs—she went to the library, and called for Newbridge—when he entered the library and saw her there, dressed as she was, he raised his eyebrows, she smiled

"Newbridge, Mr Chandler will be coming in a short while, Lady Alice is in no fit state to see him, so it has fallen to me to do so, please show him in here when he arrives"

"Of course My Lady" said Newbridge taking note of her appearance

"Thank you, and close the door on your way out" he threw her scowl, before leaving and closing the door behind him. Maria didn't have very long to wait, she could not have been there more than twenty minutes, when the door opened and Mark stepped into the library

"Mark, come in" Mark stepped inside the door and stopped dead, he couldn't believe it when he saw Maria sitting there in Richard's chair, he had to admit that she was looking ravishing, he couldn't take his eyes from her body, almost covered by the gown she was almost wearing, but it was obvious what she wanted and he was not about to go back on his word.

"I thought that Lady Alice had a job for me" he said, still not flinching or taking his eyes from her body

"Yes, well I believe that we have unfinished business dearest" she said in her usual purr

"If you will excuse me Maria, I shall return home to my wife now—I have already made it plain that there is to be nothing more between us, and I meant it" he replied. Maria knew that she would have to act quickly, she needed to complete her plan before his escape

"Come, at least have a brandy with me, I'm lonely you know, surely it would not hurt to have just one drink with me, to show that we can be friends?" Mark considered this for a few moments, he could well do with a glass of brandy, two if truth be known, and even though he had no intention of giving Maria what she wanted, what could be the harm in gazing at her body in that so becoming robe

"One drink then—but then I am going home to my wife" he said firmly, shutting the door he went to the chair, which had been placed for his benefit and sat down, Maria went to the decanter and poured two glasses of brandy, the golden liquid warm and inviting. Maria went back to the desk and handed Mark one of the glasses before propping herself right next to him on the desk—and rubbing her foot up and down his lower leg—Mark said nothing, he was expecting this, he would have been a fool not too. He could smell her perfume, it was drifting to his nostrils, and the sight before him was intoxicating—he took a swig of his brandy

"Tell me Mark, are you happy?" she asked him

"Of course, I love my wife, and she loves me" he replied

"But you enjoyed our interlude did you not?"

"Very much, you know that though don't you?" Maria was looking directly at him, she placed her drink on the desk beside her watching him as she did so

"Why then must it end now my darling, you love your wife yes, but you love my body" Mark was becoming hot and uncomfortable—it would be so easy to take her in his arms, nestle his face into her hair, and smell that wonderful fragrance—taste her lips. He had to stop thinking about her—he had said that he wouldn't and now he must stick to it—he loved Angela, he couldn't hurt her, he just couldn't, she had suffered enough already. Without taking his eyes from her luscious curves, he whispered unconvincingly

"I can't Maria, I will not hurt my wife any more than she has been hurt already" Maria leant forward and whispered in his ear

"She need never know" she slipped from the desk, slowly Mark could not find it in him to push her away—she smelt so good, and looked even better. She recognized his weakness, throwing her arms around his neck and pressing her body against his, she pressed her lips to his and kissed him, first light and whispy, then firmer until he threw his arms about her and pulled her as close to him as he could—she pulled the satin tie at her waist, releasing the robe, then throwing her shoulders back and her arms to her side, allowed the robe to fall in a heap at her feet Mark opened his eyes—he was lost, her beauty was tantalizing, would he ever be free of her charms—he wanted too—he really wanted too, but he was weak, too weak for his own good

"You see my darling" she whispered in his ear "you cannot dupe me, I only wish to be your mistress, not your wife—all gentlemen have mistresses, isn't that a known fact? Even your wife should be aware of that fact" Mark pulled her close and started kissing her once again, then she pulled away "come my love" taking his hand and pulling him up, she picked up her robe from the floor, then she tugged his hand as she opened the door and dragged him up the stairs with her, she was completely naked

"Maria" he said

"Shh—someone will hear us" she whispered

"Surely you are not ashamed of me?"

"Of course not, but I cannot afford to be seen with you like this" she looked at him and smiled—before they had reached the top of the stairs, she heard a sound and turned to see Sarah, just leaving her room—Sarah looked up and saw them, though Mark had not seen her in the dim light from the candle in the opposite corridor, he was more eager to reach Maria's bedchamber unseen. Maria made a point of moving, to allow Sarah to see that she was naked, then she stopped where she was and pulled Mark into her arms, kissing him on the lips again—Sarah tried to look away, but she had witnessed more than she had wanted too. She was embarrassed and with her hand still on her bedchamber door handle, she opened the door again and slipped back inside. Maria had done what she set out to do—with a smile on her face she pulled Mark into her bedchamber where she would spend the night in his arms.

It was dawn before Mark climbed from Maria's bed, kissing her forehead, and pulling on his clothing—he cursed his weakness, and promised never to allow it to get the better of him again. If his dear Angela ever found out, their marriage would be over before it begun—he couldn't lose her for anyone— not even Maria. Quietly, opening the door, he slipped out into the corridor, and down the stairs, he could hear voices coming from the back of the house, though he couldn't hear what they were saying, then softly padding to the side door, he let himself out into the yard. The grooms were already in the stables, he could see the light from their lanterns, his first thought was to collect his horse, but if he were to do that, then it would very soon be common news that he had stayed at Penleigh Court all night—so changing his mind, he slipped round the back of the stables, and strode along the back path—he stood a better chance of not being seen that way. Once back in his cottage, he crept upstairs, Angie was still in bed asleep, he shook off his clothing and slid in beside her—he hoped that she would never know what time he returned, and he would not tell her, not this time—he made a vow that he would never keep a secret from her ever again. He had no idea that he was now in a situation, from which he could not escape—Maria had him where she wanted him, and he could do nothing at all about it.

❧ ～✥⊙✧⊙ ⊙✧⊙✥～ ☙

Maria opened her eyes and stretched—she had heard Mark creeping from her bed, and back to his wife. A smile crossed her face, she had managed to do what she set out to do—Sarah had definitely seen them together, creeping to her room, there was no mistaking that. She would of course have a word with her later, after all, she didn't want this news to get back to Angela Chandler, well at least not for now, and it gave her bargaining power—he would never refuse her charms again, last night have proved that he was as weak as her husband had been—why couldn't she find a real man, Richard would have been different—he would never allowed himself to be drawn into something like this, although unfortunately for him she had placed her trunk in his room, otherwise she would not of been able to send that note to Drummond, and it was very unfortunate that she would now lose all her gifts from Melvin—but, although it was a shame, and a waste of a real man, he had cast her advances away, like she was no more than a harlot—and he would have to pay for that, it would be worth it, but it had confirmed for her that her dear Melvin must have been the second highway robber, the one who escaped—it was exciting to think that her own lover, had been such an exciting man. She turned over, snuggled beneath the covers again and went back to a lovely deep delicious sleep.

❧ ～✥⊙✧⊙ ⊙✧⊙✥～ ☙

Maria had been seeking an interview with Miss Kirkby all day—she could not allow her to go running to her dear friend, telling tales, not at the moment at least. She had hoped that they would meet at breakfast, but it looked as if she was spending her day with Alice—Alice hadn't even been out of her room since Richard's arrest—but it was of no account, her son would one day take the title and estate, she would see to that—and until then, as his mother, she would never be turned out. It had crossed her mind that Miss Kirkby may speak to Alice about what she had seen, but that wasn't likely either—Alice wouldn't believe it for one thing and Sarah would surely not want her friend to suffer by spreading such rumours.

She had thought to seek her out in Alice's chamber but she didn't want anyone else involved or even suspicious for now—and if Mark decided to treat her as Richard had, then she would have something to persuade him differently.

It was just before dinner when Maria walked into the drawing room, to see Miss Kirkby sat by herself, in a chair near the fire. As Maria had opened the door, the girl looked up, seeing who had just walked in, she looked away the colour flooding her cheeks like a beacon—she was obviously embarrassed by what she had seen the night before, this was all the more amusing to Maria.

"Good afternoon my dear—your all on your own this evening" said Maria gaily

"Yes Lady Maria I am, I've actually been with Lady Alice all day, she is suffering badly from the shock and the heartache of her son's wrongful arrest" she spoke without glancing in Maria's direction, clearly avoiding her gaze

"That was to be expected" said Maria

"You are not concerned My Lady?" Sarah asked tartly

"Of course, but I fear it is out of our hands—there is little we can do"

"Then I beg to differ, clearly the Duke has had no part in the dealings that he is accused of, and I would like to know who could hate him enough to have brought such terrible accusations against him" she would not meet Maria's eye. Maria had under-estimated this young lady—she was too opinionated for her own good

"So you believe him to be innocent of the crime—even though he was found in possession of stolen goods"

"Anyone could have arranged that so" Maria gave a half hysterical laugh

"Surely not, who would go to such lengths, I really don't think that is even a reasonable consideration" Sarah was beginning to get annoyed with this woman, as it was she didn't like her very much, she remembered how she had watched Richard and her walking in the garden, from an upstairs window, as if jealous of her—there was definitely something strange here, and she was sure now that Maria was playing a major role in all of this

"You don't like the Duke very much do you My Lady" this time Sarah looked straight at Maria, meeting those ice cold eyes with her own and holding her gaze

"Really, whatever would make you think that?" for the first time Maria had started to feel uncomfortable—this young lady would have to be watched

"Lady Maria, my friends and I will do everything within our power to prove the Duke an innocent man, whether or not you like him or any of us, doesn't really concern me, but what I had the misfortune of witnessing last evening, I was shocked and devastated—Mark Chandler is a married man, married to a good friend, I shall not tell her what I have seen, this time, but I promise you, that should I ever witness such behaviour in the future, then I shall inform my friend immediately. I am sorry that your husband died, but I will not stand by and watch you destroy my friend's marriage and life"

"So I am to blame for Mr Chandler's adultery—all men take mistresses do they not?

"No, they do not, and I suggest that you find a new husband for yourself madam, not steal someone else's" with that, Sarah stood up and left the room.

Maria sat for some time, looking into the fire—she didn't have to say one word, the conversation went better than she had expected.

CHAPTER TWENTY FOUR

(The Build Up)

Richard sat in his cell, he had seen nothing of his good friends for at least a week—it would soon be Christmas, but he wasn't sure whether or not he would get to see anything of it this year. He wondered just how he could have got himself into this dreadful mess—his lawyer, Grimley Hopcroft, had come to see him and he had gone through everything he knew, but he didn't hold much faith in the man, when he had told him about the Gate Lodge and passageway, and the contraband stored there, instead of seeing him eager to co-operate, the man looked at him with disdain, telling him that the less said about that the better, and that he was more likely to be signing his own death warrant for admitting his crimes. His good friends Mr Chandler and Mr Trent would corroborate his story of the caves and what they found there, though even when this was suggested, it was discarded promptly. He had told Hopcroft that he had first noticed the trunk on his return to Cornwall last December, though with it being padlocked, he had never bothered to investigate what was hidden inside, or who it belonged too. He also pointed out to Mr Hopcroft that he had been in Europe for two years, only returning in November the previous year, and that he hadn't gone to Cornwall at all until a week before Christmas when he heard from his mother that his brother had died. The problem there was that some of the goods in the trunk had been stolen from other parts of the country earlier, but the fact that they had caught one of the highway robbers and he had been hung, did not help this plea, as Hopcroft had pointed out, just because he had been absent for some of the raids, it would not save his neck from the gallows. The man had even had the audacity to suggest to Richard that Clara's ring of betrothal, would also have to be checked as they believed it had been the product of ill-gotten gains, though Richard had pointed out that he should speak to the jeweller, he would confirm Richard's story. When Richard was asked did he have any enemies, he had thought about it before answering, after all, if he told the truth about his sister in law, he would be distinctly frowned upon, what gentleman would try and involve a lady, when he found himself in a tight spot—no, that would never do.

It was not looking good for him. He knew that this had to be something to do with Maria, but he didn't know how it all linked together, she was obviously storing the goods which Lincroft had left—Richard was quite convinced now that he was not only involved with smuggling, but with highway robbery too—he would not have put it past him, but he had already been hung, even though not for this particular crime—someone would be expected to pay the price and this one looked as if it may well be him. Now he could only sit and wait to hear from his friends, he hoped to God that they would come up with some answers. He could only hope that Hopcroft would at least check out all the details he had given him, though he certainly seemed to make for a better prosecution than defence.

Jasper and Russell had been going round town to try and find something which would prove beyond doubt that Richard had played no part in these activities—but up to now, they could find nothing. Everything they tried to use, was discounted in some way or other, and until they had some good news for him, they didn't really want to visit him again, they must just keep searching. Jasper had written to Mark on several occasions, and he wrote every other day to Sarah—he couldn't wait to see her again—he had told his friend all about her, though Russell himself was taken with his own sweet Clarissa. Sarah had been keeping Jasper informed of the situation at Penleigh Court. Mark was a gem, he was keeping everything going very well, including trying to find something to prove without doubt Richard's innocence—he knew that Richard was innocent, but proving it was more difficult. Sarah had told him how she was worried about Mark, that he had been seduced by Maria, and that she had had words with Maria, though Jasper was already aware that Maria was his mistress, he could say nothing. In a way he had been glad of the situation, or they would have had a much harder time, trying to escape the Gate Lodge. Then there was Alice, she had not left her bed since hearing of her son's arrest—Sarah feared for her health—it was certainly deteriorating. She talked of Angela and Clara, and how they had become firm friends, poor Clara, she was terribly distraught—and for the last few days, she had also shut herself away, the girls didn't know why, she would not even see them, let alone speak to them about it all. Everything seemed to be falling apart. Richard's hearing was set for January eleventh, the day before they were due to throw a ball to introduce Clara, as Duchess of Warren to all the local gentry—they had all been looking forward to the event, and now that would have to be put on hold, if not cancelled entirely. There was so little time, but they must turn something up soon.

Mark sat in his office, his head in his hands, things were becoming very difficult as Maria had manipulated him once again—he had such a good resolve to never go near her, and everything had ended up going out of the window—he had to admit that his times shared with her were pure delight and joy, he had only shared the same delights with his wife, but as much as he loved her and enjoyed every minute spent with her, his time spent with Maria was so exciting, she was a good teacher, that he would never deny. His problem now was how to be free of her, he had started to think that he never would be, but he couldn't keep on taking chances like the one he took last night—he couldn't bear to think of his dear Angie getting hurt, she had been hurt enough already, and he had promised to make sure that she would never be hurt again, and yet he had done something which could hurt her more than all the physical hurt, that Flora Kirkby had dealt her. It had to stop, it really had to stop. He must tell Maria that he had no intention of meeting her again, and this time he would stick to his word.

As he sat pondering on his own problems, the office door opened and Miss Kirkby stepped inside

"Miss Kirkby, how nice to see you, what can I do for you?"

"I need to speak with you a moment Mr Chandler—it's very important" Mark tried to study her face, to see if he could read anything there, but her face was serious, not even a quirk of the lips—he could read nothing there

"Of course, please take a seat"

"Thank you" she said taking the seat opposite him.

"So, have you some good news for the Duke?" he asked

"No, I'm afraid not. I'm sorry Mark, I shall come straight to the point—I have to tell you that I saw you—last night, Lady Maria in a state of undress, and yourself, I saw her kiss you—I was shocked and disappointed with you sir" Marks face fell—the blood drained from his cheeks—he had thought that no-one had seen them, he certainly hadn't seen Sarah, and he had never expected this.

"I see" he answered "Then I'm sorry that you had to witness my little—indiscretion" he spoke so softly it was hardly a whisper and he was staring into space now, before carrying on

"I suppose that you will speak to Angela about it, being her friend and all" he asked

"No, I shall not hurt that poor girl more than she's already been hurt by my own mother, but I shall warn you, as I have Lady Maria, that should I ever be witness to such behaviour again, then I shall have no choice but to speak with Angie—she loves you so much Mr Chandler, I thought that you loved her, but clearly that's not the case"

"Please Miss Kirkby, I love Angie with all my heart and soul—I was dazzled by Lady Maria when I first arrived here, and things got out of hand, I have tried to put an end to it all, but she is a very persuasive woman, very persistent"

"I can imagine—but I have now told her the same as you, so my advice to you is to keep away from the woman, if you truly love my friend, it should not be too difficult for you—as it happens, I don't like her one bit, and I fear that she has a hand in these dealings with the Duke, though I have no proof of that. I like you Mr Chandler, and I believe that you make Angie very happy, please don't let her down, I beg of you"

"You are right—I thank you for not ruining our lives, by holding your tongue, I shall not be resuming my liaison with Lady Maria—of that you can be sure"

"I am relieved to hear it sir, if you need anyone to talk too, you may always talk to me—I will do anything I can to help you and Angie, you only have to ask" she looked at Mark and smiled, before standing and excusing herself. Once she had left, Mark sat on for a while—he felt embarrassed and ashamed—how could he be so stupid, he could be throwing away the best part of his life, for nothing more than a little excitement which he could easily live without—he would do exactly what Sarah had suggested.

Sarah decided that although it had turned really cold, it was dry—she had not seen Clara for days now, and she was very worried about her, she had been spending a great deal of time with Alice, but the poor woman, she was in such a state of shock and nervousness, that Sarah worried for her health. Angie had called several times, and she had also spent some time with Alice, but Alice had just clung to her and cried—Angie had broken down herself after leaving Alice's room—she felt so helpless, though she would do anything she could for the woman who had shown such kindness to her. So, when Sarah suggested that her and Angie call at the rectory to see their friend, Angie had been happy to do so. The day being cold and crisp, was a good day to walk to the village, it wasn't so far after all. Sarah left the house, buffeted by the wind, dressed warmly with her thick cloak wrapped tightly around her. When she arrived at Angie's cottage, Angie was already watching for her from the window and came straight out so that they could be on their way. They walked the short distance from the village to the rectory and knocked on the door. Daisy answered the door

"We have come to visit Miss Penrose" said Sarah, Daisy bobbed a curtsey

"I'm afraid Miss Penrose is not receiving anyone" the girl said. Ada Penrose must have heard the girls at the door speaking with Daisy and came up behind her and ushered them inside

"I'm afraid that Clara has taken all this very badly—she is heartbroken and more distraught than I have ever known her before—to think that she fell in love with a highway robber—it makes me feel sick to my stomach" she said

"Begging your pardon madam, the Duke is innocent—there has been an awful mistake, one of which I'm sure will soon be resolved" said Sarah firmly

"Yes, well, with so much evidence against him, how could he not be guilty?"

"He is proclaiming his innocence and we are sure that he is indeed so"

"Then let us hope that you are right—my husband prays every day for his release, though I'm not convinced, but for Clara's sake I hope that you are right" she said "Now, I shall take you up to see Clara, she has been refusing to see anyone up to now, but I'm sure that if anyone can cheer her, you will do so, though I would prefer you not to say too much about Richard Penleigh, I don't think that it's a good idea to remind her of the—well incident" Sarah and Angela looked at each other before following Ada Penrose upstairs to Clara's room, she knocked at the door and entered, the girls close at her heels. Once they were settled beside Clara, who was lying on the bed, Ada Penrose left, but before she went from the room, closing the door behind her she turned to the two young ladies and said in a whisper

"Remember now, no mention of that man" then she left. Sarah looked at Angie rolling her eyes and shaking her head, before turning to the girl laid in the bed

"Clara dear, how are you?" Sarah asked

Clara turned to them, tears already forming in her eyes—she looked pale, thin and listless—the girl was ill.

"I don't know" then she burst into tears, sobbing her heart out

"Please dear, don't cry, Richard will be set free, I'm sure of it" paying no heed to Ada Penrose's warning, Angie went to her and threw her arms about her, cradling her tight. Once her sobs subsided, she looked up at her friends her eyes red and bloodshot, with huge puffy bags beneath

"It's of no matter now—whether or not he lives, he doesn't love me, he never did" she sobbed again

"Oh Clara, you are so wrong, he loves you, he wanted to marry you, he has put a beautiful ring on your finger, how could you say that he doesn't love you"

"I was merely a pastime for his pleasure"

"What makes you think like this Clara" Sarah asked

"Lady Maria told me so" Sarah's eyes flared with anger

"What has that woman been saying to you?"

"She told me that she has been his mistress since he first arrived here, and that he was planning to marry her all along—her baby, the boy she had recently, it's Richard's son, and he was going to marry her to legitimize the child, and give her two daughters a father—I know how much Richard loves those little girls, and with a son of his own, a son and heir, then he has everything he needs. How can I stand in his way, and the very fact that I'm only a vicar's daughter, Lady Maria is better suited as a Duchess than I"

"This is utter nonsense Clara, I know that it is, if the Duke had any interest in that woman whatsoever then would he not have married her already, before she had his son?" said Sarah—she was so angry, to think that dreadful woman had said such things—she was beginning to think that there was definitely something going on with Maria, why would she want to do such a thing, unless she was jealous of Clara—that had to be it, why else would she be so vile

"But she insisted that it was all true, and that I was stupid not to be able to see the truth of it all, and when I thought about it, I could see that it did indeed fit" said Clara, her large eyes open wide now

"Have you written to Richard, you should write to him and ask him, after all now he has nothing to lose—he will tell you the truth, I shall speak to Mr Trent, he will speak to him about it next time that he visits, if you would like me too?" said Sarah trying to persuade her friend to see sense

"I don't know—I don't want to bother him with my stupid fears, poor Richard has much worse to worry about, and I'm sure that he wouldn't want to hear from me now" she said

"But I'm sure he will be eager to set this matter straight—I know that he loves you, anyone can see that, he will set your mind at rest, and very soon, I promise that we shall find a way to set him free, though you may have to put the wedding on hold for a little while, you will still become the Duchess of Warren, of that I'm sure" Sarah persisted

"Alright, if you think that it is important enough to bother dear Richard with, then perhaps I shall write to him" she relented, drying her tears

"Good. Now, we want you to stop worrying about that dreadful woman, and help us to prove the Dukes innocence if you will" Clara gave a watery smile, she wasn't wholly convinced, but at last she was sharing her troubles with her two best friends.

Sarah sat alone in her room, there was so much going round in her head, but one thing she was sure of was that Maria played a part in all of this somewhere, she seemed to be causing havoc with everyone—she was a very manipulative, domineering woman, and Sarah disliked her intensely, and she wasn't frightened to let her know it. To think that she had said all those dreadful things to her dear friend, had turned her into a wreck, and had poisoned her mind against her fiancée who was depending on them for his life. She had known what it was like to live with a manipulative bully, her own mother was surely that. She had written to her dear Jasper this morning, and now she had so much more to tell him. She wondered what would be happening if Jasper were still here with them, he had gone running off to London, but he wasn't having a great deal of success, he would have truly been more use here, she was sure of that, with the way things were going here. Someone knew what was going on, someone had to know—and she was determined that she would get to the bottom of it all. She went to her writing desk and pulled a fresh sheet of paper out, then picking up her pen, and dipping into the ink, she started writing to Jasper to tell him of all that had been happening that day. Once this was done she decided to ask Gracie to take it for her, she could rely on Gracie, she was a sweet girl and would do anything for her mistress, she would see that this note reached its destination safely, she certainly wouldn't want it to fall into the wrong hands. Then she left her room and went downstairs ready for dinner.

On entering the drawing room, she found Maria already seated there, beside the fire, all on her own.

"Good evening Lady Maria" she said, Maria looked as she entered

"Oh, good evening Miss Kirkby, it looks as if we are to be the only ones eating again tonight"

"Lady Alice is not well enough to join us I'm afraid" her gaze fixed on Maria as she spoke "so it is just you and I"

Maria never answered she looked back toward the fire. The silence in the room was deafening, uncomfortable—Sarah took a seat on the settee, where she opened the book which was in her hand, she would read, that would make it a little more bearable, take her mind from the unease of the situation. They had been sat in silence for about half an hour before the drawing room door opened, and Newbridge stood in the doorway—as Sarah looked up Flora Kirkby pushed her way past Newbridge and into the room, Maria stood up and went to greet the lady

"Mrs Kirkby, how nice to see you" said Lady Maria, curling her lip in that horrible way of hers

"You must be Lady Maria, pleased to meet you I'm sure" said Flora Kirkby bobbing a curtsey "Now Sarah, I hear that Lady Alice is ill, and we've all heard about the Duke—it isn't right for you to be staying in a house like this, not now anyway"

"Please mama, Lady Alice is glad of my company, especially now" Sarah pleaded, but casting a quick glance at Maria, sat watching everything going on between mother and daughter, with that ugly smile still on her lips

"No Sarah, it's not right, whatever next, having you mixed up with a highway robber—it's preposterous,—I'm only glad that he had not seen fit to make an offer for you now, or we should be the laughing stock of the area" she said looking straight at her daughter

"But mama, my trunk is not packed, I am not prepared to leave yet, perhaps Lady Alice would allow me to travel home tomorrow in her carriage, when I've had time to organize my packing at least, and had time to say goodbye to Lady Alice for her kindness"

"No Sarah, I will not hear of it, you will not stay another moment in this house—do you hear me? You are coming home with me this instance young lady, I cannot believe that you had not told me of all the going's on yourself—you should have come home before now" she said haughtily

"And what of my things mama"

"I'm certain that Lady Maria here will see that one of her maids sees to that, and returns the trunk tomorrow, is that not so Lady Maria" she asked, looking at Maria as she spoke. Maria had a smile on her lips

"But of course Mrs Kirkby, Sarah can rely on me to see to it for her" she had looked from mother to daughter and she was loving all this

"Thank you so much, you are too kind My Lady" Mrs Kirkby told Maria, then she turned to her daughter "get your cloak Sarah, we are going home now" Sarah stamped her foot in frustration

"Am I not to thank Lady Alice before I leave for her hospitality—surely it would be rude not to do so" she was clutching at straws

"There is no need Miss Kirkby" Maria had turned her icy blue stare on her "I'm sure that Lady Alice will be sleeping now, you would not wish to disturb her I'm sure, she will understand, I shall personally speak to her in the morning" she said with a satisfied smile. Sarah could not help herself any more, she turned to Lady Maria

"This is your fault isn't it?" she asked her "You have ensured that I am sent home—you shall not get away with this Lady Maria, you shall not" she said

"How dare you, speaking to a lady in this way, where are you manners my girl" said her mother, then looking to Lady Maria she said "You must forgive my daughter for her sharp tongue My Lady, she should not have spoken to you in such a way, and after your kindness to her" and turned to her daughter, pushing her toward the door, her face like thunder

"Do not upset yourself Mrs Kirkby, I'm sure that Sarah will understand that it's for her own good, once she is safe in her own home again, I cannot possibly act as her chaperone, and really Lady Alice has taken to her bed, it is for the best" the two ladies smiled at each other

"You are very kind and understanding My Lady—and now we shall go and leave you in peace" said Flora Kirkby

Sarah had no choice, she strode off before her mother and up the stairs to collect her cloak. A few minutes later both mother and daughter were being accompanied by Lady Maria to their carriage, Sara walked briskly past Lady Maria, without as much as a glance in her direction. She climbed straight into the carriage, where in the darkness, a tear spilled from her eye, and ran down her cheek—she sat back in the corner of her seat and bowed her head—she had no desire to look or speak with the woman sat opposite her, she knew only too well that she would have to suffer her tirade and more than likely a slap across the head, once back home, so for now she could cherish the silence.

Maria sat down once again beside the fire, a permanent smile fixed on her lips—stupid girl she thought, did she really believe that she would get the better of me. She was no match for a woman, one who was set on having her own way. She would not tell Alice until the morning, she would visit

her room and tell her that Flora Kirkby had arrived, eager to take her daughter home. There was no need for further explanation. No one need know that she had sent a note to Mrs Kirkby, asking her to remove her daughter as soon as possible due to Alice being taken ill and no longer able to act as her chaperone. She had certainly taken it seriously, it hadn't taken her above a few hours before she had raced over here to collect her. The interfering girl—she couldn't allow her to stay and meddle in things which didn't concern her, and she wouldn't have it. She heaved a sigh of relief, but now she could have dinner, and an early night—she had to plan her next move.

<hr/>

Jasper and Russell sat together in the library in Russell's town house, with a glass of brandy in each of their hands, they were now planning what they should do next, all their investigations had led nowhere, and although they knew that Richard was out of the country for the best part of the time that this highway robber would have been employed, the authorities would not believe that he wasn't linked in some way to the other one who was caught. Newgate gaol was a terrible place, they didn't know how Richard could bear it—from what he had said the food was no more than slops, it was little wonder that he was looking thin and pale—he couldn't go on like this much longer. They had visited him but three times, and although they had tried their hardest to prove that he wasn't even in the country at the time of the robberies, the magistrate was determined he had the right man.

"I have received another letter from Miss Kirkby" Jasper told Hinton

"Dare I ask what she writes?" he asked casually, not taking too much notice with other things on his mind

"It seems that not only is Chandler still visiting Lady Maria, but the woman has now upset Miss Penrose, she has only gone and told her that Warren was to marry her instead of Miss Penrose, and that the baby which she gave birth to" he looked from the letter to Hinton as he spoke, "is Warren's son" he stopped mid—sentence, "I don't believe it Hinton, surely if Warren had a son, he would have told us" he looked to Hinton, waiting for a reply "Without a doubt, I don't know what this woman is playing at but she's certainly causing a few problems for everyone" Jasper went back to the letter once again—then he swore, Hinton looked across at him, looking for a reason for his language, Jasper looked up at his friend once again "Of all the damnable things the woman has done, she has had Miss Kirkby carried off home to Truro, by her loathsome mother" he said. Russell was trying to make sense of what his friend had been saying "Who has Trent?" "Lady Maria, she sent word to Mrs Kirkby, who happens to be a vicious woman by the way, to collect her daughter from Penleigh Court, stating that Lady Alice is not able to act as her chaperone—so my poor Sarah has been carted off home against her will, away from her friends and everyone—it really is too bad Hinton"

"It sounds to me as if this Lady Maria is something of a tyrant herself, though I've never met her of course"

"I have to say that I've never thought of her as anything like that—she's a very attractive woman—though, she has been causing a few problems lately it seems" said Jasper—he never took life seriously

"I think that the woman could be trouble—when you write again Trent, you should warn your friends to beware of the woman" said Russell thoughtfully

"It seems that Sarah wishes us to speak with Warren and see what he says about Clara, she needs the truth, though I have to say there is no doubt in my mind that he is totally smitten with Clara—but for my dear Sarah, anything—even a visit to that hell hole" he said with a sigh

"We will go in the morning then, and afterward, I think that we need to make our way to Cornwall—I'm convinced that's where we will find the answers Trent" said Russell to his friend

"I had best get home and instruct my man to pack then" Jasper agreed

Angela left the cottage, stepping briskly up the lane in the howling wind it almost took her breath away. She was going to visit Clara, she was still worried about the girl, and couldn't believe Lady Maria could have said such terrible things to her. She had found her to be pleasant enough—why would she be so nasty to her new friend Clara. She turned in to the rectory gates, and going to the heavy front door, she knocked hard and waited for the door to swing open—it was the sweet little maid Daisy, Angela liked her, she felt a certain rapport with the girl

"I have come to see Miss Penrose if you please" she said smiling

"You had better come in then" Daisy stood back to let Angela pass and bobbed a curtsey—Angela still wasn't used to servants curtseying her, after all, it had always been her to curtsey to others, not the other way about

"Thank you" she said, waiting in the hall for Daisy to return, as she had rushed off up the passageway and into one of the rooms

"Would you like to come through Madam" Daisy said calling softly to Angela from the passageway. Angela followed the maid into the drawing room, where her dear friend Clara sat, her needlework in her hands. Once she looked up and saw Angie stood there she jumped up and rushed to greet her—throwing her arms about her before taking her hand and leading her to a settee, where they could sit and talk together. Although she was still concerned over Richard, her friends had convinced her that Lady Maria had lied to her, though she couldn't for the life of her think why, how could anyone be so cruel and what would be the reason to do so—her mother too had now taken a disliking for her beloved fiancée, since his arrest, and she had without any compassion, branded him guilty—although her father was certain that the man was innocent, he prayed for his release daily

"It's so good to see you Angie, I hoped that you would come" said Clara, smiling at her friend

"Of course, I am so pleased to see you feeling better again" Angie said smiling back "I must say that I'm still very shocked that Lady Maria could have been so awful to you, I can't think why she said those dreadful things, it sounds as if she were jealous of you and as for Sarah, when I called to see

Lady Alice, she told me that the dreadful Flora Kirkby came to Penleigh Court just before dinner the other evening, and took Sarah off home with her—out of the blue, I shall miss her as she was my one and only friend until we met you—her mother treats her nearly as bad as she treated me"

"I don't know, you said you think that Lady Maria is jealous of me, why she should be jealous of me—I know that Richard had told me he wanted to marry me, and he bought me this ring to mark our betrothal" she immediately looked down to the gem on her finger, touching it with love "perhaps she had expected Richard to marry her after his brother had died—I know that he loved her two daughters, he had told me about them lots of times, he used to spend a great deal of time with them and he was looking for a small pony, so that he could teach them to ride—he so loves children. And now, there isn't going to be a wedding at all, let alone children for us are there?" Clara said, her lip quivering, before bursting into tears and sobbing. Angela put an arm about her friend—and tried to comfort her

"Please don't cry Clara, I'm sure that they will soon realize that the Duke has no part in these terrible crimes, and that they have made a terrible mistake—then you will get married and have lots of children, and be happy again, just like Mark and me" Angela really was happy with her new life

Clara looked up at Angie, through her sobs she said

"I don't believe that he will, I'm so afraid Angie, they will take him away from me forever—I don't think that I can bear it—I love him so much"

"I know you do, and he loves you too" there was silence for a few moments then Angie said "I thought that we should go to Penleigh Court and see Lady Alice this afternoon" Angie was determined to cheer Clara up, and she loved visiting Lady Alice. Then Clara suddenly said

"I had a note from Sarah, she says that Lady Maria wrote a note to Mrs Kirkby urging her to take Sarah away immediately—I do think that is so odd, don't you?" she asked her friend

"Why would she do something like that?" she asked

"I don't know Clara, but I do know that Flora Kirkby will be quite awful to Sarah, and she won't allow her any letters from Mr Trent, she will forbid it—but I don't know what we can do about it either" said Angie with a little shudder

"I will come with you to see Lady Alice, I will fetch my cloak" Clara went off, but she was back in minutes, her cloak wrapped around her the hood pulled over her head to shield her from the bitterly cold wind. They had soon set off, and were headed in the direction of the village, and then on up to Penleigh Court.

Maria stepped inside the estate office, she had got rid of Sarah, so there was no reason not to set up a meeting with Mark—she had done what she had set out to do, and she would make sure that Mark knew they had been seen, and she could now use that against Mark—she would tell him that Miss Kirkby would speak to his beloved wife, if he didn't go along with her wishes.

"Good morning Mark—have you been hiding from me?"

"Not at all Maria, I have been busy, but you already know that"

"Too busy to spare time for me"

"I'm afraid so—to tell you the truth, I shall not be meeting you anymore, things have gone on for too long as it is, and I see no reason to carry it on any further" he looked straight at her, her lip started to curl in that hideous fashion of hers and her eyes were ice cold, her gaze unfaltering

"This is becoming very tedious you know, we have had this conversation so many times—may I remind you that if you have any ideas of ending this relationship, then perhaps I should have a word with your young wife" a smile formed, but not a natural true smile, this was something ugly and forced

"Not this time Maria, did you know that we have been seen, Miss Kirkby saw us going to your bedchamber, the last time I came to you—she has already made sure that I know about it, she has told me that she will go to my wife if I see you again, and I'm not prepared to hurt my wife or risk my marriage, not even for you"

"You are a fool—I mean what I said, and I shall let your wife know that her friend has known about the relationship too" she obviously thought that she could twist him round her little finger, and to be fair, up to now she would have been right, but not this time—he had already made a vow, which nothing would make him break—perhaps he should have a word with Angie himself, she would be upset, but at least it would be out in the open, and there would be no more threat to hold over his head, this woman was evil, he should never have allowed her to influence him in the first place

"It makes no difference Maria, this time I mean what I say, I should be glad if you will leave now and allow me to get on with my work" Mark was more nervous and affected than he would care to admit, but all the same, he would stick to his resolve, and that was final

"Then I shall go but do not say that I haven't warned you—and of course you forget that the Duke is not coming back, and when he is hung, then you will be out of a home and a job, you and your dear wife, that's if you still have one of course"

"I shall take my chance of that—Richard will not die if I can possibly prevent it, and I shall do my very best to see that he doesn't—in that you can be sure" with that she turned on her heel and left the office. Mark was more disturbed by her visit than what he had allowed her to believe, as she had left closing the door behind her, he sat at his desk, his hands shaking,—he wasn't sure how he was going to deal with this, but he wouldn't give Miss Kirkby a reason to do it for him. When Angie had told him what she had said to Miss Penrose he had been appalled, there was of course no truth in it, but why was she jealous of the girl, she was attractive, and intelligent, she had so much, she could easily find a new husband, in fact the men would fall at her feet, and then, the way that she had gone to Flora Kirkby, to rid herself of Miss Kirkby, that was understandable he supposed, after all, she had no problem standing up to the woman, that was a sheer vindictive thing to do, well, she wasn't going to ruin his life—he wouldn't allow her to do that, he had made up his mind and this time there would be no going back, whether Maria liked it or not.

CHAPTER TWENTY FIVE

(Secrets Unfolded)

Mark Chandler sat in his estate office, he had just returned from checking some work that had been done to Hilltop Farm—he was very pleased with the way that it was all going and he knew that the Duke would have felt the same way. He had been so keen to get everything done before winter, although that didn't seem likely, as the weather could turn at any moment, while the weather allowed them too, they would push on with the many tasks required.

Mark was marking up his ledgers, logging each completed task and the cost—he was particularly good at keeping books, it was after all what he had been trained for. While sat at his desk, head bowed over the ledger before him, he did not hear the door open, or see the man stood before the desk. As he looked up, he was startled for a second

"I'm sorry Mr Chandler sir, I didn't mean to interrupt but I wondered if I may speak with you for a moment" said Newbridge

"Of course, please take a seat" the old man sat himself down across the opposite side of the desk to the estate manager

"How can I help you" Mark said, now giving the old man his full attention

"Well sir, I'm not sure where to start—it's just that there's been talk, rumours, I thought as you would want to hear what's being said sir, seen as the master isn't here at the moment and the mistress is indisposed" he was edgy and finding the conversation difficult, Mark had no mind to make things worse for him

"You have done the right thing, coming to me with anything which is bothering you—if I can help, I surely will" he said

"Well sir, I see things and hear things, in my job you understand, sometimes you can ignore things sir, but other times you cannot" the old man stopped, he looked deep in thought, trying to find the best way to broach the problem at hand

"I fully understand Newbridge, you can speak to me, anything said in private will stay that way of course"

"Yes, thank you sir. Well sir, it's to do with Lady Maria sir, I don't like to tell tales about people, but she has been acting very strange sir, I know that she's been well, beg your pardon sir, but she's been nothing short of evil to the master, I've heard her with my own ears, I wasn't listening deliberately you understand, but the way she was shouting, you couldn't be off hearing it all—she threatened the master she did and from what I can make of it, she wanted him to marry her, and when the master said he couldn't do that—she went off her head, like a mad woman. I know that the old Duke treated her bad, but she's a wrong 'un and that's for sure. Then there's all that talk about that bloke who worked for the old master, the one that they hung, she was as thick as thieves with the bloke, and talk has it that he was as thick as thieves with the one who hung just before the new master arrived, he was a highway robber. I can tell you too, that it was her as sent a note to that Mr Drummond, and that's a fact—no, she's a one to watch she is—I just wanted to warn you Mr Chandler sir, don't you go trusting her will you, you keep away from that woman, I know it's none of my business what you do and all that, but she's no good—and when I think of the young master, and where he is now, I dread to think" the old man was looking at Mark in earnest—this was his way of warning him off Maria, but he didn't need to be warded off—he had already started to see some of her handiwork, though if she was the one who sent that note to Drummond, then it must have been her who had set Richard up—he shuddered to think of it

"Thank you Newbridge—I shall remember what you have said, and I shall also be watching her a bit closer now—if what you have told me is right, then I think that Maria is the one who has caused the Duke's arrest—you also say that Melvin Lincroft was friendly with Oliver Townsend, the highwayman, hung a year ago?"

"Oh yes sir, no doubt about it, the head groom, he's friendly with my daughter sir, and he saw the man about here all the time—there's no mistaking—they were in something together"

"Well Newbridge, I thank you for the information, if anything else happens you will keep me informed won't you? I intend to get to the root of all this one way or another" Mark said, thinking about all the things which the old man had said

"It's a pleasure sir, but you watch her, they do say that she'll end up like her mother before her—I wouldn't want to see you in a fix like the master" he said, rising and going to the door

"I shall indeed be careful Newbridge, you can depend on that—good day to you"

"Aye sir, good day" the old man opened the door and slipped out.

Mark sat for a while, trying to digest everything which had been discussed, he had been warning Mark, so he must have known he had fallen for her charms, and was warning him to end it before it was too late, which is exactly what he planned to do. There was also the reference to her mother, Mark would have to take ride into Truro as soon as possible, it was very important that he find out about her mother—perhaps it would answer some of the questions which were on everyone's lips.

Russell and Jasper finally arrived at Penleigh Court, they had visited Richard before leaving for Cornwall, and it had taken them two days travelling to get here. Richard had told them that they must stay at his home, he wouldn't hear of his dear friends having to stay at the local hostelry, and he was sure that his mother would make them welcome. Jasper had asked his old friend some questions about his fiancée, though he didn't ask about his mother, so they had also promised that they would keep an eye to her too. They hadn't however, given away the true reason for broaching the subject, he didn't want his friend to worry about that on top of everything else. Richard had made it quite plain where his love and loyalties lay, and he asked his two friends to keep an eye to his precious Clara for him, and although he said nothing to them, he still had his fears that Maria was behind all of this, but stuck in there he couldn't prove anything. He was also very worried about the eleventh of January, until the hearing, he just hoped that would be time enough to find out exactly what had been going on.

Once they had completed their visit and had assured their friend of their intentions, they climbed into Russell's carriage and left for Cornwall immediately.

On arrival, they alighted from the carriage, and Russell followed Jasper into the house, Newbridge had opened the door to them, before organizing two rooms to be made ready, and directing the footmen to their master's bedchambers to deliver their trunks. Jasper was ready for a drink, and after hearing that Alice was resting in her room, Jasper led Russell to the library and poured two glasses of Richard's brandy for them both—he smiled as he remembered his friend stating that they should not empty his cellar. Russell was going through all the things which they had learned and he was particularly keen to meet Lady Maria, the woman who had been seemingly causing all the problems—Jasper still found it hard to believe that a woman that was so attractive could have caused such bedlam, but he had always been shallow, it was part of his charm.

They had downed another couple of brandies each, before a knock came at the library door, both gentlemen turned towards the door, when the door opened, a very tall man slipped inside

"Good afternoon gentlemen, I hope that you don't mind, but I hear that you are looking for information to help my master" he said looking from one to the other of them

"And you are?" Russell asked

"James, the Duke's valet—at your service" he replied bowing to them

"How can we help you James?" Russell asked

"Well, I thought that you would like to know about that trunk, the one with all the jewels, I think I know a bit about it" he said

"Indeed, then you best tell us what you know" said Russell

"That damned woman—the one that was married to the Duke's brother, that Lady Maria, I caught her in the Duke's bedchamber, and not just once either—the first time I had only gone into the dressing room to collect a jacket that needed cleaning, and I heard all this noise, when I went in, there she sat, as bold as brass, on the carpet with the lid of that trunk up and messing about with whatever was inside—though I didn't know what was inside then, she soon shut it and padlocked it again when she saw me. I asked her what she thought she was up to in the master's bedchamber, and she just said she was looking for him—but I knew that she wasn't looking for him, no more than I'm the King of England. When I told her that he wasn't there, and I waited for her to leave, she gave me the ugliest look you ever did see—but I didn't care, I wasn't going to have her rummaging through his stuff like" he said looking from one to the other of the gentleman

"You say that you saw her in there more than once" Russell prompted

"That's right—the next time I saw her it was the morning of the day that my master was arrested—I came in here to sort out clothes for his evening dinner party, and there she was, as large as life—she was going through the master's things—I told her that she had no right in the Duke's room, and she said that she was waiting for him to join her—well, you could knock me down with a feather you could—it was hardly likely that he would bother with a sour faced witch as her, when he was planning to marry that pretty young thing from the rectory—I know that he's never been averse to a pretty woman or two, but this one was something else. She got in such a temper with me, asked me if I knew who I was speaking too she did, and threatened to have me thrown out the house—I told her, not your house madam, the Duke's the master here—not you, and I'll thank you not to threaten me—she didn't think much to that, she started screaming at me like some sort of raving lunatic, then she came over here—her face was evil, that's the only way I can describe it, she spat at me, before raising her hand to slap my face, but I caught her hand and threw her out—she was screaming down the corridor that she'd make me pay, but she didn't frighten me. Then, that very night, when everyone was seated round the table, that Drummond fellow turned up and found a key, that I had never set eyes on before, and opened the lid of the trunk, that's when all those jewels and gold came to light. With a trunk full of stuff worth what that was, why would the Duke have needed to sell the house in Bond Street to raise enough money to keep him going until he married—right worried about it all he was, after the old man done the dirty on him"

"I have to agree with you James, none of it makes sense, unless this Lady Maria has something to do with it all, and she certainly seems to be off her head, the more we hear of her, the more it's apparent that she's mad"

"There was also her relationship with the old man—they fought like cat and dog they did—she would shriek at the top of her voice and the old man would shout louder—threatening to kick her out without a penny he was, just about every day—well, couldn't help hearing it all, got a bit sick of it to tell the truth, then last Christmas night it was, I can't forget that, I saw him, creeping along the landing and into her room he did—she must have invited him to her bed, perhaps she thought she could buy his favour as his mistress, anyway, a week later and he was dead—funny old business, talk about a black widow, that's what they do 'aint it, takes their pleasure then eats their mate, that's what she is, I never did believe that she didn't have something to do with it, haven't got any proof of course, but you mark my words, she was behind it, same as I reckon she's behind it all, and no mistake"

"Well James, you could be right—thank you for coming to us, we will certainly look into this, I fully intend to get to the bottom of it all. Did you tell Drummond about any of this?" said Russell, Jasper sat quietly saying nothing but taking it all in

"No sir, I told no-one, that Drummond fellow wouldn't have believed me, he would have thought that I was just saying something to get my master off the charges. Well, if you'll excuse me gentleman, I shall go back to my work, but I reckon if anyone can help the Duke now, it's you—my master trusts you both, so that's why I thought that I could trust you too" said James

"Yes you can indeed trust us, if there is anything else that you can think of, then I trust that you will come and find us again" said Russell

"Oh I shall indeed—good afternoon gentlemen" he bowed his head and slipped out of the door, leaving the two friends looking at each other in silence, they were both pondering on what they had just learnt.

That evening, knowing that Jasper and his friend had arrived, Mark went into the house, he slipped through the side door and went in search of Newbridge. He soon found the butler, and asked him where the other two gentlemen were, Newbridge informed him that they were in the drawing room, awaiting dinner, Mark thanked him and went to seek them out. As he entered the drawing room, Jasper jumped up once he saw him

"Chandler my friend, it's good to see you, come and meet my good friend Hinton. Are you staying for dinner this evening?"

"It's good to see you too, good evening Mr Hinton" Mark said bowing to him "I'm afraid that I won't be dining this evening, in fact I should really have left for home by now, Angie will be expecting me, but I wanted to see you first and enquire of the Duke's welfare"

"What a pity, perhaps we can convince Lady Alice to invite you and Mrs Chandler one evening, I hear she's taken to your wife as her own"

"Indeed, she has been extremely good to both of us. You have no doubt heard that Miss Kirkby has been ordered back to Truro with her mother, it's rather a pity as I know that she was looking forward to your return" said Mark looking to Jasper. Just at that moment the door opened and Maria entered the room—she looked from one gentleman to the other, the conversation stopped abruptly, and all the men focused on the elegant lady, who had walked into the room, head held high and back straight

"I seem to have interrupted something—would you rather I leave the room again?" she asked

"Not at all Lady Maria—and in any case, I'm now on my way home" said Mark, trying to avoid meeting her gaze

"Oh please, don't leave on my account" she replied in a whisper taking a seat near the fire. Mark said a hasty goodnight, with the promise of a further discussion the next day, after all, he was eager to tell his friends what he now knew but he was equally desperate to escape Maria

"Lady Maria, can I introduce you to my good friend Russell Hinton" Jasper said to her, moving forward to where she was seated

"Good evening Mr Hinton, so you will both be our guests for Christmas?" she asked

"Indeed we shall My Lady" Russell answered, watching her closely and taking every bit of her appearance in

"I'm afraid that you will have to put up with my company alone this evening as Lady Alice won't be joining us, she is not feeling up to it, but no doubt she will wish to meet you once she feels a little better" she said directly to Russell

"I'm sorry to hear that she is unwell" said Russell inclining his head "It must be very difficult for her, having the Duke indisposed at the moment" he persisted

"Yes, well there is little that anyone can do about that is there not?" she said, her ice blue eyes fixed on Russell's face

"On the contrary madam, I am quite confident that we shall see the Duke released before long" Russell had heard of Maria's dealings, and had been quite disturbed at what he had heard, he fixed her stare, he was not about to allow her to intimidate him—for a few seconds their gaze was locked in silence before Maria finally spoke

"Then I wish you well sir" she spoke softly and looked away, the smile on her face fixed and unnatural. Russell moved away from her, he had won that battle, although he felt that there was much left unsaid, but there was still some way to go to win the war.

The following morning, the rain was pounding the window panes once again, Mark had decided that he must go to Truro, he needed to speak with Mr Truscott, he would be able to make enquiries to the history of Maria's real mother—if anyone could find that information, Mr Truscott could. Since Newbridge had visited him a few days before, it had played on his mind what he had said, he had been led to believe that Maria's parents had both died, that's why she had gone to live with her aunt and uncle, but clearly rumour didn't agree, he wasn't sure how much was just talk and speculation and how much was actual truth, but perhaps this held the key to the truth—and if that was so, then he must look into it. His plans to ride to Truro were not such a good idea, and he was certain that Lady Alice would have no objection to him taking the carriage, especially when he was on an errand that may eventually free her son. He entered the stables and spoke to the head groom, who was able to confirm that the carriage had not been ordered for today, but there was also the older coach, which although less robust, would be suitable enough for his task—so he requested that it be made ready to leave within the hour—he was eager to be on his way without delay, there was little time to lose.

Very soon he was rattling and jolting along the rough rutted road, on his way to Truro, the rain still pattering on the windows of the carriage. He sat back against the red soft plush of the interior, thinking about the task in hand, he had wanted to speak to Jasper and Russell the previous evening, he had even stayed late to speak with them, but Maria had put paid to that—blast the woman, any other time she wouldn't have shown her face, but the one time he would have welcomed the privacy, she had turned up and thwarted his plans. He was beginning to believe that she did indeed have a hand in all this somehow—he had learnt that she had been Lincroft's lover, it seemed to him that she would do anything if she could improve her own situation, and in meaning anything, he wasn't sure how far she would be prepared to go. He had seen a side to her that he didn't particularly like—it had frightened him in fact, she had no thought or compassion for anyone, least of all those who didn't comply with her wishes—she was indeed a dangerous woman.

The carriage suddenly jolted to a stop, he had lost track of time, but he had arrived already—the coachman had jumped down off his seat, opened the door and pulled down the steps for him to alight. The rain had not let up at all, it was still beating against the coach—he had taken an umbrella from the stand in the office before he left, he was glad of it now, though there was not far to go. He told the coachman to meet him in an hour at the hostelry in town, then he turned and made his way towards the offices of Truscott and Penn.

As he stepped into the small waiting area, old Mr Truscott opened his small office door and looked to see who had just entered.

"Mr Chandler I believe" he had said, studying him over the top of his spectacles

"Yes that's right sir, I came in hopes of speaking with you this morning—it is rather urgent" Mark stressed

"You had better come in" he said, Mark entered that familiar little office where he had sat once before, and was studied for the job of his dreams, now the little old man took the same seat behind the desk, while he sat opposite him, but this time he was the one doing the talking

"As you must already be aware sir, the Duke is unfortunately detained by the authorities but we believe that he has been wrongly accused. I have reason to believe that Lady Maria Penleigh is involved in this sorry business, and it has reached my ears that there is something strange to do with her mother, that could help us to free his lordship. So, I am here to ask if you could make some discreet enquiries for me" the little man had been studying him intently while he was relaying the details, once he had finished his tirade, a silence fell between the two men for several moments, before Mr Truscott spoke

"I'm afraid your request is rather a strange one sir, whatever you're reasoning, would it not be better to ask the lady herself, rather than have the matter investigated" he said

"This is a very delicate matter, I don't believe the lady would wish to impart the information willingly sir, and I wouldn't ask, but it is important, at least to the Duke, it is a matter of life and death so to speak, depending on the outcome, this could lead to the Dukes release you understand" he was choosing his words carefully

"If it is for the Duke, then I shall see what I can do—I make no promises of course, had it been his father, then I would have said that his guilt was possible, but knowing the young Duke, like you I can't believe that he is guilty of the crimes with which he has been charged—so I shall do what I can for you. Once I have some information, I will write with the details" he said looking at some papers in front of him

"Thank you sir, I'm very much obliged to you—but I should sooner return here personally for the outcome of you investigations" said Mark, thinking that he couldn't allow anyone else to intercept such information

"As you wish Mr Chandler" the old man replied "then I suggest that you return here one week from today—that should leave enough time to look into this matter for you.

"Thank you Mr Truscott" now he stood, before the old man changed his mind "Until next week" he gave a little bow, then he turned and left the dingy little office.

<hr />

Mark returned to Penleigh Court, the carriage took him directly to the stables where he alighted and strode round the corner and into the estate office, as he entered he stopped dead in the doorway—there, sat in his chair at his desk, was Maria. As soon as his eye fell on her, his stomach lurched—he had not expected that, and she was the last person now that he would have wanted to see.

"Maria—what can I do for you?" he must try and keep things civil, he didn't want to upset her un-necessarily although he had no intention of falling in with her wishes

"Do you really need to ask? Surely you have not forgotten so soon" she said smoothly

"Of course not, but I have not changed my mind, it is over Maria, there is no more to say"

"That's where you are wrong, you are here to do a job, I am the mistress, you will do as I say" that awful curl of the lip again

"I am weary of this conversation, it has become tedious, I am employed by the Duke, and now I must get on, I have no time for all this"

"Do not dare to dispense with me—I am not finished with you" her voice was gaining momentum, and rising by an octave

"Maria, we have already discussed this matter more times than I care to remember, I am a married man, and have no intention of hurting my wife—not in any way. As I told you before, we have shared a pleasant interlude together, but now it's over—there is nothing more to say on the matter, so if there is nothing else, then perhaps you would leave me now, and allow me to carry on with my work"

"Where have you been in the carriage—who has given you permission to use it—you are a servant here—nothing more" she was grasping at straws—if Mark didn't know better, he would be feeling sorry for the woman. She stood up, and walked round the desk, to where he was standing, she slipped her arms about his waist and looked straight into his eyes, then she pressed her body against his, and her lips hard on his—he tried to push away, but she held him firm, he unclasped her hands and pushed her back against the desk

"No, I have said no, and I meant it—now please go" he went to the door and opened it wide, the rain still beating down was blown inside but he stood beside the door, holding it ready to close after her—she stared at him and started to walk toward the door, and before he could prevent it, she had raised her hand and brought it down hard against his cheek—it stung, and he immediately raised his hand to his cheek

"You have not heard the last of this—you had better watch out Mark Chandler, for I shall make you sorry for this day" she said as she stepped outside into the rain and wind.

Mark slammed the door shut, before taking his seat behind his desk—he placed his hands to his head, his cheek still burning from the slap that she had administered. He was in no doubt now that she was involved in all this, her behaviour was volatile to say the least, he was convinced that she had been the cause of the Duke's arrest, and probably for something which he had refused her. He sat for a while, his mind all over the place, he couldn't concentrate today—so he decided that he would go to the library and have a glass of brandy, he needed something to calm his nerves, then he would find his wife, he knew that her and Clara should be meeting Lady Alice, so he would join them for a while. He made his way to the library and poured himself a large brandy, before sitting at the Duke's desk. He must have been there an hour or more, before getting up and going to the drawing room to find the ladies, but to his horror, as he stepped out of the library, Maria was descending the staircase—he deliberately ignored her presence and carried on to the drawing room as he had planned to do—he could hear her footsteps behind him, but he had no intention of acknowledging her as he opened the drawing room door and stepped inside.

Clara had visited her friend that afternoon, Angela was happy and excited, this was to be her first Christmas in her own home, though Lady Alice had suggested that they spend Christmas Day at Penleigh Court, especially now that there would be house guests for the season. Clara suggested that they visit Lady Alice this afternoon—after all, they hadn't seen her for a couple of days, and they had become very firm friends, Angela looked on the older lady as a mother, which delighted Alice—their one regret that Sarah couldn't be there to share their friendship. Angela fetched her cloak and wrapped it around her, it was such a wet and nasty day, and they would have to walk to Penleigh Court.

Once they arrived, Newbridge showed them into the drawing room

"I shall let Lady Alice know that you are here" he said closing the door behind him. Clara and Angela sat on the settee next to each other, warming themselves by the fire, which was throwing warm shards of orange, red and yellow rippling in the grate. The girls held their hands out to the flames, which were glowing and welcoming. It seemed to be an age before the door opened and Lady Alice stepped inside, on seeing the girls she went over to them hugging each one in turn, before seating herself opposite them in her armchair

"How are you my dears" Alice asked looking from one to the other of them

"We are well thank you Lady Alice" said Clara

"Good. And have you met my guests yet?"

"Not yet, although my husband had told me that Mr Trent had returned with a friend of his" said Angela

"Yes, they are my son's good friends—I'm hopeful that they will help to see him released—I know that they are intent upon that purpose" said Alice

"I'm sure that they will—I'm so glad that they have come" said Clara. At that moment the door opened and Jasper entered followed by the other gentleman who the woman had not met—on seeing the young ladies Jasper rushed forward to greet the two ladies sat opposite Lady Alice, taking each hand in turn and raising them to his lips before remembering that his good friend was stood right behind him

"Forgive me ladies, I would like you to meet my good friend Russell Hinton" and then to his friend

"May I introduce Miss Penrose and Mrs Chandler" he said casting his hand out to identify each in turn. Russell bowed his head to each of the young ladies before saying to Clara

"I believe that you are the Duke's fiancée Miss Penrose, I have to say that he is a very fortunate man, to have such an attractive young lady waiting for him" the colour rose in her cheeks

"Thank you sir" she replied smiling

"Warren has been keen to hear how you are and also how you are Lady Alice" he said turning to Alice then. Alice just smiled, but Clara was eager to hear more

"Is Richard in good spirits sir?"

"As well as can be expected, though he speaks often of you, and his feelings for you Miss" a large beam spread across Clara's face, if she had any doubts of his affections, they had just been dispelled

Lady Alice had met Russell Hinton at breakfast, and she had taken a liking to the gentleman, there was something about him which was stable and firmly rooted—someone she felt that she could trust, just as she did with Mr Chandler. Alice rang for tea, the young people were chatting gaily between themselves, Alice watched them closely, wishing that she had been blessed with a large family, having young people around her made her feel less isolated than she had been for many years, and there was also the little ones who still visited her regularly. Once the tea arrived Alice set about pouring it, while the gentlemen handed it round to the ladies. Just as they had settled down to sip their refreshment, the door opened and Mark entered, followed closely by Maria—Alice greeted both of them and Mark went to stand behind his wife, and resting his hand on her shoulder, while Maria took a seat next to Russell. Alice poured out more tea for the two newcomers, before picking up her cup and taking another sip

"So Mr Chandler, how is the repairs going, the Duke had hoped that they would be complete by winter, but there were rather too many for that I fear" said Alice, looking straight at Mark

"Indeed, the work is going very well, but to have it completed will take rather a while longer—but by spring most of it should be done" he said

"And the budget, you have been able to stick to it?"

"Yes, that has been a blessing, things have been fairly straight forward at least up to now" he replied

"And is there any news on my son's predicament? I had hoped that he would be free to enjoy Christmas with the rest of us" she asked, looking round the room

"We are doing our best My Lady, though with Christmas just over a week away, I fear that may be a little too optimistic" said Mark, answering for the party

"I think Alice dear, that we should not count too highly on seeing the Dukes freedom, after all, you will be devastated if it is not meant to be" said Maria, now joining the conversation—everyone turned to look at her, though not one of the group agreed with her

"But surely My Lady" Russell said looking straight at her "It is what we are all working toward, is it not?" he was watching her eyes unfaltering as he spoke

"Of course, but my thoughts are only for Alice's welfare, after all it has made her ill with worry—I think that we have to prepare ourselves for the worst, it would be more sensible don't you think?" she had turned to Russell as she said it

"I believe that there is plenty of time to turn this situation around, and I for one am not convinced that Warren is guilty of the crime he has been accused of" he said firmly

"And what of the evidence Mr Hinton, do you deny that isn't convincing either?" Russell studied her face, from those ice cold eyes, to the set of her mouth

"The evidence in this case could easily have been planted, by the real highway robber" this time it was Mark that spoke—Maria's cold blue eyes shot a glance in his direction

"So who would you think the culprit Mr Chandler, Lady Alice perhaps, or myself, or maybe James, the Duke's man?" she said, waiting for a reply, but studying him closely, for a moment the group was silent, no-one said a word, then Mark said

"The Duke is innocent, I'm sure of it, and I shall do everything within my power to prove the fact, it's a case of learning the truth of the matter" Angela lifted her hand and patted her husband's hand, which was still resting on her shoulder. Maria's lip curled, that horrible, ugly smirk that Mark had seen so many times before—and in that second he knew that she was about to say something that he would regret

"Truth and what do you know of the truth—for the man who speaks of truth and yet tells so many lies" this time the whole group looked to Mark for a reply, though Jasper's face coloured, guessing what she was referring too

"I have no idea what you mean Lady Maria" Mark said, trying to keep his voice even, though he too had a rush of colour to his cheeks

"Perhaps I should explain sir" she replied tartly, now Angela spoke up

"Indeed you should Lady Maria, how dare you speak to my husband like this" she said—Angela was always so very quiet and not in the habit of getting into any sort of dispute, but this woman's obvious verbal attack against her husband was more than she could take. Maria, cold staring eyes still fixed on Mark said

"Your wife seems to think you are the fount of honesty, but we know different do we not Mr Chandler?"

"What nonsense, perhaps we should agree to disagree My Lady, before this gets out of hand" Mark said quickly, trying to end the conversation, but Maria wasn't having any of it—she had started and now she would have her say—she had waited for this moment for a while, delaying due to Mark's weakness, but this time she would not delay further—Mark had thwarted her for the last time, only this afternoon he had made his position clear, she would no longer hold her tongue, it was his own fault and he could blame himself.

"Then you have told Mrs Chandler of our relationship? That we are lovers? That is the truth, and you seem to hold such store by the truth, yet you can lie to the person whom you profess to love?"

There, she had said it, her face was aglow with a sense of pride and achievement—he could never say that she hadn't warned him, that lip curling into some grotesque smile, her eyes were so cold and piercing, he feared she could turn him to a frozen mass, worse than he had ever experienced before. Angela's face changed as she realized what this woman had said—her hand flew to her mouth and she jumped up from her seat, and ran to the door and out into the passageway, with her husband close on her heels—Clara also sprang to her feet and followed her friend—the small group that were left sat in silence, even Lady Alice didn't know quite what to say. Finally Russell turned to Lady Maria, who sat with that satisfied smile still on her face

"That My Lady, was totally uncalled for—Mrs Chandler I'm sure did not deserve your brutality" he said, the line of his mouth set

"I'm ashamed of you Maria, if you must have your fun, why could you not have found it outside of this place, but to hurt that poor dear girl this is unforgiveable—perhaps you should consider moving into the Gate Lodge permanently" said Alice at last, this was the first time that anyone had cause to witness her anger

"That is not your decision Alice, I am mistress here, my child will own this estate and take the title, and I shall be mistress, your days are numbered and once your dear son hangs, then it will all fall to me" now her mask had fallen, she was showing herself as she really was

"I don't think that you should speak to Lady Alice like this My Lady, as I understand it, you have been given a home here, you and your children and the Duke has taken you under his protection, yet you treat him and his family with such disdain, that is despicable in my eyes" Russell hated rude people

"What business is it of yours? No one asked you here—and to put it bluntly you are not wanted here—do you hear me, you nor him" pointing to Jasper "you are neither wanted here—the Duke will hang, and when he does, this will all be mine—all of it mine" her voice was becoming hysterical now—Jasper had never seen her in this light before, and he shrank back, he chose to avoid unpleasantness of any kind, unlike his friend

"Nevertheless, until that day comes, and we will do what we must to see him freed, this house belongs to my dear friend the Duke of Warren, and you are as much a guest here as we are" he would not allow her anything

"We shall see, you Mr Hinton are trying to thwart me just as he did, now look at him, he learnt that I won't stand for it, and so shall you" she was shrieking now, a woman demented, Alice sat fixated to the shaking mad woman

"Are you telling me that you were responsible for the Duke's demise?" Russell persisted

"As if you don't know it—of course I am, I couldn't allow him to take what is rightfully mine—I even offered to marry him, to share all this with him, but he thwarted me, I saw that he wanted me his eyes told me so, yet that chit from the vicarage came on the scene, and he put her before me—how dare he, and she no more than a common chit—well now he will pay for his mistakes with his life, and I shall make sure of it" Russell stood up and grabbed her hand, and dragged her from the room, Jasper jumped to his feet and went with them, the woman was shrieking at the top of her voice, leaving Alice sat, staring at the fire, her mind far away.

Chapter Twenty Six

(The Facts)

Angela ran from the drawing room, with her unfaithful husband close behind her, and following them both was Clara. Mark was calling her name, but she couldn't deal with him near her right now—she just had to get away, she opened the front door and ran out into the rain and cold, without taking her cloak—Mark still following her. Within minutes Mark had caught up to his wife and ran in front, thrusting his arms out and taking hold of her arms, to stop her from going further—the rain was beginning to soak them to the skin, and Mark wanted to lead the two women somewhere dry and warm, Angela tried to dodge away from him, but he wouldn't allow her too. She couldn't look at the man she loved, her heart was broken and she was sobbing so hard she could hardly catch her breathe. Mark threw his arms about her, and pulled her against him, and after putting up a fight, she fell listless and broken, into his arms, Clara stood beside her good friend, she couldn't look into Mark's face, how could he have hurt the poor girl so, she had been so happy, how could he have thrust her world into such despair.

Mark led her to the office, where he sat her down pulling her close in his arms to try and soothe her sobs.

"Angie, my darling girl, I love you so much, I never meant to do anything to hurt you" he whispered into her beautiful auburn hair—Clara stood behind her, unsure of how to handle this situation, once the sobs had ceased a little she tried to lift her head and speak, Mark could see the torment in her eyes, the one thing he had vowed to do was to look after her, see that she was never hurt again, and yet, only a month into their marriage, and he had already broken his vow, and left his dear wife vulnerable to a parasite, waiting in the wings to cause as much misery as she could—but it was no-one's fault but his own—he could not blame Maria, it was his own fault for allowing her to tempt him so

"My darling I'm so sorry—I never meant to hurt you this way"

"Why did you do it? Why did you tell me that you loved me, and why did you marry me, when you didn't want me at all?" she cried between sobs

"But I do love you, more than anything else in the world"

"Did you tell her that you loved her too?"

"Please Angie, my dearest, I have never loved anyone but you—she was a mistake, a terrible mistake"

"Yet still you went to her, to her bed, I know that I'm not an expert in these things, but I don't know what I've done to make you treat me so" she said, her eyes red and her skin blotchy.

"You have done nothing wrong my love, would I could start again, I should never have been so stupid"

"But the damage is done—I don't know whether I can forgive you—yet I know that I have too, your my husband, and in spite of everything I love you so much" Mark pulled the girl hard against his chest, kissing her hair and forehead

"And I love you too—please believe me Angie, I want no-one but you, not ever again" he said, looking into her face, her lovely face, Angie couldn't stand it any longer, she was frightened of losing the one man in all the world that she loved, so she threw her arms about his neck and returned his affections. Clara decided that she should leave the two of them to sort things out without her, although her heart was breaking for her friend, she could see how much they really loved each other, and men had a habit of taking mistresses, not that that would be much comfort to her dear friend, so she crept out the door, trying not to disturb them, and made her way back to Alice. Mark and Angela spent an hour or so, just making up their differences, before Mark requested the carriage to see them home.

Christmas was looming, just five days to go, Alice had decided to throw a dinner, what with her house guests and all the trouble that there had been with the Chandlers, she felt that they could all do with something of a more pleasant nature, to lift all their spirits. Angie and Clara had visited her a couple of days after that terrible scene, both Clara and Alice had had a good talk to Angela, Alice had pointed out that she should think no more about it, she could see how much Mark loved her, and that was all that counted—as for Maria, she had proven to be someone whom Alice had no desire to associate with anymore—Alice didn't trust the woman, she had seemed overcome with madness, she was pleased now that her dear Richard had turned the woman down, God only knew what would have happened had he agreed to marry her. Angie was still a little upset, but that was to be expected, but she was desperately trying to forgive her husband his indiscretion, everyone can make a mistake so she must give him another chance—Mark felt privileged that Angie had agreed to try and put it all behind them, and he certainly wouldn't make a mistake like that again. Maria was keeping away from everyone, knowing that she would get no sympathy from anyone here.

Mark had gone back to Truro, this time he rode his horse, although the wind was whistling, at least it was dry and fine, there was no winter sun today and it was bitterly cold. As soon as Mark arrived he left his horse at the hostelry stables and made his way through the town, to the offices of Truscott and Penn, he wasn't sure that the old man would have any news for him, but he hoped that he did. Once inside the building, Mr Truscott once again came out to meet him

"Mr Chandler, please come in" Mark followed him into that same dusty dank little office and seated himself in the same chair, the piles of books and paperwork, still as they had been a week ago

"Were you able to uncover any information which might be of use?" Mark asked the old man

"You were right in thinking that there was a hidden secret—it was believed for all intents and purpose, that Lady Maria's parents were both dead—the father died as you know, and left the mother and daughter in a penniless state, the mother was frantic, not knowing what she could do, so she had spoken to her sister who had no children, they were a wealthy couple, but there were rumours that the man was less than honest in his dealings. The mother wrote to her sister, asking them to take both herself and the girl in and to give the daughter a season and find her a good match, but the uncle refused to take his sister in law, though it was agreed that they would do what was asked for the girl, on condition that it never be known that the woman had become a mad pauper, and that she would never make contact with the girl again, the mother had no alternative but to agree to it—but had gone into a decline, she had been very ill, but while she was thought to have become ill and died, the pain she suffered was mental not physical illness—it seems that she had already started a mental decline before her husband died, but once her full situation was realized, she was overcome with madness, giving the uncle no alternative but to have her committed to the Dartmoor asylum, for the safety of all around her, notwithstanding her own, and where it appears, she still lives today" the old man stopped and looked at his companion, his beady little eyes watching him closely

"I see—so the mother is mad, is there a possibility that her daughter could be touched with the same complaint?" he asked

"I'm afraid I'm not a doctor, but it is generally believed that this madness had run in that particular family for several generations, though not every generation was affected" Mark sat quietly deep in thought—that would make sense, the way that she had acted was that of a woman who was seriously unbalanced, there seemed little doubt that she was indeed following in her mother's footsteps—so rumour was correct.

"I thank you for that information sir, it has been a great help" said Mark standing "I shall not take any more of your time"

"I'm glad to have been of some help—is there any news of the Duke?" he asked

"Not just at the moment, though I believe that there soon will be now" Mark replied

Eliza Laval

"Good day to you Mr Chandler"

"Good day to you Mr Truscott" Mark turned and left the solicitors office.

<hr>

Shortly after Mark had returned to his office, Russell and Jasper entered. Jasper hadn't seen much of Mark the last few days as he had been to Truro several times to see his sweet Sarah. Flora Kirkby was not overly happy with her daughters suitor, but they did wish to see her married, and he was a gentleman of means—so it would seem churlish of her to forbid their friendship, and besides, her daughter had not been swamped with suitors of any sort, so she allowed Sarah her visits, under her own supervision of course.

Mark welcomed the two gentlemen who had just arrived, since having returned from Truro with the news which old Truscott had found for him, he was eager to impart it to his friends, and to see if they had news of their own that would be of use.

"Well Chandler, have you any news" asked Jasper

"I have some, but I'm not sure how it all fits, though I believe it to be relevant"

"We have also had some information which may be relevant" said Russell, Mark then asked him what they had learned, Russell did the talking

"The afternoon that we arrived, we had a visit from James, Warren's valet, he told us that Maria was the owner of the trunk in Warrens bedchamber, and that he had caught her in there on two occasions—Warren had already made it quite plain to us that there had been no union between him and Maria, so it seems to me that she was responsible for the trunk, and possibly the goods inside"

"Then it is truly as I fear, I am convinced that Maria is central to the Duke's problems"

"I have to agree with you Chandler, now what is your news?"

"Well I too have had a visit, from Newbridge, the man is very knowledgeable about the family and what is going on in general. He came to me specifically to tell me that it was Maria who had sent the note to Drummond on the afternoon that the Duke was arrested, he also made a statement that rumour had it that she was going the same way as her mother—well, by all accounts her mother was thought to be dead, so I took the liberty of visiting the family solicitor Truscott in Truro, and requested that he investigate the mother, which he did, and I have only just returned, a little while ago, as old Mr Truscott found that her mother had not died at all, she had been committed to Dartmoor asylum soon after Maria came to live with her aunt and uncle, who apparently was wealthy, though how he came by his means, was rather dubious. He also stated that it was thought that this madness was something which ran down the generations, though there were generations which it missed totally"

"Then that all ties in does it not, the woman is as we thought touched with madness, and it seems fair to say that the trunk of goods belonged to Maria, not to Warren" said Russell

"Exactly. There is also something else, there was a man called Oliver Townsend he was caught red handed so to speak, holding up a carriage one night last year—well from what Newbridge tells me, this man was always lurking about here at the time, apparently he was friendly with Melvin Lincroft, who was the estate manager before me, who was hung when he was caught as leader of the smuggling band in the area. Newbridge also insinuated that Maria had been very close with Lincroft too—could she have been his mistress? It would not surprise me—if that is the case, then the goods which she had in her trunk could have belonged to Lincroft, but because she couldn't use them herself, or let anyone know that she had them, then she used them to spite Warren—Newbridge said that she had been threatening him, if the madness came upon her then who's to say that she wouldn't go so far"

"I have to say Chandler that I agree with you—but I certainly think that we should speak to Drummond about all this" said Russell, suddenly Jasper seemed to remember things

"The passage leading to the Smugglers Cove, leads to the Gate Lodge, which was the home of Lincroft, and he left the place to Maria—which would indicate that there was something going on there don't you think?"

"Indeed I do Trent, but we now have to persuade Maria to admit to her crimes" said Russell, trying to think how best to go about this

"We have to get her to admit it in front of Drummond—so that there can be no doubt about it, though I would expect her to be committed rather than hung for her crimes" said Mark thinking about it all

"With less than a week to Christmas, I think we should get back to London Trent, there is no reason that we cannot return for Christmas but we must speak with Warren now—what with the information that we know already chances are that Warren could offer some that we don't already know, if we can just piece everything together, this could be our chance to have our friend freed, and back with his family where he belongs" said Russell

"I must say that you are quite right, though London is a long way to travel and at this time of year" Mark considered

"I think that we should go on horseback, if we leave at Dawn tomorrow, we would make London by nightfall, spend a day to complete our tasks and we could return the following day" Russell was looking to Jasper for agreement

"Then we must leave at dawn" replied Jasper at last.

Russell and Jasper arrived in London late the previous evening and had made arrangements to meet up at ten o clock, to go and visit their friend in Newgate gaol. At least this time they had something positive to tell him, there were several things now which before had laid uncovered but now were facts which would help in setting the Duke free, and particularly Jasper was very excited about doing just that.

As agreed, and furnished with their sweet smelling handkerchiefs, they entered Newgate gaol, the guard was a different one to the one which had been there previously, and he questioned them on their business there, before allowing them to go and find Richard. As usual, once Richard saw his friends he stood up and strode to the bars to talk with them

"I didn't expect to see you here today, after all, I thought that you were going to Penleigh Court for Christmas my friends" said Richard, looking from one to the other

"Well we would have been there, but we managed to learn some things which we believe may help us to get you out of this hell hole" said Russell. Richard's head jerked up to his friend, he had become eager to hear what he had to say

"What have you learnt" he asked, fixing his gaze on Russell's face

"That your sister in law has had a great deal to do with all this" he replied "and we have also learnt that her mother, who everyone thought was dead, is actually rotting in Dartmoor asylum, and from what I can see of things, she is going the same way" said Russell "and that's why we've come here now, to see if you can shed any light on the situation at all, obviously you have displeased her, for her to be determined to see you ruined, and not only that—she has tried to poison your fiancée's mind against you, she told her that you were leading her on, and that you were planning to marry her, and that her son, recently born, was also your son" Richard's face was now like thunder

"She has said what?" he asked "so Clara believes that I have betrayed her?" his face was pale and oh so drawn as it was, with large dark circles underneath his eyes, he looked tired and worn, and old in that moment, his eyes seemed to go black as they came out at Russell and Jasper

"You need not worry about that—Miss Penrose knows now that it was all lies" said Russell hastily "she is eager to see you, she truly loves you"

"To think that I wanted only to assure the woman that she would have a home and be protected for as long as she needed it, but she wasn't satisfied with that, she wanted me to marry her, I could not do that—I would not spend the rest of my life with that woman—even if I had not had the good fortune to have met dearest Clara" he said

So as we suspected, you thwarted her plans, but her hysteria and madness have turned her into something far more sinister" said Russell

"What of Chandler? He must be careful, you must warn him, he succumbed to her charms for a while, and no doubt that Trent has told you how he had insisted on using that relationship with her, even though he wanted it ended, to get us out of a scrape, when we found the passageway" he said

"Yes, Trent has told me all about that, I'm afraid that she has already told Chandler's wife that she was his mistress—and it caused the obvious devastation to the poor girl, but I hear that she is trying to forgive him for his part in it all, we all sincerely hope that they will survive this interlude"

"The woman truly is mad" replied Richard, remembering her shrieking at him "I had hoped that Mrs Chandler would never have to have known about it all, but I should have known that Maria would take her spite out on Chandler, for incompliance to her wishes"

"Well my friend, we have now found out for sure that Lady Maria was responsible for sending the note to Drummond, as Newbridge has assured Mr Chandler of that, and we have also had a visit from your valet" said Russell

"From James? And what does he know of anything?" asked Richard

"He has twice caught the woman in your bedchamber, and on one occasion she was with the lid of the trunk open—there can be no mistake that she was responsible for the trunk and the contents, and for informing Drummond as she did" said Russell looking to Jasper as if for agreement, Jasper looked directly at Russell and nodded his ascent

"But why did James not tell me this" Richard said, looking from one to the other for an answer

"I have no idea Warren, he probably intended too, but with all the preparation for the dinner party that evening, it probably got forgotten" said Russell, hazarding a guess

"We also learnt that Lincroft and Lady Maria were having an affair, probably the reason for leaving the Gate Lodge to her on his death. He was also very friendly with that man who got hung last year for highway robbery, Oliver somebody or other, so it seems that the chances were, Lincroft was the highway man who got away—the goods probably belonged to Lincroft and Lady Maria took them for herself once Lincroft had gone" said Russell, after having gone over it all with Jasper and working it all out between the two of them

"I should have guessed—I knew that Lincroft was definitely involved with the smuggling ring, in fact, I believe that he was the ring leader, and that would make sense with my father setting him up in the Gate Lodge in the first place" said Richard. Russell was trying to piece that together, but where did the old Duke come into it?

"I'm sorry Warren, you said that your father gave Lincroft the Gate Lodge, but I'm not sure that I understand why?" said Russell, looking to his friend for enlightenment

"My mother told me that my father set up the smuggling ring in the area— the caves which we found were initially his concern—once he grew too old to take the lead position on the raids, he allowed Lincroft to be the one to take that side of it on—when my father died, then it all fell to Lincroft, including the heavy profits. When my father's will was read, there was unexpected money in his account which was hardly there from legitimate means—he would have been lucky to have been able to cover his gambling debts, yet the large sum was a great surprise to us all" Richard said

"So you believe that it was through illegitimate means that he was as wealthy as he was? I see" said Russell

"Perhaps you should also know that Lincroft was my half-brother—my father's illegitimate son" Richard declared

"Lincroft, the Duke's son" Russell looked at his friend sharply

"I'm afraid so, he was the produce of rape—I cannot even say that he was born to one of my father's mistresses"

I'm sorry Warren—there is so much of this that I would never have guessed" replied Russell, now deep in thought as was his friend Jasper, who's eyes had grown wide with the latest revelations

"Yes, well my mother has been aware of much of this for many years, she told me what I know, she has been through a great deal more than even I was aware of" said Richard "and I am still not satisfied that both Edward and my father died through accidents—I just have a feeling that there is more to both their deaths than have up until now been exposed, though I just cannot piece together enough to make any sense of it all—I would guess that Maria knows exactly the facts of the matter, but it would be a case of how to make her talk—I can't see her admitting anything to do with Melvin Lincroft, and I fear that he has played a part in all this somehow" Richard had said what he had not meant to discuss with anyone—the thoughts which just went round and round in his head, especially while he was in this awful place, God only knew he had plenty of time for speculation

"Well, in the light of what you have also now told us, I think that we have a very good case to hand to Drummond—we should return to Cornwall as soon as possible—if all goes well, we should have you freed from here in no time" Russell now knew that his friend's chance of freedom, was only a breeze away

"Then I shall patiently wait to hear the good news—in the meantime, I shall have a word with Mr Hopcroft, it will at least give him something to work on for the time being, and he may be able to get some answers to the rest himself" Richard felt as if a weight had now lifted from his shoulders, although still not out of the woods, he was hopeful, and hope was the most important thing for him at this present time. Russell and Jasper said their goodbyes, and left without losing any more time—they must return to Penleigh Court, and inform Drummond of all they had now learnt— perhaps he would find a way to clarify the old Duke and his son's deaths.

The two gentlemen went round to Russell's town house, Russell had decided that the best way to proceed, was to send a note to Drummond, which would go ahead of them, asking that he call at Penleigh Court the following evening—it would mean that they would have to ride hard to reach Penleigh Court by the following morning, and they would leave the moment he had written the note and sent it. Once the note was done, the two gentlemen took a brandy from the decanter on the side, before going to the stables for fresh horses, in which to ride for Cornwall with all speed.

The journey was long and arduous, but they kept going, slowing down through that night—they had taken several short stops, at different inn and hostelry's along the way—the weather was cold, but they were wrapped in greatcoats, and pushed their way on, riding at times against the wind and the bitter cold air. Luckily it wasn't raining and although the wind was in the North, the snow had only threatened until now.

As they turned in past the Gate Lodge and on up the long sweep of drive to Penleigh Court, the first flakes on white fluffy snow was beginning to fall from the sky—the wind still bitterly cold, was blowing the white flutters into their faces, making it difficult to see where they were going—it was still very early—there were no chinks of light from the monstrous building in front of them, everyone was still sleeping, including the servants, who were always up at the crack of dawn

"Thank God we returned when we did Trent, I'm not sure that we would have made it if we had waited until this morning to leave London" he said to his friend

"Indeed, but what are we to do now Hinton, we are still too early to gain access to the house and our rooms" said Jasper who's only intent at this moment was climbing between the sheets of that warm and comfortable bed waiting for him

"I think you will find that the servants will soon be waking, we will go to the stables and wait in one of the empty stalls there until they arrive, the horses require food and water in any case" he replied, but before they had dismounted the sound of bolts being thrust back, before the door to the stable block quarters, swung open and the head groom a taper still in his

377

hand, stood in the doorway, straining his eyes to make out the identity of the two figures stood there with their beasts. Once the man's eyes became accustomed to the light, he realized who the two figures were his master's guests—he quickly lit the lantern, which he held in his other hand

"Good morning gentlemen—you're about early this morning?" said the man, looking from one to the other of them

"Indeed we are, we have just ridden direct from London, so our horses need immediate attention" replied Russell

"Then you best give me the reins, and I shall see to it" said the man, taking both sets of reins and leading the two sweating and frothed beasts into the stable for something to drink and some food. Russell and Jasper walked across the courtyard, and tried the side door, it was open, someone must be awake in the house—the two gentlemen were exhausted and cold, so they headed for the stairs and their long awaited beds—they would probably sleep until lunchtime, but that was no matter, as long as they had a chance to speak to Lady Alice and warn her that they had invited Drummond to call at the house that evening, then it shouldn't cause too many problems, and if they could have Richard freed, Lady Alice would be more than happy. Once they reached their own rooms, Jasper was soon in his bed and fallen into a deep and peaceful, long awaited sleep, but Russell could not seem to stop all the thoughts from circulating round—he slept fitfully, waking every short while—his good friends words kept coming back to him—they may have solved the immediate problem, but the death of his friends father and brother were now beginning to torture his mind too, he had never even considered it before, but since Warren had planted the idea in his head, he couldn't shake off the feeling that there were still horrors to uncover—he wouldn't rest until all was made clear—they would have to force Lady Maria's tongue somehow.

⁓ ◦ ⁓ ⦿ ⁓ ◦ ⦿ ⦿ ⁓ ◦

It was gone noon before Russell, unable to fall into a peaceful sleep, decided to rise—he washed and dressed and descended the stairs, he needed a brandy—he still couldn't put the full story together, but perhaps after a brandy or two, and a bite of lunch, he would speak to Lady Alice and see what she could make of it all, he needed to speak with her anyway, as he had still to tell her of Drummond's visit that evening, and he didn't want it to come as a shock to her, been as his last visit had been so awful for her, and according to Warren, the poor woman had suffered more than enough at the hands of her husband. After tossing back two glasses of the warm amber liquid, Russell stood up and made his way to the dining room—lunch would be served any time now.

As he entered, both Lady Alice and Lady Maria were sat at the table—so he bowed to them before taking a seat beside Lady Alice. He had no desire to speak frankly before Lady Maria, the less she knew of it all the better at this stage—so he made polite conversation and bided his time.

"Did you go to London after all Mr Hinton, I had not expected you back so soon" asked Lady Alice

"Yes indeed madam, and a very successful visit it was too" he said smiling

"Good, and did you visit my son while you were there?" she asked

"We did, he is in quite good spirits My Lady" he replied, being very selective as to his answers, but Lady Maria was taking note of his words, that awful curling of her lip, and malevolent smile—it made him uncomfortable when she pulled that face, he knew that something was about to be said, so he braced himself in readiness

"You are not still hoping for his freedom surely Alice, you must not get your hopes up you know, it will be all the harder to bear when the time comes" she said looking from Lady Alice to Russell. Russell would not allow her that—he couldn't speak freely before her, but he had to stop her gloating

"With the greatest respect My Lady" he said looking directly at the obnoxious woman "I'm sure that Lady Alice has every right to be optimistic for her son and his welfare, and surely we are all hopeful that the Duke will shortly be freed" he said

"I merely see no sense in Alice making herself ill and raising her hopes for something that . . . . is so unlikely" she stated looking straight into Russell's eyes—the stare was fixed between them, Russell gave a shiver, the coldness of her eyes, belying her words. Nobody spoke for a long moment, then Russell said

"Unlikely perhaps, but not impossible I think" with that he turned his head to address Lady Alice "would you care to join me this afternoon in a game of cards My Lady" he suggested, anything to get the woman alone for a while, so that he could warn her of Drummond's visit

"That would be wonderful Mr Hinton, I didn't know that you play" said Lady Alice happily

"Indeed I do" he said with pleasure, though he could not forget Lady Maria's words, nor could he shake off the feeling of being eyed closely and summed up.

Once lunch was over, Maria beat a hasty retreat—leaving Russell and Alice to retire to the drawing room for their game of cards. Russell stood for a bit, beside the window, watching the flakes, now much bigger and coming down much faster, covering the gardens and all that was visible in a thick white cloak—as he watched, and still thinking about his friends suspicions, he said to Alice, who was now seating herself at the small green baize card table that Newbridge had set up for them

"I hope that you have no objections My Lady, but I have taken it upon myself and sent a note to Mr Drummond, requesting that he would visit the house this evening, many new developments have come to light, and I truly believe that Warren could soon be freed, though at present, I believe that the less who know of this the better—that was my reason for not mentioning this at lunch I'm afraid" he said this as he seated himself on the opposite side of the small table to Alice

"I see" she replied "And you really believe my son's innocence can be proven?" she enquired

"I really have no doubt of it My Lady, but the sooner we can speak with Mr Drummond, then the sooner the Duke will be freed" he said confidently

"Then I have no objection whatsoever sir, you have been so very kind, I don't know what would have happened had it not been for yourself, and Mr Trent—Mr Chandler has also been very kind, I have in fact invited them to dine with us this evening also" she said musing

"You also have some of your own servants to thank My Lady, Newbridge has brought certain facts to our attention, as did the Duke's valet James" he relayed to her

"Good, then I shall leave it in your hands Mr Hinton, but in the meantime, I may have to beat you at our game of cards" she was smiling now—he could see that this lady was quite competitive in her own way, but had little chance to show it. They played cards for almost two hours, before Jasper joined them—on entering the room, Alice decided that she had managed to take enough money from Mr Hinton and was more than happy with the outcome—it had been a very long time since she had enjoyed this little pastime, especially with such a young and charming gentleman.

CHAPTER TWENTY SEVEN

(The Truth)

It was early evening they had all dressed for dinner and had met in the drawing room, Mark and Angela Chandler had arrived, there was a little strain and tension between them, but Mark was very attentive to his wife, and she very civil to him. They all sat round a roaring fire in the grate, when there was a knock at the front door. It was a knock fit to wake the dead, the room fell silent, as voices drifted through the not quite closed door, before Newbridge followed by a familiar face, stepped into the drawing room. Newbridge introduced a very wet Rufus Drummond, with a white cloak, which seemed to fall away to small puddles as he stood in the doorway

"Good evening, ladies and gentleman" he said bowing to each in turn, before resting his eyes on Russell who had now risen from his seat to meet the man's gaze

"Mr Drummond I presume" said Russell, taking in the man's appearance "perhaps you would care to remove your cloak sir and take a seat with us here by the fire for a while" said Russell, going to the door and asking Newbridge to do the honours. Once this was done, Russell offered Mr Drummond a seat, before once again seating himself close to the fire

"Thank you Mr . . . ." said Drummond

"Hinton, Russell Hinton sir" he replied

"Ah, you are the gentlemen who sent me the note then" he returned. The room was in quiet, nobody spoke, but all eyes in the room were now on Rufus Drummond

"Yes, thank you for coming on such an awful night Mr Drummond" he said

"Oh tis nothing, my work has me out on worse nights than this My Lord" said Mr Drummond looking around the company seated

"Now, what is it that is so urgent sir?" he asked, eyes fixed on Russell now, waiting to hear all that he had to tell

"I have to tell you that you have arrested the wrong man—the Duke is innocent, and I'm sure of this now" Russell said

"Ah, he is a friend of yours?" Drummond stated, now with a strange smile on his lips and disbelief in his voice "then if he is innocent, how do you account for the evidence sir?" he asked Russell

"Perhaps I should give you some facts sir, and then you may account for the rest yourself Mr Drummond, I mean only to help you arrest the right persons and let my innocent friend go free" he said firmly

"And the facts as you see them are what sir?" he asked Russell

"Mr Lincroft, who has now been hanged for his crimes, was a known friend of Oliver Townsend, who I believe I am right in saying was the man hanged last year for highway robbery—he was a regular visitor here at Penleigh Court, Mr Lincroft was the head of the smuggling ring hereabouts, the passageway from the caves on the beach leads to the Gate Lodge, you have surely found this out for yourself already", there was a look between the others sat in the room, although as Russell cast his eye over to where Maria sat quietly taking each word in, one of her ugly smiles began to alight on her face. "Henry Penrose, the late Duke, was also a known part of the smuggling ring, I believe that is so, is it not Lady Alice" said Russell looking to Alice for assent "I'm afraid that is so Mr Hinton" she said "and Mr Lincroft was the illegitimate son of Henry Penleigh, and once Henry was unable to carry out his smuggling activity further, he chose his illegitimate son to take on the leadership for him, still sharing in the profits—hence you will find great supplies of the contraband, as you are already aware" Drummond's face was studying him intently now. He ploughed on "Lady Maria, was Lincroft's mistress" he said this, his gaze wandering to where she sat, listening intently, but still she said nothing "So it seemed only natural that he should leave the Gate Lodge and access to the goods, to her on his death" still she sat without movement, taking it all in "Lady Maria we believe, had a son not long ago, the child was thought to be her late husband's child, but I believe that child was Lincroft's instead" that was it, now she was going to have her say, she would not stay quiet for longer

"Then Mr Hinton, I'm afraid you are so very wrong—the child was nothing to do with Melvin—my son is indeed a Penleigh" again that smirk on her lips

"But you have already lied about the father of your child have you not madam" this time he was addressing Maria direct

"I don't know what you mean" she answered, the smirk still apparent

"Then allow me to enlighten you, I believe you told Miss Penrose, that your son belonged to Richard, but we know that it could not have been his child, you were not even lovers, so this could not have been so" said Russell ploughing on

"I'm sure that I never said any such thing to Miss Penrose, she must have misinterpreted my words" this time Angela spoke, she had had quite enough of this dreadful woman, who was also now her arch enemy

"There was no misunderstanding, you deliberately set out to cause a rift between Miss Penrose and her fiancée, you won't get away with your lies" she said ferociously, aiming her words directly at Maria "And if that was not enough for you, you then had to take my husband too, and try to entice him away from me, but you haven't won, you never will, I hate you for what you have done to me and my friends, the way that you had Sarah removed, Miss Kirkby was taken back to Truro against her will because of you, and all because she would stand for none of your nonsense" Russell hadn't bargained on this outburst, but all the same, it didn't do any harm. Maria was sat almost purring, like a cat that had the cream, she obviously felt very pleased with herself

"The Duke has told us how Maria has done many spiteful things in which to gain what she wants" he carried on, silence still remained, apart from the ticking of the clock on the mantelpiece but this time not looking at the woman set a little apart from the rest "I believe that Lady Maria is in need of Dr Somerville's services, after all she seems to be affected with a . . . . madness which overtakes her at times, and after learning of the truth about her poor mother, who we all supposed was dead, to learn that she is in fact very much alive and living at an asylum on Dartmoor" he stopped, had he gone too far, but he had to ensure his friend's release, then Maria jumped from her seat, his aim was to force her tongue, and he hoped that this had done the trick

"How dare you—how dare you slander me or my family Mr Hinton, you are supposed to be a guest in my house" she screamed—everyone was watching as her tantrum began to get the better of her

"I'm sorry My Lady, I misunderstood, I thought that this house belonged to the Duke" said Russell calmly looking straight at her—her ice cold eyes were hard and frosty, more so than he had ever experienced before, and she took on a faraway evil look on her face, though different to the one they had become accustomed

"This is my house, it's my son's and until he is old enough to take charge, I shall do it for him—the Duke is all that stands between me and this house now—and you are not going to stop me taking what is rightfully mine" she screamed

"But madam, as I say, this house is not yours, nor your son's this house belongs to the Duke, and so it shall stay" he would not allow her to browbeat him

"And also" he said turning now to Mr Drummond "It was Lady Maria who sent you the anonymous note, calling you here to arrest the Duke, Newbridge approached Chandler over this, and what's more, the trunk which held the highwayman's treasure, also belonged to Lady Maria, the Duke's valet has assured me of this, and that the lady had been twice caught in his lordships bedchamber, during periods when the Duke was employed elsewhere, and with the lid of the trunk open—indicating that she not only owned the trunk, but also the key, is that not so Chandler?" he asked, this time looking to Mark for agreement

"I'm afraid that is exactly so" he replied casting a quick glance at Maria now

"This is ridiculous, it is all nonsense, whatever are you likely to say next to conjure up such lies against me, what have I done to make you hate me so much" she said, her voice rising to a crescendo and looking round the room, one to another, such pretence all of a sudden, for what, to gain sympathy?

"Every word spoken My Lady has been true—and you know it only too well—why don't you just admit it and be honest" said Mark staring directly at her

"How dare you, you are no more than a servant, what are you doing here anyway, nobody wants you here" she was shrieking

"My wife and I are here My Lady, on the invitation of Lady Alice" he said calmly, more to the company than to the woman, who was losing her temper by the moment

"You all think that you are so clever don't you, well you are not so clever after all, you may think that you know it all, but you know very little—but if you are sure you want to know, then know you shall" she was screeching again

"My father died, leaving my mother and myself penniless, once my father's debts were paid there would be nothing left for either mother or myself, my mother was devastated, her distress was overwhelming, so she wrote to my aunt and uncle, requesting that they help us, they had no children of their own, and plenty of money, it would have meant nothing for my aunt to have helped her own sister, but my uncle although agreeing to take me in, to give me a season, and to find me a good husband, refused to help my mother—he had hated my father, and my mother had gone against them when she married my father, so they saw her cut off from the family. My mother was driven to insanity, banished from her home, and sent to live as a servant in a house close by, as a seamstress, to think that she had been mistress of her own home, and here she was living like the servant she had become, because of a man—insanity, it had been in the family tis true, but my uncle drove my mother to the asylum—before forbidding me to visit her ever again. I didn't get my season, before my chance came, my uncle had met Henry Penleigh, and they had done a deal and reached an agreement over me. I was instructed by my aunt that the Duke had seen me and wanted a match between his elder son and myself. I didn't want the match—Edward was a coward and a fool—but I was given no choice in the matter, I was told to treat Henry Penleigh as if he was the king, and I must do everything he would have me do, and I would then become a Duchess. Marrying his son was supposed to be an honour, and I was a very lucky girl to have him. So, to get this position, and for my uncle to put up the large dowry that accompanied it, I had no choice but to marry Edward Penleigh. The man was not worthy of me, in any way—I hated him, and after a few weeks of marriage, Henry was doing his best to get me into his bed, he wanted a mistress under his roof, and Edward, apart from the few times that he was compelled to share my bed, wanted nothing much to do with me so I sought my own company elsewhere—well, even Alice didn't live in the same wing as her husband, let's face it, they spent years not speaking, let alone living together. Once I was with child, I was left to get on with it—so, I met the estate manager, Melvin Lincroft—and very soon we became lovers, oh yes, he was wonderful, everything that my husband wasn't, and it took my mind off the constant hounding from Henry, except once the child was born, and it was a girl, Henry was not happy about it—he turned on us both, and insisted that we try again—so, I had to tell Melvin that I couldn't see him until I was with child again. Melvin's friend Oliver used to visit him sometimes, he wasn't like Melvin though, he was a peasant, and no mistake, I didn't like him much I have to say, I told Melvin as much too—I also told him he shouldn't associate with the likes of him, but he just laughed at me and told me that he was our ticket out of this place. Well, it soon happened, thank God, I found myself with child again, so that Melvin and me could take up our relationship once again. He was so good to me, giving me jewels, beautiful jewels, though I wasn't allowed to tell or show anyone—I guessed that he gotten them by not entirely honest means, but I didn't care, he treated me like a queen, though I never got to spend all night with him, the fact that Henry was always trying to get me into his bed, made me want to spend my nights more and more with Melvin, but he wouldn't allow it—I never knew why. Once I had given birth to another wretched girl, I decided that Edward was probably incapable of producing a son and heir. Henry was horrible to me—he started to threaten me, he had chosen me for his son, to give him a son and heir and for Henry's pleasure, and I fulfilled neither. I used to go to the Gate House to meet with Melvin, we would make love in nothing more than the jewels which he would dress me in, before the fire in his drawing room, I don't know why but he never wanted to go upstairs ever. On more than one occasion Oliver was there—he would creep in and watch us, Melvin didn't care, but I did—he would make noises about Melvin sharing me, but that wasn't going to happen. Then I heard that he had been caught and hung for highway robbery—Melvin was as mad as fire, he didn't want to talk about it, but I was glad he was gone. One afternoon, we had been together, when I arrived back here, my husband found me and he told me how he had come looking for Melvin, he had gone missing and he wanted something done, so he went to the Gate Lodge to find him, instead of knocking on the door and waiting, he opened the front door and crept inside, he must have seen us in the drawing room, before the fire, me with all my lovely new jewels which he had just given me, but that was it you see, he didn't care about me, or that he found me with his estate manager, I know our marriage was only of convenience, but he just didn't care, imbecile that he was, all that bothered him was the jewels—he told me that I was wearing stolen goods, things that had been stolen in highway hold ups, he had recognized the necklace as something stolen, which the authorities had already been making enquiries about, Mr Drummond had spoken to Henry about it, he told me that he would not keep quiet about this, he was going to report it to the authorities himself, so I would have to tell them where my jewels came from, dear Melvin would be finished—well I wasn't going to have any of that—I knew then anyway, that my Melvin was the other highwayman who had escaped the hangman's noose, I would never allow them to hang him" she looked at Mr Drummond as she spoke, so I thought up a plan, I couldn't discuss the matter in this house, what with all the servants that didn't like me either, they would soon get word of it, and have my lover strung up, so I asked Edward to meet me along the cliff path, above Devil's Point—he loved that route—so it was easy, I told him that I needed to speak to him, about the jewels—he said that it wasn't advisable to go there at that time of year, but I insisted, and eventually he agreed. I waited for him, I stayed behind bushes, out of the way—it was a cold and windy day, and I thought that I would take a chill, but eventually he came—he climbed from his horse and led him along the path—I waited until he was close then I stepped out behind his horse, the horse reared—it was on a bit firmer ground than

Edward, as the horse reared, Edward turned, let go of the reins, and slipped, he fell to the rocks below—his horse ran off, leaving me standing there looking over the edge of the cliff at my husband's body below—I was free of him, I laughed out loud—now I was free to go away with Melvin, but when I suggested it, Melvin just said that he wouldn't leave—his father needed him, that's when he told me that Henry was his father, well, it certainly explained a lot of things, he said that he needed to stay, but one day we would go away together, abroad somewhere, then I would be able to wear my jewels out, to show them off, but for the time being I had to be patient. That was easier said than done, after all, Henry was still after making me his mistress, and I didn't want him—or need him. Then, just before Christmas, Richard turned up, I hadn't expected that, he was too full of his own life before, but suddenly he turns up here—even Henry wasn't too pleased to see him, but as soon as I set eyes on Richard I wanted him, and he wasn't married, so I decided that I must have him marry me—he soon took a liking to my girls and because Henry was trying to push him to marry, I tried everything to show him that he would never do better than me, but he wouldn't have it, he made me angry, Henry bullied me terribly and Richard stood up for me, so I had to keep on trying. Anyway, Christmas night, after a huge fight with Henry, I went to bed, and a little while later, I was asleep, but something woke me up, it was a man climbing into bed beside me—when I woke up, it was to a man making love to me, but I was facing the opposite direction to him, so couldn't see his face, but he was a large man, I had convinced myself that it was Richard, he had changed his mind, so I allowed it to happen, then I realized that it wasn't Richard, but Henry in my bed, so I tried to fight him off—he held my wrists until I thought that they were broken, he bruised my body, my face, my neck, chest and legs, he overpowered me, he was too strong, I had no defence against him—afterwards, he had climbed out of my bed, and laughed at me—he had laughed at me—in that moment I swore I would kill him—so I bided my time, made a plan and on New Year's Day, when he was at his happiest, so pleased with himself, so arrogant but worst of all, he had taken me as his prize and he would never allow me to forget that, so at the shoot, lording it with all those vermin he mixed with, I dressed in some of my late husband's clothing, took a rifle from the cabinet, and some shot, and I hid behind the hedge in the lane, and waited, they had their backs to me, I wasn't seen, I waited until the guns started to fire, then I lifted the rifle and aimed it at his chest, and squeezed the trigger—I saw him fall to the ground—once everyone went to see what was happening, I made my way back to the house, relieved he was gone—I was a good shot, my father had taught me well" suddenly she stopped her oration, her eyes fixed and cold, thinking of something now far away. Mr Drummond was impatient, he wanted to know the rest, when she still didn't speak, he prompted her

"And then Lady Maria" she didn't answer him immediately then she spoke loud and clear once again "Melvin was angry that Henry was dead, I wasn't going to tell him anything of what I'd done—and Richard was keeping him busy for some time, in the afternoons when we would have normally met, Richard was robbing me of my lover, and he was still refusing to comply with me—he had even started to see that chit from the rectory, why would he spare time and care for her, when he did not offer me the same courtesy—it wasn't for the want of trying either—then the horror struck me—I found myself with child again—this child I didn't want—I knew who's child it was, and I had no intention of giving birth to Henry Penleigh's bastard. So, I had to think of something to tell Melvin, and decided that I could just about get away with having another child by my husband, it was the most logical thing to do. Shortly after my poor Melvin" she turned to Mr Drummond "It was you wasn't it? You arrested him and had him hung—I hate you, oh how I hate you—you ruined my life, you took away the only man who truly loved me and I shall never forgive you" she was screaming at the top of her voice again. It was so strange how she could go from talking to shrieking, but it must be down to the insanity that overcame her. After a few minutes, she carried on "Melvin had gone, and Richard, I wanted to teach him a lesson, if he would not give me what I so wanted, I would see him die, my life had been ruined and I should show him what that felt like. Melvin left me his house, our house, Richard wanted to get his hands on it again—it was all part of the estate, but Henry had given it to his other son, and now it was mine—I would have gladly given it back to him, if he had made me his Duchess, but still he would have none of it. Then Mark arrived, a young man who was pleasant enough, wet behind the ears of course, he had no idea of the world or women, it was easy to seduce him, I didn't have to try very hard at all, he wasn't Melvin, that was for sure, he was barely able to keep me happy, but it was better than nothing and he was passable in his looks—no I had to have Richard, but then it would be difficult to find anyone comparable to him, so I decided to be grateful and accept my lot for a while, at least until the damned child was born. I had several more attempts at trying to convince Richard that I would make him a far better wife. Alice had been holding tea parties for young ladies, to try and find him a wife, but none of them were good enough for him, I watched him with one of them, out there in the garden, Sarah Kirkby, she was mad for him, I could see it from the window in my room, but he showed her no real interest, yet that chit at the rectory, only had to look in his direction, and he was putty in her hands. He had even promised to take me riding, but had not kept his word, though he took her riding, he took her for a picnic, all the things which he should have been doing with me. Once my son was born, I made up my mind that I must try again, I couldn't let him make a fool of himself marrying that simpering ninny, but Alice encouraged him—she didn't like the girl any more than me yet she encouraged him, throwing a dinner party for her family indeed, it infuriated me—I wouldn't allow him to marry her—even if Alice did, so I decided with Melvin dead, I had little to lose, I had moved all the jewels from the Gate Lodge to my trunk in Richard's room, I could never wear them here, and I didn't want to go abroad, not without my dear Melvin—so, I sent the note, and I planted the key in his room, it wasn't difficult to set up—I told him that I would see him dead, and sooner that than see him marry that little bitch. When Mr Drummond arrived, he was able to find everything as I had planned it to be—so he was arrested, and he would hang for his injustice to me. I told that stupid girl that he was to marry me, and that my son was his, it wasn't difficult to persuade her, and as for that virgin" she said this nodding her golden locks in Mark's direction "he was insistent that we should end our affair, I had let it go, been as he wasn't up to much anyway, but then one afternoon, he had crept into my house, and into my bedchamber, luring me to join him, I had never thought him capable, he had only just married, and he had made it more than plain that he wanted no more, yet here he was, begging me to go to him—how could I refuse?" she looked toward Mark as if for an answer, and he eager to give his explanation said

"I had no choice Maria, you see, we had that day found the passageway, which ended in your house, my two friends the Duke and Jasper Trent were with me in the little box room on the second floor, and we had to get out—so to allow my two friends to escape, I lured you to your bedchamber, and kept you occupied until my friends had gone—that was the only reason that I did what I did, I'm afraid it wasn't for the want of you" he looked no longer at Maria, but he had turned to his wife now, she sat with tears in her eyes yet a smile had crept across her lips—he had gone to such lengths to see his friends safe—the feeling of betrayal and mistrust disappearing from her, and in its place, a feeling of pride, that her dear Mark had shown so much loyalty—she was ready at last to put it all behind her and start again with the husband that she loved so much. Maria's face fell, once the reality formed in her brain, her anger rose, and she jumped to her feet picking up a candlestick, the nearest thing to hand, and ran at Mark, holding up the candlestick, high above her head, she would wipe him out for the traitor he was—Russell was quick to his feet, he grabbed her arm from behind, forcing her to drop the solid silver to the ground—in the next moment, Rufus Drummond had stood up, and took hold of the woman, he had two of his men at hand, waiting in the hallway for him to complete his business, Jasper went to the door and invited them in, they took hold of Maria, leading her from the room—she was shrieking words of abuse, and trying to pull away from the hold of the two gentlemen, though her strength was nothing compared with theirs, but she was putting up something of a fight, in fact, she was fighting like a tiger to free herself from their hold—Alice sat in her chair, a teardrop spilling from her old eye and down that frail old cheek—she had never felt for Maria as she may have, she had never trusted her but she hated to see the girl being dealt with in this way, she was after all the mother of her grandchildren, and what of them now. Her mind still fixed on the poor wretches life—she had not had a good life, so much of it dictated by other people, leaving her no control over the important choices she was left to face—and her own husband, Henry, she knew he cared not a fig for the way he treated anyone for that matter, but she had found herself the second victim of his rape, and forced to give birth to his illegitimate child—she took her handkerchief and wiped her eyes, now filling with tears—Angela went to her and putting an arm around her shoulder, tried to comfort her—she gave in to the girls care, and sobbed against her shoulder, while the gentlemen talked with Mr Drummond, who had ventured back into the drawing room, Maria was to be taken to Newgate gaol, but they would hold her more locally until the following day. Rufus Drummond told the gentlemen, that she would like as not be committed to the asylum, and would end up as her mother before her. Once this happened, she would never be allowed to return to society, and would spend the rest of her days there, but at least she would not be hung, and she had murdered twice.

Mr Drummond left at last, and Newbridge was asked to have dinner served, as he had had the kitchen put it on hold while the confession was in progress. Dinner was a quiet affair, very little was said, and little food was eaten, although Jasper ate quite well, as he was very hungry. Once the meal was over, Mr and Mrs Chandler called for the carriage to take them home, and Gracie to help Alice to her bed. Jasper and Russell retired to the library, content with the outcome, and to celebrate with several glasses of brandy, the knowledge that their dear friend would soon be on his way home.

CHAPTER TWENTY EIGHT

(Welcome Home)

The following morning, Richard awoke to a visit from Mr Hopcroft, he had come to Newgate especially this morning, to give the Duke the good news, that he was to walk free. The snow that had fallen the day before was lying like a thick white carpet, and with the overnight frost, the silvery trailing fingers, sparkling in the morning sunshine.

Richard had hoped that his friends would have some success, but he had never believed that they would have managed to set him free so soon. He left the stinking hole stepping outside in the sharp, brisk winter breeze, shivering as the cold seeped through his worn clothing. He made his way toward his Mayfair home, he desperately needed a bath, a meal, and a glass of that warming amber liquid. Once inside Reeves came to greet him, overjoyed to see him walking free

"Welcome home Your Grace, it's so good to see you" he said smiling all over his face

"Thank you Reeves, now if you would be so good as to arrange for me to take a bath and to change these clothes, as you see they are no more than rags, I have been wearing them since my arrest" Richard noticed that the old man's face, although trying to keep the smile that was fixed there, had started to screw up his nose in distaste—the smell was obviously reaching his nostrils, and it was far from pleasant, he knew that only too well

"I will indeed My Lord, and I shall inform cook to prepare a good breakfast for you once you are ready" he said, eagerly stepping backwards away from the Duke

"Yes, thank you—that would be most welcome" Richard knew only too well how he smelt—he had never suffered such depravity in his life before, and if he had anything to do with it, never would again

Reeves went off to give the orders, clearly he couldn't wait to be off on his errand, while Richard made his way to the library, he had long since dreamt of watching that golden amber liquid, swirling round in his glass, and the feel as it's warmth slipped down his throat, he had wondered if he would ever again experience its pleasure. He lifted the stopper from the decanter and poured some of the liquid into a glass, but eager to taste its healing qualities, he tossed it straight down, before pouring himself another glass. Some moments later the library door opened and Reeves entered

"Your bath is ready for you now Your Grace"

"Thank you Reeves, I shall be leaving for Penleigh Court a little later today, they would not welcome me in this state, I'm sure" the old man smiled, he could well agree with that, though he was too good mannered to say so. He left the room, leaving the door open for his master to follow.

Richard climbed the stairs two at a time, stretching his long legs, though he was well aware that his clothes would probably hang from his body, as he hadn't eaten a proper meal, since his arrest. He went to his room, and looked through some of his clothes, choosing something warm to wear for his journey to Cornwall—he had no intention of going by carriage, he wanted to ride there so he would set off as soon as he had eaten, as he planned on arriving tomorrow morning, after all it would be Christmas Eve. Once his bath was ready, he undressed and stepped into the warm soothing water, he relaxed and found himself closing his eyes, tiredness started to overcome his body, but he couldn't afford to sleep as he had a lot of miles to cover, before reaching his destination, and he fully intended being there for Christmas this year, his lack of sleep over the last few months, would easily have induced him to sleep for a week, but there would be time enough for that later, for now he must concentrate on arriving on time—he thought about his dear sweet Clara, how he longed to see her again, though he was anxious as she may not welcome him in the same way, after his friend told him of the things which Maria had said to Clara, perhaps she would not wish to marry him anymore, but he had to believe that she would have seen it for the lies and embroidery that it was.

Once bathed and dressed in the fresh clothes, that he had himself taken out for his journey, he went downstairs to the dining room, where Reeves had laid a single place setting for him, and the silver dishes were already sat on the dresser with hot food just waiting to be eaten, he helped himself to a large helping of ham and eggs and devilled kidneys, before seating himself at the table, the food tasted so good—he had almost forgotten just how good, he had finished it in seconds, and returned again to the silver dishes, lifting each lid and serving himself a second helping, he then ate several slices of toast, with a strawberry preserve and a whole pot of coffee to himself. He had started to feel so much better already. Though still feeling an overwhelming sense of fatigue, he went out to the stables and ordered his horse Brutus, be saddled and made ready for him to go—once done, he jumped up in the saddle and set off.

He rode long and hard, but by nightfall, he was so cold, and almost falling asleep in the saddle, that he decided that he had little choice but to stay at a hostelry for the night, after riding a little further, just the place came into view—it looked warm and welcoming, so leaving his horse with the stable lad, he booked a room for the night. The place looked clean and cheerful, and the proprietor offered him a small table near to the fireplace—he found himself closing his eyes, from the warmth of the fire and utter exhaustion. He ordered a good hot meal of beef broth, with a chunk of warm crusty bread and a large tankard of best ale. By the time he had eaten he immediately rose, while he was still able and made his way up the rickety staircase, to the room appointed him. The room was sparsely furnished but clean, and a fire was burning in the grate, but the most delicious sight of all was the large welcoming bed, he slipped out of his clothing and throwing back the sheets and blankets, slipped into a clean and enticing bed—it wasn't the most comfortable he had ever slept in, but at this moment in time, it was sheer bliss, he laid back against the pillow, but within seconds his whole body had relaxed and he had fallen into a deep and comfortable sleep.

The following morning he awoke later than he had hoped too, though he truly needed the sleep, it was almost lunchtime, but the proprietor had some food brought for him, a large hunk of freshly baked bread, still warm from the oven, with cheese and ham, and some game pie, and a tankard of best ale to wash it all down—he hoped to reach Penleigh Court by lunchtime, but clearly that was not to be, so he ate the food, while warming himself by the roaring fire, before setting off once again to complete his journey—with any luck he would still be able to arrive before dinner, and he had now had a good rest, leaving him wide awake and ready to face what lay ahead.

The sky looked heavy once again, but the snow didn't fall, he was thankful for that at least, he pulled his greatcoat closer round him to hold back the biting chill as he spurred Brutus on. As he passed Gallows Cross, he couldn't resist peering at the gibbet, standing empty now, and letting his mind imagine how it may have been for him, but he must not dwell on those things, he was here, and free—he turned back to the road, and headed on up the hill, he came almost level with the rectory, he couldn't possibly ride past the door without calling on his Clara, he hoped that she would still be pleased to see him, and although he was desperate to see her again, he was apprehensive as to his welcome. He pulled his horse in through the gateway, before jumping from the saddle, tying the reins to the post he knew so well, before striding across to the front door—he had great hopes for this Christmas, last year had been so different, only a year ago when he had first seen the one woman in all the world who he wanted to marry, his arrival at Penleigh Court and meeting Maria for the first time—who would have thought that she would have been the cause to all the families problems, he shook himself, that was all over now, and he had no intention of letting this Christmas be the blight that last year was, he would never allow anyone to poison his family again. He knocked on the door, within moments Daisy opened the door

"Good afternoon Your Grace" said Daisy a warm smile on her lips

"Good afternoon Daisy—I wish to speak to Miss Penrose, if you would just let her know that I'm here"

"I'm sorry My Lord, Miss Clara is visiting Lady Penleigh, she has gone with Mrs Chandler, not an hour since"

"Thank you Daisy, that's splendid, then I will see her when I get home" he replied "Good day to you"

"Good day Your Grace" she said, then turning and closing the door behind her, the smile still touching her face, she had always liked the man, and she knew how much he made Clara happy

Richard mounted his horse and pushed on up the hill, the snow had started to fall now, it was blowing a blizzard, Richard remembered what it had brought with it last year, and smiled to himself—it wouldn't be long until he saw that sweet face, with those large brown orbs, pulling him in, it was what had kept him going through that terrible time, locked away in that stinking pit, and now he was about to claim his prize, he looked about him, his horses hooves clip clopping over the little stone bridge and through the now familiar village before heading on up to Penleigh Court.

On his arrival home, everyone was surprised to see him so soon, from his mother, to the servants, who ran in circles to please. The tree and the house had been decorated ready for the occasion, and there were gifts, all wrapped in pretty paper, and tied with ribbons, underneath, his mother stood in the great hall with Angela and his dear sweet Clara. As he opened the door and entered, the first person he set eyes on was dear sweet Clara, she looked more alluring than she ever had before, he stood still and eyed her, his eyes not straying from her face, she turned and saw him, and in seconds she had run towards him, throwing her arms around his neck, as he threw his arms around her and lifted her off her feet—he planted a kiss on those luscious inviting lips, uncaring of propriety or who was watching them, though he felt eyes, all around the room, fixed to them. If he had any apprehension as to his welcome, he need not of bothered, indeed, it all seemed worth having been locked away, just to receive such a warm welcome. Alice caught her breath as she noticed how thin and pale he looked, but she was pleased that he was home where she could now see to it that he was brought back to his health and strength once again. He went to his mother next, giving her a long hug and kissing her old and now very pale and wan cheek. There were tears in her eyes, and he knew then what she must have suffered, believing that her only son had been taken from her, then he took Angie's hand and planted a kiss upon it, thanking her for looking after the two women who meant more to him than anyone else in the world. The moment was touching all their hearts.

After the initial welcome, they went into the drawing room where Alice rang for tea. They were soon joined by Richard's good friends, and also Mark, who knew that his wonderful wife was visiting Alice that afternoon. Alice had invited them for Christmas, and she had also invited vicar Penrose and his wife, with Clara, she was so pleased that she had now—this Christmas was to be the best ever for her family. She had also written to the Kirkby's inviting them to Christmas lunch, but Flora Kirkby had declined the offer, after all, there was no reason to spend Christmas with a family who were criminals, or at least that's the way she saw it. Jasper was disappointed, but he would manage for the one day, and besides, he could visit Sarah on Boxing Day, when many of the gentry met in Truro for a Boxing Day hunt, Jasper would ride over and see Sarah then—though he didn't relish meeting with her mother again. He told Richard a little later that he was going to ask for Sarah's hand in marriage, though he was a little nervous of her mother, he wasn't sure that she would be very pleased, although his breeding was of the best.

Christmas Day and the snow was still falling, they attended church, just as they had last year, and vicar Penrose and his family returned to Penleigh Court, along with Mark and Angela Chandler. They were a very happy group, Alice was in her element, playing hostess to the party, and Richard was the topic of the day. This was the Christmases that he had remembered, lots of people, good food and pleasant company. The carol service went ahead as usual and there were more attendees than normal—though Maria's aunt and uncle did not venture near this year, they had obviously heard that she had gone the same way as her poor mother. Nanny Anson had joined the party with her three charges, though she would return to the nursery after the carols with baby Edward, but Richard insisted that his two nieces were older now, and they should stay with the family and enjoy the day, there were presents all round, giving and receiving, though the only present that Richard had to give this year was for Clara, his mother had given him a pair of beautiful diamond earrings, which had belonged to his grandmother, they were laid in a red velvet box, she wanted her son to give them to his betrothed as her Christmas gift, Richard knew in that moment that his mother had truly accepted Clara as he had always wanted her to do, she had been welcomed into the Penleigh family at last, Richard had pressed the little box into her hand, urging her to open the lid, when she did, she looked from the jewels before her to Richard's face, and the tears coursed down her cheeks, even Ada Penrose caught her breath, she had never owned anything so beautiful, and she was overjoyed that her daughter should, she threw her arms round Richard and hugged him, but he knew that she would have been just as happy that he was home with her—she had all that she wanted there in front of her, this beautiful gift was the bonus. Richard stood up and suddenly noticing the his two little wards watching him, he seated himself so that they could scramble upon his knees, he looked at Clara, as he bounced the girls, one on either knee—they were squealing with delight—Clara watched, a smile fixed on her face, thinking what a good father he would be to their own children. Even Ada Penrose had cast aside her animosity towards Richard, and had once again embraced him as a son in law. Mark and Angela sat together, he could not do enough for her, holding her hand, and eager to do anything she asked of him, and she seemed to have managed to put that whole awful affair behind her, Alice watched them as the girl looked up at her husband with such warmth and love in her eyes, Alice knew that feeling, she had once felt the same for her own husband, though he had not returned her feelings. Richard's two friends were full of fun and excitement—and eager that everyone should join in their pleasures of the day.

When the day drew to a close, and it was time for everyone to take their leave, Richard went to the door with the Penrose family, the snow was still falling heavily outside, and the wind was now blowing the flakes all over the place. Vicar Penrose's carriage had been brought around to the front door, and the coachman was waiting for them to alight—he was covered from head to foot in the white blanket. Richard caught hold of Clara, and with all eyes still firmly fixed to them, he pulled Clara under a sprig of mistletoe, with large white waxy berries, and planted a long lingering kiss on her lips. There were sharp intakes of breath, but neither of them cared at all, they would be married within the fortnight, and now nothing would stop them. They said their goodbye's and Richard stepped out into the cold white world outside to hand his precious beloved into the carriage, before returning to his other guests. The Chandler's also left soon afterwards, and Alice retired, happy and exhausted. The three men went to Richards library and polished off the full decanter of brandy before finally they retired to bed, Richard stumbled to his room and into his warm, welcoming bed—within minutes he was fast asleep, no more haunted dreams—now his sleep was deep and peaceful—no more demons lurking around in his head—his future was bright, and he was happier than he had ever been in his life.

EPILOGUE

The next twelve months found many changes but much happiness. Jasper Trent had gone to Stephen Kirkby and asked for his daughter's hand, her father had jumped at the match, considering that this gentleman was from such good stock—and his daughter was rather left on the shelf, although, he believed that his wife had more to do with that than met the eye—she could be an overbearing woman at times. She had not been quite so pleased about it all, and wasted no time telling her husband so, but she had to admit that Sarah did seem very happy, more than she had ever been before, even though the man was so closely linked with the Duke of Warren and all that bad business. They were married very soon, on the eighteenth of March, a dry and warm spring day, though there was a stiff breeze, their wedding took place at the local church in Truro, before he whisked her off to travel Europe for an extended honeymoon.

Russell Hinton had persuaded the Martin's to travel to Penleigh Court, where they were guests of Richard Penleigh, to attend his wedding to Clara. Russell and Clarissa were married as planned in June, the twenty sixth of June to be precise, they left afterwards for a honeymoon in Italy, where they planned to meet up with Jasper and Sarah. Richard had not seen them together for over a year, but he could see that they were made for each other, Clarissa was a down to earth, country girl really, very practical minded, just like his dear friend Russell, they would make a good couple.

Alice was the happiest she had been in years, her and Clara got along better than she could ever have expected, the girl wasn't fully versed to play her role, and Alice had great pleasure in helping her fulfil her part as Duchess of Warren. She got to help with all the arrangements, and Clara welcomed her help. She had even been able to have her seamstress make up new gowns for her, so that she could once again socialize—and she took great pleasure in spending time with her two grandchildren, and she even came to accept, with Richard's encouragement, Henry's illegitimate son by her daughter in law, though she did find it difficult, she couldn't deny that, but it wasn't the child's fault after all—she also built on her relationship with Angela, so much so that Angela spent more and more time with the woman who was nothing less than a mother to her. Alice's happiness was indeed full.

Mark and Angela's marriage continued to flourish, Angela had forgiven Mark for his betrayal, she had even come to believe that he had only done what he did to help his friends—even though this was not strictly the full story, but it helped her to put it all behind them. Mark was a devoted husband who loved his wife like nothing he had ever loved before, and by April Angela realized that she was with child—this seemed to make their happiness complete—they were both certainly thrilled, and when Angela told Alice, she too was overjoyed at the prospect, now she would have another child looking for guidance, and Alice was more than happy to offer her assistance. Mark was delighted, he had no care whether the child were a boy or girl, he was delighted with whatever God blessed them with. The following January Angela gave birth to a healthy baby boy—to the delight of everyone, who they decided to call Peter.

Richard and Clara got married as they had already planned on the fifth of January, everyone was overjoyed for them, they had been through so much in a short time, and they deserved any happiness that would come their way. The wedding was large and a great reception was held at Penleigh Court for the couple. They were planning to travel Europe for the summer months, but that wouldn't be until after the ball, which was to be held in Clara's honour—she had never known anything like it before, she was so happy, she hadn't believed that such joy existed. Richard was attentive and loving and would do anything for his lovely wife. They had planned to leave shortly after the ball, and the welfare of his mother was left in the capable hands of Mark Chandler, who had agreed to take care of her as his own mother. They had not been away long, only a month, when Clara realized that she too was with child. They were delighted another child in the nursery, but this one was their very own. Richard should have been hoping for a son and heir, but he really didn't mind what gender the child was, as long as it was healthy, it would certainly be loved and cherished. Clara's child was born in November, a healthy boy, who they named Charles, after Alice's father. The whole family were happy and excited, and Richard's wards too—they were growing up fast, the girls were eager for the baby to play with them though that wouldn't happen for some time. Even Edward was growing fast, he was doing very well, and already showing signs of taking after his father, he certainly had a will of his own. Richard spent as much time as possible, with his extended family, he had bought a pony for the girls to ride, and he had decided to buy another to allow them one each, they were proving to be good little riders, and quick learners, he had also discussed with Clara the need for a governess—after all, there would now be four children to teach, and that number could rise if they were fortunate enough to have more children. Alice was in her element, she had even broached Richard that once Mark and Angela's child was old enough, it would make sense if the governess duties were extended to their children too. Richard was more than happy with that arrangement, after the birth of their son, he came into the full amount of money that came with the estate—so he had promised Mark that any sons they had, would have a full education, which he was more than willing to pay for. Mark and Angela were thrilled—Clara had undertaken teaching Angela to read and write, something which she had never foreseen happening, but she very soon got the hang of things, although she would never be fluent, she could manage enough to get by.

Their lives very soon settled down, and all the things which had happened had dwindled into the background—nobody ever referred to that horrible time again, and Henry Penleigh was no more than a bad memory to all who knew him. The tyrant Duke was replaced with a well loved and respected one, and when Penleigh Court held balls, soirees and dinners, as they did frequently, everyone receiving invitations were honoured to be a part of it all. Once again, Penleigh Court was the place it had once been, and Richard knew that one day the Ritson estate would also come to him—he was a lucky man and blessed indeed.

Lightning Source UK Ltd.
Milton Keynes UK
UKOW03f0746031213

222251UK00002B/120/P

9 781491 881149